A Perilous Moment

Their eyes met and Lily took a hesitant step backward. "If you intend another speech about what a difficult situation we are in and how we must conduct ourselves, then you may save your breath. Our courtship is nothing more than a temporary arrangement. I realize that it is in both our best interests to appear no more than cordial. That way no one will think it strange when the time comes to go our separate ways. We can simply say we didn't suit." She glanced past him toward the path and nervously cleared her throat. "If you don't mind, I would really like to leave. This was a trying day and I'm very tired."

"I'm not tired in the least." Remmington took a step closer and the hem of her gown brushed against his legs. She tried to back away, but he grasped her elbows and held her in place.

"What are you doing, Remmington?"

He stared down at her a moment, then murmured his answer as he lowered his head. "Appearing cordial."

She opened her mouth to let out a startled cry but he was quicker. He caught the sound as his lips covered hers in a hard, possessive kiss. . . .

Bantam Books
by Elizabeth Elliott

THE WARLORD
SCOUNDREL

Scoundrel

—— ✦ ——

Elizabeth Elliott

BANTAM BOOKS
New York Toronto London
Sydney Auckland

Scoundrel
A Bantam Fanfare Book / February 1996

ISBN 0-553-56911-2

Published simultaneously in the United States and Canada

*Bantam Books are published by Bantam Books, a division of Bantam Doubleday
Dell Publishing Group, Inc. Its trademark, consisting of the words "Bantam Books"
and the portrayal of a rooster, is Registered in U.S. Patent and Trademark Office
and in other countries. Marca Registrada. Bantam Books, 1540 Broadway, New
York, New York 10036.*

PRINTED IN THE UNITED STATES OF AMERICA

RAD   0 9 8 7 6 5 4 3 2 1

Happy Birthday, Mom!

Scoundrel

---✦---

One

London, 1813

"Shameless, that's what she is."

Lily Walters tried to ignore the whispered insult. She focused her attention on an imaginary spot along the far side of Lord and Lady Ashland's ballroom, her steps precisely measured as she made her way across the room. More than five hundred people crowded the enormous assembly, the music of the finest musicians in London muted by laughter and conversations all around. A lavish buffet table stood to her left, while the dance floor dominated the opposite side of the ballroom. Lily told herself that gossipy young women like the four who stood near the buffet table were to be expected. The venom they whispered behind their jeweled fans couldn't affect her.

A young woman named Margaret Granger made sure her voice rose above the whispers. "Poor Osgoode barely in his grave three months, God rest his soul, and already she's back in society as if he'd never been. Have you heard of anything so improper in your life?"

Lily felt her face turn red. She wished Margaret and her friends had the decency to gossip behind her back like everyone else. Even though the room swelled with music and conversations, their voices were impossible to ignore.

"Dear, misguided Osgoode," Margaret continued. "He gave his life in that duel, and she doesn't even have the decency to mourn the man."

"A duel?" one of her friends asked. "I thought Osgoode fell victim to footpads."

"At dawn in Regent's Park?" Margaret asked. "I believe the facts speak for themselves. Indeed, I asked my fiancé about the matter and he thinks it obvious that Lord Osgoode died in a duel."

"Your fiancé? Margaret, do you mean to say you are engaged?"

The other girls broke into excited whispers, but Margaret waved away her friends' pleas to tell them more. "No, I'm afraid I can say no more. Remmington asked me to keep our discussions about the engagement private."

Lily missed her step and nearly tripped. She recovered her composure with a sidelong glance toward the buffet table. Only Margaret watched her. The blond smiled and tossed her curls over one shoulder, then she whispered something to the girl standing next to her. Lily steadied herself with a deep breath and kept walking, realizing that Margaret's venom could indeed hurt her.

At last Margaret's conversation drifted into the blur of voices that competed with the orchestra, but Lily still felt its effects. An odd ache tightened her chest and her throat seemed so constricted that she could barely breathe. The cool wind that stirred the palm fronds near the wall of French doors wilted inside the ballroom. The heavy, humid air trapped the scent of stale perfumes and the underlying smell of too many people crowded together in one place. She snapped open her fan, but the forced breeze didn't seem the least refreshing.

A flash of color caught her eye and she turned toward a pair of palm trees that flanked one set of French doors. In an ocean of pastel ballgowns, only Sophie Stanhope would wear such a startling shade of fuchsia. She caught another glimpse of the bold color through the fronds and hastened her steps.

"Lady Lillian!"

Lily groaned, but she pasted on a vague smile and turned to watch Lord Allen stalk toward her. He'd stood near one of the wide Grecian columns that supported the ceiling and now he all but ran to reach her side.

"I vow you are the last person I expected to see here tonight, Lady Lillian."

Lily couldn't say the same of George Allen. No matter where she went, their paths always seemed to cross. He was a nice enough young man, yet bothersome at times. She told herself that it shouldn't matter if his bulging green eyes always appeared too eager, or if his hair looked dirty even when it was clean. Having endured the judgment of others, Lily refused to judge a person by appearance alone. Still, tonight's combination of a peacock-blue suit and dark purple vest made her eyes hurt. Although his clothing appeared expensive, he always managed to have something missing or undone. Tonight he lacked the bottom button of his vest and its absence drew her eye to the snowy white shirt that peeked through the gap. Yet another fashion failure for George.

"You must promise me your first dance," he announced. His gaze swept over her sea-green ballgown then came to rest on the jeweled bodice.

"Why, how kind of you to ask, Lord Allen. I'm afraid I promised my first dance to Lord Artonswell. Or was it Lord Williams?" She unfurled her fan and tapped the gilded edge against her lower lip, her expression one of wide-eyed innocence. "I misplaced my dance card and cannot seem to remember the order of things."

"Then you must promise me your next free dance."

"I believe that would be the dance right after the first waltz." Lily gave him a charming smile, knowing the first waltz would follow the first elephant parade. Everyone knew the stuffy Ashlands never allowed the orchestra to play the waltz.

Lord Allen frowned. "You *must* allow me to escort you on a tour of the gardens. They are quite spectacular and I'm sure you wouldn't want to miss them."

"What a lovely idea." Lily tried to appear thoughtful and flustered at the same time. Her smile faded to a sulky pout and her fingers twisted one of the auburn curls that brushed against her shoulder. She didn't attend this ball to flirt or dance with the likes of Lord Allen. The sooner she put an end to this farce the better. "Papa forbade me to step outside without his escort. Shall we see if he's available? He's in the card room with Lord Howland and his friends just now, but perhaps they would enjoy taking the air as well."

"Oh, I don't think that would be the thing, to disturb your father and his friends," he said quickly. "Surely the earl wouldn't—"

"Yes, you're quite right. Papa simply wouldn't approve if I disobeyed him." She tapped his arm with her fan and gave him an admiring smile. "How charmingly proper you are, Lord Allen. I vow, 'tis most refreshing. I shall look forward to dancing with such an inspiring gentleman."

"Why, thank you." He gave her a broad smile and adjusted his vest with a sharp tug. More of his shirt escaped through the opening.

"I shall see you after the waltz, Lord Allen." She gave him an airy wave, then turned and walked away before he could think up anything else they *must* do.

When she finally reached the palm trees she stopped short, startled to find not only Sophie, but Sophie's Aunt Clara and Lord Poundstone as well. In appearance, Lady Bainbridge and her niece closely resembled each other. They had the same wavy brown hair and the same green eyes, but their taste in clothing differed drastically. Lady

Bainbridge's pastel blue dress only made Sophie's bright gown look all the more glaring in comparison. Standing next to Lady Bainbridge was Lord Poundstone, a portly gentleman of middle age who shared Sophie's interest in Egyptian artifacts. At any other time, Lily wouldn't mind his company. His presence tonight was yet another omen that nothing would be simple. She reminded herself to smile, then called out a cheerful greeting. "Good evening, all."

"Lady Lillian!" Poundstone spread his arms wide. His ruddy face grew even redder as he bowed over her hand. "How delightful to see you out again. We've missed you at the Antiquities Society meetings."

From the awkward bow and odd creaks, Lily guessed that Lord Poundstone was trying to diminish his ever-expanding girth with a corset. His pained expression made her wonder how he managed to get any color at all to his face.

"I vow I shall not miss another," Lily said with a curtsy. "Such sophisticated company I've missed these past months, sir. The discussions are always so very dignified and important. I feel quite improved after each session." She paused to add a wistful sigh, thinking it a nice touch. "Unfortunately, I cannot seem to grasp the theories of hippogryffs as readily as our Miss Stanhope, nor remember all those difficult names of Egyptian kings and dynasties. But I must say, Lord Alfred serves an excellent tea at each meeting. His settings and fare are most impressive."

Poundstone corrected her in a superior tone. "That's hieroglyphics, Lady Lillian."

"Ah, yes," Lily murmured. "I stand corrected. I must remember to write the word out several times. That often helps me recall difficult words such as hyrogliffys."

"Is that a new fan, Lily?" Lady Bainbridge asked, cutting off Lord Poundstone's attempt to correct Lily a second time. "How very unique. I must take a closer look at the workmanship."

Lily handed her fan to Lady Bainbridge. "I am simply

bursting to tell my dearest friends about Madame Justine's newest shipment of silks. I hope you will not repeat this conversation, my lord, for all the ladies will call at Madame's shop first thing in the morning if they hear a word of this gossip, and our selection will be severely depleted." She lifted one hand to shield her words as her tone imparted the importance of her secret. "The shipment is from France, my lord. Can you imagine? Sophie and I shall soon be wearing smuggled goods! I vow the very thought makes me light-headed."

"Indeed," Poundstone replied. He craned his neck to one side and raised his hand to acknowledge someone on the other side of the room. "I would love to share this gossip, Lady Lillian, but I fear I've made a prior appointment in the card room with Lord Greyvall. He'll be dreadfully disappointed if I don't show soon."

Poundstone mouthed a few polite apologies, then made a hasty retreat, leaving the ladies to discuss their smuggled goods in private. All three women gave a sigh of relief.

"Thank goodness he's gone," Sophie said.

Lady Bainbridge spoke to Lily, but her keen eyes swept over the room to make sure none observed them. Her hands moved inconspicuously along the spine of Lily's fan. "I know you were expecting only Sophie tonight, but my husband is very anxious about the latest message you translated."

"I'm sure he is," Lily said. She knew the reason for Sir Bainbridge's impatience. The message concealed in the spine of her fan contained news of Napoleon's latest troop movements on the Continent. Yet even Sir Malcolm Bainbridge, the director of Special Projects for the War Department, could not read the original message until Lily provided the translation.

Lady Bainbridge tucked the slip of paper into her glove, then she returned Lily's fan. "I'll leave you two young people alone now. Do give my best to your father, Lily."

After her aunt's departure, Sophie's expression became secretive and she turned again to Lily. "You will never guess who is here tonight."

"Who?" Lily asked. She shifted closer to the palms. Hopefully, no one would notice her standing there. She didn't want to be caught up in an endless round of dances, or the meaningless social pleasantries that took place at these events. In another hour she could leave, but at least she could keep Sophie company in the meantime.

"He's very tall, sinfully mysterious, and dangerous, too, some say. My best friend happens to think him the handsomest man in England." Sophie tapped her chin and gazed up at the ceiling. "Now who could that be?" She gave Lily a teasing glance, and her smile faded. "Whatever is the matter? You're white as a sheet."

"Nothing," Lily lied. "I'm just not feeling very well this evening."

Sophie didn't reply. She just kept staring at Lily, waiting.

"Oh, all right. I overheard Margaret Granger say that she is engaged to the Duke of Remmington."

Repeating Margaret's announcement was almost as devastating as hearing it the first time. Lily had always nurtured the impossible hope that Remmington would someday notice her, that he would at least ask for an introduction. Just as well he hadn't, she told herself. She had her work to consider. Highly secretive work at that. A man like Remmington would never fit into her life.

"Remmington and Margaret Granger," Sophie mused. "The gossips will be in the boughs. Everyone was beginning to think he would never remarry."

"Oh, don't look so melancholy," Lily chided. "The day I admitted my infatuation with Remmington was the same day we decided to find out what brandy tasted like. I didn't mean half of what I said. Besides, what duke would want to marry a woman who gets tipsy and admits to her friend that she finds him appealing? Margaret Granger would never make such silly confessions under the influence of spirits. The perfectly proper Lady Margaret will make him an excellent duchess."

"She will probably make a better wife than his first," Sophie agreed. "His first duchess was legendary for her secret lovers, although they were hardly a secret. They say she died giving birth to a child that could not possibly have been fathered by her husband, he being in the West Indies for too many months prior to the event. He did happen to be on hand when she passed away. There are some unsavory rumors about exactly how she died."

"Remmington had nothing at all to do with his wife's death," Lily snapped. "By all accounts, he turned a blind eye to her infidelities. He is not the sort of man whose passions can be stirred by jealousy or revenge, at least, not the way you imply. Although what business it is of ours, I'm sure I don't know."

"I didn't realize you knew him so well."

"You know very well that I do not."

"I know you like the man," Sophie insisted.

"Like him?" Lily made an annoyed click with her tongue. "We've never actually met. How could I like him when I don't even know him? Most people think he's cold and arrogant, and it's no secret that he's a shocking libertine. Last year he flaunted his affair with Lady Penton so openly that Lord Penton finally took his wife on an extended journey to the East Indies. Then there was Lady Saint James, Lady Farnsworth, and many others, I'm sure."

"Good Lord!"

"Shocking, is it not? How could I think him attractive? Really, I'm quite over that silly infatuation. In fact—"

"Yes, of course!" Sophie smiled brightly, her gaze directed over Lily's left shoulder. "We shall visit Madame Justine's shop first thing in the morning. Those silks sound positively heavenly."

It took only a moment for Lily to realize that someone stood behind her. Even without Sophie's bizarre behavior, she knew she was being watched. From behind her, a deep voice made her breath catch in her throat.

"Good evening, ladies."

"Good evening, Your Grace," Sophie murmured.

Sophie's response and curtsy were properly respectful. Lily turned and stared up in rude silence until Sophie's elbow nudged her into an awkward curtsy.

One dark brow rose as The Duke of Remmington watched her curtsy before him, otherwise his features remained impassive. Lily hoped her expression reflected the same degree of polite boredom. It was an unlikely hope. She was far too unsettled by his sudden appearance.

She'd caught an occasional glimpse of the darkly handsome duke at balls and parties over the past few years, yet whenever he happened to look her way, his gaze quickly skimmed past her, a silent dismissal of a woman who failed to stir his interest. Yet she'd always hoped. Hoped that one day he wouldn't look beyond her, hoped his depthless gray eyes would linger for just a moment. Perhaps then he would feel some spark of the same attraction that made her remain for hours at the dullest ball just to catch another glimpse of him. It seemed some strange manifestation of her own longings and imagination that he stood before her now.

How many times had she dreamed of meeting him? How many times had she rehearsed the clever things she would say to impress him? She couldn't think of a single word to say, much less anything clever.

As Lily gazed up at him, she realized he was taller than she'd thought. The top of her head came only to the middle of his chest, and she had to tilt her head back to study the strong line of his jaw. A hint of dark stubble shadowed his face, the resulting impression both dangerous and masculine. Her gaze lingered on his mouth. The full, perfectly shaped lips managed to look hard and soft at the same time. Disturbed by thoughts of what it would be like to touch those lips, she forced her gaze to travel higher. His eyes weren't exactly gray. They were a silvery shade of blue, the color of rare Damascus steel. Fascinating.

"I wonder if I might have an introduction, Miss Stanhope?"

Lily's gaze flew from Remmington to Sophie. "You *know* each other?"

Sophie's brows drew together in a slight gesture that spoke volumes. Lily knew her blurted question sounded rude, but at the moment she didn't care.

"We met at Lady Barton's a few weeks ago," Sophie replied. She turned again to Remmington. "It would be my pleasure, Your Grace. This is my friend, Lady Lillian Walters, the Earl of Crofford's daughter. Lily, the Duke of Remmington."

"Your Grace," Lily murmured. She remembered to extend her hand, although the gesture looked hurried and clumsy.

Remmington lifted her fingers in a deft movement and bowed over her hand. Even though she expected the kiss against the back of her hand, the pressure of his lips against her lace gloves startled her. Was it just her imagination that made her think he lingered over the kiss?

She stared at the spot where his lips had touched her and watched as he released her hand, watched in amazement as her hand remained extended in midair. It took a conscious effort to force the errant limb to her side.

"The pleasure is mine, Lady Lillian. I wasn't sure if you ladies would appreciate my interruption. The two of you looked quite engrossed in your discussion." One brow rose again, as if he'd asked a question. Or perhaps it was a sardonic gesture that said he knew they wouldn't mind his intrusion.

Lily smiled weakly and wondered if he knew just how much she appreciated his decision to interrupt them. She found his deep, rough-edged voice as fascinating as his face. The sound mesmerized her as she continued to study his features. His size and dark coloring broke all the rules of what society deemed fashionable, but there was a natural masculine grace about him that had nothing to do with fashion or manners. She suspected he could make himself as much at home in a taproom as he could in a ballroom. He regarded her with a combination of wordliness and intelligence that made her breath hard to catch. He looked at her as if he knew everything about her—hopes, dreams, secrets. She wondered if any were safe from that penetrating gaze.

"You are not disturbing us in the least." This at last from Sophie, after another awkwardly long silence. She pushed her elbow into Lily's side again, but Lily remained helplessly silent.

Why couldn't she open her mouth and say something?

"I almost didn't see you behind all this greenery," he remarked. One hand swept out to indicate the palms. Lily's gaze followed the gesture, distracted for the moment by the unstudied ease of his movements. "But I felt certain you, Miss Stanhope, would be the only woman daring enough to wear such a remarkable shade. That color is quite . . . stunning."

Sophie glanced down at her dress and said hesitantly, "Why, thank you, Your Grace."

Lily wondered if he'd just complimented or insulted her friend. She suspected it was his intent to leave them guessing, the glimmer of a cynical side to his personality disturbing, but not surprising. This was the Duke of Remmington. He could do or say almost anything he pleased, and did both with great frequency.

"Are you ladies enjoying Ashland's little do?" He tilted his head toward the dance floor. "It seems the world is in attendance."

"The Ashlands always have a crush," Sophie answered. "It's been quite pleasant so far. Lord Poundstone and I had a rousing discussion about the artifacts that arrived from Cairo last week. Are you interested in Egyptian antiquities, Your Grace?"

"I know very little of the subject, Miss Stanhope." Remmington's glance flickered Sophie's way, then returned to Lily. "How about you, Lady Lillian?"

Lily remained hopelessly silent. What had he and Sophie been talking about? Something about Egypt? She'd stared so intently at his eyes that she forgot to pay attention to the conversation. Surely it only seemed like an hour of silence before he explained the question.

"Do you share Miss Stanhope's interest in Egyptian antiquities, Lady Lillian?"

"No."

"Lily and I were just on our way to find a glass of punch," Sophie said, taking control of the conversation. Lily silently blessed her. "Would you care to join us?"

"Actually, I would much rather join one of you ladies in a dance." He executed another bow while his gaze held Lily's captive. "Would you do me the honor, Lady Lillian?"

Lily didn't remember if she answered the question, but he extended his arm to escort her onto the ballroom floor. The spell he wove around her seemed to lose its potency the moment she stepped forward, probably because she had to concentrate on where she placed her feet so she wouldn't trip over them. It occurred to her that Miles Garrett Montague, the twelfth Duke of Remmington and holder of many lesser titles, was the last man on earth she should dance with that evening. He was very likely engaged to Margaret Granger. She had no right to feel so giddy over the attentions of another woman's fiancé. And she had no business feeling any sort of interest in a man as clever as Remmington.

That didn't change the fact that she felt as if she walked on air as he led her onto the dance floor. What harm could there be in one dance? What harm could there be in pretending, just for a few moments, that they were a couple? No one would ever know how aware she was of even the smallest details of her first encounter with Remmington, how she couldn't stop staring at him. She studied the pattern of a small scar that marred his chin, then closed her eyes for a moment to savor the slight scent of tobacco, brandy, and some other indefinable male scent that drifted across her senses.

Beneath her hand and the smooth silk fabric of his sleeve, she could feel the impressive muscles that made her seem small and slight in comparison. She felt those same strong muscles along his shoulder when she placed her hand there to begin the dance. Male strength and virility surrounded her, his nearness a tangible sensation as potent as finely aged brandy. The first few strains of music drifted across the room and Lily's eyes widened with delight as she realized the orchestra was beginning a waltz.

Because he was one of the few men who could smile down at a lady five and a half feet tall, it took her a moment to wonder why he was smiling at all. And why was there a hint of triumph in his eyes, as if he'd known all along that they would dance this intimate dance? She knew the Ashlands didn't approve of the waltz, but they would make certain the orchestra played anything a duke wanted to hear. The vague suspicions about his long-awaited interest crystallized into a cold, hard lump of certainty. If her suspicions were right, she didn't interest him in the least. She'd spent the last few minutes gazing cow-eyed at a man who intended to use her. His devastating smile made the butterflies in her stomach sink like lead weights.

She schooled her features to reveal none of her suspicions and to wipe every trace of her foolish infatuation from her face. Her gaze focused on his shoulder, and she made herself pretend that he was but another dandy who sought her hand for a dance, no more than a casual acquaintance. It was a difficult task and she didn't quite succeed, but at least her thoughts were no longer scattered and she felt a little more in control of her emotions.

"You appear quite pleased about something, Your Grace." She made the words flow like warm butter, pleased to note a new, wary edge to his smile. For a moment she dared to hope that he hadn't noticed the way she'd stared at him when they met, or that he would simply think her empty-headed. If he'd thought to sweep her off her feet, he was about to find out that his ploy didn't work. She lowered her lashes in a coy gesture that she'd watched many women practice on him when they flirted. "To what do I owe the favor of your smile?"

He looked puzzled by her remark, as if distracted by the fact that they were conversing at all. His smile faded. "What gentleman would not be pleased when a beautiful woman is in his arms for the waltz?"

"Indeed." She inclined her head to acknowledge the compliment and studied his face unhurriedly, feature by feature. She didn't really know what she was looking for. A trace of compassion? Or perhaps some hint of interest in his extraordinary eyes? Whatever it was, she didn't find it. His true opinion of her remained his own. Though his compliment sounded genuine, hers rang cynical and insincere. "And what lady could help but be pleased, when she is dancing the waltz with a handsome gentleman?" She raised her brows in a superb imitation of a shrug and continued to glide gracefully through the dance. "Of course, the lady would also be contemplating the gentleman's fiancée, who is surely devising any number of slow, painful tortures at this moment. Tortures applied best to the woman being danced with for the sole purpose of making a certain Lady Margaret jealous."

The corners of his mouth tightened and she watched him nod to an acquaintance as they moved past another couple on the dance floor. At last his gaze returned to her face, his displeasure apparent. "How did you know?"

Her smile hid the sting of his words. She'd wanted so badly to be wrong. He wasn't supposed to be this callous and unfeeling. He was supposed to be kind and courteous, the epitome of everything she might admire in a gentleman.

He wasn't even polite enough to lie.

In her mind, she'd made him into a man so perfect that it hurt just to look at him. For three long years she'd admired a man unworthy of three minutes of her regard. The news of his engagement to Margaret Granger paled in comparison to the pain that now gripped her heart. It wasn't Remmington's fault that he wasn't the man she thought he would be, but she still felt cheated.

"Do you see the elderly gentleman standing near the punch bowls?" she asked, with a nod toward Lord Porter. She waited until Remmington caught sight of the eighty-year-old gentleman. "Aside from my father, you and Lord Porter are the only two men who seem capable of speaking exclusively to my face this evening, and not to other parts of my person."

Remmington looked startled by her boldness, but at that moment Lily didn't care what he thought of her. She was caught off guard when his face broke into a smile and he laughed out loud. The deep sound drew the attention of other couples on the dance floor.

"Oh, that was a nice touch," she murmured. "Everyone will believe we've just shared an intimate secret. I believe Lady Margaret's imagination just moved on to sharp objects."

He returned her smile, a warm expression that conveyed his pleasure. Why wouldn't he be pleased that she cooperated so willingly with his scheme? Lily gritted her teeth and felt her smile turn brittle.

"You are taking this rather gracefully, Lady Lillian. Most women would surely slap my face and create quite a scene if they'd guessed my intent."

If only she had the nerve to create a scene! She would very much like to scream. Instead she kept her voice soft and pretended she couldn't care less that he was using and humiliating her. She wouldn't give him the satisfaction of knowing how easily she fell into his trap. "Perhaps I find it refreshing to dance with a man who doesn't ogle me throughout a dance."

The warmth of his gaze took on the cooler cast of suspicion. "You don't appreciate the fact that men find you attractive?"

Lily took offense at the question. He didn't find her attractive. Remmington didn't appreciate her looks beyond the fact that they would make Margaret jealous. He had no idea what hid behind them, probably wouldn't care if he did. It was almost comical how they'd both misjudged the other. At least she'd discovered his true character before she made a complete fool of herself, though his actions said he thought her that still. She was tempted to give him the setdown he deserved, to prove how wrong he was about her.

"Do *you* appreciate it, Your Grace?"

He gave her a quizzical look. "Pardon me?"

She caught her breath as they made a daring sweep of the dance floor, and then blurted out her explanation before she could change her mind. "I asked if you appreciate being pursued for what you appear to be, rather than for what you are."

He stared at her in silence, then avoided her gaze entirely. Although he held her just as closely, she could feel the distance grow between them by the moment. "You are proving entirely too insightful, Lady Lillian."

He looked as if he meant to say more, but Lily didn't give him a chance to elaborate. She didn't want to hear any more of his cutting remarks. She wanted to be away from him as soon as possible, before she did something truly foolish. Tears would be the final humiliation, and she could feel them sting her eyes already. "And you, my lord, are surely aware that Lady Margaret holds me responsible for swaying Lord Osgoode's affections from her court. If there is any doubt in your mind, let me assure you that it is extremely unpleasant to be the subject of your fiancée's gossip."

"Lady Lillian, I—"

"Please spare me the explanations." She refused to look at him, wished she would never again have to see that handsome face. Instead she fixed her attention on a very small, loose thread on the lapel of his jacket. "Explanations are entirely unnecessary, Your Grace. Whatever games you play with your fiancée, I do not wish to be a part of them."

The music faded away and Remmington brought their dance to a sweeping halt, but he didn't release her. She glanced up at him, then she quickly looked away.

The odd light in his eyes made her nervous. It was as though he'd looked into her very soul. She didn't want him there. She especially didn't want his pity. "Your Grace, the dance is over. You mustn't ruin your plan at this late date by looking so displeased with me."

They also looked conspicuous on the nearly empty dance floor. Lily could almost feel people stare at her as they whispered more gossip behind her back. Why did he do this to her? What had she done to deserve such treatment? So she'd fancied herself half in love with him. This was more than ample payment for that folly.

Remmington executed another practiced bow, then tucked her hand beneath his arm to escort her from the floor. His pace slowed as they neared Sophie and the doors that led to the gardens. It was then Lily noticed the small crowd that had formed around Sophie. Its members varied in age, but all were male. Her heart sank. She would be forced to accept their invitations to dance or risk even more gossip about the reasons she'd danced with Remmington.

George Allen inclined his head toward Remmington as he approached the couple. Lily felt herself shrink away from the barely concealed note of triumph in his voice. "I believe Lady Lillian promised the next dance to me."

"Lady Lillian has taken ill," Remmington said in a clipped voice. "You will have to claim your dance another time."

Lord Allen's smile disappeared.

"Tell me it isn't true," he demanded of Lily. He reached out to take her arm, and glanced up at Remmington at the same time. Whatever he saw there made him take a hesitant step backward.

Lily didn't take time to wonder why Remmington had provided the excuse. She took advantage of the opportunity and held one limp hand to her forehead. "Quite true. I'm afraid it's the headache."

"Good evening, Allen." Remmington dismissed the young lord with a curt nod. He glared at Lord Allen until he bowed and backed away. None of the other rakes dared approach after that cool dismissal.

Sophie pushed through the crowd to join them. "What's this about not feeling well?" She looked from Lily's forced smile to Remmington's dark expression, and her mouth drew to a thin line. "A good dose of fresh air always clears my headaches. If you will excuse us, Your Grace, I promised Lily that I would show her the new fountains in the Ashland gardens. Lord Poundstone assures me that they are most impressive."

"Of course," he replied, his tone stilted. "Thank you for the dance, Lady Lillian. I hope . . ."

His voice trailed off. Lily wondered if he contemplated some sort of apology for his awful behavior, but she didn't give him time to think up anything less insulting than his reasons for insulting her in the first place. She didn't want to hear one more word from him.

"Good evening, Your Grace."

Lily turned on her heel and pulled Sophie along by the elbow as she walked briskly toward the gardens. They crossed the wide terrace that ran the length of the house, and then descended the steps into the gardens before Sophie pulled her to a halt.

"Are you *mad*?" Sophie demanded. "You just gave the Duke of Remmington the cut direct. The Duke of *Remmington*," she repeated, as if the name alone could bring Lily to her senses. "He can ruin you!"

Sophie clapped her hand over her mouth, then looked around them. She pulled Lily away from the steps and into the lilac bushes near the terrace where she lowered her voice to a whisper. "He can make certain you never receive another invitation to anything important, Lily. What were you thinking?"

"That it was an excellent time for a walk in the gardens." Lily pulled her arm from Sophie's grip. "Don't fret so much, Sophie. I don't think any real harm was done."

"No harm? You insulted him in front of four hundred people!"

"I suppose I did."

"A month ago you declared yourself in love with him!" Sophie shook her head. "What happened?"

Lily felt a blush stain her cheeks. "The only reason he danced with me was to make Margaret Granger jealous."

"The bounder," Sophie whispered. "Are you certain?"

"He admitted as much. Can you believe his nerve?" Lily shook her head, a silent answer to her own question. "I wasted years pining for a man who is rude, arrogant, and insensitive beyond belief."

"You did the right thing by giving him the cut. The man deserved much worse."

Lily sighed and discovered she really did have a headache. She rubbed her temples. "Unfortunately, I doubt anyone will ever give him the setdown he really deserves."

"We can always hope." Sophie linked her arm through Lily's and smiled brightly. "There is no reason to let him ruin our evening. Why don't we walk through the gardens? I wasn't lying about the Ashlands' fountains. They really are wonderful. Shall we find them?"

It was a blatant attempt to change the subject, but Lily didn't mind. She'd had enough of the Duke of Remmington for one night. She turned toward the gardens, but the sound of a woman's voice from the terrace above them froze both women in midstep.

"There you are."

Lily exchanged a horrified glance with Sophie, then she stepped closer to the bushes and peered upward through the branches. From her vantage point, she saw that a man stood directly above them with his back to the terrace railing.

Remmington.

How long had he been there? Before Lily's mind could form an answer, Margaret Granger appeared on the terrace, followed closely by Lord Allen. She could see them clearly in the moonlight. Margaret looked furious.

Lord Allen looked uncomfortable. He kept tugging on his cravat, looking anywhere but at Remmington.

"Lady Margaret was feeling a bit out of sorts. Said she simply must have a breath of fresh air." With that explanation made, Lord Allen lowered his gaze and fell silent.

"I was certain I'd find you here," Margaret purred. "I vow everyone saw you leave the ball just a few moments after Lady Lillian and Miss Stanhope." Margaret looked around the terrace and out over the gardens, her expression innocent. "I do hope we're not interrupting anything."

Remmington leaned against the stone railing and withdrew a cheroot from his breast pocket. He took his time about lighting it, then he tilted his head back and released a puff of smoke that turned blue in the moonlit night air before it slowly drifted away. "Does it look as if you are interrupting anything, Margaret?"

"One never knows," Margaret said. "Especially when a certain lady with a questionable reputation is involved."

"I'm not certain I take your meaning. Would you care to explain?" His words were softly spoken, dangerously so. Margaret didn't seem to notice.

"You may not be aware of this, Your Grace, but the lady is still in mourning. She shouldn't be here tonight, much less enjoying herself in a frivolous dance."

"As no one has died recently in your family, I take it we are speaking of Miss Stanhope or Lady Lillian Walters?"

"Of course it's not me." Margaret's face twisted into a scowl. "My reputation is spotless, as well you know. It is Lady Lillian who behaves indecently. People are talking quite freely."

"I hardly think one dance is cause for talk," Remmington murmured.

"You'd be surprised." Margaret snapped open her fan to beat a furious rhythm in the air. Her blond curls billowed out around her face. "I overheard quite a few interesting comments. Everyone noticed the looks exchanged when you danced with her. Many are saying she's found herself a new lover."

"Truly?" Remmington sounded amazed by the news. "Me, perchance?"

"I'm only telling you this so you will know what people are saying so shamelessly behind your back." Margaret clicked her fan closed and began to tap it against her hand. She looked very much like an overset governess reprimanding her charge. "One person said they thought it very bad form for a man to dance with his mistress in the presence of the lady he's courting."

Margaret crossed her arms and waited for Remmington's answer to the charge. Lord Allen studied one of the potted rosebushes with embarrassed intensity. The tip of Remmington's cheroot glowed bright orange while everyone waited for his reply. His voice remained quiet when he finally answered, his words spoken very slowly, but Lily recognized the underlying menace.

"If I hear one word of the preposterous lie that Lily Walters is my mistress, I shall meet that liar at dawn in Regent's Park. If the liar is a woman, I shall make certain she is never again received in decent society. Do I make myself clear, Margaret?"

Margaret took a step backward, as if she finally realized his anger. "Very clear, Your Grace."

Remmington pushed away from the railing and stalked off. Lily watched the trio return to the ballroom. Margaret hurried to keep up with Remmington's long stride; Lord Allen trailed behind.

"Oh, my," Sophie whispered. She wore a look of fascinated horror as she gazed up at the terrace. "Do you think he overheard our conversation?"

Lily rolled her eyes. "Of course he did." She smoothed her gown and tried to contain a wave of self-pity. This was the ultimate humiliation, an end to her infatuation with Remmington that would haunt her forever. She would never be able to face him again, or even remain at the same ball or party they both might happen to attend. Unfortunately, Remmington received an invitation to every noteworthy event. Her social life was at an end. "If you don't mind, Sophie, I believe I'll find Papa and see if he's ready to leave. I don't think I can handle much more excitement this evening."

"You aren't going to let him chase you off."

"Of course not. The message I came here to deliver is in the safety of your aunt's hands, I am undoubtedly the subject of every gossip in that ballroom, and I managed to reveal my most humiliating secret to a man I thought I cared for." Lily shrugged her shoulders. "I would say I have accomplished everything that I possibly could in one evening. What reason do I have to stay?"

Two

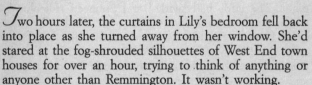

Two hours later, the curtains in Lily's bedroom fell back into place as she turned away from her window. She'd stared at the fog-shrouded silhouettes of West End town houses for over an hour, trying to think of anything or anyone other than Remmington. It wasn't working.

At least her father hadn't argued over her abrupt request to leave the ball. The earl of Crofford disliked parties almost as much as Lily did, and he'd decided to spend the remainder of the evening at his club. If the earl fell into a philosophical debate with one of his friends at White's, it would be hours yet before he returned home.

Lily's slippered feet padded across the soft Aubusson carpet, and she sat down before a vanity table that was tucked away in one corner of her room. The servants often remarked on the oddness of the room's decor, for the vanity was the one small concession to femininity in the starkly furnished bedroom. A green and blue plaid covered the massive, old-fashioned bed, while dark chests with heavy brass handles were lined up against one wall, as orderly as a row of soldiers. A few contained the personal articles of clothing normally found in a woman's room, but most were stuffed with writing papers, inks, and any number of ancient documents and odd mementos. Books and papers covered every available surface and a flat, rectangular stone tablet balanced precariously atop two of the chests, its weathered granite face covered with hieroglyphics. The chiseled miniature pictures were strange in their foreignness, yet beautiful in their simplicity.

Altogether, it looked a very masculine room, one that a man would feel comfortable in. Lily's delicate, feminine beauty looked completely out of place. But the room was hers, and the furnishings reflected much more of her personality than her appearance ever would.

She arranged the folds of her blue silk robe around the stool and stared into the oval mirror that hung above the table. She hated her hair. It so perfectly complemented the practiced expressions she'd worn earlier that night. The curls had swirled and bounced ridiculously when she bestowed empty smiles on Lord Allen and Lord Poundstone. Her fingers tugged at the braid and curls until her hair spread across her shoulders in a rich auburn cape. She pulled a brush through the long tresses, and tears came to her eyes.

Remmington thought her a fool. Everyone thought her a fool. She was greatly tempted to show everyone how wrong they were, to do something so outrageously intelligent that no one would treat her like a witless doll ever again. Detailing her theories about hieroglyphics at the next Antiquities Society meeting would do nicely. Admitting her role in the war effort would remove any lingering doubts.

That was impossible, of course. Staring at the witless fool she'd created, Lily knew she would be stuck with her until the war ended.

A muffled sound from somewhere within the great

house caught her brush in midstroke. The hairs at the nape of her neck stood on end. Ever since she'd arrived home that evening she'd had a strange sense that something was wrong, a sense of something sinister in the quiet night. She caught sight of her frightened expression in the mirror and shook her head. Doubtless the noise was caused by a servant who'd bumped into a wall or door on the way to the water closet. It was far too early for her father to return home.

The brush began its long strokes again, her expression wary now as she listened for any other unusual noises. But it wasn't a noise that sent a shiver of dread down her spine. It was the mirror's reflection of her bedroom's door handle as the brass lever moved ever so slowly. Her heart leapt to her throat as the door opened noiselessly from its frame in agonizingly slow degrees.

Her father was home early. He always checked on her when he returned from his club. She should just call out and let him know she was awake. Instead she sat frozen to her seat, trembling like a leaf. The flames of the candles that flanked her vanity flickered in the draft, as if to warn her of the intruder. Her eyes remained locked on the reflection of the door, watching it open just a crack, then wider, wider still, the dark hall shrouding whoever stood there. The clock over the mantel that she hadn't noticed just moments earlier began to tick so loudly that the sound filled the room, drowning out even the loud beats of her heart as it pounded against her chest.

The mirror reflected a man as he stepped into the doorway and Lily sighed in relief. His green-and-gold-trimmed livery announced his place among the Earl of Crofford's servants, but the sight of his face trapped the sigh in her throat. It was not a face at all, but a strange Oriental mask, the painted features twisted into a hideous caricature of a smile. A low, menacing laugh came from the depths of the mask as he stalked toward her. Lily opened her mouth and screamed in terror.

• • •

It was nearly two in the morning when Remmington left his club in the company of his friend Harry, Viscount Gordon. While they waited near White's cloakroom for their coats and hats, Harry asked for a ride home.

"If it wouldn't be an inconvenience," he amended, his boyish face lit by a winning smile. "Afraid my mother and sisters absconded with the family carriage to attend Ashland's do."

"No inconvenience at all," Remmington assured him. That wasn't quite true, but he wasn't entirely certain that Harry could afford the blunt for a hired carriage. Harry's father left behind a mountain of debt when he died last winter. Like many in his situation, Harry's only hope lay in the time-honored tradition of marriage to an heiress. Surprisingly, Harry seemed in no hurry to repair the family fortunes.

"Heard an interesting bit of gossip tonight." Harry draped his greatcoat over his shoulders. "Rumor has it that you singled out Lady Lillian Walters for a waltz."

Remmington frowned. Lily Walters was the last thing he wanted to be reminded of at the moment. She'd haunted his thoughts all night. Before he could answer the unspoken question, two more patrons approached the cloakroom. Both were friends of Harry's, anxious to relate stories of their success at the gaming tables that night. Nodding a brief greeting to the two young gentlemen, he told Harry, "I'll wait for you outside."

Remmington made his way to the club's entrance and gave a silent signal to the doorman that ordered his carriage to be brought around. A liveried servant hurried down one of the side streets where carriages that belonged to the club's patrons were lined up to await their owners. It would take a good quarter hour for his driver to maneuver through the clogged side streets. Remmington propped his foot on a nearby bench and withdrew a cheroot. In the puff of smoke that followed, he pictured a woman with hair that reminded him of a magnificent autum day and eyes the color of warmed sherry.

Tiger Lily.

He liked the sound of the name. Like the flower, she was earthy and sensual, lovely and sweet-smelling, and just as easily crushed. Her beauty had attracted his attention more than once over the past few years. He had a weakness for beautiful women, and none could surpass Lily Walters. She radiated innocence and lush sensuality, a combination almost impossible to resist. He'd made it a point to avoid her, all too aware that he had no place for a woman like Lily in his life.

Until tonight.

Tonight he had purposely sought her out for the most selfish of reasons, his actions justified by the sure knowledge that she would never guess his motivations. It wasn't her intellect that drew men to her like bees to honey. In fact, many considered her slow-witted. He wondered where they'd come up with that notion. The wit he'd encountered tonight was razor sharp. She had guessed one of the reasons he sought her out within moments of their encounter, then commenced to make a mockery of his conceited plan. He'd humiliated her. He recalled again his brief glimpse into her eyes at the end of their dance. It would be a long time before he could forget that look of wounded betrayal. Later, on the terrace, he found out just how deeply he'd hurt her.

There were other ways to break off his courtship with Margaret Granger, other women he could have danced with to make Margaret realize his interest in her would not last much longer. In a moment of weakness he'd chosen Lily Walters, unable to resist her beautiful smile any longer. Dancing with Lily had turned out to be more effective than he could have imagined. He hadn't known about Margaret and Osgoode, or that Margaret would accuse Lily of being his mistress. He'd done what he could to ensure that Margaret would not repeat slanderous gossip, yet he couldn't help but imagine the expression on Lily's face when she overheard Margaret's accusation.

Guilt was a new em   n to his jaded senses. He

didn't like the feeling at all. It wasn't like him to involve innocents in his plots. Indeed, he'd almost forgotten that innocents still existed in this world. He should have walked away from Lily Walters the moment they met, the very instant she'd looked up at him. She'd stared at him as though he were a mighty conqueror, or some long-lost lover returning from the war.

It was a heady feeling to be the object of that beauty's attention, to realize that she was attracted to him. In the past he'd watched her bestow charming smiles on countless men, yet he'd never seen her look at one with such open desire. How he'd wanted to kiss her then, to see if she would taste as sweet as she looked. He'd had to settle for a chaste kiss on the back of her hand.

He stared down at the glowing tip of his cheroot and watched the smoke curl lazily upward. The remembered scents of roses and sandalwood drifted across his senses, and the memory of temptation. He recalled what Lily felt like when he took her into his arms for the waltz, how his hand unconsciously measured her small waist, then tested the curve of her hip as far as he dared. The heat of her had penetrated him everywhere. The offhanded compliment she gave him about not staring at her figure still made him smile. Lily Walters had a figure that no man could help but stare at. She filled a gown as few others could, and the lush swell of her breasts made his mouth go dry. He'd looked long and often at that tempting display. She just hadn't caught him at it. He wondered again if she could possibly be as innocent as she seemed.

"Sorry to keep you waiting," Harry apologized, as he walked over from the club's doorway. Remmington's carriage pulled around the corner at the same time. "Jamison is set on my sister, Prue, and he never wastes an opportunity to point out his potential qualities as a husband. Can't seem to comprehend the fact that I must get her older sister, Claire, off my hands before I can make settlements on the younger ones."

Remmington pushed aside thoughts of Lily and forced a smile. "I'm often thankful that my parents were adept at producing males. Sisters must be a great nuisance." He gave Harry a speculative look. "Any plans to see to your own marital affairs in the near future?"

"I have my eye on a lady, but she has yet to notice that I occupy the same universe. Perhaps I should start pestering her brother with endless lists of my husbandly qualities." Harry grinned and shrugged the matter of his marriage aside. "What about you, Remmington? You must be an old man of thirty by now. Any plans to set up your own nursery?"

Yes.

The voice came unbidden from inside his head, a soft, feminine voice. It was Lily's answer when he'd asked her to dance, filled with hopes he hadn't understood at the time. What a fool he'd been. What a fool he was now, to regret what could never be. Always the fool where beautiful women were concerned. Some things never changed.

"I'm in no hurry to remarry," he said, walking with Harry toward the carriage.

"Well, I'm in no hurry to find myself in a state that makes most men I know positively morose. Although I'll admit that—" Harry stopped in midsentence. "Good God. Will you look at that."

Remmington turned around. One could see almost anything on the streets of London, but his face registered surprise at the sight that greeted him.

The new gaslights of Saint James's Street revealed the shadowy form of a woman as she raced down the middle of the foggy street, her figure vague and muted in the dim light. He watched with an eerie sense of the surreal as she drew nearer and her features became distinct.

The fog that surrounded her began to drift away, a trick of the eye that made her look as if she emerged from the night itself. The voluminous folds of a dark blue robe billowed out from her waist like silk sails in a brisk wind. The skirt of a pristine white nightgown revealed itself beneath the robe, and her flight outlined long, lithe legs against the smooth fabric. Waist-length auburn hair floated over her shoulders in fiery waves. One slender hand held the skirt of her robe and nightgown above the path of her slippered feet while the other hand clutched her throat. The expression on her face was one of sheer terror. She glanced over her shoulder several times, as though certain the hounds of hell were on her heels.

The girl was less than fifteen feet away when Remmington swore under his breath, recognizing the shadowy figure at last. He thought she was running right to him, but she changed direction at the last moment, obviously intent on the entrance to White's. Two long strides from the side of the carriage and he intercepted her. He caught her with one outstretched arm and her breath came out in a whoosh. He pushed her toward Harry and the waiting carriage.

"Get her inside, man. She can't be seen on the street!" Remmington spun around to face the club's doorman. The liveried servant's mouth hung wide open. He pressed ten pounds into the man's palm. "One word of this incident and I will know where to direct my anger."

Remmington didn't think it possible, but the man's eyes actually opened wider as he stared at the money.

"No! My father!" the girl cried out. She tried to pull away from Harry's grip. Her voice sounded strained, and she put her hand again to the high, ruffled neckline of her nightgown. She turned her attention to Remmington, both hands at her neck now as if she found it painful to speak. "He's . . . inside."

"No, he isn't," Remmington replied.

Harry stared down at the woman in silence, his expression incredulous. "Good God! Lady—"

"Shut up," Remmington snapped. He turned Harry toward the door to his carriage. "Just get her inside before anyone else sees her."

Harry pushed Lady Lillian into the plush carriage and took the seat opposite hers. Remmington followed a moment later, then he signaled to the driver with a rap on the roof before he sat next to Lily. She clutched at his arm as the carriage lurched forward, but pushed away from him as soon as she regained her balance. Her breath came in quick pants and he could feel her tremble. The fear in her eyes made him uneasy.

"Would you mind telling us just what you are doing on the streets at this time of night?"

"Must find . . ." She lifted her hand to her throat. Her words died on a hoarse whisper. ". . . Papa."

He reached out to push aside the lacy frills that concealed her neck. She slapped his hand away, but not quickly enough. The ugly red marks on her throat made him swear under his breath. Someone had tried to strangle her! Rage flowed through him, instant and potent, but he forced his voice to remain calm. "Who did this to you, Lily?"

Harry leaned forward. He'd also noticed the bruises. "Give us the name and we'll take care of the blackguard."

"Don't . . . know. Must . . . find—"

"There, there, Lady Lillian," Harry said. "We'll take you home to Crofford House and get to the bottom of this foul deed." Harry leaned forward to place his hand over hers, but Lily jerked away and pressed herself even further into the corner of the carriage.

"No!" She shook her head.

"We're not going to hurt you," Remmington murmured. "We only want to help you, Lily. Are you afraid that whoever did this is still in your house?"

Her gaze moved slowly to Harry, then back again before she finally nodded. Remmington covered her hand before he remembered that she'd refused the same meager comfort from Harry. He was absurdly pleased when she didn't draw away from him. "How many were there?"

"I saw . . . one," she said with difficulty. "I screamed . . . no one came. Please take—"

"How many servants are in residence?"

"Seven."

Remmington frowned. Not an unusually large

number of servants, but enough that one should have heard her cries for help. Harry's comment echoed his thoughts.

"It seems unlikely that just one man could take care of seven servants."

Lily tugged on Remmington's sleeve. "Papa is at White's."

He winced at the sound of her raspy voice, then slowly shook his head. "No, Lily. I saw your father leave White's an hour ago. Where else might he be?"

Her expression grew uncertain. "I don't know."

He exchanged a worried glance with Harry, then nodded toward the trapdoor in the ceiling. "Tell the driver to take us to my house."

Harry stood up to carry out the order, but Lily shook her head. "I cannot—"

"We will stop just long enough to get some of my men," Remmington told her, "then we will go check on your servants. If your father doesn't turn up in the meantime, I will send someone out to search for him."

She nodded, but her hands were clenched in tight fists, her lower lip caught between her teeth. There was a look of bewildered fear in her eyes. As he gazed down at her stricken face, he was nearly overwhelmed by the need to take her into his arms and keep her safe. He wanted to kill the man who had done this to her.

"Can you describe the man who attacked you?" His frustration deepened when she shook her head. "Can you remember anything at all? The color of his eyes? His height or size? Are you certain it was not a servant, or someone you know?"

Her breaths became more rapid and shallow with each question. She held one hand to her throat, the other to her forehead.

"Take a deep breath," he ordered, worried she would faint. He knew from his experience in battles that anyone frightened this badly would respond more readily to command than to pity. "That's right. Now take one more and you'll feel better."

She took several before her breathing returned to a more normal rate. "Too many . . . questions. No answers."

He didn't quite believe her. She had to remember something. She must be too shaken to recall the answers clearly at the moment, but he didn't know how to calm her down.

"We need a plan. Give me a moment to think this through." Unable to concentrate when he looked at her, he pushed aside the carriage curtains and gazed out at the night. He closed his eyes and pictured the marks that lined her throat. By tomorrow, they would be dark, vicious bruises. He couldn't imagine that any sane man would take that slender throat between his hands to deliberately choke the life from her. He could think of any number of things a man might want to do to a beautiful, defenseless woman, but murder was not one of them.

His hands became fists as he wondered just what sort of man she'd encountered. Perhaps she'd stumbled across a common thief, startled him enough that he'd turned on her. Only a fool would rob a house when the family was in residence, yet who else would try to kill her? It was a daring plan, but a definite possibility. If a thief knew that Lily and her father were at a ball, it would be logical to assume they would remain there until the very early hours of the morning. Yet that night Lily had gone home early, and Remmington knew the reason why.

His gaze returned to her. If he hadn't interfered in her life earlier that evening, she might still be at the Ashlands' ball. Without thinking, he reached out to stroke her cheek. "Don't worry, Lily. You're safe now."

The carriage drew to a halt and he heard the driver announce that they were at his town house. He gave her hand a squeeze, then he opened the door and jumped down from the carriage and raced up the steps.

Lily's fear returned as soon as he left her side. More than anything, she wanted to find her father. What if he returned home and encountered her attacker?

She squeezed her eyes closed to shut out the thought. Instead, she forced herself to remember every moment that led up to the attack, to examine every detail for hidden clues. Until Remmington began to ask questions, she'd thought only of that horrible mask and the terrifying need to escape. She hadn't thought about small things such as the culprit's hair color or his build. He'd seemed larger than life at the time, but now she didn't think he was much taller than she. She couldn't recall seeing his hair. A black hood attached to the back of his mask covered his head completely.

She pictured the mask just as she had seen it in her mirror—the ghostly white porcelain face, ceramic red lips that curled at the corners into an endless smile, and enormous black eyes pierced in the very center with peepholes. She couldn't see anything of his eyes in those peepholes, nothing that would hint at anything human beneath the mask. Sheer terror had held her motionless, then the sound of screaming, and the odd realization that it was her own.

Her hand moved to her hip to feel a bruise there, then she remembered how her hip had struck the corner of her vanity when he threw her to the floor, the sound of her vanity as it toppled over. She had lain on her back, the weight of her attacker straddled over her chest, his knees pressed against her shoulders to keep her pinned to the floor. He fastened his hands around her throat, an unbreakable vise that squeezed and choked, then she couldn't breathe at all. Then the pain of his grip was unbearable.

Lily closed her eyes even tighter to remember, to go beyond the blurred vision. What she recalled made her stomach roil. Suddenly the crushing weight on her chest had been gone. He had kept hold of her neck with one hand while he reached behind him with the other to pull up the skirts of her nightgown. He released his hold on her throat just when the blackness threatened to overcome her. His hands moved to the fastenings of his pants, then he shifted his weight from her shoulders and freed her for a moment.

She had felt something in her hand, realized that sometime during their struggle she'd grasped one of the candlesticks that had fallen next to her from the vanity. The candlestick was very old and very heavy. She gathered all her strength to swing it upward. There was a dull, almost hollow sound when it connected with the side of his head. Then there was a dim memory of him crumpling to the floor. Her lungs were bursting. She couldn't fill them with enough air.

Somehow she knew he wasn't dead. It was that fear, that certainty that spurred her to action. She'd struggled to her feet, but staggered no more than a few steps before she felt his hand wrap around her ankle. The candlestick was still clutched in her hand. Without a thought, she brought it down on his wrist. His bellow of pain gave her the strength to run, to flee that nightmare and take her chances on the street. She tried to remember if he'd followed her. There was a moment when she glanced over her shoulder as she raced down the stairway and—

The carriage door snapped open and Remmington stepped inside. An instant later, his hand covered Lily's mouth to cut off her startled cry.

"It's only me, Lily!" He sat next to her in the carriage and pulled her onto his lap, his hold on her gentle despite his harsh words. His hand came slowly away from her mouth. He looked worried that she would start screaming. "You're safe. I won't let anyone hurt you. Breathe, damn it."

Lily nodded and tried to obey the order, taking deep gulps of air.

He glared at Harry. "What the *hell* did you do to her?"

The barely leashed violence of his voice startled Lily. She glanced up and saw that Harry had braced himself against the back of his seat. He looked just as alarmed by Remmington's tone.

"N-nothing! She's been sitting here quiet as a tomb the entire time you were in there."

The two men stared at each other, then Remmington finally nodded toward the trapdoor. Harry obeyed the silent order and signaled to the driver by rapping on the roof. A moment later, the carriage lurched forward.

Lily eased herself off Remmington's lap and onto the seat, but he kept one arm around her shoulders, as if to anchor her to his side. He reached out to tilt her chin up and waited for her to meet his gaze. She realized that he was careful to avoid her injured throat, that he was surprisingly gentle for such a large man. "Are you all right now?"

"You startled me," she whispered. "I was . . . remembering." She closed her eyes as a shudder racked her body. "Awful."

He forced her to look up at him again. "What did you remember? Tell me anything that might help."

"I hurt him." She touched the side of her head where she'd struck her attacker. "He's bleeding. He might still be there."

Remmington looked at Harry, then nodded again toward the trapdoor. "Tell him to hurry."

Lily watched Remmington step down from the carriage and looked up at Crofford House, then he turned to help her down. His gaze remained locked with hers even after her feet touched the ground and his hands lingered on her waist. For a moment she had the odd sensation that he wanted to pull her closer. He released her abruptly and turned away to wave down a large traveling coach that pulled up behind them.

She walked over to one of the wrought iron carriage posts that lined the street and wrapped her arm around the cool, damp metal as she gazed up at the stately brick structure of her home. It struck her that she'd never been so afraid of a place so familiar. She was standing outside her own home, terrified to step inside, her safety in the hands of a man she'd sworn she would never speak to again. Life made little sense at the moment.

Her gaze moved to Remmington's traveling coach and her eyes widened when she caught sight of the driver. He was the most ferocious-looking man she'd ever laid eyes on. He wore a red silk scarf that was fashioned into a bandanna and tied over his head. A gold hoop earring flashed from one ear, and a bold red sash broke the monotony of his black breeches and shirt. He leaped down from the driver's box with catlike grace.

The door to the coach opened and more burly men began to emerge. Rather than the neat livery of a nobleman's servants, they wore an odd assortment of clothing, accented by bold stripes and bright colors. Like the driver, several wore earrings and bandannas.

"Pirates!" Lily whispered.

"Sailors," Harry corrected her. He stood right behind her. "Remmington's family owns a shipping line. They're from his ship, the *Reliant*. Another odd quirk of his. He hires them on as servants when they're in port. Can't say as I'll be sorry to have them at my back tonight."

As she watched Remmington direct the men into her house, she wondered just when Harry expected to find them at his back. One of the men stepped forward to address Remmington and Lily forgot about Harry. If Remmington's driver won a contest for looking fierce, this one would win for sheer ugliness. He was no taller than Lily, but he was just as brawny as his companions. Hardly an inch of his face lacked a scar, and his large cauliflower nose did nothing to enhance his appearance. Curly red hair sprinkled liberally with gray sprung out from his head in every direction.

Remmington lifted a hand to acknowledge him. "Digsby, make sure the entryway is secure, then we'll bring Lady Lillian in to direct us through the house."

The curly-haired man gave them an extremely formal bow, then he led the other men up the steps and into the house. A moment later he reappeared.

"The entryway seems in order, Your Grace." Digsby

bowed again with one hand over his waist, the other extended toward the interior of the house. "It appears quite safe for Lady Lillian to enter."

Lily was so astounded by the refined speech and the elegant manners that came from such a coarse-looking man that she didn't hesitate when Remmington took her elbow and led her into the house.

"Where is the library?" Remmington asked. Lily pointed to a set of double doors, and he pushed them open to look inside. A lamp on the desk burned brightly, and he took a cursory glance around the book-lined room. He sounded appalled by whatever he found there. "Good God."

"What?" she asked anxiously.

Remmington stepped to the center of the library and turned in a slow circle to complete his survey. "He ransacked the place."

"Oh, no!" Lily hurried into the library. She checked the floor-to-ceiling bookcases, the desk and tables, even the floor. Her puzzled gaze returned to Remmington. "Everything is in order."

"The library always looks like this?" His hand swept out toward several piles of papers stacked on the floor near the desk, each balanced over a foot high. His other hand indicated similar piles placed dangerously close to the fireplace. Lily nodded.

Remmington glanced around the room once more, amazed by the chaos. He assumed there was some sort of desk underneath the books and papers that were piled around and on top of a rectangular piece of furniture. Near the fireplace, the backs of two chairs rose above more papers. There appeared to be a sofa beneath a pile of scrolls that spilled onto the floor, and the bookcases were just as disorderly. At least half the contents of the shelves lay scattered around the room. They left gaps as ugly as missing teeth in the bookcases.

"Your Grace?" Digsby inquired from the doorway. He tilted his head toward the hallway. "Could I request your presence in the kitchens?"

"Keep an eye on her," Remmington told Harry. "I'll let you know what turns up."

After Remmington left, Lily lit several more candles, then rearranged a pile of papers so she could sit in one of the wing chairs that flanked the desk. Harry spied the cut-glass decanters on the sideboard, and he poured a healthy portion of brandy into a glass.

"Here, drink this." He held the glass out to Lily. She shook her head, but Harry pressed the glass into her hand. "It will probably soothe your throat," he explained, as he nudged the glass toward her lips. "It certainly couldn't hurt."

Lily wasn't so sure when the fiery liquid hit her throat, but she didn't have long to worry about the brandy. The sound of loud voices caught her attention. Remmington appeared in the doorway, her father and Digsby right behind him.

"Papa!" Lily launched herself into her father's arms. Remmington led the older man to a wing chair.

Although he was in his middle fifties, Crofford still appeared lean and fit despite his sparse gray hair, but tonight his angular face showed its age. Eyes the same sherry color as his daughter's reflected the strain of fear. Harry cleared the books and papers from the chair to make room for the earl while Lily sank down to the floor near her father's knee.

"Thank you, Digsby." Remmington dismissed the servant with a nod. "Let me know if you find anything unusual in the rest of the house."

"Your Grace," Digsby murmured. He bowed again, then removed himself from the library.

"Could I pour you a drink, sir?" Remmington reached for the brandy decanter.

The earl accepted the drink, downed the contents in one gulp, then handed the glass back for another. Remmington refilled the glass and waited while the earl took a long sip. "Can you tell us what happened?"

"The damned bounder was masquerading as my driver." Crofford shook his head. "Had plenty of time to think things over during the past hour. My driver, John, was on the box when we went to Ashland's. I paid little attention when I set off for White's, yet now I realize he was careful not to let me see his face. I think that might be when he made the switch. When we arrived back here, he opened the door and stuck a pistol in my face."

"Did you recognize him?" Remmington asked.

"No, he'd put on some sort of mask. An ugly Oriental thing," Crofford added. He rubbed his forehead. "It's the type of mask the Chinese use in their theater, I think."

"It seems likely that he wore a mask to avoid being recognized," Remmington said. "Are you certain it wasn't your driver?"

"My driver is an Irishman," Crofford told him. "I'm certain this man is English. The mask muffled his voice, but he spoke without any trace of an accent."

Despite Crofford's conviction, Remmington wasn't convinced of the driver's innocence. Of the earl's seven servants, they found six tied up in the kitchen with their employer. The driver was the only servant unaccounted for now and during the attack.

He watched the earl stroke his daughter's hair in an absent gesture and felt a stab of jealousy that he could not do the same. He recalled how soft she had felt when he held her in his carriage, the velvety texture of her cheek when he touched her face. The room suddenly felt warmer, and he rubbed his palm against his thigh, as if he could brush away those memories. He didn't want to feel anything for Lily but sympathy. He forced himself to focus his attention on the earl. "What happened next?"

"He held the weapon to my head and said we had business inside the house. Thought he meant to rob the place." There was a catch in Crofford's voice, and he had to wait a moment before he continued. "He had far more devious plans than that. Knew every one of my servants by name and where to find each one at that time o' night, the clever bastard. First he ordered a footman to rouse the staff and send them to the kitchen, then he made the cook tie everyone up while he held the pistol on me. He made sure the knots were tight before he gagged us all. Trussed us up like Christmas turkeys. If I'd known then . . ."

Lily took one of his hands into hers and laid her head on her father's knee. She made a beautiful, sad picture there, one Remmington knew he would remember for a long time. He saw the tracks of tears wet the earl's face, and everyone waited while he sipped his brandy, a visible struggle to retain his control.

"Seemed like hours later when I heard Lily's screams." Crofford gazed intently at his daughter, the lines of his face etched into the agonized expression of a father who could do nothing to protect his child from danger. His voice dropped to a bare whisper. "The screams seemed to go on and on, but it was even worse when they stopped. I thought . . . I thought he . . ."

Crofford covered his face with his hands. A soundless sob racked his shoulders. Lily lifted her head and gently pulled her father's hands from his face to force him to stare into her eyes. "I'm . . . fine, Papa."

The words sounded forced. The earl grimaced and reached out to trail his fingers along the ruffled neckline of her nightgown. "Fine?" He brushed his thumb with infinite care over a dark bruise that showed on her throat. His voice turned harsh with shock and sorrow. "He nearly killed my baby! He could have—"

The earl's expression grew hard with resolve. He held his daughter's face between his weathered hands, his voice quiet with determination. "Did he hurt you anywhere else, Lily?"

She shook her head. "No!"

A discreet knock at the library door interrupted the awkward moment. Harry opened it only a crack, then just a bit wider to allow Digsby into the room.

"Tell us what you found in the rest of the house." Remmington poured another brandy for himself. He welcomed the distraction of Digsby's presence. The earl's worry brought to mind an ugly picture, one he hadn't fully considered before now. The way Lily blushed and looked away from her father could mean she was simply embarrassed by the questions. Or, it might mean that she meant to spare her father the truth. He stared down at his clenched hand and decided it would be best to set the fragile glass of brandy aside for the moment.

Digsby bowed then began to recite his report. "We attended to the earl's household staff and they seem recovered. No one inside the house sustained serious injury. Unfortunately, we found a rather unpleasant surprise in the stables. According to the cook, the gentleman we found there is one John Larson, the earl's driver." Digsby's eyes shifted to Lily, who was still seated on the floor. He lowered his voice to a tone only Remmington could hear. "It appears that someone strangled him, Your Grace."

"John is dead?" Crofford asked anxiously.

Digsby waited for Remmington's silent approval, then nodded his answer. "We haven't summoned the undertaker, my lord. I thought you might wish to take those matters into your own hands."

"Did you find the earl's carriage?" Remmington asked. With the driver dead, the servants were cleared of suspicion. The town servants, he amended, thinking the size of the earl's staffs at his country estates would be considerable. There was a reason the man had worn a mask. If he hadn't, Remmington felt certain the earl or Lily would have recognized him.

"No, Your Grace," Digsby answered. "The stables contained two barbs and a phaeton, but no carriage."

"What about Lady Lillian's room?"

"Signs of a struggle, Your Grace. I found a rather weighty candlestick with traces of blood on the base. There were a few spots on the carpet and marks on the hallway wall along the stairwell. It appears the injured person put a hand to the wound before he made his way down the steps. A hand along the wall to support himself would account for the stains found there. The cook says they heard their mistress flee the house and he felt certain he heard the culprit exit the premises a short time later."

"Was there anything else of interest in the house?"

"Not in the house, Your Grace, but in the side yard." Digsby's manner remained calm and collected, as if the subject was of no more concern than the weather. "There is an area directly beneath the library window where the bushes were pushed aside and the undergrowth trampled. We found more than a score of these, but as they were all the same I brought only the largest."

Remmington accepted the stub of a cheroot from Digsby's extended hand, then held the half-smoked cigar to the light for closer examination. He passed the object under his nose and remarked absently, "Expensive." He held the cheroot up for Crofford's inspection. "I don't know about you, sir, but I can only smoke two of these in a night. Actually, one is more than enough. It would appear the culprit was at your house several times. It would account for his knowledge of your staff, though not entirely. Whoever he is, the man is thorough."

"He is a murderer!" Crofford declared, his hands balled into fists. "I will not sleep until he is locked away. My daughter will never be safe until then."

"I fear you are right." Remmington's expression turned grim. "Unfortunately, it seems he is rather clever as well."

"Clever or not, I will see him caught and hung for his crimes." Crofford looked from Harry to Remmington. "I can never thank both of you enough for what you have done tonight. When I think of Lily alone on the streets, after what she'd faced in her own home ... He could have killed us all. Trussed up helpless as rabbits, he could have slit every one of our throats."

"Your lives were in danger," Remmington agreed. A muscle in his jaw tightened as he looked from Crofford to his daughter. Lily still looked badly shaken. "We are just glad we could be of service."

"I'll have extra men brought up from Crofford Hills," the earl announced, with a nod that seemed to agree with his decision. He propped his elbow on the arm of his chair and raked a hand through his hair. "Your assistance tonight is much appreciated, Your Grace. And yours as well, Lord Gordon. I am in both your debts and would be even more so if I could impose upon you to keep this matter as quiet as possible. The scandal would be quite embarrassing, don't you know."

"Of course," Harry answered. "You have my word on the matter, sir."

"And mine," Remmington added. "Rest assured that none shall hear a word of the incident from my men, either. They can be trusted to hold their silence."

"Appreciate that." Crofford nodded gravely.

"Would you like my men to stay until your staff arrives from Crofford Hills?" Remmington offered. His gaze rested briefly on Lily. He could feel their time together drawing to an end. He didn't want to leave her, but she was with her family now. He had no right to stay.

"I don't worry about that madman attacking in broad daylight," Crofford began. "But I would rest considerably easier if your men wouldn't mind hanging about till dawn."

"I'll inform Digsby of the arrangement. Just let him know when they're no longer needed. He and the other men can return in my traveling coach."

A short, uncomfortable silence passed as everyone realized the immediate danger was over. There was no longer a need for Remmington and Harry to remain at Crofford House. Harry cleared his throat, then found a grim smile as he swung his greatcoat over his shoulders.

"I say, Remmington. We should be off and let these people get their rest. Been a rather eventful night for all of us."

Remmington nodded, but his eyes remained on Lily. "You are sure you will be all right?" He meant the question for Lily, but it was Crofford who answered.

"Quite fine, thanks to your help, Your Grace, and yours, Lord Gordon." Crofford patted his daughter's shoulder, then rose from his seat and escorted the men to the door. "If there's ever anything I can do to repay you, anything at all, please do not hesitate to let me know."

Remmington took a last look at Lily, nodded once, then he stepped into the hallway and closed the door behind him.

Three

---✦---

"The charade is over, Lily."

A transformation came over the earl the moment the two men departed. Gone was the air of fear and distraction. In its place was grim determination. Lily moved out of the way as her father pulled his chair up to the desk. He rummaged through his desk to find his quill pen and a sheaf of paper.

"Have a seat." The tip of his quill pointed toward a chair on the opposite side of the desk, then he bent over the blank sheet of paper and began to scribble at a furious pace. "I'll have a footman take this letter around to Sir Malcolm at dawn. It will tell him what happened tonight and inform him that you are already on your way to the safe house he keeps in Brighton. We need to get you out of London. Quickly."

"What is a safe house?" Lily asked. She nudged aside a pile of papers with her hip as she settled onto the chair.

"It's a place where no one will ask questions, where you'll be safe until we catch this man and uncover the reasons for his attack." He tore a corner from one of the papers stacked on his desk and wrote down an address. "This is the direction to the house. Inform the servants there that you will be staying by invitation of a Mr. Short. It's a code and they won't ask any more questions."

"But—"

"I want no arguments from you, Lily. Every fear I've harbored for the past four years came true tonight. It was a mistake to give Bainbridge my permission to involve you in this business in the first place. I knew no good could come of it." He glanced up from his writing long enough to scowl at her across the desk. "It seems I was right."

"Sir Malcolm is careful to keep my involvement a secret. We can't even say for certain that this happened because of our work. You cannot blame yourself, Papa. The man who attacked me is responsible for what happened tonight, not you."

Crofford dismissed her opinion with an impatient wave. "Bainbridge could sell coal in Newcastle. He convinced me that you would never be in any danger. I must have been out of my mind. I should have put a stop to it years ago, before your very life was at stake."

"But my work is important, Papa. You said yourself that my talent with codes is rare."

"True, but you will not put your talent to use again anytime soon." He added a final paragraph to the letter. "Nothing is more important than your life."

"What about Robert's life?" she asked. "I'm the only one in England who can break his Cross code. It will be months yet before you master the formulas."

He looked up at last and slowly shook his head. "Your brother can take care of himself, Lily. Bainbridge will notify Robert that he is to use the new Maze code until we resolve this situation. The French haven't developed a new code in months, and I am perfectly capable of deciphering anything they might come up with."

"You know I can break the codes faster than you can." It wasn't a boast, but a statement of fact. If the truth wouldn't persuade him, guilt might. "What about the lives that depend upon deciphering those messages as quickly as possible?"

"I cannot take care of the world," he said, "and its fate does not rest solely on your shoulders either. We shall manage as best we can in your absence. What do you think we would do right now if that madman had succeeded tonight? Your absence would be a permanent one. Do you think I will allow you to risk your life that way again?"

The finality of his tone worried her. "If you truly wish to send me away then I will go, but do not take my work away from me. Please, Papa."

Crofford set aside his pen and folded his hands on the desk. "We will not lose the war in the few days or weeks you are away, Lily. But you must face the fact that I cannot make any promises right now. If tonight's attack is related to your work, that means the French know your identity and you will not be safe until the war ends. If that is the case, then I'm not sure what we will do. Undoubtedly, your work will come to a halt. You need to prepare yourself for the possibilities."

Lily felt herself nod. For the first time, she realized just how much her life had changed over the past few hours. She might have to stay in hiding until the war ended. She couldn't picture it.

"You've been through more tonight than any young woman should go through in a lifetime," he continued, his tone subdued, "and you will be forced to endure even more over the next few weeks. You're a strong girl. Right now your very life could depend on that strength. Can you be strong for me, Lily?"

She nodded again.

"Good. Now I want you to go upstairs and pack no more than one trunk. You will take the morning mail coach to Brighton, and more than one trunk will attract undue attention. Dress in something black with a veil that covers your face. The mourning clothes you wore to Great-aunt Amelia's funeral should do nicely. I think it will be best if you appear a recent widow, too overcome by grief to engage in polite conversations."

"The Brighton mail coach? A *widow*!"

"Sending you in a Crofford carriage emblazoned with the family coat of arms would hardly keep your location a secret. Hired coaches are notoriously slow. They rarely make a trip without breaking down at least once. Think, Lily. The mail coach is the fastest, most reliable means of making this journey in secret."

"I'm to go alone?"

"Not completely, my dear. Every respectable lady travels with a servant. Take along your maid, Gretchen. She doesn't seem the talkative sort. Considering the events of this night, she'll go along readily enough with the widow story."

"You won't go with me?"

"No, Lily. I must stay here. I'll make sure everyone thinks you are here as well, stricken with an illness of some sort that has you bedridden. If the fiend breaks into the house again, this time we'll be prepared. I won't risk your life so foolishly by having you here within his grasp."

"Come with me, Papa. You mustn't endanger yourself." Lily reached across the desk to grasp his hand, but he eyed his daughter's other hand, the one that rubbed her throat. He shook his head.

"I'll be in little actual danger. The men I'll send for are not from Crofford Hills. They'll be Bainbridge's men, all more than capable of handling ... the situation. I can cover your absence, but the man will not show himself again if we both leave."

"Why can't I stay with Sophie and the Bainbridges?" she asked. "Close by where you can reach me if I'm needed?"

"Staying with the Bainbridges would be like leading a fox to the henhouse. The only thing you need to do now is hide. I want you to promise that you will do nothing to endanger yourself. I will worry enough for your safety."

Lily looked ready to continue the argument, but at last she nodded. "I promise, Papa."

"Excellent. Now go pack your things. I don't want you to miss the coach."

Lily packed her trunk as quickly as possible. She sent a sleepy Gretchen off to her quarters to do the same. Less than half an hour later, two haggard-looking footmen carried her trunk down the stairway followed by Gretchen who toted her own bulging satchel. Remmington's man, Digsby, still lingered in the foyer. The library door stood open and her father emerged at the sound of her arrival.

"Digsby reminded me that my carriage is missing at the moment. It will be almost impossible to find a hired hack at this time of night. Digsby feels certain the duke would insist that his driver see you safely to the Two Swans, and he graciously offered the use of Remmington's coach in his employer's stead. I told him you plan to stay with Great-aunt Amelia in West Wycombe until this dreadful business is over." He gave her a meaningful look and her nod said she understood the lie. "I will let you know the moment we apprehend the villain. Until then, I'll feel better knowing you're safe with Aunt Amelia. Now let's get you to the carriage. I don't want you to miss the coach for West Wycombe."

When she stepped outside, Lily noticed that her trunk was already loaded onto the back of the duke's carriage. Digsby hurried forward to hold open the carriage door.

"My lady." He executed another of his proper bows as he held open the carriage door. Lily wondered if Remmington hadn't taken lessons from the man. They both executed the move flawlessly.

The driver was at their side in an instant to take Gretchen's satchel. He was one of the earring wearers with the colorful bandanna. Not the most likely-looking driver, but Digsby was hardly a likely-looking butler, with his scars and wildly untamable hair. His rust-colored curls danced about in the evening breeze with a life of their own. But he was propriety itself as he handed Lily up into the carriage. Gretchen followed, then the earl filled the carriage's open doorway. Their good-byes were hasty. She knew her father wanted her away from the house while there was hope that her attacker would not observe her departure. Moments later the carriage pulled away. Crofford House and everything else Lily valued were left behind her.

Little more than four hours earlier she had struck down the man who had tried to kill her. He might be recovered from his injuries by now, ready to hunt her again. An uncontrollable shiver racked her body, and she lowered the black net veil to hide her fear from Gretchen.

The maid seemed excited over the prospect of this journey, and she had readily agreed to accompany her mistress to an unknown destination. Only a handful of the earl's town servants accompanied the family to Crofford Hills when they retired to the country, and Gretchen was not among that number. Lily wondered if the girl had ever been beyond the boundaries of London. She was about to ask that question when the carriage rolled to a stop.

"We can't possibly be at the Two Swans already." Lily leaned forward just as Digsby appeared at the carriage door with an explanation.

"Pardon me, my lady."

Lily anticipated the bow before it came. Lord, the king's servants didn't bow as much as this man did. "Yes, Digsby?"

"Jack reminded me that my missus will worry, as quickly as we left earlier this evening. As long as we had to pass by His Grace's residence, I thought you might not mind if we stopped ever so quickly to put my wife's worries to rest."

"You're married, Digsby?"

Well, that wasn't very tactful, she decided, glad for

the veil that hid her embarrassment over her rude question. No reason the man wouldn't be married. After all, Vicar Robbins said there was someone for everybody. A wife for Digsby proved the point.

"My wife is employed as the cook, my lady." Digsby kept his hands at his sides and stood at rigid attention. Lily finally realized he was waiting for her permission.

"You must certainly put her mind at ease," she offered, with a wave toward the door. "Do hurry, Digsby. We haven't much time."

"My lady." He dropped into the bow she was starting to find annoying.

Digsby walked up the steps and disappeared inside the house as Lily lowered the window curtain on the carriage door. Veiled or not, she was uneasy about the possibility of being seen in front of the duke's residence.

Remmington was inside that house, just a few steps away. Why did the knowledge bring with it a small rush of excitement? Lily frowned and leaned away from the window. Their brief but eventful acquaintance was at an end.

At least she didn't have to worry about seeing him again until she returned from Brighton. That might be weeks. Perhaps months. He would very likely be married in the meantime. She must use this time to forget Remmington and her childish infatuation with him. That thought made her sigh, for she could sooner forget her name. She missed him already; his air of authority, the gentle way he held her, the tenderness in his expression when they stood before Crofford House. She'd wanted him to put his arms around her then, to draw her closer, to—

"Are we really in a duke's carriage?" Gretchen asked. The maid brushed her hand over the tufted seats and reverently touched the velvet upholstery of the walls. The brass trim of the doors and fittings sparkled like gold in the soft light that glowed from the carriage lantern, and rich mahogany gleamed along the trim.

Gretchen shot Lily a guilty look and returned her

hands to a prim position on her lap, her eyes downcast. "Sorry, my lady. I didn't mean to be so forward."

Lily smiled. She doubted whether Gretchen had known an *un*forward moment in her life. "I don't mind your questions. Yes, it is a duke's carriage. He's the employer of Jack and Mr. Digsby, and the other men at the house tonight."

"Is he one of your suitors? The duke, that is." Gretchen fidgeted uncertainly when Lily took a moment to reply.

"No. He is courting another lady." Lily wondered how they'd gotten onto this subject. "Don't you have a beau yourself, Gretchen?"

"Oh, no, miss. I had one a long time ago, but he married my best friend. Wasn't much interested after that. I'm not the sort to draw a man's attention anyway."

"Well, I don't agree," Lily said kindly. She inspected the maid with a critical eye, looking for some trait to praise. The girl's hair was a nondescript shade of brown, her eyes murky green. She had the sort of face that would look very motherly in a few more years. Though not obese, Gretchen was certainly on the plump side. "You've a very nice complexion and a pleasant face, Gretchen."

"Why, thank you, miss." Gretchen's cheeks glowed from the praise. "I'm afraid the men don't seem to see it that way. Then again, could be the right one hasn't seen me yet!"

Lily began to chuckle over Gretchen's outlook on men, but the laughter caught in her throat. The carriage door snapped open and a hand reached inside to wrap around her wrist. She could barely draw a breath before she found herself yanked out of the carriage.

"Remmington!" Lily tried to keep her feet underneath her as he pulled up the steps toward his house. He didn't acknowledge his name, barely seemed to notice that she was at his side as he towed her along. His mouth was set in a straight, determined line, the dark expression on his face nearly frightening. She looked lower and realized he was wearing a black satin robe. His strong, bare legs emerged from the folds of the garment with every long stride. "Good Lord. You're on the street in your robe! Have you lost your wits?"

"I seem to recall you in a similar state not so long ago," he said in a faintly mocking tone. His stride didn't break as he continued into the house. He passed through a door into the library, slammed the door shut behind them, then led her to a low couch and pushed on her shoulders until she sat down.

"You're staying here."

Of all the things he could have said to her, that was the last thing she expected to hear. In fact, it wasn't even on the list. "I'm *what*?"

"You're staying here. In my house." He planted his hands on his hips and stared down at her. The look in his eyes dared her to defy him. "Digsby told me that your father sent you packing to some elderly aunt's house in the country. I've never heard of anything so ludicrous in my life. Until I can talk reason into your father, you'll stay here."

"I will do no such thing!" As she stood up to face him, it dawned on her that Remmington thought he was doing her a favor. He'd rescued her once tonight, and now he seemed to feel responsible for her safety. She appreciated his concern, yet how could she tell him that she didn't need to be rescued? The windows reflected long, gray shadows and she knew her time was about to run out. The mail coach would leave in less than half an hour. She had to leave.

Physical strength wouldn't win this argument. Her wits would. Or rather, what would appear to be a lack of them. Men could be persistent when they set their mind to something, yet she could be equally evasive. She calmly drew the netting aside and arranged the veil over her hat. "I do appreciate your concern, Your Grace, but I simply cannot remain here another moment. My coach will leave the Two Swans no later than seven o'clock, and I must be on my way."

He studied her for a moment, a puzzled expression on his face, then he shook his head. "There's no hurry. You aren't going to West Wycombe on a public coach."

"But of course I am. Papa planned this himself. He would be very upset to learn that you detained me, that I am in your house unchaperoned. Can you imagine the scandal should anyone learn of this visit?" It wasn't hard to look horrified by the possibility. Men fought duels over far less serious matters. He must know the possible consequences, yet she decided to give him a reminder. "My family would surely demand satisfaction, for my reputation would be in shreds. It would mean social ruin for us both. Please don't be stubborn about this, Remmington. I'm leaving."

"You're not."

Lily gritted her teeth. "You can't keep me here."

"Really?"

The implication that he might use physical force to get what he wanted made her hesitate. The thought alarmed her, yet what he wanted wasn't so very offensive. He meant to keep her safe, and he'd obviously decided to do whatever it would take to insure as much. If only the situation were as simple as it appeared. He deserved gratitude rather than an argument. Unfortunately, her feelings on the matter didn't change any of the facts. She had to leave.

"I believe kidnapping is a very serious offense," she said. "My maid will go straight to my father when I don't return to the carriage. His gratitude will be short-lived when he learns you are holding me here against my will. He will very likely press charges."

Remmington shrugged off her warning. "I'm certain your maid is having a nice hot cup of tea in my kitchens at this very moment. Digsby is already on his way back to your house to collect the rest of my men. He will also inform the earl that I wish to have lunch with him at our club to discuss certain changes in your travel plans. If he insists on sending you to West Wycombe, then I will take you there personally. It won't be any great feat to get you back into my carriage without being seen, and to West Wycombe without being recognized." His gaze lowered to inspect her somber mourning clothes, his tone disdainful. "I doubt even Great-aunt What's-her-name will recognize you in that awful getup."

Lily didn't take offense over the insult. His plan sounded reasonable. It would be much safer to travel in Remmington's carriage than in a mail coach. She could even picture herself in his coach. He would have his arm around her again, and her head would rest against his shoulder. The gentle swaying of the coach would lull them both to sleep, but he would hold her securely in his arms, safe in his care. She released a wistful sigh. His plan tempted her. Unfortunately, there were just a few minor flaws in his scheme, such as the fact that Great-aunt Amelia had died three years ago, the woman had never lived a day in West Wycombe, and he must never learn her true destination.

She had to leave.

"You've done more than enough already," she said, trying desperately to think up a logical argument. "I cannot allow you to inconvenience yourself any further on my account. Gretchen and I will be quite safe on the mail coach. I expect the journey will prove uneventful, probably even tedious. You know how very dull long journeys can be. There is no need for you to endure that long ride to West Wycombe, my lord. If you are truly so concerned about my safety, I shall have my father send you notice of my safe arrival. Of course, you are more than welcome to accompany me to the Two Swans, although I daresay you might be recognized. You know how crowded the inns can be when the mail coaches depart. And of course you are hardly dressed for an outing, so that might not be such a sound idea after all. We are rather pressed for time, you see. I think it best if we go on ahead to the Two Swans without you."

Remmington frowned, then he turned the tables on her. "It is done, Lily. You will not set foot from this house until after I speak with your father. You may make yourself comfortable here in the library until that time, or avail yourself of a guest room to rest for a few hours. Considering the fact that neither of us has slept tonight, I highly recommend the rest. I intend to sleep a few hours myself until my appointment with your father. I'm certain you'll want something more comfortable than that dress to sleep in, so I'll have your trunk taken upstairs to your room. You may rest easier knowing I will have one of my men posted outside your door. Would you like a cup of tea, or perhaps even a glass of sherry before you retire?"

It was Lily's turn to frown. "I'm leaving."

"Are we back to that again?" He rolled his eyes. "Lack of sleep begins to make me irritable. I've presented a sensible solution to your dilemma. Until I can escort you to West Wycombe, you will be much safer here than you would be on the mail coach. Now, it's time for you to decide. Either you walk upstairs to the guest room, or I carry you there. One way or another, I intend to be asleep in my own bed within a quarter hour. Which will it be?"

"I want to leave!"

His expression made Lily wonder if she should have tried tears in the first place. They wrought a remarkable change in his manner. In an instant, the determination in his expression faded to a look of uncertainty and concern. He reached for one of her hands to give it an ineffectual pat. "You are overset, Lily. Little wonder after everything you've been through."

She began to cry harder. Remmington looked hesitant for a moment, then he drew her into his arms. The black satin of his robe felt warm and sleek beneath her hands. She turned her head to rest her cheek against the soft material, all too aware of the hard flesh it covered. The temptation was too great. Lily felt herself melt against his chest, conceding the argument, surrendering herself to his care.

He couldn't know what he'd just done. Her father would be beside himself when he learned she was here.

What could he possibly say to Remmington's offer? She wondered if there was a safe house in West Wycombe. The possibility seemed remote.

"There will be no more talk of the mail coach," he said. "I'm taking you upstairs. It's obvious you need sleep to recover from your ordeal. In any event, it's nearly dawn and you'll never reach the Two Swans in time."

"I will." Her tearful declaration carried little weight. It would take a miracle to get her to the Two Swans before the coaches departed. They both knew it.

"You won't," he countered. He lifted her into his arms, then carried her from the library.

The sudden shift from standing upright to being carried made her dizzy. In truth, she couldn't say if it was the change in position, or the man who held her that accounted for the reaction. She pushed against his chest. "Put me down this instant. This is indecent!"

"I'd call it sensible." He ignored her feeble struggles and carried her up the stairs. "Your father's harebrained scheme to send you off on a public mail coach is what I would call indecent."

"But you don't understand!"

He gave her a wry look, then nudged open one of the doors that lined the hallway at the top of the steps. They entered a feminine-looking bedchamber that smelled of stale lavender. He placed her none too gently on the ruffled bed, then stepped back to cross his arms. "I understand more than you think."

The certainty of his words made her breath catch. He'd kept her too distracted to concentrate on what she said. Had she let something slip?

"You are worried about my reasons for keeping you here."

"I am?" She stifled a sigh of relief. Her secret was safe for the moment.

"Yes, you are." He walked over to the fireplace and absently rearranged the small figurines that sat on the mantel. "Some men might use this opportunity to take advantage of a woman." He looked at her over his shoulder. "I am not that type of man. You will be as safe with me as you would be with your father. Perhaps safer, given his notions about protecting you." He held up one hand to cut off the objection she tried to make. "We got off to a bad start at the ball last night. I know I hurt your feelings. Look at this as my way of making amends. I will take you to West Wycombe tomorrow, then we can make a fresh start of things when you return. If you can manage as much, I would like you to forget what happened at the Ashlands'."

Their ill-fated meeting at the Ashlands' ball was the last thing on Lily's mind. Finding some way to get from this house to Brighton and not inadvertently end up in West Wycombe was her biggest worry at the moment. Already the bedroom windows reflected the rosy colors of dawn. She sighed in defeat. It had been such a simple plan. He'd managed to unravel it completely.

"You have no choice but to stay here," he said, as if he'd read her thoughts.

She stared out the window and refused to look at him. "You've left me no choice."

She didn't hear him step closer to the bed. His touch startled her when his hand captured her chin, a silent command to look up at him. "Don't be afraid of me, Lily. I'm only thinking of your safety."

His fingers brushed across her cheek and she finally lifted her lashes to look into his eyes. She could lose herself in those inky depths. Every emotion she'd ever felt about him rushed to the surface; anger and admiration, yearning and desire, jealousy and hope. No matter what went before, the attraction she felt for him remained.

His hand cupped her face in a gentle embrace that drew her closer. His gaze reminded her of the hypnotic attraction that drew a moth to a flame. She closed her eyes and drew a ragged breath. That fire could destroy her.

At last his hand slid away and she breathed a sigh of relief. She had hoped he would kiss her, *wanted* him to kiss her. It shamed her to know he could affect her so easily.

"I think it's best if I leave now." His voice sounded strained and her gaze traveled no higher than the scowl that curved his lips. "There will be a guard in the hallway." He pointed toward a door next to her bed. "My room is through this door. I thought you might rest easier knowing that no one will be able to enter your room." He hesitated a moment, started to say something, then changed his mind. Shaking his head, he said, "It's been a long night, Lily. Try to get some rest. I'll wake you when I return from my meeting with your father."

Four

—❖—

Remmington paced his library like a caged tiger. He wanted to break something. How could he have been so stupid?

"Your Grace?" Digsby asked from the doorway.

"About time you showed up." He'd sent for Digsby less than a minute ago, the same minute he'd arrived home from his meeting with Crofford. "Wake that damned woman and send her down here immediately."

"Would the damned woman be Miss Gretchen or Lady Lillian?"

Remmington glared at him. "Don't play thick-skulled with me, Digsby. I've had my fill of dealing with fools for one day and I still have—" His next order came from between clenched teeth. "I want Lady Lillian in this room immediately."

Digsby bowed and retreated as Remmington picked up the brandy he'd just poured. For a moment he considered flinging the glass against the door as it swung closed. It was tempting, but instead he drank the fiery liquid, then slammed the empty glass down on his desk. "Of all the stupid, asinine, inconceivable . . ." Remmington continued to mutter as he paced the floor and recalled the events that led to his fury.

Ensconced in one of White's private rooms, the meeting with Lily's father shouldn't have taken more than a few minutes. He'd intended to inform Crofford of the change in his daughter's travel plans, then return home and take Lily to West Wycombe posthaste. He'd known when he left her room that morning that he had to get her out of his house as soon as possible. A guilty conscience could override baser instincts for only so long. She would turn white as a sheet if she had any idea of the thoughts that went through his head every time he touched her. He wanted her. Badly.

His simple plan to rid himself of temptation went awry from the start, from the moment he informed Crofford of Lily's whereabouts and announced his intention to have her travel to West Wycombe in his carriage.

"Good God," Crofford had whispered. "That won't do at all, Remmington. No, not at all."

"You cannot intend to send her on the mail coach," he pointed out, puzzled by the earl's objection. He'd expected gratitude, not a look of horror. "There are few incidents on the mail coaches these days, yet there will be no question of her safety in a Remmington coach. No one will suspect she is inside, or have any clue as to her whereabouts. It is simply the most logical option."

"No, you don't understand," Crofford said. "Lily mustn't go to West Wycombe."

"Do you care to tell me why not?"

"Certainly."

He'd waited patiently for the explanation, and wondered in the long silence if Crofford misunderstood the question.

"Aunt Amelia isn't in West Wycombe." Crofford's announcement was blunt, his explanation almost rushed. "I sent for my solicitor this morning to arrange additional funds for Aunt Amelia's allowance, and the man reminded me that the lady went on holiday to Italy over a month ago. Afraid it slipped my mind entirely last night, what with all the commotion. Surely you understand how difficult it is to keep track of relatives. One never knows if they're coming or going. I didn't become too concerned, because I already had your message stating that Lily's travel plans had changed, and that I shouldn't worry. I thought perhaps she missed the coach and it was all for the best because Aunt Amelia isn't in West Wycombe. And you see? It was all for the best. Aunt Amelia isn't in West Wycombe at all. Lily would have been quite at sixes and sevens in West Wycombe."

Remmington stared at the earl in silence. He wondered if the man realized what a menace his daughter was to anyone's peace of mind. Sending her off to stay with an elderly aunt was hardly a sound idea. Sending her on a public coach was unthinkable. If he hadn't interceded this morning, Lily would be stranded in West Wycombe at this moment, alone and probably very frightened. He was tempted to tell the earl exactly what he thought of his half-baked plans. If Lily were his, he wouldn't allow her out of his sight.

When a question that wasn't insulting came to mind, he tried his best to contain his sarcasm. "So where do you intend to send Lily, now that you are reminded of Aunt Amelia's holiday to Italy?"

"Italy is rather pleasant this time of year." Crofford rubbed his chin. "Lily could secure passage on one of the ships that leave from Brighton. The mail coaches run there, too, don't you know. I'm certain she could manage the trip with little difficulty. No need to bother yourself over this matter, Your Grace. If you would be so good as to escort Lily to the Two Swans tomorrow morning, she can continue her journey with this slight change of itinerary."

"Slight?" Remmington lifted one brow. Had the earl lost his mind? "Crofford, your daughter is in no condi-

tion for a long sea voyage. You should not send Lily anywhere by herself right now. You should travel with her."

"Don't you think I want to be with my daughter?"
Crofford dropped his elbow to the table and rubbed his
forehead. "I can't leave London, Remmington. My plan is
to draw her attacker into the open by making him believe
Lily is still in the house. Yet if he discovers that Lily fled,
he will start searching the most obvious places. If I am
with her, there will be no guesswork at all concerning her
whereabouts."

"Isn't there somewhere else you can send Lily? Somewhere this man won't think to look for her?"

"Nowhere I could be certain of her safety. I don't
want to send her away at all, but she isn't safe here.
Hopefully, we'll catch this madman within a day or two,
and this entire business will be a blessed end. I want my
daughter back."

Remmington didn't want to give her back. Crofford
had a sound plan to catch the man who threatened his
daughter's safety, but he seemed incapable of a plan that
would keep her out of harm's way in the meantime.

"Unless you can think of a destination more suitable
than Italy, she's safer with me." Remmington closed his
mouth too late. What possessed him to make such a suggestion?

"It would be an enormous imposition." Crofford
shook his head. "You've done quite enough already."

Remmington sighed in relief.

Crofford continued to stare down at his folded hands,
then straightened in his chair. He nodded slowly, his expression enthusiastic. "Of course, it does make sense. No
one knows she's there. And it would only be for a few
days."

Remmington felt a twinge of panic. The earl was seriously considering the idea. Not that the thought of
keeping Lily didn't appeal to him, too. It was the thought
of her father knowing of the arrangement that appalled
him. She would be as untouchable as ever, yet just as
tempting. It would be torture, an insane test of his will-

power. "Of course, I'll understand if you consider the offer too outrageous. Her reputation would be in shreds if anyone learned she was in my house unchaperoned."

"I thought you said your servants were not the types to gossip."

"You won't find more discreet servants in London." Remmington mentally kicked himself over the too-prompt answer. He should be bragging of the rumormongers in his employ. "Yet I would understand any father's hesitation to place an unmarried daughter in my care. I fear my reputation with women is far from exemplary."

Crofford's expression turned dark. "Are you saying that you made this offer simply as a means of seducing my daughter?"

"Of course not! I have no intention of seducing your daughter." In fact, that was what he wanted to avoid. To be accused of plotting her seduction was insulting. He leveled Crofford with a stare that would make lesser men shiver. "You have my word as a gentleman."

"Fine. I accept your word." The earl leaned forward, his expression solemn. "After all, no *true* gentleman would take advantage of a woman in such circumstances."

The two men stared at each other across the table, the air charged between them. Remmington finally broke the silence.

"Your daughter is safe, Crofford. In case you aren't aware, rumors have me very nearly engaged to Lady Margaret Granger."

"I'd heard that," Crofford murmured, undaunted by his glare.

"Lily has nothing at all to fear from me."

"I'm glad to hear that, too."

"She's safer in my home than she is in her own!"

"I believe you're right, Remmington. I accept your offer to keep Lily in hiding. You've put my worries completely to rest."

Remmington shook his head. Just recalling the conversation with Crofford made him furious. He moved to one of the long windows in his library, braced his hands on either side and stared out at the garden, unappreciative of its stately beauty.

He'd been duped. Looking back on the meeting, he felt certain he'd walked right into the old man's plot, had an ugly suspicion that this arrangement was Crofford's intent from the start. Crofford must have known that his men wouldn't abandon Lily at a public inn. Looking at the situation from Crofford's viewpoint, his town house was the perfect hiding place. No one would ever guess Lily was here.

"You sent for me?"

He grimaced at the sound of the small, hoarse voice. With a sigh, he turned to face her. She didn't look very appealing at the moment. The coil of her hair had come undone already. The long strands framed a face swollen from tears, and she still wore the ugly black gown she'd obviously slept in. She looked a mess. He felt the reluctant stirrings of pity. None of this was her fault or her doing. Her father might be manipulative, but he would swear that she played no part in any plan to insinuate herself in his household. She was an innocent, left alone and vulnerable in the care of a man she barely knew. Her father should be horsewhipped.

He fought down an urge to cross the room and take her into his arms. Then again, why not? That would prove beyond any doubt that her father's trust in him was misplaced.

In that moment, the conversation he'd overheard in the Ashland gardens came back to haunt him. Did Crofford know of Lily's infatuation? A father could demand marriage if a man compromised his daughter. Could the earl possibly be that devious? It would be the most elaborate plan ever conceived to force him to the altar, yet he couldn't entirely set the suspicion aside.

If there was any hope of weathering this situation un-
scathed, he must make it clear to Lily from the very start
that their relationship would be businesslike. He would
do nothing that might encourage her affections. He
would turn away if she looked up at him with that combination of innocence and longing that he found so appealing. Innocent looks could be deceiving. His own
experience had taught him that much, and he never
made the same mistake twice. He would ignore the rush
of heat he felt whenever she came near him, and he
wouldn't stare at her whenever he knew she wasn't looking. For the time being, he was her guardian and he
would not so much as touch her.

With his resolve firmly in place, he pointed to the
high-backed chair near his desk. "Sit down."

Lily seated herself without argument. Her head ached,
her throat hurt, and her eyes felt so swollen that she
could scarcely keep them open. But she was here to find
out what her future would hold, to discover how her father intended to get her on the Brighton mail coach without arousing Remmington's suspicions. Holding her
throat against the pain of turning her head, she looked
over her shoulder at her host.

Remmington stood before the window nearest her,
the long streamers of afternoon sunlight at odds with his
dark clothing. He wore a charcoal-gray riding jacket and
matching breeches with a pearl-gray shirt and cravat.
Sunlight reflected off brightly polished black Hessian
boots. It seemed everything he wore came in some shade
of black.

Even the room itself appeared more cheerful than its
owner, now that she had an opportunity to study the
place in daylight. Deep blue walls were trimmed with the
white woodwork of floor-to-ceiling bookcases. Not one
gap showed between the books, an indication that all the
leather-bound tomes were in their proper places. The
books were not only arranged according to size, they

were also grouped according to the color of their bindings. Amazing.

Turning in her seat to survey the room as a whole, Lily realized that everything appeared exactly right. Even the furniture was placed at precise angles. The wood glowed with rich highlights from a recent polishing, and the scent of lemon and beeswax made the room smell as fresh and clean as it appeared. Except for a few papers spread on Remmington's desk, the room looked as if it never saw any use. She wondered how he could concentrate in such a barren place.

"There have been certain changes in your travel plans." Remmington's clipped voice interrupted her thoughts, and he walked around the desk to take the seat across from her. "In fact, you no longer have travel plans."

She released a sigh of relief. "It won't take me long to gather my belongings. I'm sure there will be some risk in returning to Crofford House, but Papa will have a sound plan to deal with the culprit. I hope my stay hasn't inconvenienced you too much." She stood up to take her leave.

"Your stay hasn't begun to inconvenience me." He pointed again to her chair. "Sit down, Lily."

"But—"

"You aren't leaving." He picked up a folded paper from his desk and tapped it against his fingertips. "I want you to listen very carefully to what I'm going to tell you, Lily. I dislike repeating myself."

His voice reminded her of the tone her father used to address servants or small children. Perhaps he shared the opinion of many men that the weaker sex also had the weaker brain. Considering her circumstances, that wasn't such a bad misconception to encourage. She managed to keep her expression blank as she gave him a solemn nod.

"Your father and I decided that it's best if you stay here." He didn't give her a chance to absorb the shock of his announcement, but continued before she could object. "Your great-aunt took herself off to Italy, and your father cannot think of another safe place for you to stay until he tracks down the culprit responsible for this situation. I think it important to set a few rules at the outset of this arrangement so we will both understand what is expected of the other. First, I do a great deal of work in my library in the mornings and I will not tolerate interruptions of any sort. Second, I—"

"You cannot be serious!" Her voice broke into a harsh croak but he ignored the sound.

"Quite serious," he said. "My estates and business ventures require my undivided attention in the mornings and I will not put up with distractions. I have a very orderly schedule that will not be interrupted by your stay if you simply follow—"

"I'm not staying here." She crossed her arms and sat back to wait for his agreement.

"Your father anticipated that you might be doubtful of the arrangement." He tossed the folded paper across the desk. "His letter should help clarify the situation."

Lily snatched up the letter and broke the seal. "My father would never agree to such a ludicrous plan, Remmington. You must be . . ." Her voice trailed off as she read the contents of her father's letter.

Dearest Lily:

After a long discussion with Remmington, I am convinced you will be safer in his keeping than with Aunt Amelia in Italy.

I am certain His Grace knows my concerns about this agreement, yet he has convinced me that your safety is of the utmost importance.

I have his word that nothing of an improper nature will take place while he is entrusted with your care, that your honor will not be compromised in any way.

After much thought, I've decided you're to stay in hiding at Remmington's town house until your attacker can be brought to justice.

I fear you'll not be safe in your own home until this madman is in custody, or until his reasons for such a bold attack become known.

Remmington has promised that your stay in his home will remain a tightly guarded secret, that not even a breath of scandal will arise as a result.

I wish I could be there as well to lend my support, but you know the reasons I am staying here.

I hope that you can trust Remmington as I do.

It certainly seems there is nobody better qualified to keep you safe at this time.

I can think of a <u>halfdozen</u> reasons why you will object to this plan, but know it is my wish that you stay with Remmington until this dreadful business is resolved.

Yrs.,
Crofford

Lily understood immediately why her father underlined the word *halfdozen*. It was the sixth word in the sentence and an alternate word for six. It was also the clue to the letter's simple code. She scanned the note again, reading only the sixth word of each sentence. *Remmington knows nothing. You're safe. Stay there. Trust nobody.* Her hand trembled as she placed the letter on Remmington's desk.

"You must be very convincing, Remmington. That, or my father has taken leave of his senses." She tried to reconcile herself to the fact that she was staying. One part of her felt a sense of elation. The other part, sheer dread.

"I assure you that I was not the least convincing, and

I agree completely that your father's senses are sadly lacking where you are concerned."

Her chin rose several inches. "How dare you insult my father!"

"I am stating facts, not insults. You must also take into consideration the fact that I have had less than three hours' sleep in the past two days and now find myself the guardian of a young woman I hardly know. Forgive me if I seem somewhat irritable."

Her thoughts raced forward. She would be forced to face him every day, perhaps several times a day. How long could she pretend indifference? How long before he realized that she was as stupidly infatuated with him as she had been before they met? It was a lowering thought. "You cannot want me here. My presence will be a dreadful inconvenience."

"I agree completely."

"Good. Then I'm leaving."

"You're staying."

Lily shook her head. "My father was wrong to ask so great an imposition. I will not impose further on your hospitality by asking that you honor his request. We are already indebted for your assistance last night. Anything more is beyond presumptuous. The strain of the situation must be affecting my father's judgment. Under normal circumstances he would never consider asking such a favor. I'm afraid I must—"

"Your father didn't ask."

"Then why—"

"The reasons are none of your concern. I gave your father my word and I intend to keep it. Now as I was saying, there are certain rules in this house that I expect you to follow. After my morning work is complete, I ride in the park each day for precisely one hour. Lunch is served at one-thirty sharp. I may or may not be out during the afternoons or evenings, depending upon my engagements for that day. Regardless, dinner is served at eight o'clock without fail. There will be no special arrangements for your meals. If you wish to eat, you will present yourself in the dining room at one-thirty and eight o'clock. And I do not care for tardiness."

Lily leaned back in her chair, stunned into silence. Why had Remmington agreed to this plan? Why did he involve himself in the first place?

"During the day you may have use of the parlor," he continued. "My library is off-limits entirely. There are other guest chambers on the second floor that you may explore if you find yourself in need of diversion. My bed-chamber is also off-limits. The servants' quarters are on the third floor, and you will respect their privacy there. The music room and conservatory are on the fourth floor, although both are in considerable disrepair and should also be avoided."

It occurred to her that he was treating her like a child, listing all the rules of his house as if he were afraid she might break something. What happened to the man who promised to keep her safe, who put his arms around her and offered her comfort? This man seemed more concerned with the safety of his house than with her own.

"Your stay will hopefully last no more than a few days, so I see no reason for you to venture out of the house. There are twelve servants in residence. You will not interfere with them in any way. They take their or-ders from me, and they will not have time to cater to your whims. Your maid is your responsibility and should also be instructed not to interfere with my servants. If you follow my rules, we should get through this situation quite nicely," he said in conclusion. "Do you have any questions?"

Lily wanted to ask at precisely what time of day she could cosh her host over the head for his rude arrogance. If he remained this obnoxious throughout her stay, she wouldn't have any trouble at all dealing with her feelings for him. She fixed him with her best guileless, empty gaze and blinked once very slowly. "It seems so very much to remember. Perhaps I could follow your rules more successfully if you wrote them down."

"Very well." He spoke through clenched teeth. She marveled that he did it so well. "I shall write them out. I take it you read?"

"Of course," she answered. "I may not be the fastest reader, but I'm certain it will take me no more than a day or two to read your list. By the end of the week I shall likely have parts of it memorized." She tried hard not to smile over his groan. "Could I send a message to my father? I would very much like to assure him that I understand his concerns and will do as he asks."

"I'm afraid that won't be possible." He picked up the earl's letter and shoved it into the top drawer of his desk. "We've agreed to meet or exchange messages only when absolutely necessary. Someone is bound to notice if we begin meeting on a regular basis. Your father and I are no more than passing acquaintances. A sudden association now would seem unusual. We must also consider the possibility that your attacker is someone either of us might know. We do not want to arouse his suspicions, especially if your absence from Crofford House is discovered. I will take every precaution to see to your safety, Lily, but I would not care to lure your attacker to my home where my own servants' lives will be threatened. With any luck, you will return to your father within a few short days, and a message now—"

"I understand your reasons," Lily interrupted, wondering if he rattled on because he thought her incapable of understanding the word no. "We certainly wouldn't want my insignificant little message to endanger your servants."

He ignored the sarcastic tone of her voice. Leaning back in his chair, he studied her over steepled fingers. "There is just one more matter we need to discuss. As your temporary guardian, I am bound by my word of honor to protect your reputation as well as your person. This is a very unusual situation. Residing under the same roof, there are bound to be times when we might be tempted to forget that there is an outside world, that this situation is temporary. Extremely temporary. As you know, I am committed to another lady. We must both remember that there can be nothing more between us than friendship."

Lily made herself smile. She knew there could be nothing between them. Until the circumstances of her attack decreed otherwise, she'd had no intention of seeing him again. She'd even worried about how she would avoid him. He was making things simple. That didn't lessen the sting of his rejection.

"You needn't worry that I will expect anything more from you," she said.

"Excellent. I'm glad you understand." He glanced up at the Chelsea clock that sat on the mantel. "You have three hours until dinner. I trust you will find something to occupy yourself until that time. Perhaps you could supervise your maid while she unloads your trunk or some such thing. To avoid arousing suspicion I intend to go about my business and social engagements as usual. Thus I shall be out the remainder of the afternoon and much of the evening." He surged to his feet and walked briskly to the door, holding it open, not bothering to disguise the fact that he was anxious to rid himself of her company. "Now if you will excuse me, Lily, I have work to do."

Five

❖

"He doesn't want us here." Gretchen frowned as she placed one of Lily's freshly pressed gowns in the armoire. "That pompous Digsby won't say a word on the subject, but Jack said straight out that His Grace wants us gone. As if we have some choice in the matter!"

Lily kept silent. It hadn't taken long for Gretchen to settle into their temporary home. In less than two days, she'd already heard more gossip than Lily would ever hear from Remmington's servants.

The maid shook out another gown and gave the skirt a sharp snap. "Sometimes I don't think men know what they want. First he forces us to stay here, then he puts it about that he wants us gone."

"I hope you haven't gossiped about me with the duke's servants." She'd already warned Gretchen about that. Although the maid didn't know about the family's government work, Gretchen knew more about what went on at Crofford House than Lily wanted Remmington to know.

Gretchen's disgruntled expression turned to injured dignity. "Of course not. I agree with you completely, my lady. The less they know of you, the better. As a matter of fact, I've decided that they don't need to know all that much about me, either. They're a strange lot, my lady. If you ask me, he employs this band of cutthroats to scare people off. Jack told me that the duke doesn't receive anyone in this house except his brother and cousin. With the kind of hospitality he's shown us, one wonders if the man even has any friends to call upon him."

Lily shrugged. She'd gossiped enough about their host. He was a private man, and she couldn't find fault with him if he employed unsavory-looking servants to help insure his privacy.

She thought of her father, how he'd often complained about the people who constantly badgered him. People could be very ingenious when it came to money, yet the Crofford fortune would pale next to Remmington's. She could only imagine the number of people who tried to enlist him in their cause.

That was another reason she couldn't forget what had happened at the Ashlands' ball. Surely he knew how it felt to be used. Was he so jaded that he no longer cared whose feelings he hurt? If that was the case, his concern for her the night of her attack made little sense. Not that his concern had lasted all that long; he'd gone back to being rude and arrogant soon enough. But the glimpse of that other Remmington, the one who was capable of warmth and kindness, that was a man she wanted to know, a man she could care about.

What was she thinking? Fanciful thoughts, indeed. Who wouldn't be kind to a woman in the circumstances he'd discovered her in that night? So he was capable of compassion. That didn't mean he wanted her affection. He'd made it clear that he wanted nothing more from her than polite conversation. She doubted whether he wanted even that.

"I think I shall wear the pink gown today, Gretchen."

"A wise choice, my lady." The maid searched through the armoire, then held up the gown to brush at a few stray wrinkles. "The high neckline will hide those awful bruises on your throat. Are they still very painful?"

"My neck is still sore, but it looks much worse than it feels."

Gretchen shook her head. "Poor thing. You should stay in bed another day."

"I feel better now. It wouldn't be right to keep asking for trays when I'm perfectly capable of presenting myself in the dining room for lunch."

"They do seem fixed on people eating downstairs." Gretchen planted her hands on her hips. "I didn't want to tell you this yesterday when you felt so poorly, but at first the cook refused to make up a tray for your dinner. The man acted as if I'd asked for France on a platter. I explained to the great oaf that you were too ill to leave your bed. Then I had to remind him that your throat was too injured to swallow the tremendous hunks of beef he'd planned to serve."

Lily didn't voice her opinion that the cook was probably trying to follow Remmington's order that she eat her meals in the dining room. "I thought Remmington's cook was a woman. Digsby's wife, to be exact."

"Oh, no, my lady. Digsby lied to you straight out. The cook is a giant of a man with a bald head and a gold ring in one ear." Gretchen made a face. "He goes by the name of 'Bull.' "

Lily's brows rose for a moment, then lowered again into a scowl. She'd been duped! Digsby had lied to her about their reasons for stopping at Remmington's. If not for his interference, she wouldn't be in this awkward situation. "Rather an unappetizing name for a cook, is it not? Many cooks are rumored to have fierce tempers. I wonder if this Bull is temperamental."

"I can assure you that he is, my lady."

Gretchen braided her hair while Lily thought over

her best means of retaliation. She decided to pay Digsby's "wife" a visit right after lunch.

The thought of lunch dampened her spirits. This would be the first meal she would share with Remmington since her arrival the night before last. She hoped he would go out again today, but that reprieve seemed unlikely. According to Gretchen, who somehow knew everything that went on in the house, he'd spent the morning working in his library and he was still there. Lily wished she could continue her work rather than go down to lunch. She'd spent her morning poring over one of the scrolls she'd packed in her trunk. At the moment, the ancient scrolls sounded much more appealing than the thought of facing her reluctant host.

"My lady, you really must sit up straight for me to braid this properly."

Lily waved the maid away with an impatient hand. "Let's not pin it up today, Gretchen. Those wretched knots make my head ache."

"We are still in Town," Gretchen reminded her. "Most gentlemen would expect to see a lady's hair properly done up."

Gretchen was right, but Lily didn't want Remmington to think she'd gone to any lengths to impress him with her appearance. "Just tie it back with a ribbon, please."

Lily stood in the doorway of the dining room at precisely one-thirty. Her hopes sank when she spied Remmington at the end of the long table. Her luck had run out. She would be forced to endure his ominous presence for a good hour. This time she'd made a vow to keep her wits about her. He had a way of making her forget herself, forget her secrets. She couldn't afford any more mistakes.

Her gaily striped pink gown clashed with the predominant burgundy tones of the dining room. Remmington's dark attire was more suited to the stiff formality of the mahogany-lined room. Dressed in his usual shades of black, he rose to greet her.

"Good afternoon, Lily. Won't you join me?"

The greeting sounded more automatic than genuine. His frown confirmed as much when he indicated the place next to his at the table. Lily tried hard not to stare at him. He was always more handsome in person than the image she called to mind when they were apart. She'd determined to ignore his effect on her, to use the anger she still felt from the Ashlands' ball to protect herself. It wasn't working. Her heart beat faster with every step she took toward him. "Good afternoon, Your Grace."

"Your voice sounds better." He held out her chair as she took her seat. "Your injuries must be healing."

Lily rubbed her ear, and wished he wouldn't lean so close when he spoke to her. She managed a shrug. "I suppose they must."

She regretted the answer almost immediately. She was supposed to be nothing more than a fragile social butterfly. That woman would have played on his sympathies, complained long and loud while affecting delicate health. Too often in his presence she forgot who she was supposed to be and became who she wanted to be. That had to stop. She'd revealed too much already.

Their lunch arrived almost immediately, trays and dishes that two servants stacked on the sideboard under Digsby's direction. The servants departed but Digsby remained. He served cheddar soup for their first course, then returned to his station near the sideboard. Only the clink of their spoons against the fine bone china disturbed the room's lengthening silence.

Remmington was staring at her.

A quick peek beneath her lashes confirmed the premonition. Why was he watching her? The constant scrutiny became uncomfortable. Her back stiffened, and she concentrated on her table manners. The simple act of moving her spoon from the bowl to her mouth soon became an exercise in politeness.

The sudden sound of Remmington's voice startled her. "Why didn't your father send you to Sir Malcolm Bainbridge for safekeeping?"

Lily's spoon dropped into her bowl and broth splattered onto the fine Irish linen that covered the table. She nearly tipped the bowl over when she made a grab for the spoon. A blush warmed her cheeks as she dabbed at the spill with her napkin. "How clumsy I am!"

Digsby hurried forward to cover the mess with a linen towel that was draped over his arm. He nodded toward the empty seat across from hers. "If you wouldn't mind taking the chair to His Grace's left, my lady?"

Lily obeyed the thinly disguised order. Digsby had another bowl of soup at her new place almost before she took her seat. Remmington ignored the debacle. Judging by his bland expression, she would have thought that watching a guest nearly upend a bowl of soup onto herself was nothing out of the ordinary for him.

"The Bainbridges?" he prompted. "You seem close to Miss Stanhope and her family. I cannot help but wonder why your father didn't send you to Sir Malcolm, rather than to an elderly aunt."

"Papa didn't want to impose on the Bainbridges," she said quickly. "He thought it wiser to have me leave London entirely, to stay somewhere no one would think to look for me."

Remmington stared at her a long moment then nodded, his expression enigmatic. "I cannot imagine what your father and Sir Malcolm find to talk about. Does the earl have an interest in the military?"

The question was a reasonable one. Lily tried not to panic. "Uh, no, Your Grace. Not to my knowledge. I'm sure they discuss the usual male topics."

"Male topics?" Remmington echoed. "Do tell what those might be."

Lily searched the ceiling for an answer. Other than an intense loyalty to their country and an interest in the spy business, she didn't have the vaguest idea what the two men might have in common. "Not being a male, I'm sure I wouldn't know the answer to that question."

"How fortunate, in both respects."

She didn't ask him to explain that odd remark. Instead she tried to retreat to safer ground. "Papa is a dedicated scholar. I believe he and Sir Malcolm sometimes discuss philosophy. One can hardly be around my father without hearing something of the subject." She glanced up and noticed that he no longer stared at her. She was probably boring him. "Do you enjoy it?"

Remmington met her gaze, his expression startled, as if she'd just answered a troubling question. Lily felt as if he were looking into her soul.

"Philosophy," she said uncertainly, wondering if he misunderstood the question. "Do you enjoy the study of philosophy, Your Grace?"

He shook his head. "The only work I can recall with any clarity is Socrates' allegory of the cave. Even so, I never really understood what Socrates was trying to convey with his references to blind men and a fire."

Lily arranged the potatoes on her plate with the tip of her fork, unable to resist the urge to correct him. "It was Plato who wrote the allegory of the cave, my lord. I've heard my father repeat the tale many times. Papa says it simply means that knowledge is limited only by people's perception of reality."

"Ah, you're right, of course." He inclined his head in a gracious gesture. "I'm afraid I haven't studied philosophy since my schoolroom days. I'd forgotten how fascinating it can be. Wasn't Plato the fellow who answered a question with a question?"

"That was Socrates, my lord. He felt that everyone had the answers to their own questions, if they took the time to examine why they asked the question in the first place." Lily wanted to bite her lip. His intense gaze reminded her again that he could make her as thoughtless as a moth near a flame. Why hadn't she noticed the calculating gleam in his eyes before now? He was testing her.

"Ah, yes," he said agreeably. With his elbows propped on the arms of his chair, he folded his hands together and leaned back. He looked completely relaxed, as lazily uninterested in her as a cat just before it sprang on its prey. "Well, I'm certain that it was Socrates who said, 'The unexamined life is not worth living.' "

Lily nodded but she remained silent, avoiding his gaze.

"I say, you seem to have quite a grasp of the subject. Surely a passing interest in your father's work cannot be responsible for such detailed knowledge. Can it?"

"Well, I, ah . . ."

"Are you a bluestocking in disguise, Lady Lillian?"

Lily felt her face drain of color. Sophie had warned her away from Remmington all these years because she thought him too clever to be fooled by Lily's pretense. This was a bad time to find out that Sophie had been right all along. She'd revealed far too much of herself to an outsider.

"It's nothing to be ashamed of," he said quietly. "I don't consider educated females at all unladylike, if that's what worries you."

"No, that is not what worries me." Lily forced herself to relax, to offer up a weak smile. "I was simply startled that you would think me a bluestocking. My father tends to prattle on and on about his work. I'm afraid a little scholarly knowledge is unavoidable in such a household. That is all there is to the matter, my lord."

"I see."

He didn't believe her. There was no reason to panic, no reason for her heart to race madly. He simply thought she hid her intelligence to avoid being labeled a bluestocking. Her hands were shaking.

"If you will excuse me?" She rose from her seat and Remmington stood up automatically, but she turned to Digsby. "Please convey my compliments to your *wife*, Digsby. The meal is quite good, but all this talk of philosophy dimmed my appetite." She inclined her head toward Remmington and murmured, "Thank you for the luncheon, Your Grace. I hope to see you at dinner."

"I will be out again this evening." His answer was short and clipped. His frown was back in full force, too. He took her elbow to escort her from the room, speaking to her under his breath. "Perhaps that will improve your appetite."

She had to escape from Remmington's house. That thought was uppermost in Lily's mind as she left the dining room. She leaned against the dining-room door when it closed behind her and took a moment to calm her nerves. She should have known that Remmington's suspicions were aroused when he asked about Sir Malcolm. How did he manage to make her reveal so much?

How many more of these encounters could she endure before she said something truly disastrous? It was only a matter of time before he started to ask questions she couldn't answer. Already he suspected her of something, but he couldn't possibly know what. In time he might guess. She had to leave.

Unfortunately, Remmington's servant Jack followed her like a faithful hound wherever she went. His pirate garb no longer disturbed her. Jack might look ferocious, but he didn't seem to have much experience playing watchdog to a lady. Lily had the feeling she made him nervous. He stood in the entryway just outside the dining-room doors, his hands clasped behind his back as he stared at the floor. Obviously, he waited to follow her upstairs where he would stand watch at her door. Sneaking out of the house wasn't an option. Getting thrown out of the house might be.

"The stairs are this way, my lady," Jack said.

Lily continued to walk down the hallway on one side of the staircase toward the back of the house. She called to him over one shoulder. "I would like to thank Cook for the fine meals. I know the kitchen staff goes to some effort to accommodate my injuries."

"I don't think that is such a wise idea, my lady." Jack shot a worried look toward the dining-room doors. "Bull's kitchen is no place for a lady."

"Nonsense. Gretchen comes and goes from there all

the time." She paused to look Jack square in the eye. "Unless you are implying that my maid is not a lady."

"Oh, no, miss. I mean, my lady." Jack shifted from one large foot to the other. "Miss Gretchen is a proper young lady, too. It's just that you're . . . well . . . I don't think His Grace would approve of this."

"I'm sure Remmington will not object. Everyone needs to hear a bit of praise now and then. Is the kitchen through here?"

Lily pushed open a door and stepped into a spacious, airy kitchen. The man who stood next to a large butcher block could only be Bull. The bald man was nearly as round as he was tall. With his attention on a large knife and a colorful pile of vegetables, he didn't look up from his work to greet them.

"Good afternoon, sir," Lily called out.

Bull replied without turning around. "I told ye to keep yer—"

"Lady Lillian to see you, Bull!" Jack's shout drowned out the cook's reply.

The burly man spun around, his knife held at a menacing angle. "What ye be wanting here?"

His voice reminded Lily of a bass fiddle, played very badly. She swallowed her nervousness and smiled. "Why, to thank you for your efforts on behalf of my maid and myself. Gretchen tells me that you made special dishes to accommodate my injuries. I do appreciate your thoughtfulness."

"Nothing thoughtful about it," Bull growled. He pointed the tip of his blade at Lily. "I gave the wench what she wanted just to get her out of my kitchen. Can't stand chattering females, and that one's the worst. You can tell her I said so."

"I'll be sure to convey your opinion," Lily said politely. Her brows drew together and her expression turned thoughtful. Her gaze inspected the man from head to toe, then she slowly nodded.

Bull glared back at her. "Do ye see something of interest, mistress?"

"You must think me quite rude." She feigned embarrassment. "I'm afraid my curiosity got the best of me. You aren't at all what I'd imagined. It was a natural mistake, I suppose, to assume you were a woman."

"A what?"

She cringed, but stood her ground. "Digsby told me that the two of you are married, and at the time it didn't occur to me to think that you might be a man. What a very unique marriage you must have. These modern ways never cease to amaze me." She shrugged as if to dismiss the matter. "Well, I must be off. Thank you again for the excellent meals, sir."

Lily made a hasty retreat from the kitchen, a little surprised that Bull remained silent after her explanation. She and Jack were in the hallway when they heard the first loud crash, followed by colorful swearing.

"Digsby and Bull aren't really married." Jack sent a worried glance over his shoulder. "Bull is sure to have Digsby's hide for telling you that lie, my lady."

Lily smiled. "Oh, I don't think Digsby would lie to me, Jack. That wouldn't be right. If you'll forgive me for saying so, you really shouldn't call your friend a liar. It's disloyal." She changed the subject before Jack could argue further. "His Grace said I could explore the house a bit. I think I'd like to start on the upper floors."

Remmington leaned one shoulder against the doorway to the music room. It took a moment for his eyes to adjust to the darkened room. Dusty sheets covered the furniture and all but one window. The panes were so dirty that the day appeared gray and gloomy, even though he knew that outside the sun shone bright. He was about to go out for the afternoon when Digsby informed him of his guest's whereabouts. Digsby knew he'd forbidden her the use of this floor. Jack stood next to him in the hallway, his expression guilty. Remmington dismissed him with a curt nod, then turned his attention again to Lily. She stood near one of the grime-covered windows as she peered under a draped musical instrument.

With smudges of dirt on her gown and her hair tied back in a neat, simple bow, she appeared very young. She bent over to look underneath the sheet and her hair slid slowly over one shoulder. Even in this dim light, the coppery locks shimmered with a vibrant life of their own. He mentally untied the bow and imagined what it would be like to wrap that thick, luxurious mane around his hands. His gaze moved lower and his breath caught in his throat. With her back to him and bent over, he was left with the view of a nicely shaped derriere. His imagination let go of her hair and moved on to that more enticing part of her. He found the unconsciously provocative pose delightful, what he wanted to do to her at that moment absolutely forbidden.

It was an unwelcome reminder that he could look but not touch. And, oh, how he wanted to touch. In the dining room he'd tried to keep himself distracted with their conversation, yet he'd caught himself staring at her more than once. He'd tried to find some flaw in her appearance that would make keeping his word a little easier. As far as he could tell, she didn't have any. She'd stared back at him with wide, sherry-colored eyes that could warm a man's soul. Her lips moved, and often as not he couldn't concentrate on what she was saying. She had a mouth meant for kissing. When he did listen to the conversation, the sound of her voice proved just as distracting. Despite the lingering hoarseness, he thought a long time about what it would be like to hear that soft, sensual voice call out to him in the night, what kind of sounds she would make when they were in bed together. He'd been fully aroused by the time he'd finished his soup.

Throughout the meal, he'd done exactly what he was doing now; imagining his hands all over her body, what she would look like beneath that prim gown, how she would feel beneath him. It was torture. He couldn't stop staring. His hands itched to touch her, his body ached to possess her. Worst of all, he knew he could seduce her.

Sometimes she looked at him with such obvious longing that every muscle in his body grew tense, braced against the urge to drag her into his arms.

Only one question remained. Just how eagerly would she respond to him? Curious about the answer to that question, he took a step toward her. Then he realized what he was about to do and stopped short. He flexed his hands, clenched them into fists at his sides, then repeated the movements several times before he felt he could control his impulses. Aware that she could turn around at any moment and catch him ogling her, he cleared his throat.

She straightened at the sound and brushed her hair over one shoulder, then absently readjusted the bow. "Oh, hullo, Remmington."

She didn't look the least bit startled to see him, or the slightest bit guilty. He wondered if she'd forgotten about his rules already.

"There's a lovely old harpsichord under this sheet." She lifted the edge of the dusty fabric. "Would you like to see it?"

"No! Don't—"

It was too late. He crossed the room in two long strides, but Lily yanked the sheet away before he could stop her. A cloud of thick, choking dust rose between them.

"Oh, dear." She waved her hands in his general direction, a futile attempt to clear the air. The dim streamers of light were smothered by her hasty action, but they gradually reappeared. The first thing he noticed was her smile.

"You find something humorous in this?"

She pointed one finger at him and laughed out loud. "You look as if you've been in some awful bakery accident!"

He glanced down at his dust-covered clothing, then looked at her gown. "I would not be so quick to point fingers."

She shook her skirts and a small cloud of dust appeared. Brushing at her face and hair produced another small shower of dust. "It seems I've managed to dent both our wardrobes, my lord. My apologies."

She didn't look very contrite. He felt his stern expression dissolve into a grin. "You should see your face."

"I'd rather not, thank you." She smiled back at him, but when their eyes met, her smile became uncertain, then it faded entirely. She suddenly seemed intent on brushing herself off, her gaze averted.

He pushed away from the door frame and held out one hand. "Come, Lily. You've satisfied your curiosity about the music room. It's time we closed the place up again."

She finally looked up at him, only to shake her head. "But you haven't even looked at the harpsichord."

Lily ignored his outstretched hand and began to walk around the harpsichord to examine it from all sides. It was a large, awkward-looking contraption, yet the rosewood carvings on the cabinet were obviously the work of an expert. Remmington couldn't care less about the harpsichord. At the moment, he was absorbed by the gentle sway of her skirts, the soft outline of her hips. A small voice in his head told him they were alone together, that he could simply close the door and none of his servants would dare disturb them. He fisted his hands again, as if that could lessen the temptation to reach for the door and swing it shut. "I seem to recall that I forbade you the use of this room. The rooms on this floor are in disrepair. You could be—"

"Early eighteenth century," she interrupted. Her fingers brushed over the strings reverently. He could almost feel her fingertips brush over his body just as slowly. The imagined caress set his blood on fire. She knelt down to look beneath the instrument and he stared at every curve her new position revealed. "Perhaps seventeenth century," she mused. "I wonder if the craftsman left his mark somewhere."

He would leave his mark on her if they didn't get out

of here soon. "You are defying my orders quite blatantly, Lady Lillian."

"Here it is!"

He leaned over as she disappeared beneath the harpsichord. She sat down cross-legged near the center, then she brushed away more dust that had collected underneath. He studied the outline of her legs against the stretched fabric of her skirt. When he rested his hand against the side of the harpsichord, he heard a small creak. His interest in her figure turned to concern for her safety. "You will come out from there this moment, Lady Lillian. Do you have any idea how much this instrument weighs?"

As usual, she ignored his order completely. "Oh, my goodness. You must see this, Remmington."

He managed to sound indignant over the suggestion. "I have no intention of crawling beneath there."

Actually, the thought was appealing. If she'd sweeten the offer by promising a kiss, he'd follow her almost anywhere. In return he'd offer to brush off the dust that remained on her face and gown. He'd go about that task very slowly, very carefully, not missing an inch. His gaze raked over her again as he tried to decide what she would feel like beneath his hands. Soft. Warm. Oh, yes, she would be very warm.

He shook his head. Where were these thoughts coming from? He drew himself upright, away from temptation, and made sure his tone was stern and fatherly. "You will remove yourself immediately, young lady."

"But this is an important find." She leaned closer to gaze up at him. There was a smudge of dirt on one of her cheeks, and a cobweb dangled precariously from her hair bow. She looked like a grubby little street urchin. An urchin with the most intriguing eyes he'd ever seen. They were silently pleading with him, her expression so hopeful that he finally threw his hands up in defeat.

"Oh, all right." He knelt down and rested his weight on his hands as he inched forward. Eventually he was halfway beneath the harpsichord. Being considerably larger than Lily, he wasn't nearly as comfortable as she appeared to be in the confined space. She pointed out a brass plaque beneath the cabinet and he twisted his head around to read the inscription.

"Do you see?" She brushed away more dust that landed in his face. "It says 'Bartolomeo Cristofori, 1693.' "

"I can read," he said tersely. His neck had started to ache from the odd angle, and he was still deciding if he needed to sneeze. If she'd really wanted his cooperation, she should offer to let him lie on his back and rest his head in her lap to look up at the plaque. Then she could brush away the dust that she'd just dumped on him. From the corner of his eye he stared at her hands and imagined the soothing strokes of those fingertips, what it would feel like to have his head cradled in her lap. That thought made him grit his teeth. "It's an old harpsichord. Sixteen ninety-three hardly qualifies it as a relic."

"But it's a Cristofori!"

"It's an old harpsichord," he repeated. He fixed her with an annoyed glare. "It will probably fall on our heads at any moment."

"Hardly," she scoffed. "Don't you know who Cristofori was?"

He didn't know and he didn't care. The only thing he cared about at the moment was the slender thread of his control that she kept tugging away from him. He'd never known what a powerful imagination he possessed. His gaze dropped to her mouth and he wondered if she would slap him if he kissed her. Aware of the double meaning behind his reply, he still managed to sound bored. "I have the feeling I'm about to find out."

Lily lifted her chin. "With that attitude, I don't think I shall tell you."

"Fine. Then we can leave." He didn't move an inch. His gaze moved along the soft curve of her cheek and down the slender column of her neck, then stopped at the edge of her high collar. He could see the outline of a dark bruise just above the neckline, and a surge of protectiveness rose inside him. He wanted to hold her in his arms and somehow take away the pain of her injuries. He wanted to comfort her again while she cried, but this time he would brush away her tears, no, he would kiss them away, make her forget her fears, forget the man who hurt her. He would—

"Oh, all right." Lily looked nowhere near tears. He tried to concentrate on what she was saying. "Cristofori invented the piano. In fact, he based the piano on the harpsichords he built, probably one very similar to this instrument. Perhaps this very harpsichord. So you see? This harpsichord *is* a valuable relic, one that should probably be on display in a museum."

His tone turned suspicious. "You seem to know a great deal about musical instruments, my lady. However did you come by such knowledge?"

She turned away to study the small plaque with renewed intensity. "Papa has an interest in antiquities. He's quite enthusiastic on the subject and tells endless stories. Just a stroke of luck, I suppose, that I remembered this Cristofori fellow."

She was lying. He was certain of it. He looked into her wide, innocent eyes and immediately began to rethink his conviction. Why would she lie about something so trivial? He watched her gaze move lower and he knew she was looking at his mouth. She wet her lips in what was probably a nervous gesture, but the affect on him was purely sensual. Her mouth was just inches from his, the look in her eyes too inviting to resist. If he leaned forward just a little—

"Your Grace?"

The sound of Digsby's voice made Remmington's head snap up, resulting in a loud crack when his head struck the bottom of the harpsichord.

"Do you, er, need any assistance, Your Grace?"

Remmington swore under his breath. With Lily beneath the harpsichord, and himself looking as if he'd gone in after her, he could well imagine Digsby's interpretation of the scene. One more minute alone and it would have been the truth. He'd come very close to seducing her beneath this wretched thing. He should have closed the door. He never should have stepped into the room in the first place. The source of this humiliating scene remained the picture of innocence, her sherry-colored gaze wide and guileless.

"No, Digsby, I can manage this situation myself."

"As you wish, my lord."

The door closed and they were alone. Digsby had guessed what they were about, damn his hide. He'd closed the door so no one else would interrupt them. Sometimes he swore Digsby could read his mind. In most situations he found the trait useful. In this one, he found it annoying. Digsby's unwelcome interruption reminded him that he had no business being alone with Lily in this room, that there shouldn't be any need to close the door. With Digsby gone, he fixed his irritation on Lily.

She brushed her hands off and began to scoot away from him toward the edge of the harpsichord. "Thank goodness your servants are not the gossiping type. We must look rather improper."

"*Rather* improper?" he echoed, as he rose to his feet. "My dear lady, every moment I spend with you in this house is *entirely* improper. I laid down some very specific rules at the onset of this . . . this visit, and already you've managed to disregard them. I wonder how you can remember the obscure origins of pianos, yet you cannot seem to recall the gist of our conversation just two days ago."

"Memory is a strange thing, is it not?" She lifted the discarded sheet and began to draw it back over the harpsichord. "I do seem to recall your order to avoid the music room, now that you mention it. Even though you wrote down all your orders, I find lists so very difficult to memorize. It seems likely that I will break more of your rules before this visit is done with. Would you mind drawing your side of the sheet over the edge?"

He yanked the cover into place. She hadn't forgotten his orders. He would stake his life on that sure bet. She stared at him with those guileless eyes, then promptly ignored everything he said. Yesterday, while he'd searched London for the man who could help him solve her problems, she'd sent her maid on errands all over the house. Today Lily took up the exploration. He had sound reasons for giving orders that would keep Lily and her maid as confined as possible in his house. He decided it was time to enforce his rules. "It seems I shall have to keep a closer eye on you to ensure that your memory remains sound."

"Oh, I don't think that will be necessary," she said quickly. "Perhaps it would be best for all concerned if you simply allow me to continue my journey. My Great-aunt Amelia has a summer cottage in Brighton. Gretchen and I could stay there."

"You're a persistent thing, aren't you?" He found her hopeful expression oddly reassuring. It seemed obvious that she'd disobeyed him on purpose, to try his patience and thus revive her argument that she should leave. If she'd plotted with her father to get herself situated in his house, she wouldn't try so hard to undo the plan. He felt an equal measure of relief and anger—relief that she wasn't involved in a plot to trick him, anger that her father still might be. He shook his head. "You will not leave this house until I receive word from your father. Until then, you will endeavor to follow the rules of my household more carefully."

"As you wish." She gave him a stiff nod. "Now if you will excuse me, I believe my appearance is in need of improvement."

His nod equally curt, Remmington watched her walk past him. Covered in dust, she still managed to look as regal as a queen. The way she ignored him made him feel churlish. "By the way, you have an enormous spider's web caught on your hair bow. Oh, and now that you've turned around, I think you have the spider as well."

Lily shrieked. She plucked the sticky mess from her hair and yanked the bow loose in the process. Her fingers combed through the freed locks, then she used both hands to give the heavy mass a vigorous shake. She peered at him sideways. "Is it gone?"

He rubbed his chin and felt the gritty dust that still covered him. "It seems I was mistaken. There was no spider."

The glare she gave him should have singed his lashes. God, she was beautiful when she was angry. It was worth her ire just to see her eyes flash with fire. Her chest was heaving rather nicely, too. She tossed her glorious mane over one shoulder, then turned on her heel and stalked from the room. What an intriguing piece of work she was. A regal queen one moment, a dusty urchin the next. He was never quite sure what to expect from her.

Unmindful that he'd recently questioned the stability of the harpsichord, he leaned his hip against the instrument and gazed thoughtfully at the doorway. His smile faded into a puzzled frown. Whatever he'd expected when he met Lily Walters, the woman who had just left this room wasn't it. All these years he'd expected to find little of substance behind that pretty face. What he'd finally discovered made him uneasy. There was a clever mind at work beneath that facade of cheerful ignorance, so carefully guarded that he'd managed no more than a glimpse here and there of the real Lily.

What was she hiding?

Six

Sir Malcolm Bainbridge leaned back against the worn leather seat of the carriage and rested his hands on top of an ornately carved walking cane. Although his hair had turned gray years ago, and a large mustache nearly obscured his weathered face, his piercing blue eyes showed no signs of age.

"These hired carriages get worse every year, do they not?" he asked his companion. "Smells as if someone spilled a gallon of rum in this contraption."

"A rank carriage is the least of my concerns at the moment," the Earl of Crofford replied. "I could not believe it when I heard you'd left town the night of the Ashlands' ball. The timing could not have been worse."

Bainbridge nodded sympathetically. "The message Lily translated required an immediate journey. Your letter reached me yesterday and I returned as quickly as I could."

Crofford raked a hand through his hair and released a long breath. "I didn't mean to snap at you, Malcolm. I haven't slept much these past days."

"No need for apologies, my friend. I understand your worries. Now that Lily is safe in Brighton, I will put every available resource on this case. We will track this man down and bring him to justice. If he is a French spy, then we will take further steps to ensure Lily's safety, and yours as well."

"Lily isn't at the safe house in Brighton," Crofford said. He proceeded to explain everything that had happened after he wrote the letter to Sir Malcolm the morning after Lily's attack, how Remmington had intervened in the plan to send Lily to Brighton on the mail coach.

Bainbridge looked startled by the news, but oddly, he didn't seem overly concerned. He even managed a smile. "I would imagine Remmington thought you a little touched with that story about Aunt Amelia."

"There is more," Crofford said. "I convinced Remmington to keep Lily in hiding at his town house. He left me no other choice. She's there now, in the very lair of the most notorious womanizer in London. If he so much as—"

Bainbridge tapped his cane on the floor to interrupt him. "Calm yourself, Crofford. The situation is not as bad as you believe. I assume you asked for some reassurances that he would behave honorably?"

Crofford slapped his kid gloves against his open palm. "Of course I asked for reassurances. He gave me his word on the matter."

"There you have it," Bainbridge said. "Remmington is a man of his word. If he gave you his word, then Lily is as safe with him as she would be in Brighton. As a matter of fact, I'll give you *my* word that she's safer."

"You extend yourself," Crofford retorted. "I don't think either of us knows Remmington well enough to say just how far we can trust him."

"I know exactly how far I can trust him." Bainbridge's gaze turned speculative. "We've been friends a long time, Crofford. You are one of the few men I trust completely. What I am about to tell you tonight can go no further." He waited for the earl's nod of agreement. "Remmington works for me on occasion. He has a ship at his disposal that can sail at a moment's notice, manned by a crew more talented than any I've encountered. Aside from getting my operatives or their messages in and out of enemy territory, they often track smugglers' ships to make certain their cargoes are no more harmful than French brandy or bits of lace."

"How on earth did you manage to bring the Duke of Remmington into your organization?"

"He volunteered," Bainbridge said simply.

Crofford mulled over that information. "I'm sure the duke is a credit to your organization, and I don't doubt his ability to keep Lily safe, yet I cannot help but worry. He has a notorious reputation where women are concerned. Now I've conveniently placed one on his doorstep. Do you really believe he will resist that temptation if the situation continues for more than a day or two?"

"Remmington would never seduce an innocent young woman."

"Perhaps," Crofford mused. "But one wonders what he is doing with Margaret Granger. Surely he has no intention of marrying the chit."

"The courtship with Margaret Granger was my idea," Bainbridge admitted. "In the course of Remmington's work for me, he came across a smuggling operation off the coast of Dover. These smugglers carry French spies, not brandy. Rather than seize the renegade ship, we've been tracking the operation to discover the spies' contacts here in England. We know already that the head of the smuggling operation is a peer of the realm, a man who had a startling change of fortunes about two years ago. To get this information, I had to have someone close to the man. Close to his daughter, to be more precise."

"Lord Granger."

It wasn't a question, but Bainbridge nodded. "His daughter doesn't know the true nature of her father's enterprise, but the courtship gave Remmington an excuse to present himself as a frequent guest at Granger's estate near Dover. He's gathered more than enough information to condemn the man, but we want to identify Granger's contacts in London before we close the net around the operation. In any event, Margaret Granger's usefulness is at an end. There are other leads to pursue. Remmington intends to end the courtship soon so that no one, including Margaret, will suspect his involvement when her father is brought to justice. Actually, I believe he intends to have Margaret break things off so the courtship will seem less deliberate. That's the only part of his plan I've questioned. Margaret is too enamored of his title to let him get away so easily."

"Granger a traitor." Crofford shook his head. They belonged to many of the same clubs, they'd even attended Eton at the same time. Although he'd never been particularly close to Granger, the news was still astounding. "What will happen to him?"

"That depends on Granger." Bainbridge waved his hand to dismiss the matter. "But his activities are not the true issue here. It is your daughter we are concerned about. As far as I am concerned, there is no one I would trust more to guard her safety than Remmington. You must trust my judgment in this matter, and put your fears to rest. If it will make you feel any better, I will make Remmington aware of my interest in Lily."

Crofford considered the offer. "Perhaps a word or two would not be amiss, but I don't want Remmington or anyone else to know of Lily's activities. The less who know of her work, the safer she will be."

"You know that I hold my operatives' identities in strictest confidence. Were these not extenuating circumstances, I would not have said anything about Remmington. Unless he suspects something is amiss with Lily, there is no need for him to know about her work."

The carriage drew to a halt and Bainbridge pushed aside the worn velvet curtains that covered the carriage window. The gaslights along Saint James's Street turned the fog a strange shade of yellow, but he could still make out the entrance to White's. He adjusted his tophat and swung his cape over one arm.

"Keep me informed of any changes in the situation. Sorry to leave you so abruptly, Crofford, but I received another message this evening and I promised to meet the man within the hour." He climbed down from the carriage and turned to smile at his friend. "After this discussion, I have a fairly good idea why Remmington's message sounded so urgent."

Sir Malcolm made his way through White's sitting room at a leisurely pace. Now and then he paused to speak with acquaintances. He spotted Remmington in one corner of the large room and moved steadily closer to the duke's table. When he lingered at Lord Shefley's table, Remmington finally held up one hand to invite him over. The two men greeted each other with casual nods.

"Won't you join me for a drink, Sir Malcolm?" Remmington indicated the chair opposite his. Bainbridge took the seat as one of the club's unobtrusive servants appeared with another glass. At a nod from Remmington, the servant poured a drink from the brandy decanter that sat on the table.

"You're looking well, Your Grace," Bainbridge remarked, as the servant departed.

"I would feel considerably better if I could enjoy my drink in a place more private." Remmington glanced meaningfully at several tables where other gentlemen enjoyed drinks and conversation. There was no one close enough to hear exactly what they were saying, but he didn't like discussing his business in a place so crowded.

Bainbridge shrugged. "A private man often draws unwelcome attention. Hiding in plain sight confounds the curious."

Remmington ignored the cryptic reply. He leaned forward to refill his own glass, his voice terse. "I've tried to reach you for two days. I have a problem, and I need your help to solve it."

Bainbridge smiled as he lifted his glass. "I am aware of your problem. Very little occurs in this town without my knowledge. If I had to venture a guess, I'd say you are searching for a means to rid yourself of a house-guest."

"You are correct, as usual." Remmington swirled his glass of brandy in a steady circle. "I have certain business ventures that require privacy. This guest will complicate matters."

"Those ventures will not suffer from lack of attention. Your guest is related to a friend of mine, and I've given my word that you are the most trustworthy of hosts. A man mustn't allow mundane business affairs to interfere with more pressing commitments. I will do what I can to ensure that your guest does not require an extended visit."

"As far as I'm concerned, one day qualifies as an extended visit. I have nothing in common with this person and I find the entire situation annoying, to say the least." It occurred to Remmington that the director's connection to Lily suddenly seemed a little too convenient. Appearances were often deceiving, especially when a situation involved Sir Malcolm. "Is your interest in this matter personal or business, Sir Malcolm?"

"When my friends have a problem, I make it my business to help them in any way I can."

Crofford and Bainbridge friends? Remmington could not think of two men who were less alike. Crofford's cronies at White's were a rather dull lot, an elderly group of men who engaged in a seemingly endless debate of the classics. On the other hand, Sir Malcolm kept company with some of the most powerful men in England. Bainbridge was the only visible member of an organization so secretive that only the Prime Minister knew all the names of the men Bainbridge employed and their positions within the War Department. Could Crofford possibly be one of those men?

Remmington almost smiled over the thought. The absent-minded earl a spy? Crofford could barely manage to keep his daughter safe. Who would trust such a man with secrets of state? No, Bainbridge's connection to Lily and her father could be nothing more than it seemed, a family friendship.

"No one is happy with the circumstances," Bainbridge continued, "but we must make the best of them. I daresay you and your guest might find common ground of some sort over the next few days." His smile grew broader. "Perhaps a shared interest or hobby will enliven your conversations."

Something else to find attractive about Lily? Remmington shook his head. There was too much already. "The thought is almost frightening." He drained his brandy, then folded his arms across his chest. "You are better acquainted with this person than I. Have you noticed anything unusual about our friend? A certain inconsistency of character?"

"Anyone will tell you that your guest is unusual. As for inconsistent?" Bainbridge shrugged. "Women are the most confounding creatures on the face of the earth. After twenty-six years of marriage, I could not begin to tell you how my wife's mind works."

Remmington glanced around the room, then leaned forward slightly. "She's hiding something."

Bainbridge readily agreed with him. "But of course she is. Clara is always hiding something from me. Damned annoying for the most part. Last week I found out she's been riding El Capitan every morning when I expressly forbade her to ride that wild animal. She said I told her that she could not ride the stupid horse in the park, so she's been trotting off to the countryside. Honestly, I never know how she will twist my words next. Keeps a man on his toes, don't you know?"

Remmington frowned. "I wasn't speaking of your wife."

"You weren't?" Bainbridge looked perplexed. "You

very well could be. If you ask me, women are much alike in that respect. They confound us deliberately."

Remmington wondered what it was about Lily that turned people insensible when they spoke of her. He tried a more direct tack. "My guest is more intelligent than she would have anyone believe."

"Nothing unusual there. The reasons escape me, but society dictates as much. I would imagine she doesn't want to be labeled a bluestocking. Knowing her as well as I do, I can assure you that there is nothing devious or scheming about her, if that is what you are worried about."

"I'm not sure what worries me," he said. "She just seems strange at times."

Bainbridge held up his hands. "She's a woman. What more need I say?" He drank the last of his brandy, then set the glass on the table and stood up. "I wouldn't let the matter concern you too much. The situation you find yourself in should resolve itself in a few days and your guest will no longer be a concern." He gave Remmington a slight bow. "Thank you for the drink, Your Grace. I hope you will allow me to return the favor sometime soon. Perhaps your spirits will be improved when we next meet."

"Perhaps," Remmington conceded, although he had his doubts.

Sir Malcolm nodded politely, then he stepped away from Remmington's table. He made his way through the room and paused again at several tables to engage in brief conversations.

Remmington frowned the entire time. He was stuck with Lily Walters. His last hope had just left the room.

The laughter woke Lily from a sound sleep. She opened her eyes and stared up at the moonlit canopy of the bed, immediately aware that she was in Remmington's town house. Somewhere in the house a grandfather clock began to chime. First the quarter hours rang out, then the hour, three deep, resonant tones. A creak followed by a soft thump told her a door had closed nearby. Probably Remmington returning from wherever he'd been all night, she thought groggily. She wondered what he could be laughing about at this late hour.

Her eyes drifted shut and the sound of laughter returned, louder now. It came from the hallway. The low, menacing sound lacked any trace of gaiety, and she knew instinctively that it wasn't Remmington. It was harder to open her eyes this time, to make them focus in the darkened room. She struggled to brush aside the shroud of sleep. The door to the hallway was the only thing she could see clearly.

The sound of laughter drew closer. The low tones repeated themselves in an almost monotonous rhythm. Her heart began to beat harder, each thump louder than the last. It was her attacker on the other side of the door. Lily was certain of it. The laughter was taunting, a wordless arrogance that said he knew exactly where to find her, that nothing would stop him this time.

Just as she opened her mouth to release another soundless scream, a pair of strong hands grabbed her shoulders, and the shock of it returned her strength tenfold. She beat her fists against a broad chest, twisted and turned in his grip, fighting for her life.

"Wake up, Lily!"

She kept beating against his chest, certain her mind was playing tricks on her. The voice sounded almost like—

"It's me, Lily. Wake up."

—Remmington. Her struggles ceased abruptly. She opened her eyes and found herself staring at a bare chest. Her fists rested against a soft pelt of hair that tapered down his wide chest to end in a vee at the waistband of his pants. She'd never touched a man's bare chest. That was the only thought that occupied her mind for what seemed an eternity, but could in reality be no more than a second or two. She uncurled her fists and laid her palms flat against his shoulders. He felt so warm, so safe and solid.

"You had a bad dream. It's over now."

Dream? Lily shuddered. Every muscle in her body went limp at the same moment. She would have fallen over if his arms hadn't wrapped around her. He pulled her onto his lap.

"It's over now." He tucked her head against his shoulder and began to stroke her hair. "You're safe, Lily. No one can hurt you here."

The sound of a soft knock on the door made her nearly leap from his arms, but he held her secure. She wrapped her arms tighter around his neck and stared fearfully at the door.

"Everything's fine," he called out to the servant who guarded her door. "Lady Lillian had a bad dream."

"Nightmare," Lily whispered. He held her tightly against his chest to absorb the shudders that racked her body. "How—" Another hard shudder cut off her question, and she leaned her forehead against his chest.

"I heard you call out," he said. "Were you dreaming about the night of your attack?"

Lily shook her head. "No. Worse. He ... he was here."

He held her tighter. The feel of his warm, bare chest should shock her. They were alone and in bed together, Remmington was half dressed, and she wore nothing more than a thin nightgown. She pressed closer to his strength, comforted by the sure knowledge that he would keep her safe.

"I'm s-sorry I disturbed you." She rested her cheek against his chest to hear the steady sound of his heartbeat. "It seemed so real."

When her trembling didn't stop, he began to rub her arms and back in soothing motions, murmuring comforting words in her ear. He probably thought her childish to be so undone by a nightmare. She didn't care. At the moment, she seemed to need that comfort. Aside from the night of her attack, she couldn't remember the last time anyone had held her, or given her so much as a hug. She was much too old for displays of that sort from her family. But perhaps it was the vague memory of childhood that made Remmington's embrace feel so soothing and familiar. There was something almost drugging about the way he held her, so close that she could hear every beat of his heart, every steady breath he drew. His scent wouldn't distract a child, nor would the firm yet supple texture of his skin. The emotions he made her feel belonged to a woman. A woman he didn't want.

She tried to push away from him. "I'll be f-fine now. Per-perfectly fine."

"You don't sound fine. You're shaking like a leaf." He drew her closer and pressed her head against his shoulder. "Have you talked to anyone about what happened that night? The night of your attack?"

Lily shook her head. "I don't want to th-think about it."

"Sometimes people dream about things they don't want to talk about." He sounded very sure of his opinion. He nudged her chin up with one finger, but she avoided his eyes. "You endured something awful that night, Lily. Why don't you tell me what happened?"

"It's over." She clasped her hands together in a tight grip. Why couldn't he treat her with contempt rather than consideration? He pitied her. Nothing more. Lily tried to concentrate on that fact, and not on the sight of so much bare male flesh. A moment ago he hadn't seemed quite so naked. Why was she suddenly aware of the pressure of his arms around her, his warmth wherever they touched? "I-I don't think I could recall it very clearly."

"Tell me." The harsh words were at odds with the gentle way he stroked her cheek. She glanced up at him and he caught her gaze effortlessly. "Tell me," he repeated, in a more reasonable tone. "I promise it will make you feel better."

Tell him what? That she wished he would care for her just a little? That she wanted to hold his affections as surely as he held her own? She didn't think he wanted to hear any of that. "I don't really think—"

He placed one finger over her lips. "Tell me what happened. What were you doing that night when he came to your room? Were you asleep?"

His finger caused an odd sensation against her lips. Her mouth felt numb where he touched her, yet overly sensitive at the same time. His hand dropped away when she began to speak. "I was awake. I really don't want to—"

His fingers covered her mouth again. "What were you doing?"

"Brushing my hair." She pushed his hand away, unable to concentrate when he touched her that way. "I was sitting at my vanity, brushing my hair, and in the mirror I saw my bedroom door open. At first I thought it was my father, returning early from White's, but then I noticed the livery he wore and a moment later I saw the mask."

She stared at his shoulder and saw the mask clearly in her mind. "It was a hideous thing, twisted into a snarling, unnatural smile. I tried to run, but he caught me halfway across the room and threw me to the floor. A moment later I felt his weight on top of me. I screamed and I thought someone would come to rescue me, but he knew no one would come."

"Go on," he urged. "What happened next?"

"I fought back. When he'd lunged at me, he'd also knocked over my vanity, and one of the heavy candlesticks had fallen nearby. I managed to grab hold of it. He let go of me for a moment and I struck him over the head as hard as I could. He crumpled onto the floor and I thought he was dead. When I turned to run to the door, his hand reached out and grabbed my ankle, and I knew he was only dazed. I ran down the stairs, then I heard him bellow something out, and I glanced over my shoulder. He was in the hallway, leaning against one wall, his hand cupping his forehead. I ran into the streets where I thought I would come across someone who could help, or that I could find my father at White's. That's when you stopped me."

Remmington grew very still. "When you turned to look at him on the stairway, you said he held his hand to his forehead. Was he wearing the mask?"

Lily's eyes grew wider. She felt hopeful for a moment, then she shook her head. "His hand shielded his face. I couldn't see anything."

He held her hand to his forehead. "Show me what you saw. How did he hold his hand?"

Lily was silent for a moment, trying to absorb the shock of touching his face so intimately. The innocent touch shouldn't disturb her. After all, she'd just pressed herself against his bare chest. She traced the line of his brow and decided that this was a more refined torment.

"He was leaning against the wall," she said, "turned from me this way." She cupped his forehead and turned his head away from her.

"All right. Describe what you can see of him."

She tried to concentrate on the task. Every thought she possessed centered on Remmington. How could she think about another man while he held her in such an embrace? Her hand brushed against a lock of his hair and without thinking, she sifted the soft strands through her fingers. She closed her eyes and forced herself to recall the shadowy figure on the staircase. "His hair was a dark color. Brown or black, I think. Papa keeps a lamp burning at the top of the stairs until he retires for the night, but it was still very dark."

"Tell me what else you see."

He submitted patiently to her examination. She avoided his eyes to study his face, to commit each detail to memory. An artist's canvas could never capture the odd combination of refined nobility and animal magnetism. In that, he was utterly unique. The attraction didn't lie solely in his features, but in some aura that surrounded him. It was a near-tangible thing, something Lily felt sure she could identify if she had longer to study him. Her hand moved to his jaw. "His chin was more rounded than yours, the line of his jaw not as strong. His nose should have been hidden behind his hand, but it must have been very large. I could see it from here to here."

She traced the bridge of his nose to his upper lip, surprised to find a damp trace of perspiration there. Now that she thought about it, the room did seem overly warm. Her fingers rested against his mouth, testing the shape. "I think his mouth was smaller than yours."

His voice sounded hoarse when he questioned her. "Is that all you can remember?"

He looked down at her then, and Lily's lips parted in surprise. She saw her own desire reflected in his eyes, the same burning hunger that made her breath quicken and her pulse race with anticipation. Something in her dazed senses realized that time was her enemy. In a few short days she would return to her father's house to lead a life that was a lie. Remmington would probably marry Margaret Granger before the year was out. She was in a time, a place, a situation that would never happen again.

She nodded, but didn't know if she answered the question he spoke aloud, or granted the permission he silently demanded with his eyes.

He hesitated a moment, then lowered his head until their lips barely touched. She couldn't move, couldn't breathe. With smooth, feather-light strokes, he traced the outline of her mouth with his lips. The kiss that followed seemed almost chaste. His lips moved against hers very gently, as if he meant to learn the shape of her mouth, or to decide how their lips best fit together. At last he drew away from her.

What happened next startled Lily, but she didn't open her eyes when she felt the tips of his fingers touch her forehead. He traced a line across her brow, circled just beneath her eye, over the bridge of her nose, then to her other temple. After a moment's hesitation, he began to explore the curve of her cheek, the line of her jaw, then he repeated the process on the other side of her face. The careful, intimate exploration left her as breath-

less as his kiss. She wondered if he'd felt the same dizzying emotions when she examined his face. He touched
the center of her forehead and drew a line with the tip of
his finger down the profile of her nose. He traced the
outline of her mouth, then the line between her lips. He
parted her lips, then dragged his fingertip over the even
edges of her teeth. Without thinking, she touched the tip
of her tongue to his finger.

She heard the sharp intake of his breath, felt her own
breath catch when he crushed her to his chest. He lowered his head, but he still didn't kiss her. With one arm
around her shoulders, he wrapped his other hand around
her hair until they were bound together by the fiery
tresses. She gasped against his mouth and he caught her
lower lip between his teeth, painlessly tugging her even
closer, then he covered her lips completely.

Nothing could have prepared her for the effect of his
embrace. A few of her suitors had tried to steal kisses,
but she found them embarrassing and unpleasant for the
most part, something to back away from. Her arms were
wrapped so tightly around Remmington's neck that they
ached. She ached everywhere. And the heat. The room
couldn't be this warm.

No longer coaxing or gentle, his mouth moved
against hers insistently, urging her lips to part. When she
gave in to the silent command, he deepened the kiss and
the tip of his tongue touched hers. She gasped and instinctively drew away, but he wouldn't release her. His
tongue returned to trace the outline of her mouth, then
again to delve a little deeper. She didn't know that people
could kiss this way. Somehow she did know that he was
introducing her slowly to the art, being patient while she
decided if she liked it or not. That decision came when
she began to mimic his actions, to explore him just as
thoroughly. He tore his mouth away as soon as she tasted
him.

"We shouldn't be doing this." His breathing sounded
rough. Her head seemed to move of its own accord, back
and forth so that his lips brushed across her ear. He

caught the lobe between his teeth and bit gently. She shuddered against him. "Tell me to stop, Lily. Now, while I can."

Lily sighed. She loved his voice, the dark, forbidden emotions it stirred in her. Tonight she felt like a different person, the woman she might be if the war had ended years ago, before she became involved in the War Department. That Lily would be free to pursue her dreams, to encourage the attentions of the man who held her heart from the moment she first saw him. She wouldn't be forced to steal his affections, knowing he felt nothing more for her than lust.

His lips traced the curve of her ear as he caressed her shoulder. When his hand brushed across her breast, she felt a startling moment of panic. Was she truly so desperate for his embrace that she would let him use her? She would simply be another of his conquests, a woman he would barely recall in a few months. The ache in her heart spread until it was almost unbearable. He was right. They shouldn't be doing this. The fire in her died a sudden death.

When he gripped the back of her neck and urged her toward the pillows, she cried out from surprise more than from pain. Remmington's gaze flew to her neck and he quickly released his grip and slipped his arm around her shoulders.

"God, Lily, I'm sorry. Did I hurt you?"

He tried to touch her bruised throat but she managed to push him away, to slide off his lap and onto the bed. He looked like he wanted to comfort her. His comforting got her into this mess in the first place. Words began to tumble from her mouth faster than she could think.

"You shouldn't be here. This isn't at all proper. You said yourself that we could be nothing more than friends, and now you've broken your word. I don't see how you expect me to follow all your rules when you can't manage them yourself. I think you should leave now."

Remmington stared at her as if she'd turned into a curiosity. His worried expression disappeared. He lowered his head and released a long, deep sigh, then another, as if he were trying to catch his breath after some great exertion. He didn't even glance her way when he said, "Stop staring at me as if I'd just slapped you."

She busied herself by untangling the sheets and pulling them up to her chin.

He shifted his weight to sit on the edge of the bed and braced his hands against his knees. "Damn it, Lily. I am not entirely at fault." He raked one hand through his hair. "I had no intentions of kissing you when I came in here. You are the one who constantly puts my rules to the test."

Lily felt her mouth drop open. "Are you saying that I am somehow responsible?"

His expression said the answer was obvious. "It's the way you look at me. That has to stop."

She glared up at him, the shame and embarrassment she felt just moments ago forgotten. "How dare you lay the blame at my feet! I didn't ask you to kiss me."

He said nothing. He didn't have to. She read the truth in his eyes.

"Why, you arrogant—"

"You must admit that your reaction was hardly that of an outraged innocent," he cut in. "We are in a strange situation, one that calls for proper behavior and discretion. A woman who didn't plan to find herself compromised would show an abundance of both. If it is your intention to keep tempting me this way to deliberately compromise yourself, then you should know that I will not feel obliged to repair the damage by making an offer of marriage."

"You think I planned what happened tonight?"

He shrugged indifferently. "Let's just say that young women with romantic fantasies are prone to reckless behavior."

"I see." She sat up and crossed her arms. "You may have a point. Asking you to dance with me the night of the Ashlands' ball was extremely reckless behavior on my part. Humiliating me in front of a roomful of people was the least you could do to show me the errors of my ways, but I stubbornly refused to learn my lesson. Next I contrived to have you sneak onto the balcony where you could overhear my conversation with Sophie and humiliate me further. Clever planning, was it not?"

"You are deliberately—"

"Of course it was. I am simply full of plots where you are concerned. Arranging an attack in my home was the crowning jewel in my elaborate scheme. How better to play upon your sympathies? Knowing how you must pity me, I then coerced your butler into bringing me here so I could insinuate myself into your household. Now I have every opportunity to compromise myself." She shook her head. "How very unfortunate that you saw through my plan. I thought that having a nightmare was a rather novel way to bring you into my room uninvited in the middle of the night. And, of course, I knew you would feel obliged to kiss me senseless."

She gasped and feigned a look of concern as she waved one hand toward the armoire. "Pray do not open the wardrobe, Your Grace. My father is hiding in there so he can spring forward and demand marriage the moment I'm compromised."

Remmington regarded her in silence. There was no longer any passion in his eyes, and a muscle twitched in one cheek in an almost rhythmic movement. "I see no need for sarcasm."

"Am I being sarcastic?" Lily shrugged, then turned her hand over to examine her nails. "How very rude."

"All right, I'll admit that I am as much to blame as you for what happened tonight."

Lily made a clicking sound with her tongue. "My, what a difficult admission. Was it painful?"

"Must you be so deliberately obtuse?"

"I resent your insult, sir. My figure is not at all obtuse."

Remmington threw his hands into the air. "That's it. I refuse to have this conversation. We can continue this discussion tomorrow, or whenever you decide to come to your senses." He turned and walked to the adjoining door.

"I will expect your apology first, Remmington."

He ignored the ultimatum. "Goodnight, Lily."

"Goodnight!"

Seven

—————— ✦ ——————

"*Your Grace?*"

Remmington rolled to the other side of his bed without opening his eyes. He hoped Digsby would go away. The taste of stale liquor was an unpleasant reminder of the previous evening. Taking the edge off his anger with a decanter of brandy hadn't been the wisest idea, he decided. Last night he'd returned from Lily's room as aroused as he was infuriated. First she threw herself into his arms, then she took him beyond the limits of his control, *then* she told him to leave. She couldn't have any idea how long it took him to summon the willpower to consider that suggestion. He'd warned her that he wouldn't be able to stop. So he'd been a little irrational. After all but inviting him into her bed, why had she found his anger so surprising?

By his third or fourth glass of brandy, his temper had cooled enough that he realized what an ass he'd made of

himself. Lily hadn't set out to seduce him, yet he'd accused her of far worse. She was right. He owed her an
apology. If he somehow managed to restore their relationship to good terms, the same thing might very well
happen again. No, he decided, the next time he wouldn't
be content with a few kisses. The next time he would
touch her. Everywhere. With his hands, his mouth, his
body. God, he still ached for her. In the cold light of . . .

He cracked open one eye, nearly blinded himself in
the glaring light, then immediately snapped it shut.

Noon. It must be at least noon. He pushed aside
thoughts of Lily for the moment, hoped he could ignore
his pounding headache long enough to escape back into
painless sleep. He felt a hand nudge his shoulder.

"Forgive me for waking you, Your Grace, but I think
you will consider the situation important."

He slapped away Digsby's hand. "What situation?"

"It's Lady Lillian, Your Grace. She's in the library."

"You're mistaken," he said groggily. "Told her to stay
out of there."

"I suspected as much, and even mentioned the same
to her ladyship, but I can assure you that she is there
now."

"I doubt she'll get into anything. My desk is locked.
I'll have a talk with her at dinner." He turned onto his
stomach and buried his head beneath his pillow. "Now
go away."

"Dinner is nearly ten hours away, Your Grace. I, ah,
ahem. I think you should know that she is going through
the bookcases."

Remmington lay very still for a moment, then he
bolted upright. The room swayed dangerously for a moment, but he threw back the covers and sprang from the
bed. "Did she find it?"

Digsby handed him a pair of trousers. "Not yet, but
I feel certain it is only a matter of time. She's been in
there almost an hour, and she seems intent on examining
every volume."

Remmington stopped dressing with one foot stuck

halfway in his pants leg. "Good God, Digsby. What happened to your face?"

Digsby touched his blackened eye with careful fingers, then grimaced through swollen lips. "Lady Lillian, Your Grace."

Remmington stared at him. "She struck you?"

"No, my lord. You really should make haste to the library. There is no telling what that lady is about."

Remmington nodded, and resumed dressing. "After I take care of Lady Lillian, I expect a more thorough answer to my question."

At that moment, Lily was thinking how good it felt to unload the shelves, to turn Remmington's library into a fraction of the chaos he'd made of her life. That morning she woke up hurt and angry, ready to make him pay for every hateful thing he'd said to her the night before. With no clear thoughts of how to accomplish that plan, the idea to vandalize his library seemed inspired. If she were at all lucky, maybe, just maybe, he would agree to let her leave. She'd settle for getting kicked out.

Digsby had paced constantly as she riffled through the books, using polite banality to argue against what she was doing. He finally retreated when he realized he couldn't sway her from the task. There wasn't a question in her mind that he intended to inform his employer. She almost looked forward to the confrontation, the opportunity to vent just a portion of her anger.

A spindly chair served as a ladder when she moved to the upper shelves. She carefully tossed down two small books, then her fingers latched onto a large book that swung away from the bookcase rather than sliding out. The book's spine was attached to five other wide volumes, each of the spines sliced about an inch deep so they would appear normal on the shelf. The false spines concealed a small, square compartment stuffed with parchments. Curious, she withdrew the one closest to her. With her balance precarious at best, she nearly fell over when she unfolded the paper. The nonsensical words were a variation of the Vigenère Tableau, an encoding system favored by the French.

A sound in the hallway reminded her that Remmington could appear at any moment. She slammed the compartment shut and climbed down, then pushed the chair away from the shelves. It wasn't until she hurried to the center of the room to stand amidst more innocent-looking books that she realized she still held the message in her hand. She lifted her skirts and tucked the message into her garter, then quickly picked up a stack of books. In that same moment, the library door crashed open and Remmington appeared in the doorway.

Still barefoot and tucking the ends of his shirt into his pants, Remmington froze in the doorway at the sight that greeted him. Any feelings of guilt that lingered from the night before evaporated. His neat, orderly library looked suspiciously like the library at Crofford House. Books were piled everywhere, dozens upon dozens of them. Much of the furniture and most of the carpet in front of the bookcases had disappeared beneath the stacked and scattered volumes. His gaze flew to the corner of the bookcases and he breathed a sigh of relief. The false spines that concealed the hidden recess were undisturbed.

Lily turned to greet him, her arms loaded down with books. "Good morning, Your Grace."

He watched her eyes widen when she took in his attire. His shirt was open to the waist, but he resisted the urge to check the fastenings of his pants to make certain he'd done them up correctly. He felt half asleep, fully hung over, and furious to be waking up to this mess. Quite the opposite, Lily appeared the picture of prim innocence in a cream-colored gown. She looked refreshed and disgustingly healthy. Even her voice sounded better. Thank God, she wasn't smiling. A cheerful smile at that moment would send him over the edge.

"Would you care to explain?"

"Explain what?" she asked.

His hand swept out to encompass the room. "Explain the fact that you somehow managed to decimate my library in little more than an hour. Explain how you are bold enough to be here in the first place, when I gave specific orders that this room was not for your use."

Lily lowered her chin. She appeared almost repentant, or perhaps guilty. "You don't have to shout, Your Grace. My hearing is quite good."

"I'm not—" Remmington took a deep breath, unable to remember the last time he'd raised his voice to a woman, or for that matter, the last time anyone had defied him so openly. He lowered his voice to a more reasonable volume. "You will replace every one of those volumes in their proper places, and you will do so at once."

"Hm. Replace them." She glanced uncertainly around the room. "I'm afraid that would rather defeat the purpose. I was searching for a particular volume, and I'm quite certain I would lose track of my place if I started putting books away before I found it. Yesterday I was certain I saw one of Mrs. Radcliffe's novels in your collection, but now I cannot seem to locate it."

"Do you mean to tell me that you've ravaged an entire library to find one book?"

"You are shouting again, Your Grace."

"I'll damn well shout in my own house if I want to!" He lowered his voice anyway. "First of all, you may rest assured that I would not have one of that woman's books in my house. Second, if you were intent on a specific book, you should have asked Digsby to retrieve it for you. Third, you have no business in this room unless you are invited into it by myself. After today's fiasco, I doubt you will see the inside of this room again for the duration of your stay."

He slammed the library door shut. A moment later he stalked over to his desk, sat in his chair, and folded his arms across his chest in one harsh, abrupt movement. "Now, you will replace every single book in its proper place. I don't care if it takes the rest of the day."

"I think you're being very unreasonable about this."

"Unreasonable would be locking you in your room for the remainder of your stay, which I'm still considering. Taking those books that are in your arms and putting them back on the shelves will start swaying my opinions in a direction you might find more favorable."

She raised her chin a degree and glared right back at him. "Well. If this is an example of your hospitality, I'm afraid I will be leaving immediately. If you will be so good as to arrange for a hired hack, my maid and I will secure a room at the Two Swans and leave for Brighton first thing tomorrow morning." She placed the books she held on a nearby table, then crossed her arms. "Considering your ugly threats and vulgar language, I'm afraid I simply must insist on the matter. You may inform Digsby that Gretchen will have my trunk packed within the hour."

Remmington directed his scowl at the top of his desk. He couldn't look at her. The urge to cross the room, to take her shoulders in his hands and shake her senseless was too strong. No, he'd have to shake sense *into* her. Her outrageous orders and demands, heaped on top of his anger, said she had no sense at all. Not one bit.

He glanced around the chaotic room and it suddenly occurred to him that no one in their right mind would search for a book in such a fashion. And now that he thought about it, she'd turned their argument to the subject of her departure rather neatly. His gaze snapped back to her face, certain he saw her flinch.

"Well?" she asked haughtily.

He propped his elbows on the arms of his chair and rested his hands in his lap. "I thought you didn't like to read."

"I said no such thing. As I recall, I told you that I am not a particularly fast reader, but I do enjoy the pastime. It seemed an enjoyable diversion and I simply came here in search of a book, unaware that I would be shouted and sworn at in such a shocking fashion." Her gaze slid toward the library door. "If you won't allow your servants to assist us from the house, we will manage on our own."

"You won't be leaving quite yet."

She took a step toward the library door. "I cannot abide threats, my lord. Now, if you will excuse me—"

He reached into his pocket and withdrew a key, then dangled it from two fingers. "I took the liberty of locking the door. I suspected you might be reluctant to stay here until you'd righted this mess. It seems my suspicions were correct."

Her mouth opened, closed abruptly, then opened again, but no words emerged. Remmington smiled and replaced the key in his pocket. He nodded toward a pile of books. "I hope you didn't make this mess on purpose, to revive your pointless argument about leaving. If so, you will have ample opportunity to think over the wisdom of such plottings while you reshelve everything."

"Another one of my plots, my lord? I should have known you would accuse me of doing this deliberately."

"Are you telling me that you are not the one who made this mess?"

"I was searching for a book!"

"I see."

She planted her hands on her hips, one brow arched over a rather pretty scowl. "Are you calling me a liar?" Rather than give him a chance to answer, she walked over to the door and began to pound on the solid wood while she muttered under her breath. "Sworn and shouted at, and now called a liar. I shall not stay here another moment."

"Digsby?" she asked the door, then in a much louder voice, "Digsby, I know you're out there. You will open this door immediately!"

"He won't let you out, you know." Remmington leaned back in his chair and propped his hands behind his head. "I would suggest you start with the red books. They belong on the bottom shelves."

"Digsby! There's been an accident! Remmington

tripped and fell, and he's badly hurt. Please open the door!"

"I'm fine, Digsby," he called out. He shook his finger at Lily when she turned to glare at him. His brows furrowed together into a mocking scowl. "I say. That was rather clever."

Her back sagged against the door and she spoke calmly, but the edge of fear in her eyes disturbed him. He looked lower and saw how badly her hands shook.

"I have to leave, Remmington. Now. This moment."

"I didn't mean to frighten you," he said quietly. "And it is not some monstrous quirk in my personality that makes me insist that you stay in this house. You know the reasons well enough, and they have not changed in the past hour. Perhaps you should sit down for a moment and calm yourself."

"I do not need to calm myself!" Lily pushed away from the door and seated herself on the low couch anyway. With her hands folded neatly in her lap, she stared straight ahead. "If you are determined to have me replace the books, then I will." She stood up again and loaded her arms with a nearby stack of books. Her movements looked jittery. With her back to him, she began to walk toward the bookcases. "And I do think it is a monstrous quirk in your personality that makes you subject me to this childish punishment."

She was nervous about something. One of the books she held tumbled to the floor and she made a hasty grab for it as she glanced at him over one shoulder. Their eyes met for no more than a moment, but what he saw there astounded him. She was afraid of him. He tried to think why. What had he done last night to frighten her so badly? He'd asked her to bring their kisses to a halt, and instead she'd encouraged him. Then she'd asked him to leave, and he'd left. Did she expect him to fall on her like some lust-crazed beast at this late date?

He thought to question her, but there was a soft knock at the library door before he could think of a civil way to ask her opinion of him. Lily started at the sound and dropped the books in her arms. He frowned over her bizarre behavior, then went to unlock the library door.

Digsby appeared on the other side. He held a small silver tray and an envelope rested in the center. "This message just arrived, Your Grace. The man who delivered it expressed a sense of urgency."

Remmington took the envelope and broke the seal, then hastily scanned the contents. He stuffed the note into his pocket. "You will remain posted inside this door until Lady Lillian returns the library to the order she found it in this morning. She is not to leave this room until that time." To Lily, he said, "I have to leave for a few hours. We will continue this discussion when I return."

Digsby closed the door behind Remmington. Without a word to Lily, he turned around, clasped his hands behind his back, and stared straight ahead. Lily returned to her chore with a sigh of relief. It had taken every ounce of courage she possessed to stand up to Remmington, to act as if she knew nothing about the secret compartment.

Trust no one. A few days ago, the warning in her father's message seemed unnecessary. Now it took on new meaning. Did he know something about Remmington that she did not? Why would he insist that she stay here if he had any doubts about Remmington's loyalty? It made no sense. That Remmington would turn traitor made even less sense. Still, she couldn't deny the evidence. Over the past few months, her father had translated several messages in this code. Even the handwriting looked the same.

Remmington might work for Sir Malcolm, she thought hopefully. That hope slipped away in a matter of moments. If that was the case, her father wouldn't send a coded message to tell her that Remmington knew nothing, that she shouldn't trust him. He must be working with the enemy. Every instinct told her it couldn't be true, yet those same instincts warned her to get as far from him as possible.

Her gaze traveled to one of the windows. If she could

convince Digsby to leave her alone in the library, she might be able to escape through a window. The library was on the first floor. The drop from the ledge to the ground below couldn't be terribly far.

When she was certain Remmington had left the house, she turned her attention to Digsby. "You needn't remain here. Rest assured that I can accomplish this task unsupervised."

The remark met with silence. She was about to suggest more useful endeavors for Digsby's valuable time when she heard a stranger's deep voice in the hallway outside the library.

"Hullo? Remmington!" The sound drew closer, and several other men apparently joined the first. All spoke in loud voices, then the first voice called out again. "I say, man. Where are you?"

Lily's gaze met Digsby's. She was certain her expression reflected the same look of trapped panic. He backed up against the library door and held one finger to his lips, then motioned her toward the wall behind the door. When she obeyed the unspoken command, he opened the door a crack and tried to step outside. Three men pushed their way into the room at the same time.

A dark-haired man strode toward the desk as he called to Digsby over one shoulder. "I say, Digsby. You look a fright. Engaging in the pugilistic arts again?" His startled gaze took in the library's disarray. "Good Lord! What happened here?"

He didn't wait for an answer, but began to fill three glasses with brandy as his friends seated themselves on a nearby couch. All three were dressed in riding garb, and they appeared to be in their middle twenties. Two of the men had light complexions and sandy brown hair. The third was taller than his companions, with jet-black hair and piercing blue eyes that matched his jacket. His deeply tanned features were remarkably similar to Remmington's.

"We're on our way to Hyde," the dark-haired man continued, his attention on the brandy glasses. "Thought we'd stop by to persuade Remmington to ride with us. It's unhealthy to pour over accounts and business papers every morning when there are finer pursuits afoot. Thought sure we'd find him here. Is he out, then?"

Digsby remained silent and the young man finally glanced up. His mouth dropped open in surprise. "I say. Lady Lillian! Whatever are you doing here?"

The other two men turned in their seats and soon all three gaped at her. Lily smiled serenely. "I don't think I know you, sir. Perhaps introductions would be in order before we engage in a conversation?"

"My apologies, Lady Lillian." He executed a deep bow, then his arm swept toward the two on the couch who rose to greet her. "These are my friends, the Honorable Mister James Howard, and his brother, Stephen, Lord Jasper. I'm Trevor Montague, brother to our esteemed absentee host." An impish grin played about his lips. "I must say, your company is entirely unexpected and quite preferable. Didn't think we'd find a lady caller at this hour. We stopped by to invite Remmington on an outing."

He left the statement hanging between them. Lily could almost hear him silently add, *And what are you doing here?*

"It's a perfectly fine day for an outing," Lily remarked. She tilted her head toward one of the windows. "I daresay Rotten Row will be nearly impassable. I heard that Lady Haviland overturned her phaeton just last week when she tried to make her way around Mr. Smith-Hampton's carriage. I cannot imagine what the man was thinking, taking a closed carriage to the park in the middle of the day."

Stephen raised his brows. "I doubt he was thinking of Lady Haviland. Anyone who takes a closed carriage into Hyde is thinking of no one but himself. It simply isn't done. I daresay Lord Haviland will demand an apology."

"One would expect as much," Lily agreed.

"Lady Lillian," Trevor broke in, "this is all very fascinating, but if you will forgive my curiosity, I cannot help but wonder what brings you to my brother's house."

"Why, to find this book of Greek fables." She held aloft a slim volume. "Remmington mentioned the book to my father, and Papa is mad to have it. His Grace offered to lend him the book, but then he couldn't locate the volume. He suggested that Papa might find the book more readily since he was familiar with the work, and Remmington graciously turned over his library for the search. Unfortunately, Papa suffered an awful attack of gout and our footman had to take him home not half an hour ago." She waved her hand toward the piles of books that lay scattered about the room. "As you can see, even with my father, my maid, and good Digsby here to assist, the volume required considerable effort to locate. It was beginning to look as if we'd be at it all day."

"Your father was here?" Trevor looked dubious.

"Why, of course," she answered. "You don't think I would be in a bachelor's house unescorted, do you?" She affected a puzzled frown. "Oh, dear. That must seem the case. What with all the commotion of the search and Papa's dreadful suffering, it did seem inconsequential. My maid is here, off somewhere at the moment to fetch tea, and we knew we could conclude the search within the hour. Oh, my goodness. What you must think, I'm sure I don't know. I can only guess His Grace's reaction, should I be the source of any rumors of impropriety attached to his name. You don't think he would go so far as to call my father out, do you?" She began to wring her hands with the hope that she looked close to tears. "I cannot imagine my poor Papa forced to face Remmington over pistols. The very thought makes me feel faint."

Trevor studied her in silence. One dark brow rose, a mannerism that reminded her distinctly of Remmington when he was being sarcastic. "Do calm yourself, dear lady. His Grace will know that *you* could never be the source of any unpleasant rumors." He turned his attention to James and Stephen and gave them a pointed look.

"However, I fear my brother's temper is quite fierce at times. He is also considered an excellent shot. It seems best to avoid the possibility of a duel. If ever the unlikely subject should arise, my friends and I will naturally attest to the fact that your father was here the entire time."

"But that would be asking you to lie."

Trevor shrugged. "This is a large house. Perhaps your father changed his mind about leaving. He could be resting in another room even as we speak." He looked again at the two brothers. "Isn't that right?"

"Right. Quite right," Stephen and James chimed.

"You see?" he asked. "Nothing at all to worry about."

"You are too kind," Lily murmured. "At least I kept my maid here as something of a chaperon, or you would think me a complete peahen." She turned her wide-eyed gaze to Digsby. "That reminds me. Would you please tell Gretchen that we shan't be needing the tea? Now that we've located our treasure, we must be on our way. Papa will be quite anxious."

Digsby didn't move so much as an eyebrow. "I really think you should stay for tea, my lady. After such a trying chore, you are sure to find a cup of tea refreshing."

"I feel quite refreshed already," she countered. "And Papa is so looking forward to reading this volume."

"His Grace will return at any time," Digsby said. "I feel quite certain he would not want to miss your visit. You really *must* stay for tea."

Lily dismissed the order with a delicate wave. "Entirely improper, my good man. My presence here is already a burden to these kind gentlemen. Please tell Gretchen that I am ready to leave."

"Is your father sending his carriage back for you?" Trevor asked.

Lily's smile faded to a puzzled frown. It was amazing that she could fall into her role so effortlessly with these strangers. In Remmington's company she'd begun to fear that she'd lost the talent. "I wonder if Papa will remember? He tends to be forgetful when the gout strikes. Perhaps we should find a hired hack."

Trevor shook his head. "That might be rather difficult at this time of day. They'll all be on Bond Street or Pall Mall. I'd offer to escort you myself, but we're on horseback."

"I'll find a hack," Stephen volunteered. "We'll have you on your way in no time at all, Lady Lillian."

"Thank you ever so much." Lily wondered if the flutter of her lashes was a bit much. Stephen gave her a jaunty salute before he left, then she turned again toward Digsby.

"Gretchen?" she reminded him. A dull flush crept up from his collar, but his expression remained unreadable. He gave her an impertinent nod before he left the library.

"Digsby seems out of sorts today," Trevor remarked. "That injury to his face seems to have affected his manners. I've never seen him behave so rudely."

Lily smiled. "Perhaps he ate something that didn't agree with him."

"Hm, I don't think so." He dismissed the matter with a shrug. "Remmington insists on employing the oddest people. I hope you didn't take offense."

"Not at all."

"Won't you have a seat, Lady Lillian?" James stood up to offer the seat he'd just vacated.

Worried that James intended to join her on the small sofa, she declined the offer. His gaze drifted over her figure with an unwelcome familiarity that she'd almost forgotten about in Remmington's company. She despised that lecherous stare. She wished Remmington would look at her that way just once. What was she thinking? She wanted no such thing.

Trevor showed as little interest in her appearance as Remmington, and she wondered if there was something about her looks that Montague men found distasteful. Remmington seemed to find her appealing only when they kissed. She shook her head and tried to clear her thoughts. "Did you attend the Ashlands' ball?" she asked Trevor, to fill the long silence.

"I arrived just yesterday from the West Indies, my lady."

"How very exciting. I would like to travel someday. Are the West Indies as beautiful as they say?"

Trevor's reply was cut short when the library door opened. Stephen walked in wearing a broad smile. "I found a hack practically on the doorstep." With a flourishing bow, he held one arm toward the hallway. "Your carriage awaits, my lady. Your maid showed up as well. She's in the foyer."

Now that her opportunity to leave was actually upon her, Lily felt a moment of hesitation. Remmington would be furious when he discovered her absence. She bolstered her courage by thinking about his reaction when he discovered one of his messages missing. The smile she gave Stephen was forced. "Thank you ever so much for your trouble, my lord. I don't know how I could have managed without your help."

Gretchen and Digsby stood in the foyer. The normally cheerful maid kept her solemn gaze on the floor as her fingers worried at one of the buttons on her gown.

"I really wish you would stay for tea, my lady," Digsby said in an ominous tone.

Trevor called out to her at the same moment. "Lady Lillian, you mustn't leave just yet."

Lily's heart leapt to her throat. She watched Trevor hold up a book.

"You forgot this in the library." He held the book out. His thumb obscured the title that was stamped onto the front cover. "You wouldn't want to forget this. Your father will be quite lost if you don't return with his book of, ah, Greek fables."

He held the book so only Lily could see what he was doing, then he slid his thumb aside to reveal the title. *Canterbury Tales.* Her gaze flew upward and she discovered that his grin was as infuriatingly smug as his brother's. He knew something was amiss. Her hand trembled as she reached for the book, and she flinched when his hand covered hers.

"I do hope our lack of hospitality isn't chasing you away. Will you let me make amends and allow me the pleasure of your company on a carriage ride through the park this afternoon?"

"I'm afraid that won't be possible." Lily tried to pull her hand away. "I promised Papa that I would read to him this afternoon."

"Tomorrow, then?"

She gave a hasty nod. "That sounds lovely, sir. You must call on my father first, of course."

"Of course."

He leaned down to kiss her hand before he released her. There wasn't the same thrill of anticipation that Remmington's touch elicited. She felt only a burning need to be away from these people. Trevor insisted on escorting her to the hack and he gallantly assisted both women into the hired carriage. Once seated, Lily turned to give the group a cheerful wave. Digsby had never looked so dour. Trevor gazed at her with frank curiosity. The Howard brothers waved back just as cheerfully. She glanced up and down the street, half afraid she would see Remmington. When the carriage lurched forward, she moved away from the window with an audible groan of relief.

"Oh, my lady," Gretchen sighed. "That was a close thing. Digsby told me how those men burst into the house without warning. Whatever shall we do now?"

Lily rubbed her forehead. "We will return to Crofford House. I've had enough adventure for the time being."

Her hand moved to her skirts to make sure the message was still tucked safely into her garter. She had an awful feeling that her adventure was just beginning.

Eight

❖

Lily's father was at his club when she arrived at Crofford House. She sent a servant to inform him of her return, then she locked herself in the library. An hour later she had Remmington's letter completely decoded. The message left her shaken. As she folded up the tables she'd created to break the code, her father burst into the library with Sir Malcolm close behind.

"*What* are you doing here?" the earl demanded.

Bainbridge's voice was just as disapproving. "Lily, you know better than to come here. You should have stayed at Remmington's."

She looked up from her work at the desk, her face pale. "Something awful happened."

Her father clenched his fists. "Did he—?"

A pounding at the front door interrupted the question followed by a loud commotion in the hallway. Then

Remmington strode into the library. The door slammed behind him. "Have you lost your mind?"

Lily shrank back in her seat as he stalked toward her. Sir Malcolm placed a hand on Remmington's arm to restrain him. Remmington's head snapped around and he glared at the older man. The tension in his body suddenly eased, as if he'd just noticed the presence of Bainbridge and the earl.

The sound of a sharp click made all three men turn toward Lily.

She'd removed a pistol from one of the desk drawers and had the weapon leveled at Remmington. "Step away from him, please, Sir Malcolm. This man is a traitor."

"Now, Lily, don't do anything hasty," her father warned.

Bainbridge was more demanding. "Put that pistol down immediately, young lady. You don't have any idea what you're about."

Lily nodded toward the coded message that lay on the desk. "It's all in this letter. He's smuggling spies into the country with the help of his fiancée's father, Lord Granger."

"You little thief!" Remmington took a step forward, but halted when Lily raised the weapon and aimed it toward his heart.

"One more step and I will save the courts the trouble of a trial, Remmington."

Crofford stepped forward to retrieve the message, and hastily scanned the contents. "Lily, this is a copy of an intercepted message that I translated last week. This doesn't mean—"

"What is *he* doing with French messages?" Lily demanded. "He has dozens just like this."

"He's working for me," Bainbridge said.

Lily shifted her gaze from Remmington to Bainbridge.

"You'll notice that Remmington's name isn't mentioned in those messages," he continued, in the same calm voice. "You just assumed he was involved because he was in possession of the messages. Isn't that right?"

Lily nodded and slowly lowered the weapon. Her puzzled gaze returned to Remmington, her voice weak with embarrassment. "You work for Sit Malcolm? But why didn't—"

Remmington interrupted her to address the earl. "You are the one who deciphers these messages?"

Crofford nodded. "I'm sure you'll understand why my involvement with Sir Malcolm's business is not widely known."

"It seems our cards are on the table," Bainbridge said briskly. He stepped forward to take the pistol from Lily's limp hands and returned the weapon to the desk drawer. "Now we can turn our attention to the matter at hand, which happens to be Lily's safety. Although I have men stationed around the house, the street is harder to patrol. Anyone could have noticed her return. We must assume the worst, and count on the possibility that our culprit knows she's here. Now, it seems best if—"

"A moment, if you please," Remmington interrupted. He pointed toward the desk. "If Crofford didn't see the copy of this message until just now, how did *she* know the contents."

Bainbridge sighed, then shrugged an apology toward Lily. "I keep the identities of all my operative in strictest confidence, unless faced with extenuating circumstances such as these. Your father and I agreed to keep quiet about your involvement, but now it seems that both your family secrets are out."

Remmington looked from Bainbridge to Lily, then back to Bainbridge. "Don't tell me she can decipher codes, too."

Lily lifted her chin. The elation she'd felt when she realized he wasn't an enemy spy died a quick death. "You believed my father's involvement readily enough. What makes mine so hard to believe?"

"You're a woman. You couldn't possibly . . ."

"Couldn't possibly what?" Her eyes narrowed.

"Come, Lily," Bainbridge broke in. "Remmington's difficulty comprehending your skills is a compliment. After all, you've done your best to make sure no one would guess where your talents lie. I'd say you succeeded admirably."

"Yes, admirably," Remmington echoed. His expression changed from disbelief to something that might have been disgust. "You are an excellent actress, my lady. You had me fooled completely. Or should I say, you made a complete fool of me. What an amusing little game you play."

"It is not a game! My work is a serious matter."

Remmington's gaze shifted to Bainbridge. "Who attacked her?"

The older man shrugged. "We don't know."

"But it is almost certainly related to the work she does for you?" Remmington didn't give Bainbridge a chance to answer. He jerked his head toward Lily's father. "I cannot believe that the two of you allowed this. There was no reason to risk her life when Crofford can handle whatever work she does for you."

Bainbridge's mouth thinned as he propped both hands atop his silver-headed walking cane. "That's just the point, Remmington. No one but Lily is capable of the work she does for me, not even her father. I do not approve of her involvement any more than her father approves of the arrangement, but there you have it. She is simply the most qualified. Lily translates messages that her father can't decipher. We would be in dire straits without her assistance."

"Come now, let's not argue." Crofford held up one hand, determined to take control of the situation. "As Sir Malcolm pointed out, we all work for the same cause, and it's time to turn our attention to more pressing matters." Deferring to Bainbridge, he asked, "How do you suggest we ensure Lily's safety?"

"Despite the fact that we have been unable to capture the culprit," Bainbridge began, "I think it safe to rule out the possibility that he is a spy."

That news made Lily sigh in relief. "My identity is still a secret," she said, with the beginnings of a smile. "I can continue my work."

"How can you be so sure the French are not behind this?" Remmington demanded. "Why would anyone else want to kill her?"

"We identified the four enemy spies related to the smuggling ring more than a week ago, and my men have watched their movements ever since. I've accounted for their whereabouts and that of their associates at the time of Lily's attack, as well as last night when we spotted someone near the house. None of them were anywhere near Crofford House at the time."

"Someone was here last night?" Lily asked.

"That's why we were so alarmed to see you here," Bainbridge said. "The culprit managed to disappear before my men could catch him. This is not over yet, Lily."

"You know who the spies are, and you haven't arrested them?" Crofford asked.

Brainbridge's mouth twisted into a grim smile. "We know who they are and every move they make. If we arrest them, they will simply be replaced with men we must track down all over again. They unknowingly tell us much more in their illusion of freedom than they would in Newgate Prison. Their time will come, but for now they are useful."

Crofford didn't look satisfied. "You are certain they are not behind Lily's attack?"

"As I said, they and the people connected to them were not involved."

"So where does that leave me?" Lily asked.

"On very uncertain ground, I'm afraid." Bainbridge shook his head. "There are two possibilities. Either the attack was done by some sort of mentally deranged criminal who chose a house and woman at random, or you have a very dangerous enemy we cannot identify. The first scenario seems the most likely. I know this will be hard for you to believe, Lily, but there are men who kill for no reason but their own sick need to destroy another life. From your description of the attack, it seems possible we are dealing with that sort of vicious criminal."

"You are alarming her!" Crofford protested. "There is no need to share your speculations in Lily's presence."

"I disagree," Bainbridge said. "Lily needs to be aware of everyone around her, to watch for anything that might seem unusual."

"You think he might be someone I know?" Lily asked.

"There is that possibility," Bainbridge conceded. "I asked your father, Sophie, and my wife to draw up lists that contain the names of every man who's shown an interest in you of late."

"Those lists must be long indeed," Remmington remarked dryly.

Lily glared at him, but Bainbridge ignored the interruption. "I eliminated most of the suspects almost immediately. The Ashlands' ball didn't let out until dawn, and most of the men on the lists were present at the ball until that time, or otherwise accounted for at the time of your attack. The few names that remained were crossed off last night. None were anywhere near Crofford House."

"So we are left without a suspect." Remmington watched Bainbridge nod. "I think Lily and I should review those lists. We might come up with another name or two."

"That's a good idea," Bainbridge agreed. "In the meantime, we must decide how to keep Lily safe. There are two options that I see. The first is to keep her in the house under guard, but I do not think that is the wisest plan. As I said, we must assume the worst, that he knows she returned here. So far all we know of him is that he is patient and clever. He also knows the routines and layout of this house. He planned his attack carefully, and waited for what he deemed the right moment to seize his opportunity. There are a half dozen guards around this house, yet he managed to elude every one of them last night. If we keep her in a place he is familiar with, we make it that much easier for him to wait for his next opportunity. If he is as clever as I think, he will know that eventually someone will let down their guard and make a mistake."

Bainbridge held one palm upward, as if he literally weighed his words. "This all assumes we didn't chase him off for good last night. If we did, then we will keep Lily locked away for no good reason. This could all be an overreaction on our part, yet I believe it is better to be safe than sorry. However, with Lily's position in the department to consider, we don't want her to draw undue attention or speculation. If she remains in seclusion and under guard, she will draw both. On the other hand, if she goes out in society, we might have a chance to turn the hunter into the hunted. Let us assume for the moment that he is someone she knows. He cannot very well wear a mask or disguise at a dinner party, or tie up every guest at a ball. Yet he might make a mistake, do or say something that gives his identity away. It's possible that he has an injured left wrist, and the blow Lily dealt to his head sounded serious enough that it might leave a noticeable scar."

"I don't like the sound of this." Crofford's worried gaze rested on his daughter. "Lily will be vulnerable."

"As long as we are careful to keep her places where he doesn't have an opportunity to get her alone, she should be safe enough. I can assign men who will disguise themselves as footmen and outriders to guard her carriage wherever she goes. Then we must make certain that someone we trust is with her at all times to act as her escort."

"That will not be a problem," Crofford said surely. "I will not allow her from my sight."

"How often were you at Lily's side at the Ashlands' ball?" Bainbridge asked. "Young people keep their own company these days when they attend balls and parties. There will be talk if Lily is constantly with her father and not with her friends. He might realize that we are waiting for him to make a wrong move. If you and Lily act no differently than before the attack, you will give the impression that you believe it was a random act and that Lily is no longer in any imminent danger. If we are to lull this man into a false sense of security, I think it best if he sees Lily with her friends, people he's seen her with before."

"Your niece is hardly capable of protecting Lily," Crofford retorted.

"True," Bainbridge agreed, "I had someone else in mind."

The room fell silent. Remmington took his gaze from Lily to look at Bainbridge. The older man's gaze rested on him already. In that instant he knew exactly what Bainbridge wanted. He also knew what it would mean if he accepted the duty. Somehow it seemed inevitable. That didn't quell the doubts in his mind. There was nothing predictable about Lily, nothing he could anticipate or outguess. The assignment Bainbridge wanted him to assume was dangerous in more ways than one. "I don't know that it's such a sound notion."

"What are you talking about?" Lily asked.

The men ignored her. Bainbridge shook his head. "If you will but consider the idea, I'm sure you will realize that it is the best plan. This also seems an ideal solution to your other problem. Or hadn't you thought of that?"

By openly escorting Lily, Remmington would make it clear to Margaret Granger that their relationship was at an end. He scowled at the implication that he needed an incentive to accept the duty, a selfish reason to offer Lily his protection. Bainbridge couldn't know that Lily would likely need protection from her protector if he accepted the assignment. The last few days with her had been torture. At night he went to bed aching for her, and awoke each morning in the same condition. Even when he tried to avoid seeing her, he couldn't push her from his thoughts. He'd spent hours in his library staring at business papers and reports without comprehending a single word. Instead he had gazed off into space and pictured what she might be doing, what he would like to do if he were with her. Whenever he did see her, his fantasies grew more potent, his body acutely aware of her nearness. Even now with her father and Sir Malcolm in the room, he would like nothing more than to take her seat behind the desk and pull her down onto his lap for a long, deep kiss. He shook his head to clear his thoughts, a gesture Bainbridge misinterpreted.

"I suppose we could find someone else," he began.

Remmington's head jerked up at the thought of another man courting Lily, even as a sham. A courtship would provide too many opportunities for a man to be alone with her. Already he doubted his own ability to resist her charms. He sure as hell wouldn't trust any other man to keep his hands off her. "I'll do it."

Bainbridge smiled. "I knew you would see reason."

Remmington refused to look at Lily, or her father. When he had time to sit down and think this through, he'd probably consider himself as insensible as they pretended to be. They had no idea what he'd really agreed to. Even Bainbridge couldn't know. Or perhaps he did.

"Crofford, I assume this meets with your approval?" Bainbridge asked.

The earl looked hesitant for a moment, then he nodded. Lily's gaze moved slowly over each man. Only Bainbridge looked pleased by whatever they'd just decided. Her father looked annoyed. If she didn't know better, she'd say Remmington looked worried. Her eyes widened when the truth finally hit her.

"Isn't anyone going to ask my opinion or permission?"

All three men answered her at once. "No."

Nine

———— ✦ ————

Lady Keaton's glass-roofed conservatory was filled to capacity with the brightest names in London society. Twinkling stars blanketed the rooftop, a perfect compliment to the brilliant sparkle of jewels that winked from the folds of snowy-white cravats and glowed in more obvious displays around wrists and necks of all sizes. Hushed conversations hummed in a steady drone, quieted occasionally by the clear, high notes of an Italian tenor. Signór Olivetti's renowned voice kept the myriad of glass panes that lined the conservatory in a constant state of vibration.

Seated amongst the other fifty guests, Lily watched for Remmington's arrival from the corner of her eye, plagued by hopes and doubts. That afternoon she'd argued with her father about the latest scheme to keep her safe. She was ready to agree with Remmington's opinion that her father had no sense at all when it came to that subject, but Remmington had turned on her, too. He'd agreed with the ghastly plan. No one seemed to care that she didn't want someone with her at all times, someone who would constantly watch her. Not when that "someone" would be Remmington. This was but another assignment to him, a courtship as meaningless as his courtship of Margaret Granger. Remmington had accepted his assignment. Lily dreaded it.

The tenor wound down at last and the guests clapped enthusiastically as they rose from their chairs. Her father offered her his arm and escorted her into the large foyer where other guests milled about. Everyone waited for Lady Keaton to lead the procession to the table.

"Remmington said he might be late tonight," her father said in a quiet voice. "I had no idea he meant hours rather than minutes."

As if in response to the earl's remark, Remmington's voice called out from behind them. "Good evening, Lord Crofford, Lady Lillian."

The sound of his deep voice sent a familiar rush of excitement through Lily. She didn't have to turn around to know he was staring at her. She had a foolish urge to smile. In the moment she took to school her features, she reminded herself that they were nothing more than casual acquaintances in the eyes of the world, that she must not say or do anything that would seem out of the ordinary.

Dressed in black again tonight, he had only a white shirt and cravat to relieve the somber color. Her secret knowledge of what he looked like beneath his jacket and shirt made her blush with remembered passion. His warm expression almost made her think that he might hold some affection for her as well. That was wishful thinking. At this point, he probably thought her the most troublesome creature on earth.

He lifted her hand for a perfunctory kiss that only reminded her of others they had shared that were far from innocent. He smiled at her, and that smile made her heart do strange things.

"You're late," Crofford told him under his breath.

"Forgive me, sir. I assure you that it was a matter of the utmost importance."

The answer seemed to appease some of her father's irritation, but his voice remained gruff. "I want her home at a proper hour. I warned Lady Keaton that I might not be able to stay for dinner." He raised his voice, aware of those around them. "I knew my gout would act up again tonight. Now that you are here, Remmington, I believe I will be on my way." He gave Lily a kiss on her cheek and murmured, "Keep yourself safe."

"I will, Papa." She tried to reassure him. "I shall see you later tonight."

Remmington tucked her arm beneath his and gave her hand a warning squeeze. "Smile, Lily. He is on his way home, not on his way to Calcutta."

Lily summoned an artificial smile. Her father walked away, and she was left alone with Remmington.

"Your Grace!" Lady Keaton waved over the heads of several guests to catch Remmington's attention. She tugged on the arm of her escort so they could move closer to her distinguished guest. "So good of you to come. You will, of course, be seated to my right at dinner."

"I'm afraid I promised to sit in for Crofford tonight as Lady Lillian's escort. With your permission, I shall sit in the earl's seat tonight."

Lady Keaton looked disappointed, then her smile brightened. "Oh, no need for that, Your Grace. We shall simply move the person I planned to seat between you and Lord Gordon to make room for Lady Lillian."

"If it isn't an inconvenience." Remmington's tone said he knew it wouldn't be.

He waited until Lady Keaton and her escort passed them, then he led Lily through the doorway into the dining room. They made their way past a sea of silver and china to the hostess's end of the table.

"I cannot help but wonder whose place I am taking tonight," Lily whispered as the other guests were busy taking their seats. She glanced toward the opposite end of the table. A footman léd Margaret Granger to her new place at the foot of the table, and Margaret looked furious over the slight. Lily also noticed that many of the guests stared at them while others murmured behind their hands or strategically placed fans. The gossip was beginning already. She tilted her head toward Remmington. "This has all the makings of an extremely unpleasant evening."

He pulled her chair out, murmuring his response in her ear as she took her seat. "Smile, Lily."

She smiled before she realized what her expression would convey. Others at the table would assume they'd just shared an intimate exchange. He'd just made his "interest" in her plain enough for anyone to see. The smile froze on her face as he took the seat to her left. "You aren't going to be subtle about this courtship, are you?"

He offered her a small platter of pineapple rings. "No."

Lily gritted her teeth and picked up the serving fork, stabbing the rings with a little too much force. "You're only using me to discourage Margaret Granger."

Remmington helped himself to the pineapple. "That isn't the only reason I agreed."

She waited for him to explain, but he remained silent. "Would you care to tell me your other reasons?"

He held her gaze for a moment, then his lids lowered and he began to study her mouth. His voice sounded distracted. "I'll tell you later. In the gardens."

When his gaze dropped even lower, Lily whispered furiously under her breath. "Stop that!"

Their eyes met and he grinned. His eyebrows conveyed a shrug. "Sorry."

"Lady Lillian?" a feminine voice called from across the table. Lily glanced up to see Lady Caroline Samms and Lord Bryant seated across from them. Lady Caroline smiled sweetly, but there was no missing the sarcasm in her gaminelike face, and she raised her voice to be heard above the din of the meal. "My dear, it's so good to see you here. I heard you were in Ireland. It's such a restful place to recuperate from great tragedies such as Lord Osgoode's untimely demise."

The entire end of the table fell silent. Caroline Samms was notorious for digging up everyone's scandal but her own. She was also Margaret Granger's best friend. Lily fixed a serene smile on her face and turned her attention from Caroline to Lord Bryant. The corners of her lips curved upward as she gave him a look that smoldered with sensuality. "Ireland is not to my taste. I find the familiar sights of England much more to my liking."

There were several gasps around the table, but Bryant responded to her provocation. He returned her brazen stare with that famous "under-look" of his that could set ladies' hearts to beating madly. It had absolutely no effect on Lily. She was too aware of Remmington's white knuckles on the table beside her.

Caroline tightened her grip on Bryant's arm until he turned his amused smile in her direction. "How very unfortunate for the Irish."

Lady Caroline immediately struck up a conversation with Lord Gower at her left, while Bryant smoothed Lady Keaton's ruffled feathers with his charm and the incident passed. Lily took a long drink of wine to cool her temper. She glanced at Remmington from the corner of her eye and watched him attack a leg of lamb.

"Your mood seems to have soured, Your Grace."

Remmington's eyes narrowed on her. "I forbid you ever to look at another man that way in my presence."

"Whatever do you mean?"

"You know exactly what I mean."

"Careful," Lily warned. She tapped his arm with her fan. "Lady Margaret will believe we're having our first argument. Her eyes haven't left us yet this evening. I must say, Remmington, your plan to use me is working out splendidly. If I were in her shoes, I would never speak to you again."

"I could care less what Margaret Granger is thinking or doing at this moment. We were speaking of you."

Lily patted her hair and smiled agreeably. "Ah, yes,

let's speak of me. Every lady loves to have a conversation centered around herself."

"You are being purposely obtuse."

"You know I dislike that word, Remmington. I've told you already that I am not fat." She tapped his arm again with her fan. "Do stop being insulting."

"Don't you dare play that game with me, Lily." He caught the end of her fan under his hand and trapped it against his arm. "And if you poke me once more with this thing, I will snap it in two."

"So sorry I'm late," Harry interrupted from behind them. He nodded toward Lady Keaton, then slid into the seat next to Lily. "Lady Lillian, Remmington. Didn't know the two of you would be attending tonight, but it's nice to see you both under better circumstances. I take it your, er, father's problem with the unwelcome guest is resolved, Lady Lillian?"

Remmington and Lily answered in unison.

"Yes."

"No."

"I see." Harry looked confused.

Lily frowned at Remmington, then turned her attention to Harry. She wanted to avoid the subject of her attack. "Other than the night of the Ashlands' ball, I don't believe I've seen you since the Antiquities Society meeting in January, Lord Gordon. The speech you gave that day was so very interesting. How is work progressing on that papyri of yours?"

"Deucedly slow, if I must say so." Harry filled his plate from a platter of roast beef. "Of some three thousand words, I've not been able to transcribe more than a handful. There is one that appears suspiciously often. I'm almost certain it's the name Ramses, but none of the letters seem to apply consistently to any other words, even though the letters in Ramses are quite common throughout any language. But there is a word that seems without a doubt to be the word 'and.' "

"That sounds like a wonderful start." She congratulated herself over the successful turn in the conversation. "You must take heart in such important progress."

"I was that far a month ago, Lady Lillian. Now I'm at an absolute impasse. Without another breakthrough, I'm afraid my work may come to naught."

Lily twisted the stem of her wineglass between her fingers and stared down at the dark liquid. "Wasn't it Lord Alfred who said the Egyptians were quite praiseworthy of their pharaohs in all their documents?"

"Hm. Can't say as I recall," Harry admitted.

"Perhaps it was Lord Poundstone." She took another sip of her wine and pretended to be distracted. "Those conversations are always so very difficult to follow at the Society meetings. But I'm certain I heard one of those gentlemen remark that Egyptians often followed a pharaoh's name with praises such as 'live forever mighty one' or 'live forever beloved of' some god or another."

"That's very true. In the Greek version of the Rosetta, 'live forever' consistently follows the pharaoh's name. It seems that would also be the case in my papyri."

Lily suspected she knew the key to Harry's papyri, but she struggled for a way to make the idea sound as if it was someone else's. "The 'R' sound is very strong, is it not? Papa says the sound carries over quite clearly in his translations from Greek and Latin manuscripts. If you think the Pharaoh's name is Ramses, then perhaps the 'R' would reoccur in the word 'forever'."

"Indeed!" Harry exclaimed. "You've given me a fresh angle, Lady Lillian. I'll bring my papyri along to the next meeting of the Antiquities Society and show you my progress."

"I would enjoy that very much, but I'm afraid I really don't understand much about papyri and that sort of thing." She smiled apologetically. "I usually attend the meetings only as a favor to my friend, Sophie Stanhope. Sophie seems truly absorbed by all those peculiar languages, although I have yet to understand why. They just look like so much nonsense to me."

"They are quite fascinating," Harry said in earnest.

"If you like, I could explain some of the fundamentals at the next meeting. They're very simple, really. I'm certain you would catch the gist of it eventually."

"That sounds lovely, my lord." Lily sighed and fluttered her fan. "I shall certainly look forward to your explanation, although I fear you may grow frustrated with me. Sophie says I just don't have the interest required to fully understand foreign languages."

"Oh, I wouldn't grow frustrated with *you*, Lady Lillian. If anything, you will probably grow bored with my explanations."

"Your food grows cold, Gordon."

Harry gave Remmington a considering look, then he shrugged and turned his attention to his plate.

Lily reached for her fork, but Remmington caught her hand and gave it a gentle squeeze. "You must not tax yourself with such weighty issues, my dear. They are better left to scholars such as Lord Gordon. Why don't you tell me about Signór Olivetti's recital. What pieces did he perform?"

She couldn't remember. Not when he looked at her with such a tender expression in his eyes. It was an act, she reminded herself. He'd just warned her not to reveal too much of herself to Harry. Now he was affecting possession, also for the sake of their audience. "Signór Olivetti performed parts of *Fidelio*."

"Ah, Beethoven," he said. "A favorite of mine. I am sorry I missed him."

When his hand slipped away from hers, she missed the casual contact. She shouldn't let his touch affect her so deeply, yet how on earth could she guard against it?

The remainder of their meal passed in silence. Between Remmington's constant attention and Lady Caroline's insolent remarks, Lily knew she was the subject of nearly every murmured conversation at the table. She wondered what would happen if she simply threw back her head and screamed her frustration. She'd probably be hauled off to Bedlam.

"I believe it's dead."

Remmington's quiet announcement startled Lily from her thoughts. She glanced up at him, then her gaze moved back to her plate and the torte she'd just shredded with her fork. She placed her silverware on the table and folded her hands in her lap. "I was just making certain."

The corners of his mouth turned upward. The other guests began to leave the table and he stood up to offer her his arm. "Lady Keaton has musicians and refreshments at the pavilion in the center of the gardens, but I'm sure we can find someplace a little more private. I belive it's time we had a talk."

Lady Keaton's gardens were a fairytale of silhouetted trees and flowers. Softly illuminated Chinese lanterns were hung among the greenery and scattered throughout the gardens. Lily couldn't imagine a more romantic setting, nor anyone she would rather be with in this place than Remmington. She decided the night was fast turning into a cruel joke.

Just outside the dining room, a mazelike path led to the pavilion in the center of the gardens. From there Lily assumed they would go deeper into the gardens, away from the crowd. His long strides indicated an impatience to get her alone, but she knew he had nothing romantic on his mind. More than likely, he wanted privacy to deliver another speech about rules and proper behavior.

"Are you late for an appointment?" Her voice sounded breathless. His pace made her nearly run to keep up with him. He slowed grudgingly. "I think we could manage to have our conversation within sight of the other guests."

"Don't be a fool. Nothing we have to say to each other is fit for an audience."

Lily came to an abrupt halt. She kept her feet stubbornly planted despite the tugs he gave her arm. "I am not a fool."

"You're not stupid," he said agreeably. "But even an intelligent woman can act like a fool at times."

Her hands became fists at her sides. "May I ask just when I proved myself so ignorant?"

"I would rather not start an argument where anyone might happen upon us." He glanced over his shoulder. "But since you asked, your conversation tonight with Harry would be one example. Without a moment's hesitation, you more or less gave him the answers to a problem he's worked on for a month. Don't you think he will begin to wonder how you came to such an important conclusion when foreign languages supposedly leave you baffled? I would see through that blunder in the blink of an eye, just as I saw through your fool's act the day we discussed philosophy. You may be good at ciphering, but the ladies on Drury Lane can rest easy. You are no great actress."

Lily lifted her chin. "I made the solution sound as if it came from other sources. Lord Gordon is unlikely to wonder over anything."

"Perhaps," he said, "but what about Lady Caroline? To be successful in your charade, you should be inconspicuous, yet you made yourself a threat to Margaret Granger with that Osgoode business, and now to Caroline Samms by encouraging Bryant's attention. With those two pillars of society turned against you, it is simply a matter of time before other women start to watch you more carefully. The ladies of society make it a point to know their rivals' faults and secrets."

"Lady Caroline made me lose my temper." She bowed her head. He was right. At dinner she'd mooned over his smiles and grown flushed under his dark gaze. All the time he was scrutinizing her every action, his mind clear of the emotions that seemed to befuddle her senses in his presence. She felt a tear fall silently to the ground. "Am I not allowed one mistake?"

"Not when your life is at stake. To survive in this business, you must never make yourself the object of so much attention. Unflattering attention, at that." He fell silent for a moment. "Lily? Are you crying?"

She brushed at her tears but refused to meet his gaze. "Am I not allowed to have feelings, either?"

"I didn't mean—"

"Remmington!"

Lily's startled gaze flew past Remmington. Margaret Granger and Caroline Samms walked toward them at a sedate pace, but she could see the spark of anger in Margaret's eyes. Remmington pushed her behind his back, probably to give her a moment to compose herself before she faced Margaret's wrath.

"Good evening, Lady Margaret, Lady Caroline," he murmured.

Caroline looked pointedly over Remmington's shoulder. A smug grin curved her lips. "Oh, Margaret, I really should make sure Bryant knows where I am. If you will excuse me?"

"Of course." Margaret's eyes never left Remmington.

Caroline turned to walk back toward the house and Lily thought it an ideal moment to make her own exit. Remmington had his back toward her, and Margaret was paying her little attention. She took a few hesitant steps backward, and then a few more. A small voice inside her head said she should stay with Remmington, that it would be a mistake to leave his side.

The look on Margaret's face made her decide that it would do no harm to wait for him near the pavilion. Remmington might even appreciate her thoughtfulness in giving him a moment of privacy with Margaret. She didn't deceive herself very long with that wishful lie. More than likely he would add "cowardly" to her list of faults. The sound of Remmington's deep voice covered the soft crunch of her slippers against the gravel pathway as she turned and walked away.

"I thought you would be at Almack's tonight, Margaret."

"Why, whatever gave you that idea?" Margaret asked.

"I was at Almack's just last week and will certainly attend many more times before the Season ends, but dear Lady Keaton has her famous dinner only once each Season. I could not bear to disappoint her."

The path took an abrupt turn and the sound of Remmington's reply faded away. The strains of a waltz grew louder as she neared the pavilion, along with the muted sounds of laughter and conversations. The path widened and she could see the lights of the pavilion, a raised platform designed to look like a Greek temple with a score of false marble columns all around that supported nothing but the starlit night air. Lily intended to stay in the shadows of the path, but changed her mind when she saw a couple walk toward her. She pasted on a smile and ventured forward.

She nodded to the couple as they walked past, then looked for a less noticeable place to await Remmington's arrival. Tall hedges formed a large, circular wall around the pavilion, with evenly spaced openings that led to more paths. Most of the guests stood near the pavilion, but a few wandered around the manicured flowerbeds that were laid out in intricate detail to form a miniature map of the vast gardens. Many considered Lady Keaton's topiary mazes the finest in England, and there were rumors that Lady Keaton installed the map after Lord Northfield lost himself in the mazes for an entire day. Lily had no intention of exploring the mazes, but she caught a flash of color from the corner of her eye and she began to edge toward one of the openings. She caught only a glimpse of the man before she ducked into the greenery, but she knew only one person who would wear a canary-yellow suit to a dinner party.

The path came to a T and she turned right. A moment later, she found herself facing a wall of greenery and the end of the false path.

"There you are. Whatever are you doing here, Lady Lillian?"

Lily whirled toward the sound of the familiar voice.

She couldn't see Lord Allen's face very clearly in the shadows, but his bright yellow clothing seemed to glow against the dark hedges. When she realized that he blocked her only exit, her heart began to beat faster. She was trapped. Her nerves didn't feel any calmer when she reminded herself that Lord Allen wasn't a suspect, that Sir Malcolm had removed him from the list because he'd remained at the Ashlands' ball until dawn.

"Lady Caroline said this path led to the house. The night air is a little chilly, and I left my shawl at the door." She looked behind her at the wall of greenery. "It seems I took a wrong turn."

"I shall be happy to escort you to the house," Lord Allen said, as he extended his arm. "We can't take the risk of you catching a chill."

Lily hesitated, then took a step forward and placed her hand on Lord Allen's sleeve. She could see his face more clearly now, the look of pleasure in his bulging eyes. It took every bit of her courage to smile at the man. "Lead the way, Lord Allen. We must rely upon your excellent sense of direction."

Lord Allen covered her hand with his own, trapping it against his arm. "My dear Lady Lillian. There is something I must tell you before we return to the house."

Lord Allen's gaze lingered on her chest, and the lecherous stare made her skin crawl. His grip on her hand tightened until it hurt. Every shred of her self-assurance disappeared. She jerked her hand from Lord Allen's grip and took a step backward. At that moment she would give almost anything to see Remmington appear behind Lord Allen.

"I didn't mean to startle you," he said. "I simply wanted to tell you that I spoke with your father tonight before he left, and I have an appointment with him tomorrow at three o'clock." He took a step closer, unmindful of the way she shrank away. "We have known each other for many years, my dear, yet I fear you have never clearly understood my intentions. Tomorrow I plan to ask your father for his permission to begin a formal courtship."

Lily didn't respond to that announcement, although it took considerable effort to remain silent. She wanted to tell him he was too late, to use Remmington's false courtship to fob him off. Something in his eyes made the words freeze in her throat.

"I can see this comes as a surprise," he said at last. He reached out and took her hand.

Lily tried to pull away from his grasp, but he proved surprisingly strong. His thumb stroked the back of her hand, and she felt a shudder of fear. Her heart beat faster and faster until she thought it would burst from her chest. She'd known Lord Allen for years, yet she didn't really know him at all.

"That's all right, my dear." He patted her hand and leaned even closer. Lily leaned away. His breath smelled of garlic and wine. "You must be overcome by your emotions right now. I can wait until tomorrow to discuss the details of our courtship."

He turned and walked toward the pavilion, with Lily forced to follow his lead until they came into view of the garden area. She came to a sudden halt, trying her best to sound as if nothing were amiss. "I fear we must part company here, my lord, or there will be talk. I had not thought of it before now, but some might think it strange to see us emerge together from this sheltered part of the gardens."

Lord Allen glanced toward the pavilion and Lily used that distraction to pull away from him. She began to walk backward, toward the path that turned to the left. "I must bid you adieu until tomorrow, Lord Allen."

Lord Allen reached out for her, but she turned and bolted toward the hedges. The path took several quick turns and she paused for a moment where it formed another T. She heard only the soft crunch of her own slippers on the gravel, but she quickly checked around her to see if Lord Allen followed. Silvery hedges rose eight to ten feet on every side, the gravel path a faint outline in the moonlight that disappeared a few yards beyond her in the shadows of the hedges. The music sounded farther away, but Lily didn't know if she'd made her way toward the house or deeper into the gardens. More importantly, she didn't hear the sound of footsteps. No one followed her.

Lily wasn't sure how long she hid beneath the trellised rose arbor. It seemed hours. She'd wandered down one path after another until she reached this small clearing. The arched arbor stood before the outer brick wall of the garden, and the thorny rose vines nearly covered the wall. The full moon provided the only light, and the faint strains of music from the pavilion seemed to come from very far away. No one would find her here. Not even Remmington. She wiped her cheeks with the back of her hand and tried to contain a fresh wave of tears.

She wanted to go home, yet she hadn't spent the night in her own room since the night of her attack. She would probably lie awake all night, her nerves tensed, her heart fluttering as rapidly as it did at this moment. If she'd trusted her instincts about Remmington, she would still be at his town house, safe. Was he even looking for her? She'd probably pushed him too far this time. She wouldn't blame him if he decided this particular assignment wasn't worth the trouble. Her breath caught in her throat when a dark figure appeared on the moonlit path and she pressed herself closer to the dark recesses of the arbor.

"Lily?"

Remmington's voice sounded oddly calm as he walked toward her hiding place. He came to a halt just outside the arbor, and she could see him clearly in the moonlight. She took a step forward, then another, then he opened his arms just in time to catch her. She landed against his chest and wrapped her arms around his neck.

"Do you have any idea how worried I've been?" he muttered, even as his arms tightened around her in a crushing embrace. For a moment he seemed content to hold her, then his hands were on her shoulders, pushing her away. "My God, Lily. You're shaking like a leaf. What happened to you?"

"N-nothing," she mumbled. "S-something." Her arms slipped around his waist and she buried her face against his chest. "Please, just hold me for a little while."

He hesitated a moment, then he pulled her tight against his chest and stroked her back in a soothing motion. "It's all right, sweetheart. I'm here now." When her breathing sounded more normal, he lifted her chin with his thumb and waited until she looked up at him. "Tell me what happened, Lily."

She shook her head. "Very little happened. Certainly nothing to warrant these childish tears."

"What happened?"

"My imagination simply got the better of me. After I left you with Margaret Granger, I took a wrong turn and ended up near the pavilion, where Lord Allen found me."

Remmington listened in silence as she related her encounter with Lord Allen. She tried to make light of the incident, but he didn't look appeased by her explanation. The sound of muted laughter distracted them both, probably the sounds of a couple trysting on a nearby path.

"Someone is coming," he announced. His eyes were intense as he stared down at her. "There is just one more thing before we go. Don't ever leave me that way again."

Before she could guess what he meant to do, his mouth covered hers in a kiss that communicated his anger and worry much more effectively than words. Her hands became fists and she began to push against his chest at the same moment he gentled the kiss. He fit his lips against hers, expertly, insistently, until her palms opened and she smoothed her hands up his chest to his shoulders, clinging to the very object that threatened her balance. She heard the sound of laughter again, closer than before.

He broke away from her. Amazingly, he didn't seem the least affected by their kiss. He took her by the elbow and turned her toward the path. "Come, Lily. It's time we left."

Ten

◆

"We'll never get out of here," Remmington muttered. Dozens of carriages lined the driveway in front of Keaton House. The street beyond the driveway looked just as clogged with carriage traffic.

"You managed our way from the mazes easily enough," Lily said, a touch of admiration in her voice. "It seemed I circled that maze for hours until I gave up and hid in the arbor."

"Two hours," he told her, frowning over the reminder of his frantic search. He hadn't truly panicked until he reached the pavilion and saw no sign of her. For two hours he'd searched the maze, his heart gripped with fear, his mind plagued by every gruesome possibility. She still clung to his arm with both hands, as if she feared he would disappear. There wasn't a chance of that happening. He would never turn his back on her again.

He led Lily to his carriage and took the seat next to

her. She shifted closer to him and he wanted nothing more than to pull her onto his lap. The carriage started forward and he nudged her hip to make a little more room between them. "Why didn't you tell Allen that a courtship would be impossible, that you already have a suitor?"

She shrugged. "He seemed to appear from nowhere, and made me realize that I was alone when I shouldn't be. I didn't have any reason to be frightened of Lord Allen, but he made me uneasy. I know it sounds foolish, but I just wanted to be away from him."

Remmington made a mental note to have Digsby put together a dossier on Lord Allen. The young dandy appeared harmless enough, and Sir Malcolm had verified the fact that he had not left the Ashlands' ball until close to dawn. Still, he seemed to be at Lily's elbow every time he saw her. It would do no harm to make certain. "Allen is not your attacker, Lily. Several people saw him in Lord Ashland's card room until almost dawn the night of the ball."

"I know that. I also know that I made a very foolish mistake by leaving your side." She bit her lower lip, then gave him a hesitant apology. "You have every right to be angry with me, Your Grace. I'm sorry you had to look for me."

Half an hour ago he'd wanted nothing more than the opportunity to yell at her, to vent just a portion of his anger over her disappearance. Now he wanted nothing more than to hold her, to stroke the smooth curve of her cheek to see if her skin was really as soft as he remembered. "Perhaps you should sit on the other side of the carriage, Lily."

"I like this side better."

"Then I'll move." He started out of his seat, but stopped when she laid her hand on his arm.

"I know you don't like being this close to me, no more than you like kissing me," she said, "but I would feel better if you sat next to me for just a little while."

Was she jesting? He searched her face for some sign that she was teasing him.

She bowed her head. "You think I'm a coward."

"You are the bravest woman I've ever met," he said simply. "And the most baffling. Whatever gave you the idea that I don't like to kiss you?"

"You were angry that night at your town house. Tonight you didn't seem especially angry, but . . ." She lifted her chin in a haughty gesture. "You needn't look so worried. There is no need for you to pretend interest in me as you did with Margaret Granger. In fact, kissing is entirely unnecessary in this courtship. It must be obvious by now that I will not improve with practice."

Remmington stared at her in utter disbelief. He held her chin in one hand and brushed his thumb across her mouth. "You are so naive that it frightens me. Don't you own a mirror? Have you never looked at yourself?"

Lily pulled away. "I own a mirror. Until a few years ago, it reflected a girl with bright red hair and a tall, ungainly body."

"That is no longer the case, I assure you."

"No," she admitted, "but I am a far cry from the women I usually see in your company." She held her hands up for examination, her fingers splayed wide. "My hands are too big to be feminine. I'm taller than almost every woman I know, and many men, too. It was worse when I was younger. I towered over the other children in our parish, a gawky, ugly girl who never fit in. I was the one everyone poked fun at, the one who could never do anything right. Sophie was the only one who didn't tease me."

He tried to picture her as an adolescent. No matter how ungainly the child, he would have recognized the promise of her beauty. "I wish I had known you then." He reached out to stroke her cheek, not a lover's caress, but that of a friend offering comfort. "I would have protected you from those childish taunts."

She stared at her hands as if she could see the past more clearly there. "The taunting didn't stop until the year I turned sixteen. My father called me a late bloomer. Over the next few years, people started to look at me differently. The compliments were grudging at first and I didn't belive them. Then I realized that Papa was right, that I was changing. Girls who once laughed at me began to put their noses in the air and turned their backs whenever I walked into a room. Boys who'd tossed me careless, cutting insults began to stare at me in ways that made me want to bathe. I didn't see how being called pretty was much better than being called ugly. Things only grew worse when I made my debut. Women I didn't know refused to speak to me. Men I didn't want to know made a great nuisance of themselves."

She looked up at him, her lips curved into a wry smile. "Don't you see? Every time someone gives me a compliment, I remember a taunt. I wonder what they will say to me when my hair is gray and my face wrinkled. I try to keep that in mind whenever I am tempted to believe empty flattery. Faces and figures might be called pretty or pleasing, but I think you must know a person's character before you call them beautiful or handsome. It's the part inside a person that matters most."

The odd pieces of her character began to fall into place; her lack of conceit or wiles, the cynical light that came to her eyes whenever he spoke of her looks. He smoothed his hand down her arm and laced his fingers through hers to cover her gloved hand completely.

"Your hands do not seem so large to me. Sturdy, perhaps." He turned her hand over and lifted it to press a line of kisses against the lacy gloves from her wrist to the center of her palm. Her fingers curled, as if to capture the kiss.

She pulled her hand away. "I believe you are deliberately trying to distract me from our conversation."

"Ah, yes," he murmured, leaning closer. "I believe we were talking about kissing."

She placed her hand on his chest. "We were talking about our courtship."

"Kisses are a much more interesting subject." His hand covered hers, trapping it against his chest. "I think you like them."

She looked at him with that enchanting mixture of innocent curiosity and desire, the light of the carriage lantern reflected in her eyes. "I don't think I should like them so much."

The confession caught him off guard. "Lily, never tell a man that you like to kiss him."

Where did that warning come from? He didn't want her to play games with him. He smiled to cover his blunder. "However, your admission pleases me. You can be delightfully honest at times."

Her eyes narrowed. "And at other times?"

"At other times, you can be quite vexing." He thought about the secrets she'd kept from him, how much they'd complicated matters. His humor faded. "Admit it, Lily. You deceived me from the moment we met."

"Oh, and you were sterling in your honesty," she shot back. "You sound much like the pot calling the kettle black, my lord."

There was a moment of charged silence, then he smiled again. "Do you realize that you are the only woman who ever argues with me?" He stroked the curve of her cheek. "Most women do their best to be agreeable in my presence."

Her eyes flashed with a spark of anger. "Most women make cakes of themselves in your presence. They are too busy impressing you with their charms to find time to argue."

His smile grew broader. "Is that jealousy I hear?"

"It is nothing of the kind. Why on earth should I be jealous? We are no more than partners in this assignment. When this courtship is over you are certain to find some other female to amuse yourself with. Our rather odd relationship will be at an end."

"I rather like the notion of being your friend." He drew her closer to his side, a little surprised when she didn't object.

"I have a feeling your definition of the word 'friend'

would vary greatly from mine, Remmington. As far as I can tell, you don't want anyone close to you."

"You are close to me right now." His arms circled around her and her eyes grew wider, as if she'd just realized the precariousness of her position. Her lips were temptingly near, but he forced himself to meet her gaze and push other thoughts aside. "I believe a friend is a person who enjoys your company, someone who will stand by you no matter what. A friend knows your deepest secrets and keeps them." He cupped her chin in his hand and brushed his thumb across her lips. Her skin was so very soft, her scent delightful. The shudder of desire he felt was his own. It was her hair that smelled of sandalwood. He wanted to loosen it and run his hands through the silky strands. He knew he was playing with fire but he didn't seem to care, couldn't seem to help himself. His hold on her tightened. "Is there anything in my definition of friendship that does not characterize our relationship?"

"Friends do not kiss each other so intimately."

"You think not?" He shook his head. "Some of the greatest love affairs in history began as friendships."

"I think ..."

He felt her warm, sweet breath against his face, and noticed the rapid pulse that fluttered at her throat. If he weren't so curious about her answer, he would give into temptation and kiss that sensitive pulse point to feel her heart beat beneath his lips, to know that he was the one who made it beat faster. Didn't like kissing her, indeed. He would like to kiss every inch of her.

Somehow her hands made their way to his chest and she pushed against him with surprising strength. "I think you are trying to confuse me. This is nothing more than a temporary arrangement. The time will come when we will go our separate ways. In the meantime, I realize it is in both our best interests to appear no more than cordial. This must be a very entertaining game for a man of your experience, but you said yourself that I am not a good actress, and I—" Her eyes widened when he lifted her onto his lap. "What are you doing, Remmington?"

"Appearing cordial." Just one more taste, he decided. One small kiss to show her just how desirable he found her.

She opened her mouth to let out a startled cry, but he was quicker. He caught the sound as his mouth covered hers, a fierce kiss that robbed them both of breath. When he began to draw away, her hands curled around his lapels to pull him closer. He felt a surge of satisfaction. His lips brushed across her mouth and his hands stroked her back as he gentled her to his touch. With each stroke she melted a little more, grew a little softer. She was so incredibly responsive. He deepened the kiss. Her hands moved up his chest and around his neck until her fingers tangled in his hair, then she smoothed her fingers along the back of his neck in a shy, hesitant caress. The affect on him was instantaneous, a quicksilver flash of desire that tightened every muscle and made him exquisitely aware of how much he wanted her.

"We shouldn't be doing this, Lily." He caught both her hands and held them securely against his chest. "We have to stop."

"Why?"

His laugh was almost a groan. "You taste too sweet."

He leaned down to brush his lips against her forehead. When she closed her eyes, he pressed feathery kisses against her eyelids. A moment later they fluttered open again. What he saw there made the breath catch in his throat. He reached out and drew her head down onto his shoulder, then cupped his hand around her face to keep her there.

"Give me a moment to calm down before you look at me that way." His voice was deeper than normal, almost strained. "You know how that affects me."

She didn't know, and told him so. His arms tightened around her.

"It makes me want to kiss you again." A moment passed before he corrected himself. "No, that isn't true.

The look in your eyes makes me want to do much more than kiss you. If anyone else saw you look at me that way . . ." He shifted and tried to find a more comfortable position, tried to think of anything that would cool his desire. "We need to talk about something else, Lily. Tell me about Lord Osgoode. I have yet to hear you speak a word of your former fiancé. Was he nice to you? Do you miss him?"

"Lord Osgoode?" She looked confused by the question.

"Forgive me," he said at last. "I didn't mean to burden you with sad thoughts. You must have cared for him a great deal."

Lily shook her head. "Lord Osgoode escorted me to two balls and an afternoon brunch. In truth, we were not all that well acquainted. We exchanged the usual social pleasantries and I did not object to his company, but I certainly had no intention of marrying him."

"I thought you were engaged."

"I thought you were engaged to Margaret Granger," she countered.

"We have more in common with each passing moment." He inclined his head to concede the point. "Who courted you before Osgoode?"

"I really don't think that is any of your business."

"Everything about you is my business," he bit out. "I still believe the man who attacked you is someone you know. I want to know if there are any more Osgoodes out there, perhaps another man whose affections you've spurned."

"I haven't spurned anyone," she said indignantly.

"Osgoode fought a duel for you. Why?"

Lily looked offended by the question. "In future, you would be well advised to obtain your gossip from a source other than Margaret Granger. I have no idea who Osgoode dueled with, but I am certain he did not duel over my hand or some slur against my honor, or anything else remotely related to me. I meant no more to Osgoode than I mean to you."

"You mean a great deal to me, Lily." The words were out of his mouth before he could think them through. The hopeful look in her eyes made him grit his teeth.

"Are you trying to tell me that our courtship is not a sham?"

He felt as if the ground had opened beneath him. He knew what she was really asking. For a woman like Lily, there was only one logical conclusion to a courtship. Marriage. He felt a bead of perspiration form on his brow and the carriage suddenly seemed too warm. This afternoon he'd convinced himself that he could enjoy Lily's company for the duration of this "courtship," then walk away as easily as he'd walked away from every other assignment. In the meantime, no one would think it odd if they shared a few intimacies, and no one but he and Lily would have to know the exact nature of those intimacies. Hell, he'd planned to seduce her.

He saw a mental image of his plan disappear in a puff of smoke. He knew now what that plan would do to her. Lily wasn't experienced or jaded enough to play at the games of love. When she gave a man her innocence, she would give him her heart as well. He didn't deserve either, and he certainly couldn't return her precious gifts.

"I want there to be honesty between us," he began. He watched the light of hope disappear from her eyes as she tried to ease herself off his lap onto the seat beside him. He held her more securely, then cupped her face with one hand. "We have enough secrets in our lives. The fact that we can share our secrets is one of the things that makes our friendship special. I care for you, Lily, but I will not lie to you, or give you any reason to think our courtship might lead to a wedding. I learned long ago that I am not a man suited to marriage, and I would rather see my brother's heirs inherit than take another wife." Her wounded look made him release a frustrated sigh. "My views have nothing to do with you, Lily. You cannot possibly know how marriage changes a person. I doubt you even know what I am talking about. You are innocent in ways I can't even remember."

"I did not think it was such a sin to be innocent," she said, her eyes bright with tears.

"It isn't a sin. It is a gift, Lily. One that you would waste on a scoundrel." One crystal tear rolled down her cheek and he resisted the urge to brush it away, half afraid it would scald him. "There was a time when I would have made you a fit husband, a time when I still believed in marriage and loyalty, love and devotion. I know better now. That isn't the way it works in our world. You have yet to learn that lesson, and I will not be the one to teach you. Damn it, Lily. You want something from me that I cannot give you."

Or could he? Did a part of him rebel against the idea of a serious courtship with Lily because he knew how easily he could fall in love with her? The attraction he felt went beyond her beauty. What he liked best about Lily lay beneath the surface. Her looks were simply a bonus, an enticement to draw him closer to his doom. Yet how long could he hold her? Catherine's betrayal had wounded his pride more than anything else. If he lost Lily to another man, her betrayal would destroy him. The reason why struck him like a blow. He was half in love with her already.

That admission didn't sit well. He could see Lily's future as clearly as she showed him her past. Her innocence protected her now, but once she married, every male in the *ton* would consider her fair game. If he were fool enough to marry her, he would still have to leave her on occasion to fulfill his duties in the War Department. He knew well enough that men would line up to offer solace in his absence. They would tempt and entice her at every turn. The longer she resisted, the more of a challenge she would become. It would only be a matter of time before one caught her eye, and that would be the end of her "love" for him. He'd rather be celibate the rest of his life than put himself through that hell. It would be better to lose her now, before he began to deceive himself with impossible dreams, before he told himself lies that his marriage could be different from the rest. Marrying Lily would be the worst mistake of his life.

Lily didn't say anything as those thoughts raced through his mind. She just kept staring at him with those large, beautiful eyes. Why he should feel so guilty, he didn't know. He was the one who made the greatest sacrifice. After tonight she probably wouldn't let him kiss her again, or so much as touch her luscious body. He'd just told her that his intentions were anything but honorable. He'd done the right thing.

Why did it feel so wrong?

This time he didn't stop her when she moved to sit beside him. He braced his arms and kept his hands planted firmly on his knees. He wouldn't even look at her to see if she was still crying. Tears would only weaken his resolve. Instead he concentrated on the sound the carriage wheels made as they rolled over the cobbled streets.

"You will find someone else," he said at last. "I know at least a dozen men who would offer marriage if you did no more than smile at them."

"I must remember to smile at someone suitable."

"That isn't what I meant, Lily." He reached for her hand, but stopped when she shrank away from him. His hand hovered for a moment, then returned to his side.

Her words sounded as brittle as she looked, as if she might shatter at any moment. "I know what you meant. You needn't say anything more on the matter. I understand everything very clearly now."

You don't understand anything, he thought with a stab of regret. He wanted nothing more than to pull her into his arms and kiss her until she forgot every damning word he'd said. He wanted to be the one she smiled at. He wondered if he would ever see her smile again.

"Have you—" Lily's voice caught and she paused to take a deep breath. "Have you worked for Sir Malcolm very long?"

He knew why she changed the subject so abruptly. She was struggling to retain her control, to pretend that she understood why he would reject her so completely.

He didn't dare shatter her pretense. "I began working for the War Department nearly ten years ago. I took over my father's duties after he and my mother were lost at sea."

Lily's stiff composure slipped a notch as a startled look crossed her face. "Your parents worked for the War Department?"

"Only my father, but my mother often accompanied him on less dangerous missions. They sailed to the West Indies on that particular voyage, but the ship went down in a hurricane some three days from port. There were no survivors."

"I'm so sorry," Lily murmured. "It must have been very difficult for you to assume your titles and so many duties amidst such tragedy. The demands on you must have been overwhelming."

He scowled at his hands. He'd forgotten how perceptive she could be. At the time his parents died there were endless offers of sympathy, but there were questions as well. Many came from his father's solicitors, a dizzying array of financial matters. Others came from servants and staff, overseers and managers, tradesmen and nearby villagers, all anxious to know how his father's death would affect their lives. He'd looked upon his War Department duties as a respite, a means to escape those demands for a time. He hadn't even known Lily then, but she saw his life as clearly as if she'd stood at his side all those years ago. She offered her compassion and sympathy when she should despise him for spurning her affections only moments before.

He clenched his teeth. "Do you plan to attend Leathcote's ball this Friday?"

She shook her head, her expression guarded. "Before all this happened, I accepted an invitation to a house party this weekend. It's actually a meeting of the Egyptian Antiquities Society. Lord Holybrook hosts the quarterly meetings at his country house near Basildon. I spoke to my father and Sir Malcolm about the house party after you left this afternoon, and they both feel I will be safe at Lord Holybrook's. The house is quite large, but there will be plenty of people about the entire weekend. Sir Malcolm thought it a good idea for me to get away from Crofford House for awhile."

In this instance, Remmington agreed with Bainbridge. It seemed unlikely that anyone would attempt to harm Lily in a house filled with people, and it would do her good to get away from London. "When does this party start?"

"The day after tomorrow. Sophie and I plan to attend together, and I'm sure my father can act as our escort. After tonight, I—I assume you will ask Sir Malcolm to find someone else to take over your duties."

He'd considered exactly that. He couldn't be anywhere near Lily without wanting to touch her. Whenever they were alone he thought about much more than touching her. Tonight's events had proved that he had little control over those impulses. Yet his reasons for remaining Lily's 'suitor' hadn't changed since this afternoon. He didn't want another man anywhere near her. He knew it was selfishness on his part, but he wanted her to himself for just awhile longer. "I will continue to act as your escort, and I will accompany you to Lord Holybrook's. How many will be in attendance?"

"Twenty or so, I should say."

He nodded, completely uninterested in the answer. With the Stanhope girl along as an unofficial chaperon, there would be few opportunities to be alone with Lily. It shouldn't be difficult to avoid meetings in a moonlit garden, or intimate conversations in the seclusion of his carriage. His frown deepened. "We'll bring along some of Bainbridge's outriders, and a few of my men as well. You will be with me during the day, and share a chamber with your friend Sophie at night. It does sound safer than keeping you in London right now." The carriage rolled to a stop, and he pushed aside the curtain to see the lights of Crofford House. It was time to leave her. He didn't want to. Tonight would be the first night they had spent apart since her attack. He wondered if the thought of spending the night alone in her own room frightened her.

Who would comfort her if she had another nightmare? Somehow he managed to sound unconcerned. "You are home, Lily."

She began to move forward.

"There is just one more thing," he said. She looked up expectantly, her lips slightly parted. God, how he wanted to kiss her. "If you prefer not to be at home tomorrow when Lord Allen calls, I would be happy to take you on a ride through the park."

She looked wary of the offer. "I do not want to impose any more than I have."

"It would not be an imposition." He covered her hand with his own, giving in to his need to touch her. "I'm sorry I hurt your feelings tonight, Lily. I would like another opportunity to be your friend." He pressed a finger against her lips when she started to reply. "You don't have to say anything right now. Just think about it. I will pick you up at two o'clock tomorrow."

He opened the carriage door and helped her to the ground, then escorted her up the stairs to her house. A butler appeared in the doorway before they reached the landing.

"Is Crofford at home?" Remmington asked.

The butler nodded.

Remmington turned to Lily and lifted her hand for an impersonal kiss against her lace glove. "Make sure he bolts the door behind you. I'll see you tomorrow." She continued to stare up at him, and he couldn't seem to look away. All he had to do was turn around and walk back to his carriage. He tilted her chin up with one finger and pressed a sweet, lingering kiss against her lips. "Good-bye, Lily."

Eleven

Remmington pushed away from the table and leaned back in his chair, his booted feet crossed at the ankles. The light from the gently swaying lantern bathed his cabin in a warm glow. He swirled a glass of brandy in one hand, his gaze captured by the motion. The color of the brandy reminded him of Lily's hair; swirling, sparkling firelight.

"You are in a very odd mood tonight, Captain."

Remmington glanced at his dinner companion, then returned to his contemplation of the brandy. "I did not anticipate being anchored off the coast of Normandy tonight. My abrupt departure made me miss an important engagement this afternoon."

"She will surely forgive you."

He glanced up to see the sparkle in Sebastian Lacroix's dark eyes, although a tankard of ale hid his grin. Lacroix knew his moods far too well, Remmington decided. He doubted if he even knew Lacroix's real name. On the other hand, his guest couldn't know that he dined tonight with the Duke of Remmington. Lacroix knew him only as Captain Smith. In the six years of their acquaintance they had developed an extremely odd friendship, each aware that it would be dangerous for either of them to know too much about the other. Remmington wasn't even certain of Lacroix's nationality. He spoke French as flawlessly as he spoke English. His dark brown hair and tall, slender build didn't provide a clue. He could be a native of either country. His loyalty, however, lay unfailingly with England. Lacroix provided information that could only come from the highest offices of the French government, and he risked his life to do so. That was all Remmington needed to know.

"What makes you think my engagement involved a woman?"

Sebastian shrugged, a Gallic gesture that said nothing and meant everything.

Remmington scowled. "I doubt she will forgive me, but that is just as well. I cannot afford any entanglements."

"Ah," Sebastian mused. "Said with a deep sigh. That is a sure sign of love." He considered Remmington for a moment then said, "I do not make light of your *affaire de coeur,* my friend. Indeed, I can readily sympathize. Do you remember the last time I went to England?"

"Almost a year ago, wasn't it?"

Sebastian nodded. "While I was there I chanced to meet with a young woman that I hadn't seen since we were both children."

Remmington wondered if Sebastian realized that he'd let an important piece of information slip. It now seemed highly likely that Sebastian was an Englishman. He tried to substantiate his theory. "This woman is English?"

Sebastian nodded. "We were speaking of my broken heart, Captain. You could have the courtesy to pay attention."

"Sorry."

"Yes, well, this woman has grown into the most breathtaking creature imaginable. I couldn't take my eyes from her. At the time I told myself it was nothing but the shock of seeing such a change in her, yet her wit and intelligence impressed me as well. Before I left England, I knew that I wanted to marry her. My good senses came to the rescue before I told her of my feelings. Her family is also in our line of work, and she knows the dangers involved. What did I have to offer her but a high probability of widowhood?"

Remmington went cold inside. Sebastian's woman sounded frighteningly familiar. Now that he knew who decoded Sebastian's messages, a meeting between the two seemed well within the realm of possibilities. "What is this woman's name?"

Sebastian wagged one finger. "You forget the rules, Captain. No actual names. We shall refer to this lady by the name . . ." He scratched his chin, then the corners of his mouth turned upward. "Venus."

Remmington clenched his fists. "What is the point of this story, Lacroix?"

"The point is that I missed the opportunity to marry the woman I love. It will probably be too late by the time I see her again. With her grace and beauty, there must be dozens of offers for her hand. She will likely marry another before I convince her to marry me."

"Why don't you send her a message?"

Sebastian frowned over his sarcastic tone but didn't remark on it. "What I must tell her cannot be put on paper, and if all goes well I should see her in another month. But that is my problem, not yours. What I am trying to relate amidst your frequent interruptions is a bit of advice. I have never seen you morose over a woman, and I cannot help but think she means more to you than you would like to admit. It is easy for men like us to make ourselves believe we cannot indulge in the normal pleasures of a wife and family, but it is the very uncertainty of our futures that should make us hasten to embrace those pleasures. I would not like to see you make the same mistake I made, my friend."

Remmington wanted to laugh at the irony of the situation. He had but to speak her name and Sebastian would realize that Lily had them both tied in knots. He smiled to cover a sudden surge of possessive anger. "You needn't worry on that score, Lacroix. I never make the same mistake twice."

The clock struck one o'clock in the Earl of Crofford's library the next day. Remmington was nowhere in sight. Lily unfolded the note that had arrived from him yesterday morning and reread it for the hundredth time.

> *Lily,*
>
> *My deepest regrets, but an urgent matter arose and I will be unable to accompany you to the park. I will call upon you Friday, at one o'clock. Please be ready to depart for Basildon at that time.*
>
> *R.*

His urgent matter probably wore a skirt. So much for his offer of friendship. She released a frustrated sigh and tucked the note into the sleeve of her gown. The voice of doubt had whispered in her head the past two days, planting suspicions about everything Remmington had said to her that night in his carriage until she felt certain of only one thing. She meant nothing at all to him. He'd toyed with her as he toyed with every woman foolish enough to get too close to him. He was late. He had no intention of taking her to Basildon. She would never see him in this house again.

"Glaring at that clock won't hasten his arrival."

Crofford made the remark without looking up from the papers that lay scattered across his desk.

Lily smoothed the corners of the scroll that she'd tried for an hour to translate. She sat on the settee near her father's desk, and the scroll rested on top of a pile of books. Her hand reached beneath the parchment and she nudged the books farther away to make more room for her work. Unfortunately, the stack was too tall and the books began to slide sideways from the small couch. They fell onto the carpet in a series of soft thumps. She leaned down and restacked the books into a haphazard pile on the floor.

Another five minutes passed as she stared unseeing at her work. The hatch marks weren't flowing into words with their usual ease. She couldn't concentrate on anything but the ticking of the clock. The soft, monotonous sound drove her crazy. Where was he?

"Oh, here's a piece of news," her father said. His finger tapped an ancient parchment, then he rummaged through a nearby pile of books. "Where is that book on Alexander the Great?"

Lily retrieved the volume from the toppled stack on the floor. "Another reference to Alexander?" She nodded toward his scroll.

"Eh, what?" He looked distracted by the question, an expression Lily found familiar. When the earl immersed himself in his work, the outside world ceased to exist. "Alexander? He's off to Egypt to find a woman. Candice, Canyphe, something like that."

Lily stretched her arm across the back of the settee, then rested her head on her arm. She looked at her father sideways. "Is he in love with her?"

"I don't know. It's all rather cryptic."

Lily sighed. "Yes, it is, isn't it?"

Crofford glanced up, tilted his head to one side to look at her, then straightened again and returned to his work. "Oscar says that Remmington took liberties with you the night before last at the front door, in plain view of anyone who might happen by."

"He kissed me, Papa. It was just a small kiss."

Her father's pen made a scratching sound as it moved across a sheet of vellum. "I'm asking myself how you would know if a kiss was large or small."

"He kissed me in his carriage, too," she admitted. "That gave me a basis for comparison."

"I see." The scratching didn't falter. "Are you encouraging this behavior?"

Lily rolled her head back and gazed up at the ceiling. "I don't think so. He catches me off guard. I don't suppose I'm *dis*couraging him." She resettled her head until she was looking down at the settee. "Oh, I don't know *what* I'm doing with him."

The scratching stopped. Silence followed, then a tentative, "Falling in love, perhaps?"

Sideways, her father's smile looked a little strange. "Is it terribly obvious?"

"When you mope about this way? Yes, I should say it is quite obvious."

Lily sat up and rearranged her skirts. Remmington didn't want her love, or even her affections. Yet he wanted to kiss her. He told her she should find someone else, and then he'd kissed her. It was a good-bye kiss. Nothing more. "You won't say anything to him, or even hint at it, will you?"

"Of course not." His pen moved across the vellum again. "However, I'd like to know his thoughts on the subject of this courtship."

"Wouldn't we all," she muttered. A sound in the hallway made her shoulders straighten and her head turned toward the door. A moment later she was on her feet.

"Sit down, Lily. It won't do to look so anxious."

Lily sat back down and smoothed her skirts while her father responded to the knock. The butler appeared in the doorway, but Oscar didn't have a chance to announce the visitor. Remmington strode into the room, then closed the door in the butler's face.

"I have something for you," he told Lily. He made his way toward her. For a moment she thought he'd brought her some sort of present, a peace offering to make amends for making her lie awake two whole nights, wondering what she meant to him. He withdrew a parchment from his jacket and placed it in her hands. "This needs to be translated immediately. We'll take it to Bainbridge when we pick up his niece."

Lily stared down at the parchment, then back up at Remmington.

"Go on." He nodded toward the parchment. "Whatever's in that thing is important. Bainbridge wants it as soon as possible."

Crofford rose from his seat behind the desk. "Why don't you work at my desk, Lily? I'll go make sure your trunk gets properly loaded."

She glanced around Remmington to look at her father. She'd forgotten he was in the room. Behind Remmington's back, he frowned and shook his head, then pointed to his chair.

"Oh. Yes, of course. I'll translate it immediately." She carried the parchment to the desk than gathered the books she needed. The earl left the library and Remmington walked over to stand behind her chair. A blanket of papers soon layered the desk, all covered with her handwriting. Most of the words made no sense. The nonsensical words formed a large cross on every page, each word joined to the word beside or below it by a common letter. She'd circled the word in the center of each cross, one of the few words on the pages that did make sense.

"Good, Lord. How do you sort through all that?"

"It's rather complex," she admitted, without looking up. "I still haven't managed to memorize the entire code. The system requires a thorough understanding of Mr. Webster's *Compendious*." She tapped the sizable dictionary that lay open beneath her left hand. Her finger rested on the word *dark*, but the word her pen scratched out began with a *w*.

"It looks like nothing but nonsense to me."

"Uhm," she muttered, unaware that her absorbed expression was identical to the one her father wore when he worked. "Ah, yes, of course. Wellington. I should have known that one."

"*Dark* means *Wellington*?" he asked.

Lily glanced up, startled to find him still standing there. "What? No, of course not. *Dark Values Over Our Regal Manor Take Greatly Less Manners* means *Wellington*. But that is only the middle translation. Here is the coded word."

She pointed to the message and a word that read *3KIRK4SAM3RUM*.

"I should have guessed." Remmington could tell from her expression that the complex code made perfect sense to her. It occurred to him she was very likely a genius of some sort. This glimpse of her extraordinary talent also reminded him that there wasn't another person in England who could decipher that message. Although he'd always considered his own work vital, the enormity of Lily's importance to the war effort suddenly struck home. At any given time, this one slight girl could hold the fate of two nations in her hands.

"I think we should stop using the numbers," she said, as she penned another row of code. "Eventually, they will give it away."

He reached over her shoulder and pointed out the same coded word in another part of the message. "Ah, you're right. Dead giveaway."

"Really?" Lily turned her worried gaze his way. When he rolled his eyes, a small frown creased her brows and she turned back to her work. Her father returned a few minutes later, and she set her pen aside. "There. All done." She blotted the final draft then folded the translation into a neat square. "Will you toss the working copies into the fire, Papa?"

Crofford nodded, a wary smile on his face as he looked from her to Remmington. "Lily's trunk is loaded onto the back of your coach. You two should be on your way. Sir Malcolm will be waiting."

The moment the coach door closed behind them, Lily knew the new status of their "friendship." Remmington pointedly took the seat opposite hers, telling her without words that their more intimate relationship was at an end. He also looked displeased with her. She tried to think why.

"How do you communicate with the person who codes these messages?"

His question set her nerves on edge. Her brother held a much more precarious position than her own, and she'd promised Robert that she would never reveal his true identity to anyone. "In the messages themselves. Usually a line or two added to the bottom of the code."

"Did he write to you in this last missive?"

"No."

That answer seemed to satisfy him. He nodded then leaned back in his seat. "How well do you know him?"

"Who?"

"Your contact," he said impatiently. "The one who writes your code."

"How well do *you* know him?"

Remmington's smile didn't quite reach his eyes. "Well enough. I had dinner with him last night."

Lily felt her mouth drop open, even as she realized that his revelation made perfect sense. "You are the one who smuggles the messages back and forth?"

"Most of the time." He moved his hand, an impatient gesture of dismissal. "You still haven't answered my question. How well do you know Lacroix?"

His use of Robert's operative name answered a question of her own. Robert didn't want Remmington to know his identity. Remmington said he didn't want any secrets between them, but this one wasn't hers to share.

"I've known him for years." She tried to sound casual. "Why this sudden interest in my contact?"

"Let's just call it intellectual curiosity."

Lily studied him in silence. Could this be another of

his games? Did he know that Sebastian Lacroix was actually her brother, Robert? If so, he also knew that she'd deceived him—again. She decided to face the issue head-on. "Is there some reason you are angry with me, Your Grace?"

He pressed his lips together in a tight line. "No, Lily. I am not angry with you. I'm sorry if I gave you that impression. To tell you the truth, it is this courtship of ours that has me on edge. I've thought a lot about our conversation the night of Lady Keaton's dinner, and I see now that you were right. The time will come when we will go our separate ways, and it will do neither of us any good to grow too . . . friendly in the meantime."

Lily bowed her head and stared at her hands. "I see."

"No, you don't." He didn't give her a chance to wonder over the strange reply. "Your notion that we should keep our relationship no more than cordial is a sound one. In my eagerness to make my interest in you obvious to others, I did and said things at Lady Keaton's that would not be considered proper behavior. My reputation with women is such that some might even mistake the nature of our relationship. I would not like to see your reputation tarnished as a result. Therefore I believe it best to do as you suggest. From now on we must avoid being alone together whenever possible, and in public you know the rules of courtship as well as I. You have my word that I will endeavor to follow them more closely in the future."

He'd just agreed to everything she'd suggested two nights ago. Surely she should feel some small sense of triumph over the fact. Instead, she felt numb, completely empty inside. "Yes, that does seem the wisest course. We must endeavor to appear no more than cordial."

He nodded, then seemed to dismiss the matter of their courtship from his mind. "I hope Lord Allen wasn't too much of a bother."

Lily frowned. "Papa said he was disappointed."

"And?"

"And what?"

"I can tell there is more. He was disappointed and what else?"

"There is nothing more, Your Grace." Her voice sounded amazingly calm. Yesterday she'd wanted to talk to him about Lord Allen. She'd wanted to admit that she'd peered through the lace curtains of an upstairs window when Lord Allen departed, that he'd turned near the street to look back at the house with the most intense expression of hatred she'd ever seen. Now the incident seemed inconsequential. She wouldn't burden Remmington with her unfounded fears and fancies. She wouldn't show him any weakness or insecurity. "Nothing at all."

They arrived at the Bainbridge town house moments later. A butler ushered them into the foyer to greet Sophie and Sir Malcolm. A silent exchange passed between Remmington and Sir Malcolm, then Bainbridge turned to his niece. "Why don't you and Lily go upstairs for a little while? We'll call you when it's time to depart."

The men retired to the library while Sophie led Lily upstairs. Sophie closed the door to her bedroom behind them and leaned against the solid oak, her hands at her back as she studied Lily's face. "I heard about your attack. Are you all right?"

"Never better," Lily lied. "It is over with and I try not to think about it any more than I must."

Sophie pushed away from the door and began an agitated, directionless pace around the room. "Uncle Malcolm told me everything that happened to you after the Ashlands' ball. It is too fantastic! And Remmington! Whatever are we doing going off to the country with him?"

"What did your uncle tell you?" Lily asked cautiously.

"That Remmington came to your rescue on the night you were attacked, and you inadvertently ended up at his town house for several nights thereafter." Sophie paused to give her a dubious look. "And now he is courting you, supposedly to lend his protection while you are about in society. Uncle Malcolm says Remmington works for him on occasion, and that we must trust him." She gave a delicate sniff. "I am reserving judgment until I hear your side of this tale."

"We can trust him," Lily murmured.

Sophie stopped pacing, her expression intent. "Did he try to take advantage of you?"

"Quite the opposite." Lily tried to force a smile then gave up the effort. "He doesn't want anything to do with me, Sophie. We have both agreed to behave properly for the duration of our sham courtship, to do nothing that will give anyone the idea we are anything more than casual acquaintances." She released a small sigh. "Including ourselves."

Sophie opened her mouth to ask another question, but a knock at the door interrupted her. A maid poked her head through the doorway to tell them the gentlemen were waiting downstairs.

Twelve

---✦---

$\mathcal{L}$ord Holybrook was clearly beside himself at having a personage as important as Remmington at his gathering. Upon arrival at Holybrook Hall, the trio were shown to suites normally reserved for visiting royalty. Lily rolled her eyes over the lavish white and gold-gilt bedchamber she shared with Sophie. The Queen's Chamber was nearly the size of a ballroom.

"I have never endured a longer carriage ride in my life!" Sophie said, as she and Lily changed into their evening clothes. She presented her back to Lily. "Undo my buttons, will you?" She kept talking as Lily worked at the small buttons at the back of her traveling gown. "Four hours with nothing but the sound of my own voice to keep me company. I think the two of you are carrying this proper courtship business a bit too far. And where you came up with the idea that he doesn't care for you, I'm sure I will never know."

"What do you mean?" Lily asked.

"He stares at you constantly, as if he is afraid you will disappear if he looks away. Didn't you notice? I've never been ignored so thoroughly. Neither one of you paid the least attention to a single word I said. I was almost thankful when you both pretended to drift off to sleep."

"I believe Remmington enjoyed your explanation of hieroglyphics."

Sophie looked at her over one shoulder, her brows raised. "On what do you base that assumption? He did no more than nod his head on occasion."

"I can tell when he takes an interest in something." Lily finished the last of the buttons and stepped away.

"Hm. I don't believe you can. Turn around so I can unfasten you." Sophie placed her hands on Lily's shoulders and nudged her around. "His interest in you is obvious, Lily. Whatever made you think otherwise?"

"He made his feelings about our courtship very clear. It really doesn't matter, Sophie. Let's speak of something else."

"Very well. Sulking is very unbecoming to your complexion." Sophie leaned forward to examine Lily's face. "It makes you look all pale and wan. Really, Lily. After years of mooning over this man, I cannot believe you are ready to give up on him so easily. It seems perfectly apparent that the two of you are ideal for each other."

"Do you really think so?" Lily shook her head. "I don't think Remmington would agree with your opinion."

"Of course he does. What I cannot understand is why he will not admit as much, or at least give you both a chance to explore your feelings for one another. Surely a man like Remmington is not afraid of getting his feelings hurt."

"I believe he wants to spare *my* feelings. He said I should not waste myself on him, that he does not intend to remarry."

Sophie fell silent for a long moment. "Well. That's the end of it, then. At least he was noble enough to be honest with you." She gave Lily's shoulder a perfunctory pat. "That's also the last of the buttons. Do you think I should wear my pearls tonight?"

Lily whirled around to face her. "I thought you said . . . I mean, do you really think I should give up on him?"

"It seems you have no other choice." Sophie turned away to hide a knowing smile. She scooped up her evening clothes from the bed and disappeared behind a dressing screen. Her voice carried clearly across the room. "He does not want a wife, and you cannot possibly consider a relationship with him as anything less."

"It isn't as if I asked him to marry me," Lily muttered, although she knew Sophie was right. There was little point in a courtship if marriage was already out of the question.

"If I were you," Sophie went on, "I would stop acting like a mute little mouse and show him that you can manage just fine without his affections. You don't want his pity, do you?"

"Well, no."

"And you don't want him to think you are some lovesick schoolgirl, do you?"

"Of course not."

"Then you must endeavor to do something other than brood when you are in his company. Start a conversation. Your work with hieroglyphics is a safe enough topic. I know you can talk for hours on that subject. And a smile or two would not cause any lasting injury."

"You may be right, Sophie." Lily gave a small sigh of defeat. It was time to stop deceiving herself, to get on with her life.

"Of course I'm right," Sophie called out. "There is just one last problem to be dealt with."

Just one? Lily thought. Her life was nothing but one problem after another of late. She mentally shrugged her self-pity aside as she turned to pick up her own ice-blue evening gown from the bed. From this moment on, she would not indulge in such lowering thoughts. She would be strong, in control of her emotions. "What problem is that, Sophie?"

"Well, it seems apparent that he overheard everything we said that night in the Ashlands' gardens. He will doubtless continue to think of you as that poor, smitten creature until you set him straight."

Lily clutched the gown to her chest. "Just what are you suggesting?"

"You must tell him that you've come to your senses, that you no longer have any designs on his affections."

And she thought self-pity was a lowering thought? Sophie's idea would be the final humiliation. "Why on earth would I do anything of the sort?"

Sophie walked from behind the screen, rearranging the ribbons that secured the high waistline of her rose-colored gown. "You don't have to use those precise words, of course. Tell him you value his friendship, that you realize there can never be anything more between you than that. And would you mind telling me why you find this so funny?"

"I'm sorry." Lily tried to wipe the smile from her face. "It's just that Remmington said almost those same words to me the day after I arrived at his town house."

Sophie looked flustered for a moment. "Well, then. It should please him to know he was right. I just think you need to make a clean break of things, Lily. I know it will be difficult, for he will continue to be a part of your life. You need his protection until they find the man who attacked you, but you do not need his pity. If nothing else, you can salvage your pride."

Lily's brows drew together.

"You must trust me," she said. "Your thoughts are clouded by your emotions right now, and I can see the situation much more clearly. As a matter of fact, it appears clear as a crystal. When you see him tonight, do what you can to relax and be yourself. Ask him to take you for a morning ride. That will provide a certain amount of privacy to tell him what you must."

Lily bit her lip. "I don't know, Sophie. I will think about what you said, but I cannot make any promises."

She and Sophie were two of the last guests to arrive in the billiards room that evening. Almost thirty people were there already, a large gathering for an Egyptian Antiquities Society meeting. Two gentlemen played billiards at the green baize table, but most of the other guests sat on the low couches scattered around the room.

Remmington's height made him easy for Lily to spot in the crowd. He stood with Lord Holybrook and Lord Poundstone near the fireplace, one arm propped negligibly on the mantel. As if he could sense her presence, his head turned toward the doorway and his look came instantly to meet hers. He murmured something to the other gentlemen, then pushed away from the mantel and walked toward her. The conversations in the room grew quiet and Lily sensed that everyone watched them. She had eyes only for Remmington. They'd been apart less than an hour since their arrival. It suddenly seemed much longer. Sophie's advice rang in hear ears, and she forced herself to smile.

When he halted before them, they gave him the curtsy that protocol required. He lifted Sophie's hand for a perfunctory kiss, but the one he gave Lily seemed to last longer. He released her hand the moment the kiss ended. "Would you ladies care for something from the buffet?"

"I'm really not hungry," Lily said.

Sophie had no such hesitations. "I'm starved." She glanced toward the buffet at one end of the room. "Ah, there's Mr. Rumford. I want to ask him about those scarabs he brought to the last meeting. If you will excuse me?"

Lily wondered if Sophie left them alone on purpose, even as she reminded herself to keep smiling. A conversation with Remmington was the next order of business. She didn't feel quite ready to accomplish that task on her own. Sophie's advice had sounded almost logical in the Queen's Chamber. Here, standing so close to Remmington, she lost her nerve. "I should say hello to our host. I haven't seen Lord Holybrook since the meeting in January. If you will excuse me?"

"I'll go with you." Remmington took her arm before she could think of an objection and led her toward the fireplace.

Well into his sixties, Lord Alfred Holybrook boasted a thick shock of snowy white hair. The wrinkles that curved around the features of his face showed more of his years, and his rheumy eyes were a pale, faded blue. He gave Remmington a congenial nod, then lifted Lily's hand for a cursory greeting. "Good evening, Lady Lillian. I'd so hoped you would join us this weekend. The meetings just haven't been the same these past few months with you. And now you've sparked another's interest." He turned to Remmington. "I vow it is a disease, Your Grace. Once the passion gets in your blood, there is no escaping it."

Lily's eyes grew wider and wider. Remmington leaned down and whispered in her ear. "Try not to look so shocked. He is talking about antiquities."

"Eh? What's that you say?" Holybrook demanded.

"I was just telling Lady Lillian that I am looking forward to learning more about Egyptian antiquities."

"Splendid, splendid. I, myself, take particular interest in sarcophagi." He lifted his ebony cane and pointed the tip toward a massive, rectangular stone object that leaned against the wall on the opposite side of the room. "That fellow arrived just last week. I've been saving him for the meeting. Dr. Alexander, the renowned Egyptologist, will arrive tomorrow. He'll have the honor of breaking the seals and taking the first look inside. I'll probably not get a wink of sleep tonight, wondering what's in there." He leaned forward to give Lily a wink. "Dr. Alexander found this one himself, so I have high hopes that it will prove genuine. Sometimes those Egyptian chaps plant fake antiquities and palm them off as genuine to unsuspecting buyers. I don't think our Dr. Alexander is so easily hoaxed."

"Would you mind if we took a closer look?" she asked. The sarcophagus would provide the perfect distraction from Remmington's disturbing presence, and perhaps the opportunity to follow Sophie's advice and act a little more like herself.

"Don't mind a bit. There are papers and charcoal sticks laid out on the side table, if you'd like to make rubbings of the designs on the sides." He patted his rounded stomach. "If you two will excuse me, I'm off to find a plate of dinner."

Lord Holybrook left for the buffet, while Lily and Remmington made their way to the sarcophagus. The stone box was about eight feet tall, four feet wide and deep; large enough to accommodate the mummiform that was hopefully inside.

Lily ran her fingertips over a seal on one side. "He's right. These are either Fifth Dynasty, or a very convincing fake."

"These little drawings are hieroglyphics?"

She looked up to watch Remmington examine one of the seals just above her head. "Very good examples of hieroglyphics. Oh, I do hope there is a mummiform and mummy inside. Imagine looking upon someone who lived thousands of years ago. What a find this would be!"

"Do you mean to tell me there's a body inside this thing?"

"This is the outer casing for the Egyptians' version of a coffin. Of course there's a body inside. That is, if we're lucky."

The look he gave her was one of mock horror. "I had no idea you were so ghoulish, Lady Lillian. Gads. You've dragged me out here to a nest of grave robbers."

His humor surprised her, and she gave him a genuine smile. "It isn't the same thing and you know it."

"Hm. I'm not so sure. Somehow I don't think this poor chap envisioned an opening party at Lord Holybrook's country house when he was laid to rest." He leaned forward to take a closer look at the hieroglyphics on the seal above her. "Do these drawings mean anything?"

Lily took a cautious glance around the room as she leaned toward him, her voice hushed. "Those are the hieroglyphics that Sophie told you about." He gave her a blank look. "Most people think they are merely decorations, but they actually form an alphabet. It is much different from our alphabet, and I don't have all the symbols deciphered yet, but I'm very close." She straightened and returned her attention to the seal. "It's very frustrating to know the answer to something, and not be able to tell anyone that there is even a question. This is too close to my work for Sir Malcolm to let anyone know of my discovery. Except Sophie," she qualified. "But she refuses to present my theories to the Society as her own. They are fairly complex and she's afraid she will muddle them up. We've discussed the issue at length, and I'm thinking about writing an anonymous letter to Dr. Alexander and enclosing my notes."

"Don't do it," he warned. "You are asking for trouble. I'm sure it is a hard secret to keep, but I don't want you to do anything that might endanger yourself. With letters and notes in your handwriting, anyone might connect the work to you."

She made a noncommittal sound, then bent down to examine the next seal. Remmington grasped her elbow and pulled her around to face him. "I want your promise that you will not send that letter to anyone."

"It is a great discovery," she argued, even though she knew his concerns were well-founded. "The world should know the truth about these writings."

"The world has been ignorant about hieroglyphics for thousands of years. A few more will do no one any harm, and might very well save you from it."

"Oh, all right." It irritated her to know he was right. "You have my promise, even though I find your arrogance annoying. You might consider phrasing your orders in the form of a request the next time."

Having won the argument, he gave her a charming smile. "I will take that under consideration, my lady."

Until he smiled at her, Sophie's plan had progressed wonderfully. She turned away before she could feel the effects of that smile. "Because of you, I might be the only one who will ever know the name of the woman who is very probably inside this sarcophagus, or the meaning of the lurid curses that are written all over this thing. If there is any truth in them, poor Dr. Alexander will not live a very long or productive life."

"What do they say?"

She gave him a smug look and wagged her finger at him. "Wouldn't you like to know? I am afraid I've promised to keep my knowledge a secret."

Remmington started to shake his head, but something on the other side of the room caught his attention. The humor fled from his eyes and he grew very still. Lily followed his gaze to see Lord and Lady Farnsworth enter the billiards room, followed by Harry Gordon. It took her a moment before she realized why Remmington would act so strangely at the sight of them. With a sinking heart, she remembered that he and Patricia Farnsworth had once been lovers. She glanced up at him and noticed that his mouth was now a grim line. A muscle in his cheek twitched reflexively. Her gaze returned to Lady Farnsworth.

Patricia Farnsworth was not a great beauty. Cosmetics enhanced many of her features and her hair was a suspect shade of blond. That didn't seem to stop men from finding her attractive. She was a notorious flirt, seen most often in the company of gentlemen who were not her husband.

Lady Farnsworth's bored gaze surveyed the room, as if looking for her next conquest. She lifted her shoulders in a perceivable sigh that was arrested the moment her gaze found Remmington. The corners of her lips curled into a sly smile. Lily quickly looked away and brushed some nonexistent dust from one of the seals.

"Hm. I believe this one says something about adultery," she muttered. Remmington didn't respond and she didn't look up at him. She didn't want to watch him stare at another woman. "Ah, and here's something about burning in purgatory for sinful thoughts."

"Somehow that sounds vaguely familiar," Remmington said. "I didn't think our Egyptian friends studied the Scriptures."

"Perhaps they should have," she replied over her shoulder. "There might still be a pharaoh or two about if they had."

"You know about Lady Farnsworth," he said in a flat voice. She kept her back to him and didn't answer. "There is no reason for you to be jealous."

"I'm not the least jealous."

"Then why don't you prove it by looking at me?"

Lily hesitated. She knew why he made the request. Looking into those dark, mesmerizing eyes of his could render her senseless, and he knew it. She turned around and stared at his chest, trying to build her courage. As her gaze traveled higher, she emptied her thoughts of all but one. He didn't want her. Their eyes met, but she kept her thoughts focused inward. "There. Satisfied?"

He tilted her chin up with one finger. His scowl made her gaze slide away from him and she caught a glimpse of lavender silk from the corner of her eye.

"Hello, Lady Lillian. Remmington. What a charming couple the two of you make."

Remmington released his hold on her and turned to face Lady Farnsworth. Lily pretended to be innocently unaware of the heated looks the woman gave Remmington as they exchanged greetings. Glancing over Lady Farnsworth's shoulder, she noticed that Harry and Lord Farnsworth were otherwise engaged at the buffet. Not that she thought Lord Farnsworth's presence would be much of a deterrent to his wife's covert flirtation. Lord Farnsworth might be a member in good standing of the Antiquities Society, but his morals were nearly as corrupt as his wife's.

"Farnsworth didn't tell me there would be such interesting guests at this gathering." Lady Farnsworth gave Remmington another sly look. "It took a great deal of persuasion before I agreed to accompany him to this godforsaken place. Now I must remember to thank him."

"Oh, yes, you must," Lily gushed. "Lord Holybrook promises the most thrilling entertainment." She lifted one hand to rest it on the sarcophagus. "We're going to open this Egyptian coffin tomorrow to see if the body is still inside."

The remark had its desired affect. Lady Farnsworth looked appalled.

"A coffin?" she managed. She backed away from the sarcophagus. "That sounds . . . I mean, do you think that's quite legal?"

"Perfectly," Lily replied, straight-faced. "There is just one slight worry. These seals are engraved with all sorts of evil curses directed at anyone who opens the casket, or anyone in the general vicinity when that happens. Or so I'm told," she added, for Remmington's benefit. "Of course, we won't let a little thing like that bother us. Not when a mummy might be inside. That's what the ancient Egyptians called the body, don't you know. I hear they are wrapped in layers and layers of linen, and inside they are perfectly preserved. At the last meeting I attended, Dr. Alexander said he once saw a mummy so lifelike that it looked as if it might open its eyes and talk. Can you imagine?" She turned a pleading look in Remmington's direction. "We will stay for the unwrapping, won't we?"

He stared down at her as if she'd lost her mind. She turned again to Lady Farnsworth to find her wearing a similar expression. "I packed my hartshorn and a goodly does of smelling salts, just in case. According to Dr. Alexander, the unwrapping might be a little much for a lady's delicate sensibilities." She tapped the edge of her fan against her lower lip. "I wonder if the unwrapping will take place before or after lunch."

That seemed to shake Lady Farnsworth from her horrified fascination with Lily's speech. She closed her mouth and gathered her skirts closer, looking worried that Lily might contaminate them. "Well, I just wanted to wander over and say hello." Her gaze moved slowly, almost reluctantly from Lily. When she looked at Remmington, she gave him a provocative smile. "I'm sure I will see *you* later."

Lady Farnsworth pivoted and walked away. Remmington turned toward the sarcophagus and ran his hand over several seals. He was laughing.

"I don't see what is so very funny," Lily muttered. "The woman all but propositioned you in my presence. You should have given her the cut direct."

"I intended to," he told her, wiping his eyes. He began to chuckle again and Lily was fascinated by the deep sound. "You scared her off before I had the chance."

Lily began to smile. "I cannot wait to see if Lady Farnsworth joins us for the unveiling ceremony tomorrow."

"Ah, Lily, if we were anywhere else . . ." The humor faded from his expression and he took a step away from her. "We've been by ourselves too long. People will begin to notice if we don't mingle." He tucked her hand through his arm. "I think it's time to take you back to Miss Stanhope, while I have a little talk with Harry."

"There is just one thing I would like to ask before we part company," she said. "Will you join me for a morning ride tomorrow?"

He considered her question for less than a second. "No. You would be an easy target on horseback. You cannot afford such a risk, and I want your promise that you will not set foot from this house without me."

She nodded impatiently. "Actually, there is something I need to tell you, but not here where everyone is watching us. Could we meet somewhere else? The library, perhaps? No one is likely to be there tomorrow morning."

"This house is filled with people, Lily. Weekend guests feel it their duty to explore a house from stem to stern. What is so important that you cannot tell me here?"

Lily nodded to an elderly couple who strolled over to

look at the sarcophagus. Remmington took her arm and they began to walk across the room toward Sophie. He withdrew the question just as she was about to tell him the matter wasn't that important after all.

"Very well," he murmured. "Meet me in my chamber, tonight at midnight."

"What?" Lily glanced around, to see if anyone else seemed to take notice of her shocked question.

"We will do nothing more than talk," he assured her. "My chamber is directly across the hall from yours. It seems unlikely that anyone will notice if we meet there."

He had a point. And it wasn't as if they hadn't already spent several days and nights alone together. With both their resolves firmly set, what could possibly happen? "All right. Midnight."

Thirteen

***

The clock in the King's Chamber struck midnight. Remmington said a silent prayer that Lily was fast asleep. Patricia Farnsworth lay in the center of his bed, her robe splayed open to reveal a nearly transparent negligee underneath. She'd knocked at his door no more than a moment ago. He'd opened the door with every expectation of finding Lily on the other side. Instead he'd found this disaster in the making. She'd darted into his room before he could stop her. To his horror, she had then made a delighted leap onto his bed.

"Ah, Remmington! How did you know I would be here this weekend?" She propped herself up on her elbows, a provocative pose that displayed her breasts to their best advantage. "I knew you did not forget me."

"I forgot you two years ago, Patricia. If you do not leave this room immediately, under your own power, rest assured that I will remove you myself."

She tilted her head to one side and gave him a pretty pout. "Are we going to play that game again?"

"No. We are not." He stalked toward the bed, intending to pick her up and do exactly what he'd threatened: toss her out. Patricia had other things in mind. As soon as his hands closed on her waist, she threw her arms around his neck and forced her lips against his mouth. Just as he reached behind his neck for her hands, he heard a soft gasp.

"Damn it!" He knew before he looked that Lily stood in his doorway. She would surely think this scene a deliberate attempt to humiliate her. There wasn't a woman alive who would believe his innocence after walking in on such an intimate-looking embrace. He gave Patricia a shove away from him and hastily turned around. Lily had one hand on the door latch, the other at her throat. Her face looked drained of color. He felt a slender thread of hope snap and drift away.

"Oh, hullo again, Lady Lillian." Patricia curled up more comfortably on the bed. "Did you come to say goodnight to Remmington, too? I'm afraid you'll have to come back a little later. He's occupied at the moment."

He spared Patricia a brief, contemptuous glance. His gaze met Lily's and he willed her to understand. "Think a moment, Lily. You know this isn't what it seems."

Her gaze locked with his for a long moment, then she slowly lowered her lashes. After Lily stared at the floor for what seemed an eternity, she took another step into the room. The door made a soft thud as it closed behind her, an ominous sound in the quiet room that had the ring of finality.

"I've never thought you stupid, my lord." She nodded once toward the bed. "This would be extremely stupid planning on your part. I assume your guest is uninvited?"

With more than enough evidence at hand to damn any man, she steadfastly believed in his innocence. She trusted him. He smiled to let her know how much that pleased him. "Precisely."

"You do realize this poses a problem."

The certainty of her words sent a shaft of wariness down his spine. "It does?"

Lily nodded. "She could tell anyone that I was here tonight. Does she know about our plan?"

"I don't think so." He didn't have the faintest idea what she was talking about.

Lily glanced toward one of the windows. "How far are we from the ground?"

"This is only the second story." He spoke slowly, trying to comprehend her train of thought. "Not terribly far, I should think."

"Pity." She turned and slid the door bolt into place. "Not high enough."

"Here now," Patricia sputtered, sitting up to secure her robe. "What are you two about?"

Lily walked toward the bed, her voice quiet. "You haven't guessed?" She stopped a few paces away and looked at Remmington. "She will guess eventually. Or Farnsworth will tell her when she spills the story to him, and then he'll go straight to Holybrook. We will never pull it off."

"You may be right." He hoped that was the correct response even as he tried to guess where this was leading, to imagine what outrageous thing she would say next. He shook his head and gave up.

Lily began to pace the floor between the door and the bed. "What about those pirates you hired to make off with the mummy?"

"Mummy?" Patricia shrieked. "You're going to steal the mummy?"

Remmington turned away from the bed so Patricia wouldn't see his smile. It had no effect on Lily. She gave him a grave look. "You see? I told you she would guess. Everyone knows the value of a mummy. Once we grind it into powder, it will be worth even more. Think of it, Remmington. That powder will fetch a thousand guineas per ounce in Calcutta. Perhaps more. Those Indian der-

vishes will pay anything for that rare aphrodisiac." She
nodded toward the bed. "I say we have the pirates take
care of her. You said yourself that the one who wears
black with the red sash is handy with a knife."

Remmington rubbed his chin. "I had no idea you
would involve me in such foul, devilish deeds, you
wicked creature. You promised me this wouldn't come to
murder, Lady Lillian."

"Well, now," she said with a grin, "it seems I lied."

"No!" Patricia leaped off the bed and made a mad
dash for the door, skirting a wide path around Lily and
Remmington.

Lily advanced on her with stealthy grace as Patricia
fumbled with the door bolt. Her voice was low and
soothing, the tone one would use to lure a wild animal
into captivity. "You aren't going anywhere, Lady
Farnsworth. If you will just step away from the door—"

Patricia finally managed to wrench the door open as
Lily reached for her arm. She disappeared into the hallway with one last small shriek. Lily closed the door and
drove the bolt back into place.

"What a bothersome woman. I cannot help but wonder what you ever saw in her."

He stared at her for a long moment as his mind
worked to absorb the events of the last few minutes.
"Lily. What have you done?"

She raised her brows into that guileless, innocent expression he remembered from their days at his town
house. "Salvaged both our reputations, I should think."

"Salvaged them?" He shook his head. "How can you
believe our reputations are salvaged? We will either be
labeled illicit lovers, or murdering thieves. Or both."

"I don't think so." She patted a stray hair into place,
looking completely unconcerned. "Do you think anyone
will believe Lady Farnsworth's tale? Really, Remmington.
You, a thief? It is too fantastic. If she tells anyone about
the mummy part, they will probably sedate her."

He stalked over to Lily and placed his hands on her
shoulders. For the first time, she looked worried.

"Are you terribly angry?" she whispered.

"Angry? Am I angry?" he repeated. He thew his head back and laughed as he hadn't laughed in years. He dropped his forehead to her shoulder and half collapsed against her, then he laughed more. At length he recovered himself enough to enlighten her. "Ah, my fierce little Tiger Lily. I am amazed by your incredible imagination."

"For a moment, I thought you were going to be cross," she muttered. He lifted his head to look into her eyes and she finally grinned. "It was rather clever for spur of the moment, don't you think?"

"It was brilliant!" He felt the laughter rolling up from inside him once again. "Lord, I will *never* forget the expression on Patricia's face. You played your part flawlessly."

"You once said I was no actress," she reminded him, with a delicate sniff. Her haughty expression was ruined by a smile.

"The ladies of Drury Lane will quake in their slippers if they ever hear of this," he predicted. "How did you ever think up such an outrageous tale?"

She shrugged the compliment aside. "I've no idea. It just came to me. But don't be modest, my lord. You deserve half the credit. I thought you played your part rather well." Holding the back of her hand to her forehead, she gave him a theatrical flutter of her lashes. Her voice was a ridiculously high imitation of his own. " 'Really, Lady Lillian. I had no idea you would involve me in your foul, devilish deeds, you wicked creature.' Nicely done, Remmington. I have high hopes for your acting abilities. You will need them to remain straight-faced tomorrow when we are accused of these dastardly crimes."

He wrapped his arms around her waist. "I am but a bit player in this farce. I will be happy to take my cues from you."

Staring into her eyes he felt his humor fade away, replaced by an emotion just as elemental. The magic of her smile made him forget his resolve, made him forget everything but the joy of holding her in his arms. What was he doing? He knew what he wanted to do. He stepped away as if she'd burned him. "We'd best have our discussion before anyone else shows up. My room seems entirely too popular tonight."

Lily winced as if he'd struck her. She thrust her hands into the pockets of her robe and backed up several steps toward the fireplace. "I . . . well, I've thought a lot about a question you asked me the night of Lady Keaton's party, and I've come to a decision."

"What question would that be?" He felt certain he didn't want to hear about anything he'd asked her that night, and equally certain that he would not like her decision. He was right.

"Just before you escorted me to my door, you asked if we might be friends." Her explanation sounded rushed, as if she couldn't say the words fast enough. "You must know that I enjoy your company, and I realize now that what I feel for you is indeed friendship. Nothing more. I wanted to apologize for making you believe any differently."

For a moment he didn't believe her. His gaze searched her face, looking for an expression in her eyes that no longer existed. He'd finally done it. He'd driven her away.

He sat down abruptly on the bed, unable to think of anything to say. In another month, Sebastian Lacroix would come to England to propose to her. He seemed a decent enough sort, and there was no question that he and Lily had much in common. Lacroix would make her happy. He tried to picture her in Lacroix's arms and couldn't. Wouldn't. He could not bear the thought of watching another man touch her. Yet he would continue to smuggle messages between them, knowing they would likely contain the endearments he wanted to say to her. What gave Lacroix the right to take Lily from him in the first place?

"If I haven't tried your patience too sorely," she went on, "I hope that we may still be friends."

He shook his head. "I do not think that will be possible, Lily."

She looked dismayed by his refusal. "It does not seem all that impossible to me. You said yourself we could be friends."

"And you said that your definition of the word 'friend' varies greatly from mine." He stood up and closed the distance between them in three long strides. He braced one hand against the mantel behind her and leaned down until their faces were only inches apart. Her eyes were very wide, sherry-colored pools of curiosity and uncertainty. He knew instinctively that she didn't fear him. He knew just as surely that she should. "As it turns out, you were right."

Lily realized his intent the moment his arm circled her waist and she tried to twist away from him. Failing in that attempt, she braced herself against the fierce intent she saw in his eyes, the punishing kiss he would surely give her. It never came. He held her firmly against his chest with one arm, and his hand cradled her face.

"Lily." He breathed her name with an aching reverence that left her stunned. "What am I to do with you?"

The gleam she saw in his eyes didn't come from anger, but from deep, burning desire. Her body reacted instantly to the knowledge. She unclenched her fists and flattened her palms against the smooth satin of his robe, feeling the strength of his chest, the hard, steady beat of his heart beneath her hands. She felt her own pulse quicken as his lips parted and he lowered his head to touch his mouth to hers. He hesitated, then his mouth brushed very slowly over her lips, once, twice, and again, a silent question, an unspoken invitation. Her defenses began to crumble. She could hear his question as clearly as if he spoke it aloud, yet doubt made her hesitate. Could she accept the terms of his friendship? The consequences? If she refused him now, would he ever make the offer again? Would she spend the rest of her life wondering what she'd missed, regretting a wondrous experience that she could only imagine? She knew he cared for her in his own way. For her, there could never be another.

She brushed the answer across his lips, a response just as hesitant, a touch just as uncertain. She accepted his invitation without speaking a word. His hand cupped the back of her head and he fit his mouth to hers, a perfect seal to their silent bargain. He savored her slowly, sweetly, drowning her in one consuming wave of desire after another. His tongue touched her lips in unexpected darts that created keen anticipation of when and where he would strike next. Her lips parted and he delved deeper, a languid, sensual exploration. At last his lips slid away from hers to the curve of her ear, his voice deep with desire. "Breathe, Lily."

She released a gasp when his teeth closed painlessly over the lobe, and only then realized she'd held her breath too long. The sound of his breathing seemed to come from inside her head, the effect dizzying and disorienting. Her legs began to weaken at the same time he leaned over to lift her into his arms. She laced her arms around his neck and tilted her head back for another soul-stirring kiss.

His lips broke away from hers when he placed her on the bed, and she felt a moment of panic, then an indescribable excitement when his weight settled on top of her. The searing kiss that followed made her oblivious to all but the delicious warmth that coursed through her body. He urged her to touch him, guided her hand beneath the lapels of his dressing gown to press her palm against his chest. His hand smoothed over her shoulder, down her arm, then around her waist and lower to her hip, then a slow return upward across her ribs until his hand was sliding across her breast, cupping it, gently squeezing.

Lily felt as if she'd touched lightning. Her arms twined around his neck and she strained against him, pressing herself closer to his hard body, yet unable to get close enough. He probed her mouth with his tongue and she made a thrust of her own, discovering an astonishing sense of power, an instinctive knowledge that she moved close to some unnamed goal. He eased his knee between her legs and she discovered a new torment.

Summoning the dwindling reserves of his control, Remmington forced himself to break off the kiss, to lift his lips a breath away from hers. "Say that you want me, Lily, that I am not forcing you into this."

She hesitated for seven heartbeats. They were the longest seven heartbeats of his life. "I want you."

"Say my name," he coaxed. He placed small, measured kisses around her mouth. "I want to hear my given name on your lips."

"Miles," she whispered. "I want you, Miles."

Their gazes met and this time she let him see her soul, the innocence and longing she'd somehow masked. This time he couldn't gentle the kiss, or keep any of his fierce, possessive desire for her from his embrace. She responded with the same abandon, offering herself completely, melting beneath him, all warmth and welcoming desire against his hard body. She suddenly grew still beneath him. He didn't know if it was the shock of realizing his intent that made her eyes widen in alarm, or the insistent knock on the door.

The knock repeated itself before he gathered his wits enough to interpret the sound. With a soft curse, he rolled onto his back and stared up at the ceiling. Desire seeped from every pore of his body. He ached with it. What he needed to ease that ache lay within his reach, within his power to possess. His hands fisted at his sides. Was he truly so desperate? Christ. Did he really want to make love to her while someone pounded on his door?

He was vaguely aware of Lily sitting up next to him, but he concentrated on a crack in the plaster ceiling. "If that is Patricia Farnsworth again, I say we toss her from the window."

"This is no time for jokes," she whispered, with a

frantic nudge at his knee. "Get Up! Help me find a place to hide."

He regarded her from beneath an arched brow. "Why on earth should you hide?"

"Stop your teasing, Miles. And lower your voice. My reputation will be in shreds if I'm found here."

She probably wasn't even aware that she spoke his name, but the sound of it pleased him anyway. He turned onto his side and propped himself up on one elbow. Lily's hair was still braided, but it was delightfully tousled. Her lips were swollen, too. Anyone who looked at her now would know exactly what they'd been doing, or what they'd been about to do. He couldn't believe she'd suggested they be friends. They were meant to be lovers. He wouldn't deny the inevitable any longer.

He'd managed to take her robe off while they kissed, and he watched her step closer to the fireplace. The fire outlined her body perfectly through the thin nightgown and he studied the shape of her legs. "Who says anyone will find you?" he asked in a somewhat quieter voice. "I have no intention of opening the door." There was another knock, louder than the last two, but he ignored it and released an irritated sigh. "I am sound asleep. Anyone foolish enough to pound on my door at this time of night should know as much."

Lily stopped wringing her hands and they fell to her sides. She gave the door a worried look. "What if they don't go away?"

He turned his hand over and studied his nails. "I daresay their knuckles will grow sore." He patted the bed. "Come sit by me while we wait for them to leave."

She looked scandalized by the invitation. "How can you think of kissing at a time like this?"

"I wasn't thinking anything of the sort," he said in an injured voice. "Shame on you, Lady Lillian. You have the imagination of a brazen woman."

"I wasn't the least brazen before I met you, my lord." Her gaze swung toward the door and the sound of a muffled male voice.

"Remmington? Are you awake?"

Lily's eyes grew round with horror. "It's Lord Holybrook!"

"Damnation." Remmington pushed off the bed. He'd assumed Patricia had told Farnsworth some version of what happened, that an irate husband stood outside his door. An irate host was another matter entirely. He strode toward the door with Lily in tow. With one finger held to his lips, he pushed her toward the wall where no one would see her. He opened the door just wide enough that his body filled the opening.

Garbed in a maroon velvet dressing gown and slippers, Lord Holybrook didn't appear very pleased to see Remmington. His bushy white brows furrowed together into a frown. "Forgive me for disturbing you at this hour, Your Grace." He glanced down the empty hallway, then his gaze returned to Remmington. "Lady Farnsworth has half the south wing awake, screeching that you and Lady Lillian threatened her life. I don't believe that nonsense for a moment, but I thought it best to check and make sure nothing is amiss." When it became obvious that Remmington didn't intend to respond to that news, Lord Holybrook cleared his throat. "Yes, well. My wife thought it best to check on Lady Lillian before we bothered you with this matter, Your Grace. She didn't want to disturb anyone's sleep unnecessarily, so she thought to use the housekeeper's key to open Lady Lillian's door. As it turns out, she found the door unlocked."

Remmington went very still. "And?"

"Lady Lillian is not in her bed, Your Grace." Holybrook hesitated, his voice uncertain. "Before my wife rouses the servants to search the house, I thought it a wise idea to check with you, to see if you knew where we might locate Lady Lillian."

The silence seemed deafening. Remmington knew what Holybrook implied, and exactly what it meant. "You have my word that Lady Lillian is perfectly safe, Holybrook."

The lines around Lord Holybrook's mouth tightened into an expression of disapproval. "You realize that Crofford is a friend of mine, that I am obliged to inform him of this ... incident?"

"I understand completely."

"Very well, then. I will tell my wife that she should check Lady Lillian's room once more, just to be certain. It is a large chamber, and perhaps Lady Lillian felt restless and happened to wander around to a part of the room that cannot be seen from the doorway. If you hear a knock on the door across the hallway in a quarter of an hour, pray do not let it disturb you." Holybrook's gaze dropped, as if he could not bear to look at him another moment. "Goodnight, Your Grace."

"Goodnight, Holybrook." Remmington took a step backward and closed the door. A strange calm settled over him as he continued to stare at the burnished wood.

"He knows," Lily whispered. She repeated the words over and over in an anguished litany.

More than anything, he wanted to take her hand and lead her back to the bed, to comfort her the only way he knew how. He wanted to tell her that everything would be all right. He didn't know if it would be. She didn't seem to notice his concern. As if in a trance, she walked past him to retrieve her robe from the bed, then she returned to the door.

"I need to be in my room before Lady Holybrook returns."

She was right. She had less than a quarter hour before Lady Holybrook would be at her door. Now wasn't the time to discuss the situation, and she didn't look ready to listen to anything he had to say. There was also the fact that he wanted to think carefully about what he would tell her, how he would tell her. This wasn't the time. He opened the door and escorted Lily across the hall.

• • •

"Yes, thank you, Lady Holybrook. I shall be perfectly fine." Lily knew that was a lie, but she managed to smile. "Good night."

"Good night, my dear." The door of the Queen's Chamber closed behind Lady Holybrook.

Just before Lady Holybrook's arrival, Lily had managed to wake Sophie and tell her what happened, that Lord Holybrook intended to tell her father that he'd found her in Remmington's bedchamber. She turned toward the bed and searched Sophie's stricken face, her voice a bare whisper. "What am I to do?"

The bedcovers twisted into knots beneath Sophie's hands. "What . . ." She cleared her throat and tried again. "What did Remmington say? What does he intend to do?"

"He said we would talk more tomorrow, but I don't think he intends to do anything." Lily bit her lip. "You already know that he doesn't want to marry me."

"But this changes everything. Your honor is at stake."

"It doesn't change anything," Lily said surely. "The very first time he kissed me, he thought I tempted him into the intimacy on purpose. He told me in no uncertain terms that he would not feel obliged to make an offer of marriage if I deliberately compromised myself." She walked to the bed and sat on the edge, her voice without hope. "I am ruined, Sophie."

"This is all my fault," Sophie whispered. "I'm so sorry. I didn't think anything like this would happen."

Lily shook her head. "This isn't your fault. It's mine. I asked to meet with him in private. I made him believe it was a matter of great importance, when it was a matter of no importance at all."

"You're wrong, Lily." Sophie slipped out of bed and picked up the candle that burned by the bedside, then she lit more tapers around the room until the warm glow of candlelight surrounded them. "Everything you told me about Remmington made me believe he truly cared for you. I thought if you denied your affections he would soon realize what seemed so obvious to me, that he is in love with you."

"He is in lust with me, Sophie. Nothing more. I should have told you as much." She managed a grim smile. "I thought you let me give up too easily."

"You aren't angry?"

"Because my friend tried to help me?" Lily shook her head. "If anything, I am angry with myself for not recognizing such a blatant attempt at matchmaking. I should have known you were baiting me on purpose, using my pride against me. You knew I would not tolerate the thought that Remmington pitied me."

Sophie nodded, her expression uncertain. "My plan seemed to be working. I caught him staring at you on more than one occasion tonight, and there was something about his expression that seemed different than the one he wore during the carriage ride. I thought he looked worried."

"As it turns out, his worries were well founded." Lily regretted the terse words when tears formed in Sophie's green eyes. She patted her friend's hand. "Do not blame yourself, Sophie. Something like this was bound to happen. I've done nothing but ignore Remmington's warnings, and thrust myself into his path at every turn. I knew the possible consequences and ignored them. Now I must pay the price."

"The situation might not be as grim as it seems," Sophie offered. "Lord Holybrook will surely tell your father, but I cannot think that he would repeat the story to anyone else, not when he knows your reputation is at stake."

"He won't have to tell anyone else." She frowned over Sophie's puzzled expression. "When Lord Holybrook realizes that Remmington doesn't feel obliged to repair my reputation, he will naturally assume that I went to Remmington's room uninvited."

"But you didn't! Remmington told you to meet him there."

"Only because he thought it would be safer than the places I suggested, that a meeting there would go unnoticed. His concern for my safety and reputation does not change the fact that I requested the meeting in the first place." Lily dismissed that part of the problem with an impatient wave. "By the end of the weekend, Lord Holybrook will know the responsibility lies with me, that as an unmarried woman and a guest in his house, my behavior is unforgivable. I'm sure he will ask that I relinquish my membership in the Antiquities Society."

"I don't think Lord Holybrook would go that far." Sophie's shoulders slumped. She knew as well as Lily that he would. Lily would no longer be considered an "acceptable" young lady, and Lord Holybrook's fondness for her would not matter. There were certain unwritten rules in society that everyone followed whether they wanted to or not.

"There is also Patricia Farnsworth to consider," Lily went on. "Lord Holybrook said she wakened half the south wing. That gossip alone might be overlooked, but people will begin to speculate soon enough about the reasons I am no longer a member of the Antiquities Society. They, too, will come to an obvious conclusion. I will become an outcast." She pursed her lips, her expression thoughtful. "You know, Sophie, you could very well be right. This might not be as awful as it seems."

Sophie looked at her as if she'd lost her mind. "It is a disaster."

"Actually, this could be a blessing in disguise. I will no longer be obliged or expected to attend balls or parties, or any of those annoying teas. No one will invite me to anything."

"You will go mad from boredom," Sophie predicted.

"Hardly," Lily scoffed. "I can devote all the time I want to my work and to my studies."

"You will become a spinster."

"You make it sound like a fate worse than death." Lily found herself smiling. "I think I shall rather enjoy being a spinster, accountable to no one, free to do as I please. Strange that I never fully considered the possibilities before now."

"You realize that your father might have something to say about this spinster plan of yours? Or Robert? If Robert hears of this, you must also consider the possibility of a duel."

Lily's smile faded. "I will explain to them where the fault lies, that Remmington is not to blame in the least."

"Really?" Sophie didn't bother to hide her skepticism. "Do you honestly believe that anyone in their right mind will belive that Remmington is an innocent in all this, a helpless victim of your lust?"

"I suppose not," Lily admitted. She stood up and began to pace, too agitated to sit still any longer. "Perhaps they would be more understanding if I told them we met to discuss some incident related to my attack."

"I doubt it," Sophie said. "Not when I tell my uncle that Remmington invited you to his room."

Lily's eyes widened. "You wouldn't. Sophie, tell me you won't do anything so foolish!"

"Foolish is your plan to sacrifice yourself for this man. No matter how you justify it in your mind, he's ruined you. I cannot bear to think of what your life will be like. He's equally to blame, and deserves to pay the same price. Then it will be Remmington's honor at stake when your father confronts him with the truth. Remmington will be forced to do what is right by you, or he will prove himself a complete scoundrel."

"Please," Lily pleaded, her hands clenched together in a deathlike grip. "Please don't do anything that will force Remmington to marry me. He would hate me, Sophie. He would be stuck with me for the rest of our lives, and he would hate me. I couldn't bear it!" She felt tears spill onto her cheeks and she angrily wiped them away. "Please say you won't do that to me."

Sophie caught her lower lip between her teeth and her firm expression crumbled. "I couldn't do anything that would make you so miserable, yet I cannot think you will be any happier this way." She buried her face in her hands. "I feel so helpless!"

Lily didn't hesitate. She sat down and wrapped her arm around Sophie's trembling shoulders. "There, there, Sophie. Everything will work out. You'll see."

Sophie managed to giggle through her tears. "I cannot believe you are trying to comfort me. You realize that *I* am supposed to be comforting *you*?"

"I think we are comforting each other." She gave Sophie's shoulders a squeeze. "Truly, Sophie. Things are not as bad as you think. I will manage through this, as long as I have your shoulder to lean upon." She tried to cheer Sophie with another smile. "If nothing else, this gave us the opportunity to experience Lady Holybrook's remarkable taste in dressing gowns. I've never seen one made entirely of pink boa feathers. When I first opened the door, I thought something from the menagerie had gotten loose and attacked poor Lady Holybrook."

Sophie returned Lily's smile, then they both began to laugh.

The next morning, Lily couldn't find anything to laugh about. It was Sophie who discovered the note Remmington had slid under their door. While Lily brushed away the last effects of sleep, Sophie read the note aloud.

"It says, *Lily, I must leave Holybrook House for a few hours this morning. While I am gone, stay close to Miss Stanhope, preferably in your room. I will see you when the Antiquities meeting begins at two o'clock.* It's signed, *R.*" She glanced up at Lily, the look in her eyes apprehensive. "What do you think it means?"

"I've no idea." She tried not to think about what it sounded like, but Sophie wouldn't let her ignore the possibility.

"Do you think he intends to come back?"

"Of course he does. I'm his latest assignment. Remmington would never shirk his duty."

Sophie shot her a wry look. "Let us hope he is more conscientious about that duty than he is of others." She held up one hand when Lily started to object. "Forgive me. I could not help myself."

Fourteen

---- ✦ ----

At two o'clock, the members of the Society gathered in the foyer outside the billiards room. Lily leaned as close to Sophie as possible. "Do you think people are acting any differently toward me?"

"You are the only one acting differently," Sophie whispered back. "Stop craning your neck. Remmington is so tall that we shall see him the moment he arrives. *If* he arrives."

Lily straightened her shoulders. "I just thought Lady Orwell's greeting seemed a little stiffer than usual."

"Lady Orwell is so stiff with gout that she can barely walk. Do *not* jerk your head around when you hear what I have to tell you, but I see Remmington off to your left. He is headed our way."

Lily's heart began to pound a frantic beat, but she managed to keep her gaze focused on Sophie long enough to compose herself before she turned to face him. She forgot to curtsy.

His gaze swept over her then returned to her face, the look in his eyes intense. He nodded almost imperceptibly, as if he'd just confirmed something in his mind.

"Lily," he murmured, as he lifted her hand for a kiss. He nodded toward Sophie. "Miss Stanhope. Are you ladies ready to attend the meeting?"

"Where were you?" Lily blurted out. She felt a blush stain her cheeks.

Remmington shook his head. "I will tell you later. Miss Stanhope, will you lead the way?"

He took Lily's arm and they followed Sophie into the billiards room. The stone sarcophagus now rested on its back where the billiards table once stood. Most of the remaining furniture in the room had been pushed aside. Chairs were set up in semicircular rows around the sarcophagus to allow guests a better view during the opening.

Harry waved to them from across the room. He gestured toward several chairs in the second row and Sophie headed toward him.

"The senior members claimed choicest seats," Harry said, "but I believe the four of us will manage well enough from here."

"That was very kind of you to think of us, Lord Gordon." Sophie pointed toward the chairs. "I believe the best view will be from the chair closest to the center, Lily."

Sophie managed to wedge herself between Lily and Remmington as they filed into their seats.

As Lily took her seat, she glanced at Remmington to gauge his reaction to Sophie's snub, but he didn't appear the least concerned. Perhaps he was glad that Sophie sat between them. Nothing good ever seemed to happen when they were any closer. She released a small sigh.

The meeting of the Egyptian Antiquities Society began almost immediately. Lord Holybrook made his way to the center of the room to address the members. After a brief greeting, he began to read an article about the Society that recently had appeared in the London *Times*.

Lily couldn't concentrate on a word. She longed for just a moment of privacy to speak with Remmington, to tell him that she would accept most of the blame for The Incident. They would have to agree on a few of the details if she had any hope of convincing anyone other than Remmington of her guilt. His reputation would do little to persuade her family that he wasn't at fault. Of course, Remmington would likely laugh in her face if she suggested another private meeting.

At last Lord Holybrook introduced Dr. Alexander and she tried to pay attention to the meeting at hand. The leading authority on Egyptian antiquities didn't look much like a rugged adventurer. His deeply tanned skin reflected the hours spent under a desert sun, but otherwise the good doctor looked unaccustomed to hardship of any sort. There was a frailness to his slender build that made one suspect a sickly childhood.

Dr. Alexander presented a short discourse about the historical significance of the site where he found the sarcophagus, then a chisel and mallet were brought forward to break open the seals. Murmured conversations began throughout the room.

Sophie clasped Lily's hand as Dr. Alexander set about his work. "Now it will start."

"You look as if you expect demons to fly forth from the seals," Lily said. "Calm down, Sophie. The curse was meant for tomb robbers. Dr. Alexander is a scholar."

"I don't think Ameana Re will view this any differently," Sophie whispered back.

Remmington leaned toward them. "Who is Ameana Re?"

"The princess who is inside that sarcophagus," Sophie answered.

His gaze moved to Lily. "You told her?"

"I saw no reason not to." Lily frowned. "Sophie is worried about the curse. We finished translating it this afternoon and it's just as lurid as I suspected."

One dark brow rose. "Don't tell me that the two of you put any stock in that nonsense?" The women remained silent. He rolled his eyes. "For two modern, educated females, a belief in ancient curses seems remarkably backward."

Cries of excitement arose in the audience and they turned their attention toward the front of the room. Six burly footmen inserted long poles through openings on the sides of the sarcophagus lid. With a great deal of strain and effort, the footmen lifted the stone lid then slid it away to reveal the contents of the sarcophagus. Other guests began to crane their necks and a few stood up. Sophie's grip on Lily's hand became painful. Lily freed her hand as they stood up and waited for the footmen to move aside. Her breath caught in her throat when they did. The mummiform still lay inside the sarcophagus. It was the most magnificent piece of artwork she'd beheld in her life.

The full-sized image of a woman covered the top of the case, so lifelike that she did indeed look as if she might speak. Surveying the mummiform as a whole, Lily realized that the entire thing appeared made of solid gold. Dr. Alexander stepped forward and reverently touched the face of the image.

"Congratulations, Lord Holybrook." Dr. Alexander tore his gaze from the figure. "Do you wish to open the mummiform?" When Lord Holybrook continued to stare at the Egyptian princess in silence, Dr. Alexander repeated the question.

"Eh, what?" Lord Holybrook said, with a distracted glance at Dr. Alexander. "Open her up? I don't think so, my good man. This is quite enough excitement for one day. What say we have the footmen hoist her out of the sarcophagus so you can do a more thorough examination, then we'll open it up tomorrow? Have to save some mystery for the closing meeting. Biggs," he called out, motioning to his steward. "Serve the refreshments, then see to our Egyptian friend here. We'll need some sturdy straps, I should think. Try the stablemaster."

The abruptness of Lord Holybrook's orders seemed to shake everyone from their fascination with the princess. While Lord Holybrook set about organizing the mummiform's removal, servants began to circulate among the guests with glasses of ratafia and cider. Remmington and Harry led the women away from the activity around the sarcophagus and found a seat for them in one of the bay windows of the billiards room.

"Perhaps you are right after all, Remmington." Sophie's gaze moved past Remmington toward the sarcophagus. "The curses don't appear to have any affect."

"What curses?" Harry asked.

"There is a curse on every sarcophagus," Sophie said. "Our underbutler is an Egyptian fellow, and he says the curses are carved into those seals along the sides. They promise all manner of vile fates to whoever opens the sarcophagus."

"Gads!" A twinkle of humor lit Harry's eyes. "If that's true, Holybrook will soon need a company of new footmen. And here those poor chaps were already put through their paces, what with maneuvering Lady Farnsworth through her faint last night. What a scene she made! I could hardly keep a straight face when Holybrook explained what had happened."

"I was curious about that myself," Lily said. "What did Lord Holybrook have to say about Lady Farnsworth?"

Harry caught sight of Remmington's scowl and his smile faded. "Oh, this and that. Nothing the least edifying to Lady Farnsworth's character, you may be sure. She and Farnsworth departed first thing this morning. Holybrook thought Farnsworth should take his wife to London where an expert in the field could treat her nervous condition."

"Oh, there's Dr. Alexander," Sophie interrupted. "He doesn't look busy at the moment. I must ask his opinion of the find."

Lily caught her arm. "I don't think you should tell

him about your underbutler's curses, Sophie. Why worry the man unnecessarily?"

"I won't," she promised. "I just want to know if he's opened any other *sealed* sarcophagi. It might make a very *interesting* story."

Harry excused himself as well. "Been meaning to ask Rumford about those scrolls he purchased. They sound amazingly similar to my own." He gave Remmington an uneasy look, but his smile came back in force when he bowed to Lily. "If you will excuse me, my lady?"

"What was that business about a *sealed* sarcophagus and *interesting* story?" Remmington asked, when Sophie and Harry left. "It sounds as if she very much intends to tell Alexander of the curses."

"Not at all," Lily assured him. "Sophie merely intends to ask Dr. Alexander if he opened any other sealed sarcophagi. If he did, she will find a way to ask if anything unusual happened to him around the same time. Sophie really does have an Egyptian underbutler named Samir, and he's filled her head with tales of tomb curses. She might not believe every word of them, but she staunchly believes it is bad luck to open a sarcophagus."

"Then why on earth did she agree to attend an opening?"

"I asked her that question myself." Lily shrugged her shoulders. "She said that curiosity will eventually kill the cat."

"I find your friend extremely odd at times, Lily." The faint amusement faded from Remmington's eyes and he clasped his hands behind his back. "As interesting as I find tomb curses, we have a much more serious matter to discuss. I asked Holybrook for permission to use his study for an hour after the meeting, and he agreed to ensure our privacy there."

Lily's smile disappeared and she felt her mouth go dry. He looked so very remote today, so very far beyond her reach. "Actually, I'd hoped for just such an opportunity to meet with you today. There are, ah, certain things we must agree on between us."

"Are there indeed?"

A dangerous light kindled in his eyes and she hurried to explain. "The obvious, of course, will be the court-ship. I realize it must end when this weekend is over, but there are additional details to consider. For example, you must not tell my father or Sir Malcolm that you sug-gested the location of our meeting. I shall simply say that the meeting was entirely my idea, which happens to be the truth, and they will assume I suggested the location as well."

The corners of Remmington's mouth lifted. "I find that assumption highly unlikely."

"Then I will say your chamber sounded like the most logical location. You did have several excellent reasons for meeting there, as I recall. They will sound just as log-ical when I repeat them as my own."

"And what will you say when they ask why you wanted to meet with me in the first place?"

"Well ... actually, I haven't quite worked that part out yet." She lowered her lashes. "I suspect I shall be a coward and lie."

He tilted her chin up with one finger and captured her gaze. His thumb brushed across her cheek. "Lily, you never cease to amaze me."

She felt sure her cowardice disgusted him, yet there was an oddly tender look in his eyes. Sophie walked up at that moment with Dr. Alexander in tow.

Sophie glared at Remmington until he let go of Lily's chin, then she pasted on a bright smile and turned to Dr. Alexander. "This is my friend, Lady Lillian Walters, and her ... and the Duke of Remmington. I just know Lady Lillian will want to hear about your experience in the Great Pyramid, Dr. Alexander. We were just discussing the peculiar rash of bad luck that seems to plague certain visitors to that wondrous country."

"Yes, indeed, Miss Stanhope, there were many strange coincidences that occurred on my journey there." Dr. Alexander lifted Lily's hand for a kiss, then turned to give Remmington a formal bow. "Your Grace. Miss Stanhope tells me you are new to the study of Egyptology. What do you think of it so far?"

Remmington shrugged. "Who could fail to be impressed after this morning's discovery?" He stepped aside to make room for Sophie and Dr. Alexander in the bay window.

The windowpanes above Lily's head suddenly exploded, sending a shower of glass into the room. Remmington reached for Lily in the same moment they heard the gunshot, a distant report that shattered the split second of calm.

The room erupted into chaos. Several men shouted at once, and two women screamed. Remmington jerked Lily to her feet and got her away from the window, behind the protection of the room's thick outer wall. He held her by the shoulders as his gaze swept over her, a quick, frantic search for injuries. A few splinters of glass clung to her cream-colored gown, but she looked unhurt. His heart began to beat again. He allowed himself a moment to cup her face in his hand, a paltry comfort to the fear that still coursed through him. The bullet had come so close to her! Inches. A few inches and she would be dead. He turned to search for any new danger, careful to keep her protected behind his back.

Dr. Alexander and Sophie still stood before the windows, and he shouted at them to move. They both ignored the order. Glazed, wide-eyed shock held them immobile, as if frozen in that moment of time. Sophie stood closest to Remmington, and he reached over to pull her to safety. Dr. Alexander stared out the window for another moment, then he looked downward, to the red stain that spread along his side. The doctor staggered a step. Remmington rushed forward to lower Alexander to the safety of the floor.

Another blast shattered through the windowpanes.

Acting instinctively, Remmington leaned over the wounded man's face and tucked his head down to protect them both from the flying fragments of glass. His head turned almost immediately, his gaze instantly on

Lily. She nodded, as if she knew he needed the reassurance that she was all right.

Shouts went up inside the house and more yells from outside. Those who hadn't fled when the shots first rang out remained strangely silent, all but one woman who wept, loud and undignified. Everyone else waited to see what would happen next. People began to look around at one another, and a few lifted their heads to peer at the shattered window.

Lord Holybrook stood up to take control of the situation. From his place near the door, he barked orders to the servants to search the grounds. Worried that Holybrook would get himself shot, Remmington reached behind him and tugged the heavy draperies closed. At least the shooter could no longer see his targets, assuming he hadn't fled. It took a certain amount of bravery for an assassin to remain in position after the first shot. Only a fool would linger after the second. Remmington hoped for a fool. A fool who would soon hang for his crime.

Holybrook left the room to direct the search. Several men volunteered to join him, an air of suppressed excitement in their expressions.

Typical, Remmington thought. A bored Englishman never turned down a good foxhunt. It obviously didn't occur to them that they might be of some use at the scene of the crime. Before anyone else thought to demonstrate a misguided sense of duty, he snapped out his orders.

"Lathrop, Sanders, and Bothwell." He motioned toward a group of young man who stared at him from the floor. "Carry Dr. Alexander to a bed. Lady Holybrook," he said, turning to look at his hostess. She'd already made her way to Dr. Alexander's side. "Show them to the doctor's room and send for a physician." He glanced over his shoulder at Lily and Sophie. What he saw made him scowl. He fixed his sights on two middle-aged women who crouched near the fireplace. "Lady Penrose and Mrs. Rumford, go to the kitchens and make certain a servant brings hot water, a clean tablecloth, and a good pair of scissors to the Queen's Chamber." No one moved. His deep voice bellowed through the room. "You have your orders!"

Lady Penrose and Mrs. Rumford rushed from the room. The men made their way forward to carry Dr. Alexander away. Remmington stalked over to Lily and knelt beside her. Both women were showered with glass splinters, some clinging harmlessly to their dresses, others sprinkled in their hair. Their whispery, floating gowns might be all the fashion, but they'd offered little protection against the deadly shards of glass. Just one small scratch marred Lily's arm, an injury so minor that earlier he'd overlooked it. Sophie's injuries looked much worse. She'd suffered a large cut on her arm and a myriad of small scratches, but the three-inch triangle of glass that protruded from her shoulder worried him most. The penetration might be much deeper.

Sophie lay immobile on the floor while Lily did her best to stanch the flow of blood around the wound with the hem of her gown. "The physician needs to look at Sophie's shoulder," Lily said in an even voice. Her calm demeanor impressed him. The sight of Sophie's injury would make most women faint, but Lily seemed to realize this was no time for hysterics. "The glass will be easier to remove if he gives her laudanum beforehand."

"Alexander needs the physician more than Sophie at this moment." His voice was harsher than he'd intended, but Lily didn't seem to take offense. He nudged Lily aside and carefully lifted Sophie into his arms. "I'm taking her to the Queen's Chamber. Lily, I want you to stay close by my side where I can see you."

The billiards room was nearly empty now. Only a handful of people still huddled on the floor. Others had fled when Remmington pulled the drapes. Harry appeared in the doorway just as they left the room. His face paled when he caught sight of Sophie's wound.

"My God." His gaze met Remmington's. "I had just ducked into the library for a spot of brandy when I heard the shots. What can I do to help?"

"Find one of my men and send them to my chamber upstairs." He brushed past Harry and didn't stop again until he reached the Queen's Chamber. There he carefully laid Sophie on the bed. "Lily, find a chemise or a nightgown to hold near the wound and another for her arm, more if you have them."

"Just take it out," Sophie whispered. She looked down at her shoulder. "It hurts terribly."

"The doctor will be here soon," Lily said, as she patted Sophie's uninjured arm.

"Lily, do as I say." Remmington grabbed Sophie's hand as she reached for her shoulder. "Don't touch it."

Lily brought over two nightgowns and he wrapped one around Sophie's arm and tied it in place with a ribbon.

"I'm going to take it out now," he told Sophie. "It might cause more damage if we leave it in."

He braced one hand against her good shoulder to pin her body to the bed. After a quick examination of the wound site, he grasped the shard of glass and carefully pulled it free. Sophie moaned as he did it, but she remained stiff and didn't fight him.

"Good girl," he murmured. After a quick look at the long, bloody shard, he tossed the glass aside and placed the second nightgown over her shoulder, his palm pressed down hard to put pressure on the wound. "All of it came out. It's a clean wound, but deep. I'm going to keep my hand on your shoulder until the bleeding slows."

"We have everything you asked for," Lady Penrose announced from the doorway. Mrs. Rumford followed her into the room, then a maid who carried a bucket of steaming water.

"I want you and Mrs. Rumford to help Lady Lillian," he said to Lady Penrose. "You will have to cut Miss Stanhope's clothing away so the physician can stitch the wound. You," he told the maid. "Find out where Lady Holybrook keeps the laudanum and bring it back here with a glass of something to drink it with."

The maid bobbed a quick curtsy and disappeared through the door. Lady Penrose and Mrs. Rumford hovered near the end of the bed.

"Come, ladies. Who has the scissors?"

"I do." Mrs. Rumford held up a pair of scissors. "Your Grace, you cannot stay here. We have to remove Miss Stanhope's clothing."

"She will bleed to death if I leave." He released an impatient sigh, then nodded to Lady Penrose. "Get the coverlet from my bed across the hall. You can use that to preserve Miss Stanhope's modesty."

Lily took the scissors from Mrs. Rumford and started cutting away one of Sophie's sleeves while Lady Penrose retrieved the coverlet. Through the open doorway, Remmington saw Harry and one of his outriders in the hall. He motioned them into the room with a jerk of his head.

"Come closer," he told the outrider. He murmured an order only the outrider could hear that sent him from the room again. To Harry, he said, "Did they catch him?"

Harry shook his head. "Jack and two of your outriders are in pursuit, as well as Lord Holybrook's servants and a few of the more adventurous guests. One of the gardeners saw a man ride off a few minutes after the shooting, but it sounds as if he had a good head start."

Remmington lowered his voice so Sophie wouldn't overhear their conversation. "Make sure Lord Holybrook knows that Miss Stanhope needs the physician's services just as soon as he's done with Dr. Alexander. In fact, tell him the wound is very likely as serious."

"The physician is tending Dr. Alexander now," Harry said, his voice just as quiet. "Holybrook had invited him to stay the weekend in case Lady Orwell's gout acted up. A rather fortunate coincidence, as it turns out. I will make sure someone tells the physician he has a second patient."

Harry left at the same time the maid arrived with the laudanum. The outrider followed her into the room, holding something bulky under his coat. Lady Penrose took charge of the laudanum while Lily and Mrs. Rumbford continued to cut Sophie's clothing away beneath the coverlet. Busy at their tasks, the women didn't notice when the outrider handed a pair of pistols to Remmington. He tucked them within easy reach under the bed, then ordered the outrider to stand guard in the hallway. Lady Penrose held up the bottle of laudanum and squinted through the green glass at its contents. She poured a dose into the glass of water, took another measurement of the bottle, then poured another splash of laudanum into the glass. Remmington sincerely hoped she knew the difference between the dose that would calm and the dose that would kill.

"That's enough, Lady Penrose." Lily obviously shared his concern, yet she continued to work with brisk efficiency, her movements steady and sure while Mrs. Rumbford hovered at her shoulder, hesitant and uncertain. Remmington knew that if he ever fell victim to a serious injury, he wanted Lily at his side. She knew how to handle herself in a crisis.

"Could you prop her up a little?" Lady Penrose asked.

Sophie's face was stark with pain, her mouth set in a tight line, but she managed to drink the medicine. "Grim stuff," she said, with a soft moan as Remmington laid her down again. She turned her head toward him. "It isn't over yet, is it?"

He regarded her for a moment in silence, then slowly shook his head.

"I suspected as much." Her voice was weak, her skin pale already from loss of blood. "Does it need to be sealed?"

"I don't think so," he told her. The news made Sophie visibly relax. "The laudanum will take effect in a few minutes. That will help ease your pain."

"I don't think I can watch," Lady Penrose whispered.

Remmington's mouth quirked downward. "You and Mrs. Rumford may leave. Thank you, ladies, for your assistance."

The two women didn't argue. They made a hasty exit.

"The curse," Sophie whispered. Her good hand fluttered on Lily's sleeve then dropped to the bed. There was a distracted look to her eyes already, the first sign that the laudanum was taking effect. "The crystal knife." Her head turned restlessly on the pillow. "I can't remember that part. Read it to me again."

"Hush," Lily murmured. "That isn't important now."

"You have to tell me! I have a right to know what will happen."

"Nothing else will happen." Lily's gaze slid away. "Not to you, anyway."

"Dr. Alexander?" Sophie whispered.

Lily nodded.

"Stop it, both of you," Remmington ordered. "This has nothing to do with a curse."

The two women looked up at him. He could tell they didn't believe him.

Lily shook her head. "You didn't read the message on those seals."

He frowned at her. "I forbid you to speak another word on that subject. At the moment, Sophie does not need a fit of hysterics over superstitious nonsense."

"I can assure you that—"

"That's all right, Lily." Sophie closed her eyes. "As you said, it isn't important right now."

Lily glared at Remmington across the bed. She mouthed the words, "You've upset her." Remmington gave her an exaggerated look of disbelief, then rolled his eyes heavenward.

"Lily?" Sophie's voice sounded slower and her lids opened only a fraction.

"Yes, Sophie?"

"I'm afraid you won't be able to lean on my shoulder for awhile."

A glimmer of tears appeared in Lily's eyes, but she smiled and patted her friend's good hand. "Then you'll just have to lean on mine."

The physician arrived a quarter of an hour later.

Sophie remained in her drug-induced sleep as the doctor stitched the wound on her arm. The physician worked cautiously around the more serious injury to her shoulder.

"This needs to be sealed," the physician said, when the wound began to bleed again.

Remmington wiped away the blood and shook his head. "You are almost done. I am sure this young lady would prefer to forego that cure. I will keep pressure on her shoulder when you are done to stop the bleeding."

The physician looked doubtful for a moment, then he nodded. "The bleeding is not as bad as when I started. Perhaps this is for the best after all."

The trio fell silent as the physician set about his work. Remmington noticed that Lily wouldn't look at the deep stitches the doctor made, but neither did she move from Sophie's side. When he finished the stitching, she helped wrap a bandage around Sophie's shoulder.

"The bleeding stopped," the physician said. "Give her more laudanum when she awakens. I'll return in a few hours to see how she's doing."

"At least she could sleep through the stitching," Lily whispered, after the physician left. "A hot iron would have been more painful than the injury itself."

"That thought did occur to me."

"I want to thank you for both of us." She nodded toward Sophie. "If you hadn't pulled us away from that window . . ." She looked up at him, her heart in her eyes. "I owe you my life."

The simple statement set his teeth on edge. He didn't deserve her thanks. He'd failed to protect her reputation, nearly failed to protect her life. Both their lives would be easier if she would only recognize his flaws and turn away from him. Her gratitude only made him more determined to do what they would both live to regret.

Fifteen

✦

The Bainbridges and Lily's father arrived early the next day. Lady Bainbridge joined Lily and Sophie in the Queen's Chamber while the men met downstairs. An hour later, Lily heard a soft knock at the door. Lady Bainbridge read quietly to Sophie from a chair she'd pulled up next to the bed while Sophie dozed in and out of her laudanum-induced sleep. Lily left her place near the bed to answer the door.

A maid with a starched white cap bobbed a curtsy. "Your father would like to see you in the Blue Room, m'lady."

Lily wasn't certain she wanted to see her father. She hadn't had an opportunity to speak with Remmington alone since the shooting. Now it was too late. She looked over her shoulder at Lady Bainbridge. Without a break in her soft flow of words, Lady Bainbridge glanced up and motioned for Lily to go with the maid.

As Lily followed the girl down the long staircase, she practiced the speech she would give her father. It sounded ridiculous. He would never believe her.

The maid pushed open the door to the Blue Room, and Lily stepped inside. Remmington sat near the fireplace in a chair that looked too delicate to support his large frame. His legs were stretched out in front of him, his elbows propped on the spindly arms of the chair. He appeared to be contemplating his steepled fingers. Her father paced the floor nearby.

She swallowed down a fresh surge of anxiety. "It's good to see you, Papa."

Both men turned at the sound of her voice. Remmington rose to meet her halfway across the room, an unfathomable expression in his eyes. He led her to the seat he'd just vacated, then stood behind her. The weight of his hands on her shoulders calmed a portion of her fears. She wondered if it was his intent to show her his support, or if the gesture meant nothing at all.

The earl clasped his hands behind his back and gazed down at her. "Remmington tells me that you survived yesterday's incident with only a few scratches. I was sorry to hear that Sophie was not so fortunate."

She nodded and waited for him to continue. This discussion would have little to do with her father's concern over Sophie's injuries, or her own minor scrapes. She tilted her head to look up at Remmington, but his expression remained unreadable. He looked so bored that she almost expected to see him yawn.

"Remmington also told me that Lord Holybrook intends to inform me of an incident that took place the night before last."

Lily couldn't look her father in the eye. She knew he wanted her denial, waited to hear her say it was some awful mistake. She bowed her head and remained silent.

"Remmington would not tell me anything more until you were present," he added. "I would like an explanation, Lily."

He didn't know. Was this some awful test? Did Remmington want to see if she would indeed turn coward? She cleared her throat and hoped her voice wouldn't fail her. "Yes, well, the whole thing started—"

Remmington squeezed her shoulders. "I can explain, sir. I wanted Lily present because this affects her. Actually, I'd planned to meet with her to discuss the matter before your arrival, but Miss Stanhope's injuries took precedence. What Lord Holybrook intends to tell you is that he discovered Lily in my bedchamber the night before the shooting."

"*What?*"

The sound of stunned disbelief in the earl's voice struck Lily like a knife. In his eyes she saw shock and denial. "It isn't as bad as it sounds, Papa. Truly, I can—"

Remmington's hands tightened again on her shoulders. "I asked Lily to meet me there. I wanted to be alone with her."

"But that isn't true! Well, not exactly true," she qualified. "I asked to meet with him, Papa."

"And I suggested my bedchamber as our meeting place," Remmington cut in. "Lily suggested several reasonable locations where no one would think the worst if they happened to see us together. I insisted upon the more intimate setting."

Crofford's eyes narrowed. "Do you realize what you are saying, Remmington?"

"Yes, sir, I do. Lily's reputation is in serious jeopardy. I once gave you my word that I would not behave in an improper manner toward your daughter, and I have broken my word. My actions are inexcusable. I hope you can accept my apology."

The earl crossed his arms. "I hope you have something more to offer than an apology."

Remmington nodded. "If you can accept my apology, I hope you will also come to accept me as your son-in-law."

"*What?*" Lily all but shouted the question. Remmington continued as if hadn't heard her.

"Yesterday I obtained a special license. With your

permission, I would like to marry Lily as soon as possible."

The earl appeared to contemplate the offer. "I do not approve of the events that led up to this, but I suppose you will make my daughter a suitable enough husband. The situation leaves little choice in the matter."

"I will ask Lord Holybrook if the ceremony can take place here," Remmington said. "The sooner we marry, the less chance there will be of unsavory rumors."

Lily rose from her chair and whirled around to face Remmington. "I cannot believe you are doing this. You said—" She clamped her mouth shut, not about to remind him that he didn't want to marry her. Not with her father standing next to her. She could see the grim determination in Remmington's eyes. He didn't want this marriage. She didn't relish the thought of being looked upon as a sacrifice made for duty's sake. The set line of his jaw boded no argument, so she tried to reason with her father. "Remmington has a noble nature and a natural tendency to protect those around him, Papa. He is deliberately taking the blame for this when he is not the one at fault. He should not be made to pay for my mistakes."

Remmington settled his arm around her shoulders and drew her to his side. He took her hand in a firm yet gentle grip. "I'm afraid your daughter does not yet comprehend that I will not let her leave this house a ruined woman. Lord Holybrook might be persuaded to silence, but I'm afraid Lady Farnsworth saw Lily enter my room as well. If we marry immediately, that will put an end to any rumors Lady Farnsworth might spread. If we do not, Lily's reputation will be in shreds by the time we return to London."

"Is this true, Lily? Did Lady Farnsworth see you enter Remmington's chamber?"

Lily could feel any favor she held in this argument slipping away. "Well, yes, but there is more to the story. No one is likely to believe anything Lady Farnsworth says about us. You see—" Remmington's thumb brushed against the center of her palm, the sensitive place where she'd once felt his lips. He continued the seductive motion even after she stopped talking, the movement hidden between their hands. Her gaze dropped abruptly to the floor. She couldn't look at her father while Remmington touched her so intimately. Neither could she summon the strength to pull her hand away. "You see . . ." What had she been talking about? Remmington kept caressing her palm, and she wanted to lean closer to him, press herself closer to his heat. She wanted him to wrap her in his arms, tell her that everything would be all right.

"Lily?"

"What?" Startled, her head snapped up.

"Lady Farnsworth?" the earl prompted.

"What about her?" She knew that was the wrong response the moment it left her mouth. "Oh. Yes. She did see me enter Remmington's room." That wasn't right either. She did the only thing she could under the circumstances. She kept her mouth closed, and bowed her head to scowl at Remmington's boots.

"It seems obvious that taking Lily about in public was a mistake," Remmington said "The shooting only makes an immediate wedding all the more advisable. The guests who didn't leave yesterday will be gone by this afternoon, and I'm sure Holybrook could be persuaded to lend his chapel for the ceremony. We could be married tomorrow. As newlyweds, no one will think it unusual if we remain secluded for a time."

"Well, Lily?" Her father waited until she met his gaze. "You have a decision to make."

Lily bit her lip. What she said now would affect the rest of her life. One decision seemed as potentially disastrous as the other. She could refuse Remmington's offer and become a spinster. She could marry him and hope that his fondness for her might develop into something deeper. His history with women was not reassuring in the least. He might find his role of knight to her damsel in distress amusing for a time, but he could just as easily grow tired of the part and of her. He could break her heart. "I would like to think about this tonight and give you my decision tomorrow."

Crofford shook his head. "I don't see any point to dragging this out until tomorrow. You are my daughter and I will support whatever decision you make, but in your heart I think you know there is only one correct answer."

Remmington's grip tightened almost imperceptibly on her shoulder. Lily knew it shouldn't, but that small, worried gesture influenced her decision.

They were married the next day.

Lord and Lady Holybrook were nothing less than delighted to play host and hostess to the proceedings, and they insisted on a lavish wedding dinner afterward as part of their wedding present. Sophie was still weak from her ordeal, but the physician allowed her to attend the ceremony as long as she promised to remain immobile on a small settee. Lord Holybrook even had footmen carry Sophie into the dinner that followed, settee and all.

"I believe all Sophie needs is a turban," Lady Bainbridge told Lady Holybrook. Sophie's aunt sat next to her on the settee to help Sophie manage her meal. "With all this fuss and her colorful wardrobe, she looks very much like a visiting princess from some exotic Eastern empire."

Propped up on satin pillows and swathed in one of Lady Holybrook's velvet cloaks, Sophie did indeed look like a princess at her leisure. "Lily's bridal crown makes her look much more the princess than me," Sophie replied. "I feel like the dotty relative who insists on wearing her nightclothes to the dinner table."

Lily didn't think she looked much like a princess. Her wedding gown was the same ice-blue dress she had worn the night they arrived at Holybrook House. She reached up to touch the wreath of flowers that held her hair in place, a lush confection of tiny pink roses and baby's breath created by Lady Holybrook's gardener. The bridal crown did make her feel exotic, different somehow. Or perhaps it was the ceremony that had just taken place, the sense of unreality she had felt as she stood next to Remmington and listened to him repeat the words that would bind them together for life. She expected to wake up at any moment, to find this was nothing but a dream.

"I thought your friend, Lord Gordon, would remain for the ceremony," Lady Holybrook said to Remmington.

"Harry left for London with the Penroses before he learned of our wedding plans," Remmington said. "Lily and I preferred a small ceremony. Our wedding in your chapel was what we'd both hoped for, and we shall always be grateful for your generous hospitality."

"You do us honor, Your Grace," Lord Holybrook said in a solemn tone. "I do not think Holybrook House has ever hosted the wedding of a duke. It shall be all the talk for quite some time."

"Wasn't your daughter, Sally, married here just last year?" Sir Malcolm asked Lord Holybrook.

"Lud, yes. What a to-do. The gel insisted on a wedding breakfast for two hundred people."

"Two hundred and twenty," Lady Holybrook reminded him, then she proceeded to tell the story herself.

The conversation drifted around the table, but Lily found herself preoccupied with her own thoughts. Already the day seemed a blur, except for that moment when she'd entered the chapel just before the ceremony began. Remmington had stood near the altar, turned to face her. The intensity of his gaze had drawn her forward until she'd stood at his side without being exactly certain how she got there.

"Some brides smile occasionally on their wedding day," Remmington said in a low voice. His hand found hers under the table. "Are you at all happy about this, Lily?"

"I think I'm still dazed by everything that happened today," she admitted. "But, yes, I am happy."

She looked up at him and watched a slow smile curve his mouth. He'd never looked so handsome, she thought, or so dangerously appealing. And now he was her husband. Soon he would take her upstairs and make her his wife in more than just name. The mystery of what lay ahead of them tonight both frightened and excited her.

The sound of her father's voice drew her attention back to the dinner conversation.

"You have quite a find on your hands with that mummy, Alfred. Greek antiquities are my specialty, but this surpasses anything I've seen. Any chance you might open it up before we leave?"

"No!" Sophie's shout drew everyone's attention. She gripped her aunt's arm as if to brace herself against a stab of pain. "You mustn't open it, Lord Holybrook. That mummy is cursed."

"Sophie, please," her aunt chided, "you mustn't strain yourself this way. You know what the doctor said." She turned toward Lord Holybrook. "Our underbutler is a native of Egypt. I'm afraid he gave Sophie some rather odd notions about mummies and curses."

Lord Holybrook nodded toward Sophie. "I can see this matter upsets you, Miss Stanhope. I don't think the mummy will mind if we wait a few weeks, until Dr. Alexander feels fit enough to oversee the opening himself."

Sophie shuddered. "Thank you, Lord Holybrook."

Holybrook nodded, then his gaze went to Sir Malcolm. "An Egyptian underbutler, eh? I hope you will allow a chat with this fellow the next time I pay a visit. Sounds like a fascinating chap."

Lord Holybrook related a few of his adventures in Egypt, and the talk of curses was forgotten. After dinner the women gathered around Sophie while the gentlemen retired to the library to share a glass of port. Lady Bainbridge and Lady Holybrook talked on and on about their own wedding days, while Lily tried to reconcile herself to the fact that she was actually a wife. Remmington's wife. If not for the special license and the somberly dressed Reverend Clarion, this might be any other night, any other gathering to laugh and gossip with friends. She couldn't concentrate on a word anyone said.

"You must be getting tired," Lady Bainbridge said to Sophie an hour later. "I think it's time the footmen carried you upstairs again. The physician said you mustn't overdo things today."

"I'm really not—" Sophie caught her aunt's warning glare and fell silent.

"Why don't you go on ahead to your room," Lady Bainbridge said to Lily. "It is getting rather late. I'm sure your husband will join you soon."

"My maid moved your things into the King's Chamber during dinner," said Lady Holybrook. "I'll send her along to help you change."

"Thank you, but that won't be necessary, Lady Holybrook. I can manage just fine on my own." Lily didn't want a maid hovering about her tonight. The attention would only make her more nervous, if such were possible.

Lady Holybrook looked uncertain, but she finally nodded. "Clara's right. It is getting rather late. Would you like me to help you walk upstairs?"

Lily didn't think it was all that late, and she couldn't imagine why Lady Holybrook thought she needed help to climb a flight of stairs. She frowned and declined the offer. All three women stared at her in the silence that followed.

"Well," Lily said at last. "I'd best take my leave."

It wasn't her best leave. She was nervous and it showed. Her chair nearly tipped over when she stood up too abruptly. That embarrassing blunder only frayed her nerves even further. By the time she reached the staircase, she wished for just a portion of the numbing calm that had sustained her throughout the day. She was trembling so badly that she seriously reconsidered Lady Holybrook's offer of assistance. Somehow she managed to reach Remmington's chamber, but once there she had no idea what to do next.

A small fire cast warm shadows in the room and

chased off the chill of the damp night air. Lily went to stand before the hearth. She gazed into the flickering orange flames as if hypnotized, holding her hands out to the heat and rubbing them together as if a blizzard raged outside the walls rather than a gentle spring rain.

No more than a few minutes passed before Remmington appeared in the doorway. He didn't speak a word as he closed the door and slid the bolt into place. She felt a new appreciation for the fright she had given Lady Farnsworth just a few nights past. They were alone. Tonight there would be no interruptions, no unwelcome visitors. In the past his presence had always calmed her, given her a sense of security and trust that he would protect her, even from himself. Tonight she felt awkward and unsure of herself, of everything unspoken between them.

Remmington didn't move from his place near the door, yet she could feel his gaze on her. Did he consider what they would do tonight just another part of his duty? She felt vaguely embarrassed by that thought.

"It seems so very long since we had a chance to be alone," she said. "I thought it would be nice if we could just talk for awhile."

Remmington leaned his shoulder against the door, his gaze appreciative as it swept over her. "Lily, we can never manage just to talk when we are alone together. That has something to do with the reason we are alone together right now."

She frowned over the reminder that he didn't marry her by choice. "Yes, well, actually I hoped to talk about our marriage."

"I'm afraid it's too late to change your mind."

The harsh undercurrent in his voice startled her, almost as much as the fact that he even worried about such a possibility. She sat down on a bench next to the hearth and began to twist the slender pink ribbons that trailed down from her bridal wreath. "I didn't change my mind about anything. I just thought ... that is, I hoped ... Would you like to sit beside me for awhile?"

He came toward her, moving with the grace of a panther. Rather than sit beside her, he found a stool near the fireplace and moved it so they sat facing each other. "All right, Lily. We'll talk." He took her hands between his own, his elbows resting on his thighs. She felt a shock of warmth at his touch, a feeling that soothed rather than alarmed her. Staring down at their joined hands, she realized how easily his hands engulfed hers. He never forced his strength on her, yet he always surrounded her with it, holding her safely within its circle. He brushed his thumb along the sensitive skin of her wrist. "Why don't I start by saying there is nothing you should be afraid to tell me. Nothing you should be afraid to ask."

He made it sound so simple. Caught up in this forced marriage, he spoke to her as a husband would who cared for his wife. She knew he felt a certain amount of affection for her. She wondered if it would be enough, if he would agree to her request. "Actually, I thought we might discuss the terms of our marriage."

"What terms?"

He didn't sound particularly pleased by the prospect of terms, yet his hold on her hands remained steady. No telltale tightening of his grip that might indicate his refusal to consider the notion, no slight loosening that could mean he'd already dismissed the idea. He waited patiently for an explanation. How on earth could she explain? "Not terms, precisely. I was thinking more along the lines of coming to an understanding."

"Lily, this is not a business transaction. It is a marriage."

"Oh, I hoped you would see it that way." She nodded to show her approval. "I realize this is not a love match, and you said yourself that you do not believe in loyalty or devotion within the confines of marriage. You see, I was just a little worried that—"

His grip did tighten then. "What, *exactly*, are you trying to tell me?"

"That I hope you will not consider our marriage just another sham," she whispered. She looked directly into his eyes, made her gaze remain steady when embarrassment made her want to turn away. This was too important for her to turn evasive or cowardly. She wanted him to understand. "I know that many couples go their separate ways once they are married, that their marriages are, in fact, little more than business arrangements. On the way home from Lady Keaton's, you gave me the impression that you didn't think very highly of those marriages. I don't, either. I want a real marriage."

For a long moment he didn't say or do anything. Then he released her hands and flattened his palms against his thighs, his brows drawn together as he stared at the floor between them. Lily returned her hands to her lap to twist the wide gold band he'd placed on her finger during the ceremony. It was a simple ring, without flourish or embellishment, not even the customary engraving on the inside. Without being obvious about it, she'd managed to slip the band off during dinner to check for an inscription, some simple word or even his initials. The inside of the ring looked as smooth and unmarred as the outside. She supposed he didn't have time to order an engraving. Now she wondered if the thought had even occurred to him.

"You have my word that I will not treat this marriage as a sham," he said at last.

Lily frowned. "You needn't play at devotion, or even pretend to love me. If nothing else, I simply hoped you would respect our friendship enough that you could give me your loyalty."

He looked into her eyes, his expression grim. "You have my loyalty."

"I don't think we are talking about the same thing."

"Yes, I think we are. I intend to be faithful to you, Lily. I will not betray the vows we made today."

He made that pledge of devotion without touching her, without revealing any emotion at all. The reason finally dawned on her. She shook her head, thinking she must be wrong. "But you think I will?"

There was a slight tightening around the corners of

his mouth, but he didn't answer the question. He didn't have to. "You don't trust me."

"Yes, Lily. I do." He reached out and brushed a lock of her hair over one shoulder. "I've seen enough of your loyalty to know that even if your feelings for me change someday, you will remain faithful to your vows. That is one of the reasons I wanted to marry you. I see qualities in you that are rare beyond price, traits I value above all others."

Touched by his speech, she still felt obliged to correct his mistake. "I know you didn't want to marry me, Remmington. I'm not so vain that you need to lie to me and say that you did."

One dark brow rose and the trace of a smile touched his lips. "Do you honestly believe I would give my name to a woman I didn't want to marry?"

His words made her hope for too much. She tried to explain them away. "Well, perhaps you wanted to marry me because you felt it was your duty, but that is different than wanting to marry someone because ... well, for the usual reasons. I know that duty and honor are very important to you."

"Those are very good reasons." He nodded a stern approval, and she knew he was teasing. "However, they aren't the right ones. I think I knew this day would come from the moment we met, when I first looked into your eyes and saw the reflection of a man I hadn't seen in a very long time." His fingertips caressed the high curve of her cheek and he smiled. "You don't have the slightest idea what I'm talking about, do you?"

Lily chewed on her lower lip and lifted her shoulders. "It sounds very nice."

"The night you believe you lured me into this marriage, Lord Holybrook's untimely arrival only made me realize that I wanted the right to speak with you anytime I pleased." He lifted her hand and placed a gentle kiss in her palm, then another on her wrist. "I wanted the right to touch you, to hold you without a hundred eyes upon us." She suddenly found herself on his lap, his arms wrapped around her, and she released a small, contented sigh. "And I wanted the freedom to kiss you without worrying that it would go too far." He cradled her face in his hand and lowered her head until he spoke against her lips. "Indeed, with the hope that our kisses would go much farther."

He didn't tell her any more of his reasons for a very long time. Yet he told her everything she wanted to know with his kisses. They went on and on, dreamy, unhurried, as if he wanted nothing more than to kiss her forever. Then she shifted restlessly in his arms and his body went suddenly rigid. A little alarmed by the abrupt change, she leaned back to study his expression. "You look a bit . . . flushed."

He made a sound deep in his throat that might have been a laugh. "You don't know the half of it." He studied her for a moment, as if looking for something in her eyes. "But I think you are ready for the next lesson."

She gave him an indulgent smile. "Have you appointed yourself my tutor?"

"That has a very appealing ring to it." His smile turned gentle as he removed the fragile bridal wreath from her hair and carefully set it aside, then he lifted her in his arms and carried her to the bed. He placed her in the center and stretched out next to her, drawing her down until they lay side by side, facing each other. "The first rule is that you must tell me everything you like, and anything you don't."

"I like puppies and I detest snakes." She was trying her best to be lighthearted, hoping she could hide her nervousness and uncertainty about what would happen next.

As if he could read her mind, he pursed his lips and his expression turned thoughtful. "Did anyone tell you what would happen tonight? Lady Bainbridge, perhaps?"

Lily felt her cheeks bloom with color. She shook her head.

His thoughtful expression turned into a scowl. "Do

you have *any* notion of what takes place between a husband and wife on their wedding night?"

She hadn't thought it possible, but she felt her face turn even redder. "We spend considerable time in the country, and it's almost impossible not to witness certain events that take place in the barnyard." She made a face, then her gaze slid away from his. "I have the feeling this will be very embarrassing for both of us."

She felt the bed shift as he rolled away from her. He lay on his back and stared at the ceiling, his hands laced together over his forehead. "I assumed someone would enlighten you, at least with the basic information."

"I'm not completely ignorant. I've translated any number of Greek manuscripts, and certain love poems were . . . specific." She bit her lip and her voice became a whisper. "Sophie's cousin told her that it hurts a great deal the first time. Is that true?"

He turned to face her, drew her closer until her head rested against his shoulder. "I think I'm glad you saved your questions for me." He began to stroke her back, soothing motions that encompassed the curve of her hip and waist. "Do you like the way you feel when we kiss?" He waited for her nod. "When we make love, it will involve many of the same feelings, only better."

She gave him a dubious look.

He smiled back at her. "Do you remember how we like to touch when we kiss?"

"I am unlikely to forget."

"I will want to touch and caress you when we kiss, and I hope you will want to return those caresses, to touch me just as intimately."

"What do you mean by 'intimately'?"

The corner of his mouth lifted and one eye narrowed as he considered his response. "You know, rather than explain everything before it happens, it might work better if you asked me questions along the way."

"I'm not so sure. You haven't told me yet if it hurts."

"It might hurt at first," he admitted, "but I will be very gentle, and I will tell you when that time comes so you won't have to worry about it until then." His expression softened. "Nothing we do will be frightening or unpleasant, Lily. I promise."

She reached up and stroked his cheek, then smoothed her hand over his white silk cravat. "I have a feeling you are being very patient with me."

Remmington thought he should receive an award. "I have a feeling the wait will be worthwhile." He smiled and lifted her hand to press another kiss against her wrist. This time he teased the sensitive pulse point with the tip of his tongue. Lily sighed in response. She was so beautiful, so innocently sensual. She sighed again. The fabric at the front of her gown stretched enticingly over the soft swells of her breasts and he lost his train of thought.

"Should I put my nightgown on now?" She sat up and pulled several pins from her hair, sending a waterfall of fiery tresses over her shoulders and down to her waist.

Lying beside her, he propped his head up on one hand and reached for her hair with the other. He captured a thick strand and rubbed the silky stuff between his fingers, always amazed that it could be so soft. He knew her skin was softer.

She looked at him expectantly. "My nightgown?"

He shook his head. "You won't need a nightgown tonight."

Her eyes widened and she shivered. He couldn't resist teasing her. "Cold?"

"No. Well, perhaps just a little."

He smiled and opened his arms to her. "Come lie down with me, Lily." He managed not to groan when she landed on his chest. His fingers brushed through her hair and found the small pearl buttons at the nape of her neck.

"What are you doing?"

"Loosening your gown. That high neckline looks uncomfortable."

"It isn't terribly uncomfortable. The bruises are almost gone."

He frowned over that reminder. He unbuttoned the gown to her waist, then rolled her onto her back and carefully folded down the neckline of her gown. The bruises were no more than faint yellow marks that would disappear entirely in a few days. He stroked the elegant line of her throat with his fingertip, then he leaned down to do the same with his lips. "I won't let him hurt you again, sweetheart."

He'd promised to be gentle, and he showed her that consideration when he kissed her. She fit her mouth to his just as he'd taught her, then her tongue touched his and he forgot all about promises and consideration. The kiss deepened and he possessed her mouth completely. Even as he tightened his arms around her, he felt her body grow stiff. He knew instinctively that she wanted to give herself to him, that he was taking what she offered too quickly. He couldn't help himself. His hips pressed against her soft body and his hand went instinctively to her breast, squeezing her until he heard her startled cry of alarm. In an abrupt movement, he tore his mouth away and rolled to his side. He lay on his back and gazed up at the ceiling, trying to calm his breathing. This patience business would take some getting used to.

She suddenly leaned over him, her hair spilling around them both, a curtain of firelight. "I was just a little nervous, I think. You aren't going to stop kissing me, are you?"

He smiled and shook his head. She was every bit as passionate as he'd hoped. If he could keep his desire for her in check, the reward would be worth every moment of the torture. Her coaxing tone pleased him as well, and he decided to let her coax him a little more. "Are you warmer now?"

"Oh, yes. Much."

"I'm very warm, too," he said in a considering tone. "Would you mind helping me out of my jacket?"

The look she gave him was indulgent, one that said she saw through his game, but she nodded agreeably. He sat up and turned to one side as she slipped the jacket off his shoulders.

"I seem to recall loosening the buttons of your gown when you were uncomfortable." He stripped off his cravat then ran a finger inside the collar of his shirt. "Perhaps you could return the favor. This shirt is extremely uncomfortable at the moment."

Lily caught her lower lip between her teeth and reached for the top button. She undid the fastening very slowly, concentrating intently on the task. At the rate she was going, their wedding night would be over before she finished the long row of buttons. He untucked his shirt and began working on the bottom buttons, leaving her three in the middle. When the last button came undone, she held his shirt together by the edges. She hesitated and he tried to reassure her. "You saw me bare-chested that night in my town house. I'm no different now than I was then."

"I know," she whispered. "I'm just not certain I'm ready to see so much of you again."

He wondered how she would react when she saw him naked. "Was the sight so ugly?"

She shook her head. "The sight was too tempting."

He grasped her wrists and pulled her hands apart, opening the shirt, then he laid her hands against his chest. "I wanted you to touch me that night," he admitted. "As much as I wanted to touch you. I wanted to explore your body with my hands. Is that what you found tempting?"

She stared at his chest with obvious longing. "Yes."

He didn't have to encourage her further. She removed the shirt by running her hands beneath the fabric, trailing her fingers over his chest to his stomach, then to his sides, up again to his shoulders until the shirt pooled onto the bed. His flesh burned everywhere she touched him. His hands moved to her gown and he caressed her shoulders and arms as he eased the gown to her waist. Only a delicate-looking chemise covered her breasts, and he took a moment to savor the sight.

His hands spanned her narrow waistline, and a smile began to tug at his lips. "I didn't think you wore a corset."

"I don't wear one very often," she admitted. "Do you mind?"

He shook his head as he reached for the straps of her chemise. A surge of modesty overcame her and she covered his hands, as if that small pressure might stop him. He placed his hands on top of hers, then closed them so her fingers curled around the small straps. His hands moved to her wrists to apply the gentlest pressure, urging her to lower the straps for him. He took over the task just below the curves of her shoulders, lowering the silk chemise in agonizingly slow degrees. She pulled her arms free of the straps, yet she made no move to cover herself.

For a moment he couldn't help but stare, then he lifted her by the waist until she stood next to the bed. The gown and chemise fell in a pool of silk and satin at her feet. Then she did cover herself, her hair draped over her breasts, her arms crossed in an age-old gesture of maidenly modesty.

"Look at me, sweetheart." The awe he felt lent a rough edge to his voice. Her eyes were dark with uncertainty when she met his gaze. He stroked her cheek with one finger, then reverently brushed her hair over her shoulders. "You are very beautiful, Lily. I would like to look at you."

His gaze didn't waver from her face as he waited for her permission. Very slowly, she lowered her arms to her sides. "I don't feel especially beautiful right now. I just feel . . . naked."

He needed to reassure her on that point, needed to tell her of the incredible perfection of her body. He couldn't speak a word. His gaze swept over her and the awe he felt turned to wonder. Her skin was the color of a flawless pearl, warmed by the firelight. He knew already that her soft breasts would fit his hands perfectly. Her waist was just as small as he knew it would be, her hips as nicely curved, and her legs as long and shapely.

Each part of her appeared almost exactly as he'd envisioned them in his daydreams, and more often than not in his bed each night. The complete image was something else entirely. Every part of his imagination flowed together into reality to form a sensuous creature beyond compare. In all his imaginings, he'd never conjured something so perfect as the woman who stood before him. His woman.

His wife.

She was his, to do with as he pleased. He could make love to her all night, kiss and caress her however he wanted, when and wherever he wanted. Just knowing he could touch her was enough for the moment. More than anything, he wanted to please her. Without taking his eyes from her, he reached behind him and drew the covers aside. He lifted her in his arms and placed her in the center of the bed. She didn't lie down, but sat up with her back rigidly straight. He was disappointed but not surprised when she drew the sheets up to her neck. He smiled, knowing he would be beneath those sheets soon enough.

Lily's gaze followed his hands as they moved to the fastening of his pants. She lowered her lashes when he loosened the first button. A moment later, she felt him slide into bed next to her.

"Shouldn't you douse the candles?" She'd tucked the sheets under her arms, but she knew he was staring at her bare back. He confirmed as much by smoothing his hand over her shoulders, pressing his thumb along her spine to her waist.

"And miss this view? I think not."

She looked over her shoulder. His pillows were propped against the headboard and he leaned against them, his gaze intense as he slowly stroked her back. From the expression on his face, she guessed that he wanted very badly to make love. Her nervousness and inexperience didn't affect his patience. Nor did it seem to diminish his desire. She thought surely the sight of her body would disappoint him. She'd always felt too tall, too awkward. Most parts of her were too big, while other parts were too small. Nothing balanced. Amazingly, he didn't seem to notice. He even seemed to like what he saw. She decided to test that theory by letting the sheets drop to her waist. His hand stilled, and he stared at her back until she turned to lie beside him, resting her weight on one elbow.

She'd always hated it when men stared at her chest. Now she knew why. Only one man could look at her this way and make it feel right. He placed his hand at the base of her neck and her heart began to beat harder, a steady rhythm of desire that grew stronger as he drew his open palm down the center of her chest. His hand cupped one breast and her heart skipped that beat. Unhurried, he explored the shape, then his fingertips brushed across the nipple. Lily felt as if he'd burned her with a painless fire. An unconscious movement thrust her breasts forward, and only then did she realize it was an invitation. He took one nipple into his mouth and stroked the other between his fingers.

A strange restlessness began to build inside her. She didn't want him to stop, yet she wanted something more, something she couldn't name. She arched her neck and he eased her onto her back, his mouth moving higher until he reached her lips. At the same time his hand moved lower, over her waist and stomach, skimming over the most intimate part of her. His hand continued down her thigh then wrapped around her knee. All the while he kissed her, his mouth open and carnal, telling her without words that his patience was nearing its limits. He lifted her knee and her leg bent as if made of butter. He propped up her leg, then carefully lowered her knee. His hand began to stroke upward along her inner thigh and he stopped kissing her.

"You are softer than anything I've ever imagined." His breath caught when he settled his hand between her thighs. He pressed his palm down at the same moment her hips arched upward. He lowered his head until their foreheads touched, then he pressed a kiss against her temple, then a more urgent kiss against her cheek, then he captured her lips. His tongue penetrated her mouth at the same moment his finger penetrated her body. Lily felt as if she'd touched the sun. Her entire body arched, wanting to get closer. He took one last, deep taste of her before he broke away from her lips.

"God, Lily. Your body is ready for mine already." He withdrew his finger, then returned to her just as slowly to demonstrate that fact. She felt her world start to come apart. "It's time, Lily." His voice held a rough, urgent edge. "Once I take your maidenhead, you will know an even greater pleasure than this."

"I don't think that's possible." She was amazed at her ability to speak. She gasped when he moved again inside her. "And I don't have any questions at all. Miles, please!"

His hand was suddenly gone, replaced by his weight on top of her, and he cupped her face between his hands. His eyes were darker than the darkest sin, his gaze so intent that she felt certain he was looking into her soul. Then she felt a blunt pressure between her legs, steady, insistent. She waited for the rending pain that Sophie had whispered about, tensing herself when her body resisted him, then he thrust hard and deep, until their hips were joined as intimately as their bodies. And still she waited for the pain.

"Is that it?" she managed to ask, not wanting any surprises. She shifted her hips experimentally and felt a cramping sensation, but it was hardly noticeable amidst the feeling of fullness, a painless, aching sensation that kept her body arched against his. When she shifted her hips again, he groaned. His hands were braced on either side of her, the muscles in his arms and chest glistening with a fine sheen of perspiration. His eyes were closed, an expression on his face that she didn't recognize, then his eyes opened and he looked down at her, twin flames of molten, burning desire.

"There is more." He withdrew from her and she felt herself sliding away with him. Her hands moved to his hips, wanting him to stay. He complied with the silent demand, entering her again just as slowly. Her head fell back on the pillows and she couldn't breathe, could only feel as he began to move inside her. She wrapped her arms around him a little tighter each time he thrust, wanting more, another penetration, and then another. He kissed her once, but his lips soon slid away, trailing down the column of her neck and over her shoulders, as if kissing her mouth were too distracting while he did such intimate things to her body.

Her toes brushed against the back of his legs, then she pressed the arches of her feet against his calves in a long, downward stroke that matched his thrust. He groaned and wrapped one arm around her waist, as if he needed to get even closer to her. Each thrust seemed deeper than the last, as penetrating to her soul as it was to her body. She soon caught his fever and the rhythm of her torment matched his own, moving her with and against him at the same time. She was so very close, so very near him, but not close enough.

Each stroke brought her closer, the last one so tantalizingly near that her fingernails raked against his shoulders, an unconscious response that seemed to unleash something within him. With one last powerful surge he thrust himself into her body, holding her hips to receive him. She felt him swell so deep inside her that the burning penetration became pleasure, the hard shudder that racked his body as much a part of her as his seed, spilling into her womb. The sensation was so unexpected that the waves of pleasure crashed in upon her, making her call out to him even as he gathered her close and moved inside her once more to prolong the terrible pleasure.

Remmington returned to reality in slow degrees. When he moved to his side he kept Lily within the circle of his arms and pressed her head against his shoulder. His hand moved in random patterns over her back, his body sated, yet still wanting to touch her, to calm her after the shattering experience. She was asleep. He still labored to breathe, and the sound of his heartbeat filled his ears. He wanted to kiss her again, tender kisses, sweet, innocent kisses meant for nothing more than the simple pleasure of touching her with his lips.

He smiled up at the ceiling, remembering how she'd asked, "Is that it?" If he hadn't been concentrating so intently at the time, remaining still to give her body time to adjust to his, he would have smiled over her bemused expression. His smile faded a little and he felt profoundly grateful that he'd taken her virginity so painlessly. He'd braced himself for hysterics. He should have known better. Lily never did anything he expected.

Smiling at the top of her head, he wondered if she would have any questions the next time they made love. It was too soon for her, of course. Too soon for him. He'd never felt this completely sated, this completely at peace. That thought alone was enough to make him frown. He didn't want to feel any closer to Lily than he had before they married. Granted, he knew that intimacy would change their relationship, but he thought lovemaking would cure this insatiable need to touch her, to hold her in his arms whenever he could.

He forced himself to loosen his grip, to move away until no part of her touched him. She murmured his name in her sleep and turned toward him, the view delightful. He wanted her. He wanted to touch her, to kiss and caress her, to make love to her again and again. He would want her until the day he died.

He rolled onto his back and laced his fingers together over his forehead. Perhaps he was wrong about the again and again part. Every new lover seemed unique the first time or two, but they rarely held his interest any longer than that. Eventually he would cure himself of this need for her, and then his life would return to normal. They would settle into a routine, and they would have a very pleasant life together. She would give him children.

The thought of Lily swollen with his child brought a heated reaction from his loins. He clenched his hands tighter over his forehead and tried to memorize the pattern of the cracked ceiling. It didn't help. The long, rambling lines took on new, erotic shapes. The more he stared at them, the more he wanted her. He felt Lily's weight shift on the bed next to him until she'd wedged herself against his side. He was aware of every pore of his body that touched hers. He caught the light scent of roses and sandalwood, and the more potent, seductive scent of their lovemaking. Somehow his arms ended up around her.

Just once more tonight, and then he would be sated. He tilted her chin up, captured for the moment by his wife's beauty.

A considerate husband would let her sleep. He wouldn't selfishly awaken her to his need.

He stroked the curve of her cheek and murmured her name.

Sixteen

---✦---

"What? We're going where?" Lily rubbed her eyes and started to sit up in bed. Then she remembered she was naked. Her head remained on the pillow, but she turned to stare at her husband as she tried to absorb it all. He stood in front of a tall chest of drawers, dressed already in a white shirt and gray pants. A basin sat on top of the chest, and a tall mirror hung from the wall. He scraped a wicked-looking razor across his face with deft strokes that looked as if they should be painful, if not fatal. Lily found it a fascinating process, but at the moment she was more curious about the time of day than the foreign techniques of shaving. The warm light of dawn streaked through the windows, the sun just barely over the horizon.

"We are leaving for Remmington Castle within the hour," he repeated.

She turned to stare at his profile, trying to gather her sleep-muddled thoughts. "But ... why?"

He glanced at her over one shoulder, a cool, impersonal look that made her wonder if she'd only dreamed the intimacies of the night before. He dipped the razor into the basin of water and swirled it in a circle. "The marriage of a duke does not go unremarked. If the news is not already in London, it soon will be. The gossips will find one excuse after another to visit Holybrook House if we remain this close to Town. I promised your father I would keep you secluded."

Lily frowned. "Are you angry with me about something?"

"Of course not. Whatever gave you that idea?" His gaze raked over her, brief and dismissive. "I'm sure you will want to say good-bye to your father. Sophie, too, I would imagine. You need to get dressed, Lily. Wear a gown that will be comfortable on the journey."

He returned his attention to the razor. She tucked the sheets under her arms and sat up, trying to decide the best way to get from the bed to her robe. Unfortunately, the robe sat on a trunk well beyond her reach. She had no intention of parading around the room naked, as if she thought he would enjoy the sight. Last night Remmington showed an intense desire to see her unclothed, but this morning he didn't seem the least interested. She knew why. Indeed, she had expected this much sooner. He'd looked his fill last night and found her somehow lacking.

She slipped her legs over the side of the bed, rearranged the sheets to cover as much of herself as possible, then inched her way to the end of the bed. The trunk was still five or six feet away. With one last glance over her shoulder, she made a dash for the robe, then back to the shelter of the sheets.

"Damn it."

Her head pivoted in Remmington's direction, but he wasn't looking at her. He was dabbing at a small cut on his neck with a linen towel, scowling into his mirror as he tended the injury. She struggled to put her robe on with one hand while the other held the sheet in place. Her bid to conceal herself wasn't entirely successful, but at last she tied the belt into place. When she looked up again, he was dabbing at another cut not far from the first.

She sat on the edge of the bed and watched the razor scrape along his cheek. "Does your valet usually do that?"

Remmington swore under his breath as another nick appeared on his chin. He poured fresh water over the towel, then wiped his face.

"Do what?" he snapped.

"Shave you."

"No."

"You don't seem overly talented at the chore."

He gave her a withering look, then jerked his head toward the dressing screen. "We now have three quarters of an hour. It's time to get dressed, Lily."

It took twice that long to rouse everyone and explain their departure, then make their good-byes. Remmington, Lily's father, and Sir Malcolm met in the library, while Lily said good-bye to Sophie and Lady Bainbridge in the Queen's Chamber.

If not for Remmington's distant mood, she would have thanked him for their hasty departure. He didn't seem the least bothered that everyone knew what they had done the night before, but Lily couldn't look anyone in the eye, especially her father. When they finally pulled away from Holybrook House, her relief was tempered by disappointment that they couldn't return to London. It could be weeks, perhaps months, before Sir Malcolm sent word that he had Lily's attacker in custody. If her husband's mood didn't improve, any length of time would seem an eternity.

The silence in the coach grew longer. They sat on the same side of the coach, but the spacious vehicle allowed plenty of room between them and Remmington sat more than a foot away from her. He continued to gaze out the window next to him long after Holybrook House disappeared from view.

"I'm sorry we departed a little late." She wondered if he truly blamed her for the slight delay. Personally, she didn't think there was any great rush. Her father didn't plan to send the announcement of their wedding to the papers until tomorrow. They could have stayed another day. Remmington shrugged and didn't reply. His casual dismissal finally sparked Lily's temper. "Would you care to tell me why you are in such a surly mood, my lord?"

He looked startled by the question, then he smiled at her for the first time that morning. "No."

He propped one foot up on the opposite seat and watched her with an expectant air.

"If you are waiting to hear why *I* am displeased with *you*," she said, "then I think the answer should be obvious."

"Is it really?" He didn't sound the least interested in the answer. He continued to watch her, his smile lazy.

She lifted her chin and looked away from him. "You should have told me last night."

"Told you what?"

Untangling the tassels of her fan suddenly seemed an important task. She arranged the silky streamers in neat rows, then risked a glance at him from beneath her lashes. He wasn't smiling anymore. He looked puzzled. She felt a surge of satisfaction. He'd left her guessing all morning about his displeasure. It was only fair that he should suffer his own moment of doubt. She took her time answering the question. "The reason for our abrupt departure this morning. After all, you can hardly expect me to guess your thoughts, or to . . ."

She couldn't think how to put the delicate subject into words. She'd thought last night was wonderful, the most incredible experience of her life. He acted as if nothing had happened. Worse than if nothing had happened. He was treating her almost like a stranger. Only one thing could account for the drastic change in his mood. Last night she'd done something wrong. The only thing worse than knowing she'd failed to please him, was having to ask him how. It was humiliating. She refused to do it. "Oh, you should have told me last night!"

His brows rose over the sudden outburst. "I did not realize you would be so upset, Lily. Had I known, I would have told you of our travel plans much sooner."

"Travel plans?" she echoed. "What are you talking about?"

"My decision to leave for Remmington Castle this morning," he clarified. "Last night I didn't want you to worry about leaving. Sophie will be in good hands, and your father and Sir Malcolm will return to London this morning anyway. There was no pressing reason to stay, yet several pressing reasons to leave." He gave her a considering look. "What did you think I was talking about?"

"The same thing, of course." Did their lovemaking mean so little to him? She supposed it must, for he'd obviously dismissed the matter from his mind. She'd thought of little else all morning. If she voiced her concerns now, he would think her hopelessly naive about the intimacies between a husband and a wife. He would be right. "I am not quite myself in the mornings. The news that we wouldn't return to London just came as a surprise."

Remmington was silent for a moment, then he brushed his knuckles over the curve of her cheek. "Considering what you've been through the past few weeks, I'd say you took the news remarkably well."

Lily felt a burgeoning glow of warmth over the praise. She glanced up at him, caught by the tenderness of his expression.

He lifted her hand and pressed a feathery kiss against her wrist. "I want to keep you safe, Lily. At Remmington Castle I know every nook and cranny, every face. Someone who might melt into a crowd in London will be marked a stranger there. It seems the best place for you."

He was concerned for her safety. She felt churlish for baiting him.

"There is also the fact that my brother will be at the

castle. Before we left for Holybrook Hall, I asked him to attend a tenant dispute in my place. I would like to tell him of my marriage before he reads about it in the papers."

"Does your brother know of your work?"

He hesitated a moment, then nodded. "He works for Bainbridge as well. My titles come with responsibilities that make it difficult for me to leave England for extended periods of time. Trevor handles the assignments that we know will involve weeks or months of work abroad."

"Will you tell him about my work?"

"I would like to." He regarded her with eyes that were more blue than gray in the morning sunlight.

She assumed he would be the sort of husband who thought it his right and duty to make such decisions for his wife. It took her a moment to realize that he was waiting for her permission. "You wouldn't tell him if I asked you not to?"

"Would you tell anyone about my work if I said not to?"

"No."

He shrugged. "Why are you surprised that I show you the same consideration?"

"Most men wouldn't." Off the top of her head, she couldn't think of one who would.

"I am not most men." He looked indignant, yet she grew wary when one dark brow rose. "*Some* men might take offense at being placed in such a low category by the one person who should think them a male superior to all others, wise in all things."

Lily rolled her eyes. "I may not be an expert on marriage, but I am not *that* naive."

He placed one hand over his chest. "You wound me, *chérie*."

He said the casual endearment in jest, yet it warmed her anyway. "At least your brother cannot object to the fact that you married a woman who is in league with spies, being one himself. I did wonder how you intended to explain our marriage, when I accepted an invitation to ride with him in the park just a week before."

His smile faded. "That reminds me. I was not overly pleased to learn you had agreed to go on an outing with my brother."

"You needn't give me that look. He refused to accept no for an answer. In that, you and your brother are much alike."

"Persistent?"

"Arrogant."

"Hm. First you class me with most men, now I am arrogant. One wonders what you will think of me after an entire week of marriage."

She smiled back at him. "Are you fishing for compliments, my lord?"

"Miles," he corrected. "I would never be so vain."

His mood perplexed her. First brooding silence, now teasing humor. She had no idea what to think of him after one day of marriage, much less a week. And still the one question she really wanted answered kept repeating itself over and over in her mind. *Did I please you last night?* He said that she shouldn't be afraid to ask him anything. She couldn't quite bring herself to ask him that. "How long do your assignments usually last?"

For a moment he looked perplexed by her question, then he shrugged his shoulders. "It depends upon the assignment. The voyages I make are most often to Normandy, and those take no more than a day or two. There are operatives in other parts of France, and those voyages may last a week or more. Then there are smugglers. For the most part, the local officials are well aware of what goes on and the names of those involved, but they turn a blind eye to the business. We track the operations to make certain the cargoes are harmless. Those assignments often take several weeks."

"But how do men like Lord Granger become involved with the transport of spies?"

Remmington frowned. "All too easily. The only thing Granger appreciates more than French brandy is a game of chance. He plays often, and he plays deep. In time his estates became so heavily mortgaged that even his smuggling activities could not keep him afloat. The officials already knew of Granger's smuggling enterprise, so no one noticed when his ship began to carry an extra crew member or two. However, we became suspicious when Granger paid off all his debt within a matter of months. We know now that there are four spies who operate through Granger. For a time we thought there was a fifth, but it seems he returned to France before we caught on to the operation."

"At Crofford House, Sir Malcolm said he didn't intend to arrest them. Isn't he afraid of the information they are leaking to the French?"

"None of their messages reached France. We kept the net open only long enough to find out how and where they obtained their information. Sir Malcolm took them into custody after we left for Holybrook House."

"Lord Granger, too?" she asked.

He seemed in no hurry to answer the question. He propped his foot on the opposite seat and laced his hands together around his knee, his expression grim. "Bainbridge offered Granger two choices. One was to hang for treason."

"And the other?" Lily whispered.

Remmington scowled at his folded hands. "Three days ago, Granger died by his own hand."

"Oh, my God."

Remmington seemed to speak more to himself than to Lily. "Bainbridge notified our operatives in France before he arrested the French spies or confronted Granger. That is part of the reason I left for Normandy so abruptly last week. Bainbridge feels his counterpart in the French government will retaliate by arresting anyone he suspects is an English spy." He took a deep breath, then slowly released it. "At any given time, we know the identities of a few of their agents, and they know a few of ours. It's a cat-and-mouse game, really. We arrest one of theirs, and they arrest one of ours. We're just never sure which one it will be."

Lily felt herself grow very cold inside. "Lacroix," she managed to whisper. "Do you think they know his identity?"

Remmington studied her face for a long, silent moment, his expression unreadable. "I warned him of the possibilities, Lily. He knows to watch his back."

"But what if ..." She couldn't go on, couldn't allow herself to consider those possibilities.

Remmington's arm went around her. He pulled her closer until her head rested on his shoulder. "Try not to worry, Lily. I know Lacroix well enough to be certain he can take care of himself. Tell me more about that code the two of you use. Why do you need a dictionary to decipher it?"

His question was a blatant attempt to change the subject, but Lily welcomed the distraction. She didn't want to think about the danger Robert faced, not when she couldn't do anything to prevent it. She concentrated on her explanation of the Cross code. As the miles rolled by, he began to tell her more of his own activities. The sound of his deep voice and the tender way he held her calmed her fears, even though they spoke no more of Sebastian Lacroix. The gentle swaying of the coach and the lulling vibration of the wheels affected her as well, and soon her eyes drifted closed.

Remmington woke her several hours later when they stopped for the night at an inn. She sensed the difference in his mood right away. Sometime while she slept, he'd shifted her onto his lap. He woke her with a kiss. Her hands laced around his neck and she began to return the kiss before she was fully awake. She realized the coach had stopped moving at the same time he broke away from her lips. He tucked her head under his chin and she heard him take several deep breaths. She wound her arms beneath his jacket and pressed closer to his warmth.

"We are at an inn called the Brass Ring," he told her, his voice oddly hoarse. Lily struggled to pay attention. He was rubbing the back of her neck in such soothing motions that she felt as if she could melt. "I sent Jack inside to make arrangements for our meal and accommodations. What baggage do you need for the night?"

"The blue tapestry satchel," she mumbled, rubbing her cheek against his chest.

She shifted slightly to press herself closer to him, but his hands were suddenly at her waist. He lifted her off his lap, then moved her onto the seat next to him. "I'm sure Jack has our room by now. Let's go inside."

Remmington helped her from the carriage and kept a firm arm around her waist as he led her across the inn's stableyard. It was nearly dusk and the yard was a flurry of activity. The Brass Ring was a large inn, a three-storied brick structure covered almost entirely by ivy. A painting of its namesake hung over the low doorway that led to the public rooms. Jack was there to give them directions to a room upstairs.

Their chamber was small, but there was a cheerful coziness to the furnishings that indicated a woman's touch. Colorful rag rugs covered the planked floor, and a table and two chairs were placed near the window. A flower-patterned cloth covered the table, and a matching spread covered the bed. Lily's gaze moved from the bed to her husband's large frame. She knew already that his feet would dangle over the end of the normal-sized mattress. The image of it made her smile until she recalled that she would be sharing that bed with him.

Jack arrived almost immediately with a large platter that contained their dinner. He placed the tray on the table while one of the outriders set their baggage inside the door, then the servants departed with word from Remmington that they would leave shortly after dawn the next morning.

Lily eyed her meal with little interest. Her stomach still felt unsettled from the long hours in the coach. Remmington's appetite didn't seem diminished in the least. He appeared almost hurried as he ate, which kept conversation to a minimum. The way he watched her throughout the meal made her nervous. One dark brow rose when she finally pushed away her half-eaten meal.

"You aren't hungry?"

She shrugged. "I never feel like eating when I travel."

"Are you ill?"

"No. I'm just not hungry." She picked up her mug of mulled wine and took a tentative sip. It was better than she expected, and she took a deeper drink.

"How are you feeling otherwise?" He set his fork down, his gaze never leaving her as he waited for an answer.

"I feel fine." She wondered at his sudden interest in her health. Uncertain what else she could say to reassure him, she took another drink of wine.

He pushed his plate away and leaned forward, his voice lowered. "Are you still sore from last night?"

It took a moment for the meaning of his words to sink in. When they did, she choked on her wine. Alarmed, he reached over and started to pound his hand against her back. The first blow almost sent her face-first into her plate. She managed to grab his arm between the third and fourth blows to stop him before he dealt her an injury. Trying to retain as much of her dignity as possible, she placed her mug of wine on the table and picked up her napkin to dab at her watery eyes.

"Are you all right?"

"I will recover. You are stronger than you realize, my lor—Miles. I do seem to have trouble remembering to call you by your Christian name. Only natural, I suppose. I've known you by your title for as long as I can recall. It's a very nice name, though. How did your parents decide upon it?"

Remmington leaned back in his chair and smiled. "Are you attempting to avoid my question, by any chance?"

"I don't think so." She made her eyes purposely wide, hopefully innocent. "I did say that I would recover, which naturally means I will be all right."

"That guileless expression is one of your most en-

...ing, my sweet, but I know you too well to be fooled ...mock innocence. You know which question I refer ..."

Lily turned her attention to the wine she'd spilled on the tablecloth. "I feel quite fine in all respects."

He caught her hand and placed a deft kiss in the palm. "Are you telling me the truth, Lily? I don't want to hurt you again. If you aren't ready, we can wait until ... tomorrow night."

"You've never hurt me," she said in a quiet voice. Her expression turned considering. "Well, perhaps just a little when you pounded on my back."

The serious lines on his face dissolved into a smile. "I do love your sense of humor."

Lily bit her lip, but she couldn't contain the question any longer. "Do you think the day might come when you could come to love me as well?"

His smiled faltered. He took her hand and stood up, pulling her to her feet. He placed his hands on her shoulders, his expression solemn as he gazed down at her. "I want there to be only truth between us, Lily."

She shook her head, knowing instinctively that she could do with a few lies instead. "If you have nothing good to say, then perhaps you should say nothing at all."

"No, Lily. I don't want you to deceive yourself, or accuse me of deceit at some later date. I want our relation-ship to be built on truth and understanding. What you think of as love rarely if ever involves those two traits." He eyed her expectantly, then his mouth quirked down-ward when she didn't readily agree with his opinion. "I learned long ago that romantic love exists only in fairy tales, yet the word itself can mean many things. We sometimes deceive ourselves with it, as I believe you are deceiving yourself now. For instance, I might say that I love strawberries in cream, but that does not mean I am *in* love with them, or that they will always be my favorite food. Do you understand what I am saying?"

"I understand that you are comparing me to fruit." She wrapped her fingers around his wrists and removed his hands from her shoulders. "I also understand that you think my feelings are childish and naive."

He sighed in defeat. "I've hurt you."

"How astute you are." Lily took a step forward and pushed against his shoulder. Startled, he retreated a step. "I am in love with you, you ... insensitive beast!" She pushed him back another step. "You lied to me last night. You said we would make love, and I lived up to my part of the bargain. Now I realize we did nothing of the sort. I made love, but *you* ... it was nothing more than an act of mating to you." Her finger poked against his shoulder to emphasize her point. "You made me think that you cared for me, when last night meant nothing more to you than duty. You used me!"

He grabbed her hand before she could poke him again. "I did *not* use you last night, nor did I lie to you. And I would not have you belittle or diminish our wedding night, just because your feelings are hurt."

"You just did both, and I don't think your feelings are hurt in the least." She gave him a challenging look. "What is your excuse?"

"You are being unreasonable, Lily."

"Unreasonable because you have no more affection for me than you do for a bowl of fruit? I did not ask to be placed on a pedestal, but I did hope to rank higher in your affections than food. I wonder what else I must compete with for your regard. If you are comparing me to food, then I must rank a very poor second to the more important things in your life, such as a favorite pair of boots or an especially fine racehorse."

He pulled her closer until their foreheads were almost touching. "That is not true, and you know it."

"I know nothing of the sort." She turned her head away from him, but he caught her chin and forced her to look up at him.

"I've never had the slightest desire to kiss a piece of fruit, or my boots, or a horse."

Lily rolled her eyes. "My relief knows no bounds."

His hand dropped to her waist, then he gave the

curve of her hip a blatant caress. "I want you, Lily. In my life and in my bed, but I will not lie to get what I want by saying I am madly in love. You have my friendship, my respect, and my affections. Those are stable emotions that make for a stable marriage. I do not want a marriage based on something as fleeting and fickle as what you think of as love."

"How can you be so cold and callous about emotions of the heart?"

He reached up and caught one of her tears on the tip of his finger, his expression grim as he rubbed the moisture between his finger and thumb. "I've learned that it's best not to delude oneself about love." The anger in his expression faded, leaving only regret. "Now I almost wish I had lied to you. The truth is painful. I'm sorry, Lily. Let me make it up to you. Let me show you that what we have is enough."

Too late she realized his intent. He lowered his head and captured her lips. Slow and drugging, he caressed her mouth more than kissed it. The gentle, insistent pressure of his hand at the nape of her neck kept her from turning away, but he didn't demand her response. He coaxed it from her. His hands stroked a path down her back, then tightened on her hips, drawing her closer to his heat. The intimate contact sent a spark of desire through her. She managed to pull away. "I don't want to mate."

He murmured his answer against the smooth column of her neck. "Neither do I. We are going to make love."

"You can't *make* love unless you are *in* love." Her voice sounded almost frantic. The kisses he brushed against the hollow of her throat made her pulse beat faster and faster.

"You are wrong about that."

The last of his words were smothered against her lips. He kissed her until her knees went weak, then he lifted her into his arms and carried her to the bed.

"I don't think we should do this." She wondered how

he could keep kissing her while he undressed them both. "I would like some time to think over what you told me."

"You can have all the time you want." His hands continued to work at the fastenings of his breeches. "Tomorrow. In the coach."

"I would like some time now." She braced her hands against his shoulders, but her grip somehow turned into a caress. Even as her brows drew together in a frown, her hands brushed downward until she reached the round, flat discs of male nipples. They hardened instantly beneath her palms. Curious, she repeated the motion and he groaned. His dark eyes were lit by an inner fire and she knew his answer even before he shook his head.

"Tomorrow."

He captured her mouth for another kiss and she forgot everything but the pleasure he gave her. He knew exactly how to increase her need, where to touch her, the places to kiss her. At the same time, he taught her how to give the pleasure she received until they both needed more. Then he caressed her with his entire body, deep and slow at first, both aware of every exquisite movement, his dark eyes locked with hers to focus entirely on their joining. He held her gaze for what seemed an impossible length of time, a trance that held her motionless as he moved inside her, the only sound an occasional gasp when he came too close to her core, too close to the flame that would soon engulf them both. He began to swell inside her, filling her more completely with each stroke. His incredible body became a contradiction; strength and power held in check, so gentle that the beauty and tenderness of his lovemaking brought tears to her eyes.

Her eyes widened and a sound of rapture escaped her lips to mingle with his masculine groan and still he held her gaze, letting her see the violent joy of his release. In that moment she finally understood the silent message he communicated with his body and with his eyes.

He'd just made love to her.

Seventeen

✦

$\mathcal{I}$t was the hour before dawn. Not quite night, but not yet day. Remmington lay on his side to watch his wife sleep. He pressed a kiss to her bare shoulder while his hand explored the lush curves of her hip. She turned away from him, but shifted closer until she'd fit her body perfectly against his. He pressed another kiss against her shoulder as he continued his exploration. He wanted to know every part of her, the shape and structure of delicate bones and feminine curves, every inch of her velvety skin. He brushed his cheek against her hair and breathed deep of her scent, then held his breath to memorize that part of her as well.

In a different time and place he would keep her in his bed day and night until he cured himself of this constant need to touch her. But it wasn't just lust that created that need. Just holding her gave him pleasure, a sense of contentment he'd never known.

In this time and place he couldn't afford to indulge his odd whims. He brushed his lips across her shoulder once more, then forced himself away from her tempting warmth. The room was still more shadow than light, but enough light that he could study her face as he dressed, even as he wondered over his strange fascination with her.

"Lily?" He put his hand on her shoulder and gave her a gentle nudge. "Lily, it's time to get dressed."

Her lashes fluttered open and her lips curved into a sleepy smile. As her gaze traveled higher, so did the covers. By the time she met his gaze, she had the bed quilt pulled up to her chin, her enchanting smile no more than a memory. The wary light in her eyes made him frown.

He turned away to stuff the clothing he wore the day before into a satchel. "I'm going to find my men and make sure they are prepared to leave. Jack made arrangements last night to have an early breakfast made ready for us. I will return in no more than a quarter of an hour to take you downstairs for our meal." He finished packing and turned to leave. "Be certain to bolt the door behind me."

Remmington spared her only a brief glance before he left the room. Her somber expression made him feel guilty, reminded him of her unanswered declaration of love the night before. No matter how much she sulked, she wouldn't change his mind or his feelings about this marriage. Lust and desire were all perfectly fine in bed, but he would not base their marriage on such flimsy foundations. He'd made that mistake once before, and if nothing else he was a man who learned from his mistakes. The heady emotions of her infatuation would fade soon enough. The day would come when she would wonder what she had ever seen in him to inspire such yearnings.

They would settle into a comfortable routine, he decided. One that would continue whenever she decided to come to her senses and realized that they were lucky to have affection and friendship between them, that few couples in society were as fortunate. They could be friends and confidants during the day, lovers at night. Only at night.

After all, he was not a man ruled by the fleeting emotions of passion. He could control the urge to go back to that room and make love to her for hours on end. He could ignore his body's response to the sight of her sleepy, inviting smile. His restraint would prove the stability of his emotions. Getting her to Remmington Castle was much more important than his body's momentary craving, and he wouldn't let it distract him.

He waited outside their door until he heard her drive the bolt home, then he turned and made his way down the staircase. A handful of the inn's patrons had opted for cheaper berths in the pub room, and the sounds of male snoring confirmed that most were still asleep. He paused for a moment at the bottom of the stairs and stared across the room to the door that led to the stables.

An hour or two's delay wouldn't put them seriously behind schedule. As Lily pointed out, they had a good day's start on any notices that might reach the papers. Still, that wasn't the only reason for his hurry. Remmington Castle had represented safety for countless generations of his family, and it seemed ingrained in him to seek the protection of the fortress in times of trouble. He wanted Lily away from danger, to a place where she would be safe from any threat.

An odd sensation tingled up his spine, followed by an urge to forget about the coach and return to his wife. This time it wasn't lust, but a protective impulse to make sure she was all right. Just as he began to turn around, the door opened and two of his outriders stepped into the pub room.

Mindful of the other patrons, his men bowed a silent greeting. In a low voice, Remmington ordered the men to guard the door to his chamber until he returned. Even though he knew the door was safely locked, he didn't want Lily alone in this place. For a moment he considered sending one of the men to the stables in his place, then decided that Lily might think he returned for something other than her safety. There was little doubt that she would be right.

Yesterday morning he'd nearly slit his own throat as he caught tantalizing glimpses of his wife while he shaved, his mirror at a perfect angle to watch her every movement. When she disappeared behind the dressing screen, he'd strained to hear each small sound she made. His imagination had conjured up the articles of clothing she donned, what they would feel like against her skin as she slipped them on, a delicious mental image of the parts of her they covered. When she stepped around the screen, fully clothed, he'd wanted nothing more than to strip her naked again. Slowly. Very, very slowly. The room upstairs lacked even a dressing screen. He could watch her as she dressed, look at every inch of her lovely body and remember what she felt like when he touched her. He could even touch her if he wanted. Oh, he would touch her, all right. He would wait until she had her clothing in place, each button fastened just so, then he would—

He would go to the stables. Right now. He had important business in the stables. He just couldn't recall what it might be at the moment.

In the stables, Jack had already fed the horses and checked the harnesses and rigging. Remmington reviewed the map Jack carried in the coach as they discussed the day's journey. Jack was extolling the virtues of a particular inn along their route when the stable door burst open, startling the horses as much as the men inside. It was one of the outriders he'd sent to guard Lily. The frantic expression on the outrider's face brought Remmington to his feet.

"Your Grace! You must come immediately! We heard voices inside your room, and I knocked on the door to ask if everything was all right, and a man's voice answered. He—he said to get away from the door or he would shoot your wife!"

Remmington was already running toward the inn, the outrider blurting out the story behind him. He raced through the public room to the stairway and bounded up the steps three at a time. Their door was at the end of the hallway and a few curious guests stood in the corridor, as well as the innkeeper, who wore a worried expression. He tried to stop Remmington as he passed, but Remmington pushed him aside, so forcefully that the man slammed against the wall.

The second outrider stood in front of the bedchamber's door, both pistols drawn, one ear pressed against the solid oak. As soon as he caught sight of Remmington, he stepped away from the doorway.

"He's been carrying on in there since Tom went to fetch you," he said in a hushed voice. "He keeps telling your wife that he is here to save her."

"Give me your cloak," Remmington ordered. "And your pistols." While the outrider stripped off his cloak, he turned to the innkeeper. "Did anyone ask about us after we arrived last night?"

"Aye." The innkeeper rubbed his dazed head. "About an hour after you arrived, a gentleman showed up and said he was your cousin, that he wanted a room near yours so he could find you this morning." He pointed to the room directly across the hall from Remmington's. "I put him in there. He looked like a gentleman and he sounded on the up-and-up. I swear, I never would have—"

Remmington cut him off with a single glare. He swung the outrider's cloak over his shoulders, then took the pistols, the one in his right hand held in plain sight. The cloak covered his left arm and concealed the other pistol. He stepped closer to the door. "Lily? Are you all right?"

For a moment there was silence, then a man's voice called out. "Is that you, Remmington?"

"Yes." Remmington's mouth drew to a thin line. The

voice sounded familiar, but he couldn't put a face to it. With a nod of his head, he gave his outrider a silent order to open the door. "I'm coming inside."

The door was unlocked, and the outrider pushed it open before the man inside the room could object. Remmington stepped through the doorway and braced himself for what he would find on the other side.

Lily stood near the center of the room, dressed in her nightgown and robe. Her assailant stood behind her, holding her by the hair, the muzzle of his pistol pressed against her temple.

His heart stopped beating.

A strange sense of calm washed over him, bringing the two people before him into sharp focus. Everything else in the room faded into a gray haze at the edge of his vision, every fiber of his being attuned to the man who threatened Lily. He saw Lily's head jerk back, pulled by the vicious grip on her hair. That act stirred an emotion he'd never experienced, couldn't identify. It began in his chest, a strange coiling sensation like that of a snake ready to strike. His entire body tensed, every muscle aware of what it must do, his entire being focused on the enemy. He'd never felt so in control.

He cocked his right arm so the pistol angled harmlessly toward the ceiling, then he pushed the door closed with one foot. He even smiled at the man who held his wife. "Good morning, Lord Allen. I believe a few explanations are in order."

"Place your pistol on the floor, Remmington."

The order came as no surprise. The look of desperation in George Allen's eyes made him comply with the demand. He lowered the weapon to the floor without making any sudden movements. He straightened again in the same fluid motion and waited, his gaze fixed on the center of Allen's forehead. He wouldn't so much as glance at Lily. The look of terror he'd glimpsed in her face would break his concentration.

"I'm taking her away from you," Allen said, his defiant words at odds with the way his voice quavered.

The threat didn't disturb Remmington. He knew Allen would not leave this room alive.

Allen's voice rose to a near-hysterical pitch. "You will never put your filthy hands on her again, Remmington. I saved her from Osgoode, and I'll save her from you. She's mine now. She will always be mine."

Somehow he knew he had to keep Allen talking, that speaking in a rational tone would calm him down enough to move the gun away from Lily's head. Yet a new fear took hold, one he hadn't considered until that moment. In Allen's nervous excitement, he might accidentally tighten his grip on the trigger. Remmington summoned every ounce of his control to keep his voice composed, his expression bland. "You don't have to go to such drastic measures, Allen. You are frightening Lily. I'm unarmed now. Take the gun away from her head and we can discuss the situation like gentlemen."

"No!" Allen let go of Lily's hair to wrap his arm around her neck. "You turned her against me, you bastard. I came here right after you left this morning. I told her that I loved her, that I would make sure you never touched her again. Do you know what she told me?" Allen's face twisted into a sneer and he tightened his arm around her neck in a sharp, jerking motion. "She told me you were *married*."

Allen squeezed his eyes closed, his expression that of a man tormented. When his eyes opened again, they glowed with madness. Remmington knew then that there would be no calm discussion of the situation. George Allen was insane.

"She was supposed to be mine, Remmington. No one can have her but me." His gaze slid to Lily and he rubbed his cheek against her hair in a loverlike caress that set Remmington's teeth on edge. "I always thought we would be married, Lily, but this way is even better. I promise to make it quick and painless, darling. You won't even know what happened."

Remmington's blood turned to ice.

"He will shoot me then," Allen said, with a nod toward Remmington. "I'm going to die for you, Lily. We will be together always."

"There is another way you can have her," Remmington said, almost before Allen finished his obscene threat. It wasn't a logical argument, but Remmington knew he wasn't dealing with a logical man. "If you kill me, she will be a widow. You can still marry her."

"No!" Lily cried. "Don't hurt him!"

Allen silenced her with a jerk of his arm, but the muzzle of his gun shifted away from her temple. He changed his mind almost immediately and the gun came to rest against her head once more.

"You would never sacrifice yourself for a woman, not even Lily," Allen scoffed. "What are you playing at, Remmington?"

"I'm the one you really want to hurt. I took Lily away from you. If you shoot her now, she will die as my wife. She will be *mine*, Allen."

"No! You don't deserve her!"

The gun turned so that the muzzle rested alongside Lily's temple rather than pointed straight at her head. Still too close. Remmington drew a deep breath and took the biggest gamble of his life. "Don't you want her, Allen? Aren't you man enough to do what you must to have her?"

"Shut up!" Allen screamed. "You can't talk about her that way!"

"Don't you want to know her as intimately as I know her?" he taunted. "Don't you want to know what it is like to have her in your bed? Or are you afraid you aren't man enough for her?"

"Shut up, *shut up!*"

The moment the muzzle moved away from Lily's head, Remmington raised the hidden pistol and fired. A second blast exploded in the room and Remmington felt a rush of air as Allen's shot lodged in the wall behind him. The thick, choking smoke of gunpowder filled the room, and an eerie silence descended in the aftermath of the deafening reports.

Remmington dropped his pistol and rushed forward through the haze. He found Lily on the floor, dragged there by Allen's hold around her neck. He pushed Allen's arm away and snatched Lily away from the fallen man. With the edge of his cloak he wiped the blood from her face, his vision blurred until he realized that none of the blood was her own. He wanted to crush her against his chest and hold her until the fear that coursed through his blood spent itself. He didn't want her in this room another moment, where she could see what he had done. The door burst open as he lifted her into his arms.

"Take care of this," he ordered Jack, with a sharp nod toward George Allen. He kept walking toward the door then out into the hallway, his gaze searching then finding the innkeeper. "Show us to a room as far from this one as possible. Now!"

The innkeeper almost ran to stay ahead of Remmington's long strides. He led them up another flight of stairs to the third floor, then to a large, airy room at the end of the long hallway.

Remmington gave the room a cursory glance then turned again to the innkeeper. "I want a bath brought up, and send one of my men with our baggage."

"Yes, Your Grace." The innkeeper bobbed his head, but he froze when his gaze moved to Lily. "Your wife! She needs a doctor!"

"My wife is not injured," he said in an even voice, the look he gave the innkeeper filled with silent rage. "Bring plenty of water and extra towels."

"Yes, Your Grace." The innkeeper fled, slamming the door behind him.

Remmington crossed the room and sat on the bed. He held Lily in his arms, but he couldn't hold her tight enough, close enough. He made himself look at her, at the horror of what he'd done to her. He began to pray, a prayer that she was still in shock, too numbed by the experience to know what she saw. She would know soon enough.

"Get it off me," she whispered, her eyes clenched shut. Her voice was very soft, nearly hysterical.

A muscle in his jaw twitched and he tightened his arms around her. "I can't, darling. Not until they bring something to wash with. It won't be long now. I promise." He felt her begin to tremble and he closed his eyes. She was alive. That was all that mattered. Yet there was one last fear. "Tell me you didn't look at him when it was over. God, Lily, tell me you didn't see that."

He said another silent prayer of thanks when she shook her head against his chest. At least she would be spared that memory. The sight of Lily held fast in that nightmare would haunt his nights for years to come.

He knew before he crossed the room that he'd fired with deadly accuracy. The bullet had ripped through the middle of Allen's forehead. An instant death, but a gory one. Held fast in Allen's deathgrip, Lily was splattered with the unspeakable mess. He'd wiped her face as best he could, but the cloak had only smeared the blood. It fouled her everywhere; her hair, her robe, her skin. A tremor shook through him. Where the hell was that innkeeper with the water?

A soft knock at their door seemed a response to his silent question. Remmington called out, and the innkeeper appeared again in the doorway, followed by two men who carried a brass hip bath. They placed the tub in the center of the room as more servants appeared with towels and buckets of steaming water. An outrider carried in their baggage, then positioned himself outside the door to stand guard.

When they were finally left alone, Remmington carried Lily to a chair that one of the servants had pulled up next to the hip bath. She didn't want to let go of him. Her fingers were clenched in tight fists around his lapels, and it took a surprising effort to free himself. He left her for only a moment to lock the door, then he knelt down beside her to untie the robe and push the ruined garment off her shoulders. She sat quietly as he worked, her limbs as disjointed as a rag doll's as he freed her arms from the garment. He picked up one of the towels and plunged it into a bucket of warm water. He'd avoided looking at her face until that moment, steeled himself for what he would see, but the sight wrenched at his gut anyway.

It wasn't her blood. She was safe. That litany repeated itself over and over in his mind as he wiped the damp towel over her face and neck. He had to wash away her horror, cleanse her of this abomination. He opened the front of her nightgown, ripping the fragile material to the hem. He pushed that soiled garment to the floor as well.

His hands were gentle as he lifted her into the hip bath, as unaware of her nudity as he would be of his own. He lowered her into the tub, soaking the sleeves of his jacket and shirt in the process. Glancing down at his clothes, he realized they were also bloodstained where he'd held her. His hands moved over the buttons, and he shrugged his jacket and shirt aside. Lily drew her knees to her chest, curling herself into a protective ball.

"No, sweetheart." His grip on her shoulders was firm yet gentle as he forced her to lean back. He slipped the pins from her hair until it fell loose over the end of the tub, then he cupped the back of her head with one hand and pressed the other against her forehead. "Hold your head there for just a moment. That's it," he encouraged her, as he dragged an empty bucket beneath her hair. She closed her eyes when he poured ladles full of warm water over her hair. He pressed her further down into the water so she could prop her head against the back of the tub as he worked a bar of soap into the wet tresses. After he rinsed her hair, she reached up to take the soap from him. She worked the soap between her hands, then scrubbed furiously at her face and neck, repeating the same actions over and over. Just when he thought to stop her, she leaned forward and washed the soap away.

"Is it all gone?" she asked, wiping the water from her eyes.

"It's gone," he murmured.

He helped her to her feet and steadied her as she

stepped from the tub. She reached for a towel, but he insisted on drying her, as impersonal at that chore as he was at her bath. In her satchel he found a chemise that he slipped over her head, then he tilted her chin up and looked into her eyes.

It was the first time she'd met his gaze since the shooting. He stared long and hard, letting himself drown in her sherry-colored eyes. The look of blank terror was gone. She would be all right. He repeated that reassurance to himself as he impressed the image of her face upon his mind, remembering the moment when he thought he might never see her look up at him ever again.

She'd very nearly died before his eyes.

It was a vile thought, too foul to contemplate. He smoothed his hands over her shoulders and down her arms to grip her by the elbows, needing to hold her, to have that small assurance that she was safe and sound.

She seemed to read his mind. "Hold me."

He enfolded her in his arms, a precious treasure he'd almost lost. She laid her cheek against his chest, soothing yet intensifying the ache he discovered there. He rested his chin against her damp hair, then turned his head to lay his cheek upon the crown of her head, content until she began to shiver. He lifted her into his arms and carried her to the bed, placed her gently beneath the covers. They lay side by side, her head resting on his shoulder, his arms holding her tight against him. Then she began to cry.

"It's all right," he murmured. "Don't hold it inside, sweetheart. Let yourself cry."

If the bath had cleansed her body, he reasoned the tears would cleanse her soul. She soaked his chest with them. He finally had to leave her just long enough to retrieve a towel. The crying went on and on, sometimes almost silent, at other times wrenching sobs.

"It's over now. He can't hurt you ever again."

She propped herself up on one elbow and gazed down at him. Her eyes were red from tears, her voice hoarse from crying. "I've made you kill a man. There will be an inquest." She collapsed again on his chest and held him tight. "There might be a trial! Oh, Miles. What if you are sent to prison?"

In the aftermath of an attack that would leave most women hysterical for days, Lily's greatest concern was his safety. Her words rendered him speechless. At length he recovered himself and began to stroke her hair. "Calm yourself, Lily. There will be no trial. I forbid you to worry about something that will not transpire."

"But—"

He shifted her from his chest and pressed a kiss against her forehead. "There will be an inquest, but there are plenty of witnesses who will attest to the fact that Allen's mind was unhinged. He burst into our room this morning a raving lunatic, threatening us both with a pistol. It was a simple case of self-defense, and that is all the authorities will ever know of the matter."

"But that isn't how it happened."

"That is exactly how it happened. No one else needs to know about Allen's other attacks. They will only make for more gossip. Allen was insane, yet anyone who was not present this morning might begin to wonder what a man was doing alone in a bedroom with my wife. Speculation might turn ugly about why that man is now dead. You will assure anyone who asks that I was present when George Allen entered our room."

Lily's eyes grew wide. "There were others in the hallway. What if one of them tells a different version?"

"There is only one version. The one I just told you." He knew there were ways to ensure as much. "I am serious, Lily. I do not want you to worry about the inquest. It will not take place for days, then it will be over in little more than an hour."

"Will we have to stay here until then?"

He shook his head. "No one from here to London has the authority to question anything I do. We will have to return to Town."

Lily looked thoughtful for a time. Her expression

grew more downcast by the moment. "The gossip. Once people find out about this, the scandal will be awful. I don't know how I will face anyone."

"With me by your side," he said surely. "Nothing will be as bad as it seems, Lily. Trust me." He was glad that she didn't dwell on the subject of Allen's death. She was alive, and now she was safe. Those were the two thoughts uppermost on his mind, and they were all he wanted to think about for the time being. "Close your eyes and try to rest, sweetheart. It will do you good to sleep for awhile."

She frowned up at him, but settled obediently at his side. She was silent so long that he began to think she'd actually fallen asleep. Then he heard her whisper.

"I was very afraid until you came to rescue me. Then you frightened me half to death when you started to goad him. I didn't know you had a second pistol. When I heard the first shot I thought—" Her voice broke and she hugged herself closer to his chest. "I thought he'd killed you! Please, don't ever frighten me that way again."

Remmington didn't reply. A madman threatened to kill her, yet she'd feared for her husband's life? He stared up at the ceiling and wondered if she would ever know that a part of him did die when he saw Allen's gun at her head. It was a very small, cynical part of his heart that thought itself incapable of love.

Eighteen

---❖---

$\mathcal{L}$ily awoke the next morning in her room at Remmington's town house. She didn't remember much of their journey to London, only that Remmington held her in his arms the entire time. She'd drifted in and out of sleep, overcome by an exhaustion more of the mind than the body. Of their arrival at the town house, she remembered nothing at all.

The familiar room gave her a sense of comfort. Nothing in the lavender-scented bedchamber had changed during her absence. She found her striped pink gown still hanging in the armoire. She found Remmington in the library with her father and Sir Malcolm. The gentlemen all rose to greet her.

"Lily!" The earl took a step forward, then stopped. "You are unhurt? Allen didn't harm you?"

She gave him a reassuring smile. "I'm fine, Papa."

Remmington wasn't as reserved. He crossed the room

to give her hand a brief kiss, his expression concerned. "You should rest today, Lily. I didn't wake you because I thought this meeting might be too upsetting for you."

"I feel quite fine," she assured him. "If you wouldn't mind, I would like to hear what my father and Sir Malcolm have to say about ... the incident yesterday."

His brows drew together in a frown. "I don't want you upset again."

"Nonsense. I am stronger than you think, my lord."

The nod he gave her seemed reluctant, but he led her to his seat behind the desk and stood at her side, one hand resting on the back of her chair. That seemed to signal her acceptance in the group.

"Remmington just told us what happened at the Brass Ring," the earl said. "I cannot believe George Allen was at the heart of this dreadful business."

"He must have slipped out sometime during the Ashlands' ball, then returned again without notice," Bainbridge surmised.

Crofford shuddered. "Good God. I let him into my house. Lily was upstairs the entire time. I cannot believe he had the nerve to ask for my permission to court her!"

Bainbridge's brows drew together in a puzzled frown. "What I cannot understand is why he didn't ask permission to court Lily before he attacked her. She was clearly unattached at that time."

"Who knows how a madman's mind works?" Remmington asked. "I can assure you both that he was insane."

"I believe I will have another talk with Lord Ashland," Bainbridge mused. "He said that he played cards with Allen until shortly after dawn the night of his ball, but I did not think to ask what time the game started. I will speak with Allen's servants as well. They might know something that could shed more light on this situation." He twisted the silver handle of his cane in an absent rhythm, his tone speculative. "Have you notified the authorities of Allen's death?"

"I thought it best to inform the two of you first," Remmington replied.

Bainbridge nodded. "I will take care of the details and notify the King's Bench. The inquest will be little more than a formality, but I will be happy to attend if you wish."

"I would appreciate your support," Remmington said. "It seems obvious that Allen was our man, but until you verify his whereabouts on the night of Lily's attack I intend to keep a close eye on my wife. I won't risk her safety again. With our recent marriage, no one will think it unusual if we do not go about in society for a week or two."

"I agree," Crofford joined in. "We cannot be too careful until we know for certain."

"I happen to disagree," Lily said. "Lord Allen was obviously the man behind the mask. I don't see why I should be kept under guard, when there is no longer—"

"You won't be locked away," Remmington cut in. "We will simply stay close to home until we make certain the man who attacked you is dead." He gave her a look that said he would not be argued with on the matter.

Lily decided that staying in seclusion and spending time alone with her new husband was nothing to complain about. She gave him an agreeable, wifely nod.

As things turned out, Remmington and Bainbridge were right about the inquest, and she'd had little reason to worry. The lord chief justice and his magistrates arrived at the town house two days after their return to London. Lily was serving afternoon tea to Sir Malcolm and her husband when Digsby announced their arrival. Remmington made it clear that she was to excuse herself from the gentlemen's company. She did so with great reluctance.

"Your Grace?" Digsby asked.

Lily felt a surge of guilt as she lifted her ear from the library door and whirled around to face the servant. She kept her voice low so the men inside the library wouldn't overhear her. "Yes, Digsby?"

"You do not need to remain here, Your Grace. I will inform you when the meeting adjourns."

"The gentlemen might want more tea," she said. "I'll just wait here in case they do."

"That is my duty, madam."

From inside the library, she heard a muffled voice. *"I'm certain this is nothing more than a formality, Your Grace. If you would be so good as to explain the events that led up to the incident."*

Lily glanced up in time to see Digsby straighten, as if she'd caught him straining to hear the justice's words. "Afraid you might miss something, Digsby?"

He didn't bat an eye. "Yes, madam."

"Very well." She stepped to one side of the double doors. "Today we shall share this duty."

They stood side by side at the doors, listening to the proceedings inside the room. Jack wandered by on his way to the kitchens, but stopped in his tracks at the sight of the duchess and Digsby with their ears pressed to the library door. When Lily caught sight of him, she lifted one finger to her lips and waved him on his way with the other hand.

In the end, Remmington was absolved of any responsibility for Lord Allen's death. Allen was judged temporarily insane for reasons unknown. If the officials thought it odd that Allen happened to be at the same secluded inn as Remmington and Lily when he turned irrational, they made no mention of the curiosity. Nor did anyone raise the question of what had provoked Allen's attack. Lily surmised that there were certain benefits to be had when one bore a title second only to the royal family's. The entire incident was written off as a clear case of self-defense. The dreaded inquest was over in less than an hour.

Just before the library door opened, Digsby stepped away to retrieve the visitors' cloaks and hats. Lily pretended to rearrange the large bouquet of roses that stood on a polished oak table nearby.

The judge and magistrates made their farewells while Remmington stood in the doorway of the library. After they left, he turned his gaze to Lily. She thought he looked a little suspicious of her lingering presence in the hallway.

"Sir Malcolm and I have a few matters to discuss, Lily. Why don't you send a message to your father that the inquest is over." One brow lifted, but otherwise his expression didn't change. "I'm sure you are already aware of the outcome."

Lily didn't deny the accusation. She gave him a weak smile before he disappeared behind the library doors. She took a step forward, then froze in midstep when the doors opened again. The smile she plastered on her face felt guilty as sin.

"Now would be a good time to send that message, Lily."

She lowered her head and brushed some nonexistent dust from her gown. "As you wish."

He waited until she turned and walked toward the sitting room. She heard the soft click as the library doors closed again behind her. She whispered an order as she passed Digsby in the hallway. "I want to know every word."

Half an hour later, Digsby presented himself in the sitting room with an ornate silver tea set balanced on the tray he carried. "Your tea, madam."

"Is Remmington still in the library?" Lily hoped her husband would want to share whatever he had discussed with Bainbridge. Her hopes crumpled when Digsby shook his head.

"His Grace and Sir Malcolm departed for their club." He placed the tray on a table near Lily, then took several steps backward until he stood in the doorway, ready to take his leave. "His Grace did mention that he would be dining at home tonight at the usual time."

She gave him a broad hint. "How unfortunate that I

could not be present at the meeting between my husband and Sir Malcolm. I am more than a little curious about what they discussed."

Digsby straightened his jacket with a sharp tug, took a step backward into the hallway, looked in both directions, then stepped back into the room.

Lily smiled. "Digsby, you may close the door if you wish."

"Madam, in this house, open doors offer a greater degree of privacy than closed ones."

She inclined her head in a solemn gesture. "You are correct, of course."

"Had Her Grace been present at the meeting behind the library doors, she would know that Sir Malcolm informed His Grace that Lord Ashland is on a hunting trip in Scotland and will not return for another week. Until that time, he cannot verify that Lord Allen did not leave the Ashlands' ball at any time on the night of Her Grace's first attack. However, Lord Allen's servants did inform Sir Malcolm that his lordship was not at home the night Sir Malcolm's guards spotted a man lurking outside Crofford House."

"I see." Lily felt a profound sense of relief. Her life was finally her own again. Yet she also felt a new wariness settle itself into her heart. Remmington no longer had a reason to stay so close by her side. "Is that all I would hear, assuming of course that I had been present at this meeting?"

"No, Your Grace. You would also know that Lord Allen's footman delivered a note to Lord Osgoode's residence the evening before that gentleman's death. The next morning, Lord Allen left the house very early for what he referred to as a 'dawn engagement.'"

Lily sat down on a small brocaded chair as the meaning of Digsby's words took hold. Osgoode had died at the hands of George Allen, with every possibility that she was the cause.

"His Grace also mentioned that he felt the matter at a close," Digsby added. Perhaps it was her imagination, but she thought she heard a note of compassion in Digsby's voice. "He expressed his relief as well, that you could put your worries about the affair to rest."

She would rather hear Remmington reassure her on that point. At least Digsby had the courtesy to tell her. "Thank you, Digsby. I appreciate your insight on the matter."

He bowed, then left Lily alone with her thoughts.

"There is no longer any need to keep ourselves in seclusion," Remmington announced at dinner that night.

With a single look, he told Digsby to refill his glass of port. Lily found that unusual in that he never drank more than one glass of wine with dinner, and they'd just started the main course. She glanced at her plate as she lifted a forkful of spring peas, with another covert look at the positioning of her gown. She'd dressed in deep purple silk that night, the gown's square bodice cut so low that she feared she would fall out of it. Remmington took no notice of the gown, her discomfort, or anything else about her appearance. She already regretted the extra time she'd spent on her hair and clothing when it seemed obvious he didn't appreciate the effort.

One of the peas began to roll off her fork and she tried to correct its balance. She knew a moment of horror when it rolled off the fork in the opposite direction. The pea landed on her chest and disappeared into the cleavage created by the tight bodice of her gown. At the same moment she heard Remmington choke on his wine. She glanced up to see him wiping his face with his napkin, checking his sleeves and jacket for further damage. She took advantage of his distraction to retrieve the errant pea and slip it between the charger and her plate. Digsby remained at his place near the buffet, his gaze on some unknown spot near the chandelier. She released a slow sigh of relief. No one had noticed her mishap.

Remmington cleared his throat. "Yes, well. As I was saying, there is no longer any reason to keep to ourselves.

I happened to run into your father at White's this afternoon, and he mentioned that he would like to host a ball in our honor the week after next. It seems the ideal opportunity to make our formal bow to society as a couple."

That news surprised her. "Papa hasn't hosted a ball since my mother died."

"Yes, he mentioned that fact. He also asked if he might impose upon you to help with some of the planning. Musicians, refreshments, invitations, and whatnot. He intends to ask Lady Bainbridge and Miss Stanhope to act as hostesses, if Miss Stanhope feels recovered enough by that time to attend. However, he felt the planning might be too much for them to take on, considering Miss Stanhope's weakened condition."

"Sophie and Lady Bainbridge won't return from Holybrook House for another two days," Lily said. "I received a note from Sophie today. She sounds much recovered, but I don't think she will feel up to planning a ball. I'll call on Papa tomorrow to begin the arrangements."

"Very well."

"I hope Sophie can manage a visit to my seamstress," she mused. "I will need a new gown for the occasion, but I never know what style or fabrics to choose. Sophie has a good eye for that sort of thing."

"I don't think you should force your friend to sit through a fitting and hours at a seamstress's shop." Remmington glanced up and she wondered if he hadn't indulged in too much wine. There was a slightly glazed look about his eyes. He picked up his fork and knife, then cut into a slice of roast beef, his attention focused on the task. "Why don't you arrange to have the fitting here at the house? I happen to have a certain eye for fashion myself, and I would be happy to lend my opinion."

She was a little surprised that he showed any interest in the matter. "Are you certain you wouldn't mind?"

He didn't say anything for a long moment, then he shrugged. "Not at all."

A quarter of an hour later, he finished his third serving of port and set the glass aside, a signal that the meal was at an end. She laid her napkin down and stood up as well, then he escorted her from the dining room. He released her hand when they reached the staircase.

"I have some papers that need my attention in the library," he said. "I will join you upstairs in an hour or two."

She tried to hide her disappointment with a forced smile. He'd made the same excuse the night before, and he hadn't joined her for nearly four hours, rather than one or two. "I shall see you then, my lord."

She was asleep by the time he came to her bed. He had her nightgown removed before she was fully awake.

"I did not think you were coming." Her voice sounded breathless. He brushed her hair aside to press light, sensuous kisses against her neck. "I know I've occupied most of your time these past weeks. Are you terribly far behind in your work?"

He made a hushing sound in the back of his throat. His hand stroked a path from the back of her knee, over her hip and waist, to settle against her breast. Then his hand moved lower and Lily soon forgot about his work, forgot about everything but the exquisite beauty of their lovemaking.

He held her for a long time afterward, and she lay very still in his arms. Each night he made love to her for hours, yet he also taught her how to return the pleasure he gave, to explore the passion they shared. She always fell asleep cradled in his arms, his hands stroking her hair or skin, his lips pressed against her forehead or temple. In the morning she always woke up alone.

When they first returned to the town house, she learned they wouldn't share a room when Digsby delivered her baggage to this one. She'd expected as much.

Only couples too poor to afford separate beds shared one—or those too much in love to be apart even at night. That certainly wasn't the case in her marriage. She rarely saw Remmington during the days. More and more, she saw him only at dinner, then afterward for a few hours in her bed. Each day he grew a little more reserved in her presence, a little more distant, the silences between them a little more uncomfortable. She pressed herself closer to his side, laid her hand over his chest to feel the steady beat of his heart, and knew in her own that she was losing him.

She bolstered her courage to ask him why. His hand continued to rub her back, gently massaging the muscles until she couldn't keep her eyelids more than half open. Her lips parted to ask the question, even as her eyes drifted closed. Moments before she was asleep, she felt him shift her onto the bed and ease his arm from beneath her shoulders. Her eyes wouldn't open, so she tried to reach for him. She couldn't seem to move, forgot why she wanted to in the first place until she felt his warm breath against her face. He pressed a soft kiss against her forehead, his words so soft that she could barely hear them.

"Goodnight, darling."

She smiled and fell asleep.

The next morning Lily ate another breakfast alone, wondering how Remmington managed to rise so early when he went to bed so late each night. He was in his library already, the door closed, with word to Digsby that he had important work to do and shouldn't be disturbed. She was almost beginning to anticipate that announcement from Digsby each morning.

After breakfast she went to the sitting room and composed a short note. In it she asked Remmington if he would take her on a ride through the park at three o'clock that afternoon. If he wouldn't make time in his day for her, she would have to schedule it. She refused to be ignored any longer. Her ploy of scheduling his time would be better than an outright confrontation, she decided. Their ride would present the perfect opportunity to broach the subject of his schedules and routines, and why he ignored her each day. She asked Digsby to deliver the note with Remmington's lunch, then departed a short time later to call on her father.

The plans for the ball and her father's company provided a welcome distraction. They spent the morning deciphering one of his Greek scrolls, then discussed the ball over lunch. She took her leave just before one o'clock, so she would have plenty of time to change and look her best for their ride.

When she walked into the town house, Remmington was just leaving. She continued into the foyer and waited for him at the foot of the staircase.

"Ah, there you are, Lily." He adjusted his cravat as he walked down the stairs, then stopped his descent one step short of the landing. His hand rested on the newel, a pose that emphasized the strong, handsome lines of his body. He wasn't dressed to go riding. "I left a note in your room. My brother arrived in Town last night, and I promised to meet him at White's this afternoon. We're having dinner there tonight as well. I hope you don't mind if we postpone our outing until another time."

She had to tilt her head back to look up at him. "I didn't know your brother was in Town."

"He sent a note around this morning. I'm afraid I committed to the engagement before I received your request."

Lily gritted her teeth. It seemed he wasn't so busy that Trevor couldn't disturb his precious privacy. That disturbed her plenty. "I see."

He gave her an indulgent smile. "If you are set on an afternoon outing, I'm certain Trevor will understand if I send my regrets."

"No," she said in a controlled voice. His suggestion would only make her feel as if she'd begged for his time. She would not beg. "That will not be necessary."

He began to walk past her, and she laid one hand

against his sleeve. "Have I done something to make you angry?"

He stared down at her hand, as if startled that she would be presumptive enough to touch him. "Of course not, Lily. I am not the least angry with you."

"It's just that you seem so ... so distant of late." Aware of Digsby, who hovered in the foyer behind them, she leaned closer so the servant wouldn't overhear her. Remmington leaned away, as if he could not bear to be near her. The reaction so surprised Lily that she forgot what she wanted to say.

"We are not becoming distant," he told her in a firm voice. "We are simply settling into a routine. Married couples do not need to live in one another's pockets." He glanced at the clock in the foyer. "I'm already late. You will have to excuse me."

He lifted her hand for an impersonal kiss, then turned and walked away. Lily stared after him in dumbfounded silence, her grip on the banister so tight that her knuckles turned white. The meaning of his schedules and pointed absences became suddenly clear. Remmington was using his bent for order and routine as an excuse to turn their marriage into one typical of the *ton*. He expected them to go their own way during the day and meet only at night, for only one purpose. She wondered if he would be a "considerate" husband once she became pregnant, and ignore her completely.

The sound of the front door as it closed behind him seemed to shake her from her thoughts. She lifted her chin and marched up the stairs. Remmington wanted a marriage of convenience. He was about to be sorely disappointed. She didn't have any intention of being the least bit convenient until he admitted that a real marriage needed some measure of love to survive. And they *would* have a real marriage.

•   •   •

Remmington found his brother at a corner table of White's, his face buried behind a newspaper. Without waiting for an invitation, he sat down and poured himself a brandy.

The paper lowered slightly and Trevor peered over the top. "Just fine, thank you." He cocked his ear to one side. "What's that? Ah, yes, a perfectly dreadful trip. Rain from here to the border. My driver complained of his gout the entire time. And your tenant problems are solved, due in no small part to my Solomon-like wisdom. Thank you for asking."

"I am not in the mood for humor today," Remmington advised.

Trevor ignored the warning. His grin stretched from ear to ear as he laid his newspaper aside. "You've made quite a name for yourself in my absence, brother. All London is abuzz with gossip of your surprise marriage and subsequent duel with George Allen. Your reputation has moved from wicked to notorious." He inclined his head slightly. "My congratulations."

"It was not a duel," Remmington snapped. "At the time I shot Allen, he was threatening to shoot my wife."

The smile disappeared from Trevor's face. "Are you jesting?"

"No, I am not."

"I'd heard some odd rumors," he mused, "but I didn't give them credit. Most people are saying that Allen dealt you a grievous insult and was foolish enough to provoke you into a duel."

"I believe Sir Malcolm started that rumor," Remmington said. "It is the story I prefer. There would be a greater scandal if the truth came out."

"Don't tell me that your wife and George Allen . . ."

"No, it was nothing of the sort. Unfortunately, many would make that mistake."

"I see," Trevor mused. "You came to your wife's rescue and no one will ever know of your heroic efforts. Is that the reason for the long face tonight?"

Remmington's scowl darkened. He surprised both

himself and Trevor by admitting the truth. "My heroic efforts are part of the problem, but not their lack of appreciation. That wasn't Allen's only attack on my wife."

He summed up the events that took place since the night he met Lily. He ended with Allen's last ill-fated attempt to harm her. "Do you know what she said when it was over?"

Trevor shook his head, fascinated by the tale.

Remmington's hand tightened around his brandy glass. "She was afraid that Allen would shoot me. She cried because she thought I would be arrested for killing the bastard."

"It sounds as if she cares for you a great deal," Trevor said.

"She fancies herself in love with me." Remmington frowned. "At least, she did. Considering the current state of our marriage, I would no longer swear to that fact. I fear my attitude of late is a sore trial to her temper."

"You are surly because your wife loves you?" Trevor held up his hands in a baffled gesture. "Tell me I've missed something in your explanation of the problem."

"She only thinks she is in love. What she feels for me is nothing more than affection, and perhaps a certain measure of gratitude. I happened to be nearby on several occasions when she needed assistance, and I'm sure that influenced her feelings for me. When she realizes as much, she will appreciate the fact that I have not become the center of her life, nor she mine. We each have our own interests, and we do not need to rely upon one another to keep ourselves occupied."

Trevor leaned back in his chair. He folded his arms and stared at his brother. "You haven't told your wife that you are in love with her."

Remmington dismissed that with an impatient wave. "I am not in love with Lily."

"Did I ever mention the fact that you tap the arm of your chair when you are telling a lie?"

Remmington stopped tapping his fingers. "I do not care to continue this conversation."

"Why not?" Trevor's brow rose. "You said yourself that you are not in love with her. It sounds as if you are doing your damnedest to prove the fact to her. Do you think that will make things any easier when she turns to another for the affections you will not give her?"

"That is enough!" Several of the club's members turned in their chairs to stare at Remmington. He lowered his voice. "If you were not my brother, I would challenge you this instant."

"I am aware of that fact."

"Lily would never betray me that way. She is nothing like Catherine."

"I guessed as much."

Remmington sat back and regarded Trevor with wary silence.

"If she isn't like Catherine, then what are her flaws?" Trevor asked. "Is she spoiled or conceited, or so vain that she falls for the first man who pays her a compliment, the first moment her husband turns his back on her? Does she eye everything you own with the eye of a money-lender? Does she confide to her friends that she finds your infatuation with her amusing?" Trevor shook his head. "No, those flaws all belonged to Catherine, so Lily's must be even more repugnant."

"I would advise you to close your mouth. Now."

Trevor inclined his head as if to heed the warning. "I always take your advice, brother. A long time ago you told me that only a fool makes the same mistake twice. I never do. However, I believe you are about to make an entirely new mistake."

Remmington clenched his jaw, not about to admit that Trevor was right. That day at the Brass Ring, he'd realized that Lily could easily become the entire focus of his life, the very reason for his existence. He would never give a woman that much power over him. He'd returned to London with the good intentions of setting order to his marriage, of establishing a routine to insure its stability.

Something had gone dreadfully wrong. He sat in his

library for hours on end, accomplishing nothing more than blank stares at correspondence and political papers, lost in thoughts of his wife. He would wonder where she was and what she was doing, what she might be wearing the next time he saw her, more often imagining her when she wore nothing at all. Each hour turned into a battle to keep himself from her until dinner, when he could feast his eyes upon her.

At dinner he always waited until she looked away, then he watched every small movement she made, studied everything she wore, and imagined the clothing he couldn't see, the whisper-thin silk chemises with their dainty little straps and perfect tendency to cling to all the right parts of her. He mentally dressed and undressed her at his table until he couldn't concentrate on anything but the ache in his loins, knowing it would be hours before he could sate the need she stirred in him. Each night she refined the torture a little more by wearing a gown cut tighter or lower, or reaching for her wine glass in a way that revealed a shocking amount of bare flesh, or dropping a small pea from her fork to let it roll down the luscious cleft of her breasts until it came to rest inside her bodice. He'd wanted to retrieve that dainty morsel for her. With the tip of his tongue. Each dinner lasted a lifetime, yet it never lasted long enough. He wanted more and more and more. He made himself take less and less.

Each night he forced himself back to his library for more brooding until he felt certain she would be asleep when he joined her in bed. He'd known from the start that he couldn't go to her room when she was awake, when she would gaze at him with her heart in her eyes. It would be too easy to deceive himself, to think that she would always love him this way. Yet what if she did? What if she looked at him every day of his life, her eyes brimming with love for him?

He recalled what she had looked like when he left her that afternoon, the sherry-colored pools of bruised pride. He'd done that to her deliberately, to keep her at arm's length, away from his heart. Somehow he'd forgotten that she was insightful enough to figure that out for herself. Oh God, what if it was too late? The mistake made?

He set his brandy glass down with an abrupt thump. "You will excuse me, Trevor. I just recalled a matter that needs my attention."

Lily stared across the library, unable to believe her eyes. She hadn't quite believed Digsby, either, when he told her that a gentleman caller awaited her in the library. She'd almost admonished him for allowing a gentleman into the house while her husband was not at home, until she heard his name: Sebastian Lacroix.

The door closed behind her with a dull thud. Robert turned at the sound and they both took a moment to study the other.

"Marriage agrees with you, Lily."

"Oh, Robert! You are safe!" Lily launched herself across the room and into his arms.

"Umph!" He staggered a few theatrical steps backward. "I see you've not lost a bit of your strength, now that you are a proper married lady."

She pushed against his chest, but kept her fingers wrapped around his lapels, needing to hold on to him, to reassure herself that he was really here. "What are you doing in England? Did the French discover your identity? Does Papa know you are safe?"

"All in good time, Lily. For now, all you need to know is that I am safe, the earl knows I am safe, and the French have no idea where I am. However, I have a few questions of my own that you can answer."

She didn't like the look in his eye, or the sudden deepening of the lines around his mouth. His hands came to rest on her waist. "Father sent word that you married the Duke of Remmington. He was vague enough about the details that I want to know why."

"Our marriage wasn't exactly planned, if that's what you mean." Lily smiled and tried to reassure him. "There is no reason for you to be concerned."

Robert's mouth became a grim line. "I know him, Lily. He doesn't think I know who he is, but I do. I also know that he has a reputation for being a rake and a scoundrel where women are concerned. If I'd had any idea that he'd turned his attention on you—" He held her by the shoulders, his expression intent. "Did he force you into this marriage? Did he compromise your honor so you had no choice but to accept his offer?"

Lily couldn't help herself. She started to laugh. She leaned her forehead against his shoulder, but she still couldn't contain her unladylike giggles.

"I don't see what's so damned funny," Robert muttered.

"Neither do I. Take your hands off my wife, Lacroix."

Robert removed his hands from her shoulders and took a prodigious step backward. Lily supposed it was the look on Remmington's face that made him do it. She placed herself in front of Robert, ready to protect her brother. Remmington looked ready to murder him. "I-I didn't think you would be home until late tonight."

Remmington didn't move from his place near the door, but his fisted hands kept tightening in a reflexive motion. "I want you out of my house, Lacroix. I don't ever want you within sight of my wife again unless I am with her."

Robert placed his hand on Lily's arm. "You didn't tell him?"

Lily pushed Robert's hand away when she saw her husband's reaction to that innocent touch. She hurried forward to flatten her palm against Remmington's chest before he could advance any further into the room. He stopped instantly and covered her hand with his own, his expression a vague resemblance of gentleness as he gazed down at her.

"You have to leave the room now, Lily."

She shook her head. "No. It isn't what you think."

He took both her hands in his, then lifted one to press a brief kiss against her wrist. "I know that, darling.

The night you found Patricia Farnsworth in my bed, I realized that your trust in me is complete, unconditional. I will never give you anything less than I receive, in all respects."

Lily's breath caught in her throat. "Does that mean—"

"You found him in bed with another woman?" Robert asked. "And you *married* him? Remmington is right, Lily. You need to leave the room."

Lily felt Remmington's strength coil around her, an almost tangible element of protection. She glanced over her shoulder, alarmed to see Robert advance on them. She wrapped one arm around her husband's neck, and stretched her arm out to plant her other hand against her brother's chest. "No! Stop it, both of you. Miles, you must let me explain."

"You don't have to explain anything," Robert growled.

Lily glared over her shoulder. "Robert, shut up before your mouth results in a serious injury." She turned to her husband. "Miles, meet my brother."

She waited to feel the tension flow out of both men. It didn't happen. They glared at each other over her head.

"Who the hell is Venus?" Remmington demanded.

"Venus?" Lily echoed.

"None of your damned business. What did you do to make my sister marry you?"

Remmington smiled. "None of *your* damned business."

Lily sighed. She stepped from between the two and threw up her hands. "I give up. Bash each other's heads in if you wish. For the life of me, I cannot understand why you want to."

She crossed her arms and waited. They both scowled at her, then at each other.

"Crofford tells everyone that his son is in Greece," Remmington said, "digging up artifacts."

"Now you know the reason for that deception," Robert informed him.

"You two don't resemble one another at all." Remmington looked at Lily, then at her brother. "I thought you were trying to seduce her."

Robert curled his lip. "That's revolting. Not that you have much right to be so indignant, considering the fact that you haven't been faithful to her."

"I haven't touched another woman since I met Lily." Remmington reached out and drew her to his side, his smile wicked. "That is to say, I haven't touched another woman the way I touch your sister."

Robert made a sound of disgust and turned a pleading look in Lily's direction. "Tell me that is not the reason you married him."

Lily tried to shrug, but the weight of Remmington's arm on her shoulders made that impossible. Instead she smiled up at him. "I rather like the way he touches me."

Robert wrinkled his nose. "I don't want to hear any more."

"Good," Remmington murmured, his gaze on Lily. "You may leave."

Lily shook her head. "But he just got here. He hasn't even told us why he's in England."

Remmington released a sigh that sounded like it came from his toes. "Very well." He led her to his desk and took his seat, then pulled her down onto his lap. He motioned toward the chair opposite his desk with a nod. "Sit down and tell us why you're here. Make it fast."

"The warmth of your welcome overwhelms me, Captain." Robert rolled his eyes, but he took the proffered seat. "Aside from the news of my sister's whirlwind marriage, I came to England because I think the French might be on to me. I received word from my contact in the War Ministry that the place is alive with gossip that they will soon have one of England's master cryptographers in custody. Every English operative in France knows how to write code." He placed one hand against his chest. "Modesty aside, I believe I am the only one they would refer to as a master cryptographer."

Remmington's entire demeanor changed. He loosened his grip on Lily and leaned forward. "You cannot think to return to France. Will you go into hiding?"

Robert nodded. "Until I receive word one way or another from my contact. He knows how to reach me here. It might be no more than a rumor."

"Do you need a place to stay?" Remmington asked. "A means for your contact to transport his message?"

Robert smiled and shook his head. "You have a strange notion of hospitality, Captain. First you order me to leave, then you invite me to move in."

"I had one of my estates in mind," Remmington clarified. He gave Robert a pointed look. "Most are a considerable distance from London."

"I appreciate your generous offers, but they won't be necessary. Bainbridge made arrangements to transport the message my contact will send, and he found me a cozy nest to hide in." He turned to Lily. "However, I do have one request to make of you."

"Anything you ask," Lily said.

Robert pursed his lips and remained silent a long moment. "I reported my information to Sir Malcolm earlier today. He told me everything about George Allen, and how he tried to kill you. I'm sorry I could not be here for you, *chérie*."

"I'm fine," she assured him. "I have a husband who is quite capable of protecting me."

"So it would seem," he agreed. "Sir Malcolm also told me that Sophie was injured in one of the attacks, that she will not return to Town for another day."

Lily nodded and waited for him to continue. She sensed a tenseness in him that seemed to increase by the moment.

"When she returns, can you get her here alone, for tea or whatever it is you women do during the day? How about Friday, at three o'clock?"

"Why?" Lily's eyes widened when Robert began to

blush. He never blushed, not since he was a boy. She guessed the truth at the same moment Remmington did. "Sophie?"

"Venus?" Remmington said. "Sophie Stanhope is your Venus?"

The rare blush deepened until Robert's face was bright red. He kept his attention focused on Lily, and she knew he was trying to maintain a hold on his dignity. "I will call on you at that time as well, and I would like the opportunity to speak with her alone. I would appreciate it if you wouldn't tell her I will be here," he added.

"Sophie Stanhope," Remmington repeated. He shook his head.

Robert scowled at him. "Just what do you find so unbelievable about the fact that my affections are fixed on Miss Stanhope?"

"Why, nothing at all. Miss Stanhope is a fine young lady. A little queer in her thinking on some subjects, and superstitious beyond . . ." Remmington looked from Robert's scowl to Lily's. "Perfectly fine woman. None better, excepting my wife."

"I'm sure I can manage to have Sophie here alone on Friday," Lily said. "And I'll agree to let you surprise her. Just keep in mind that she has a serious injury, so you'd best remember to contain your . . . enthusiasm when you greet her. I do not think she will appreciate one of those great bear hugs of yours at the moment."

"Thank you, Lily. You're a darling." He stood up and offered Remmington his hand. "As much as I hate to admit it, I don't think I'll mind having you in the family."

They both walked Robert to the back door when he explained he'd entered that way to avoid notice. Robert told them how he could be reached if they needed to contact him, then they watched until he disappeared down a side street.

Remmington slipped his arm around Lily's waist. "We have some unfinished business in the library."

The moment she looked into his face, she knew what

sort of business it involved. "The library? In the middle of the day?"

He leaned down to nuzzle her ear. "Mm. Yes. I've thought of nothing but you in there all week. Now I want you there in person. In the flesh. Very, very bare flesh."

Nineteen

✦

"*I* had no idea you found my clothing so fascinating."

Remmington deposited Lily in the center of his bed, then stripped off his jacket. His gaze raked over her purple silk gown, the one he had requested she wear to dinner. He began unbuttoning his shirt. "I find what is inside your clothing even more fascinating." She sat up and started to undo the fastenings of her gown, but he shook his head. "No, let me do that. Later."

She smiled and leaned back on her elbows, an unconscious pose that made his hands fumble at their task. The speculative look in her eyes made him slow down, aware that it was the first time she had watched him undress. Tonight there would be no more secrets between them.

"I thought you meant it when you said you intended to take off all my clothes in the library." Her delicate brows lowered into a frown, her voice thoughtful. "I'm a little glad you didn't. What we did in there felt wicked enough." She looked up at him and her expression brightened. "But I did enjoy myself."

He smiled and said nothing. At the time they locked themselves in the library, he had every intention of stripping every piece of clothing from her delectable body. By the time he'd unbuttoned her bodice, he knew he couldn't wait that long. The tantalizing sight of her partially bared figure heated his lust beyond any degree of patience. He sat her on his desk and bared her legs as well, her silk skirts frothed around her hips, her bodice pushed open to present rather than conceal. That image would never leave his mind. He knew already that he would never get another minute's worth of work accomplished at that desk.

The act of unfastening his shirt cuffs took longer than it ever had before. As he played with the cuff links, he shrugged the smooth linen off his shoulders until the shirt hung loose around his waist. The way Lily stared at his chest made his muscles tense with anticipation. He'd never undressed this way for a woman, never thought to make it a deliberate part of his seduction. She was devouring him with her eyes. He decided to undress for her every night.

"Why did you ask me to wear this particular gown to dinner?" Her voice sounded husky, more than a little distracted. "For that matter, why did we bother with dinner at all? It's not as if we ate much."

"I want this night to be perfect, in every way." He slipped his shirt off and let her stare for awhile. He scratched a nonexistent itch at the center of his chest and smiled over the way she wet her lips. "The dinner we shared tonight is the one I've thought about every night since we arrived."

"Oh." Her brows rose. "Really?"

He felt himself nod. Tonight he wanted everything just right, in every precise detail that he'd tortured his imagination with over the past week. So far, the night couldn't progress any better. Except, perhaps, for one part.

After Lily's brother left, he'd apologized for the way he ignored her and promised that sort of behavior was at an end. But he'd delivered that vow right after they returned to the library, while they were in the midst of another distracting activity. He wasn't entirely certain his words made any sense. Other than that, he couldn't ask for a more perfect night. Since Robert's departure, he'd made love to her in his library, had lain on her bed like a lazy cat while he watched her dress for dinner, had seduced her at his dinner table, and now would make love to her again in his bed.

Once that was accomplished, only one part of his plan would remain incomplete. The best and most important part. After they made love, he would dress her in that lacy white nightgown he liked so well and then she would sit on the edge of his bed. He would take her hands in his and admit in simple, heartfelt words that he loved her, that his whole world revolved around her, that he hadn't had a life before she came into it. With all their appetites sated during this night of pleasure, she would know his words came from his heart. Of course, such a heartfelt confession might stir new hungers, and he might have a wish to seal his vow with more than a few kisses. As he recalled, that particular nightgown possessed an enchanting row of pearl buttons down the front.

He rubbed his hands together.

"I think Digsby is suspicious of the reasons you locked him out of the dining room." Lily glanced down at her dress. "And your wine ruined the bodice of my gown. Did you see the look he gave me when we left the dining room? I shall probably find a bib at my place tomorrow morning."

"I doubt it." His hands moved to the fastenings of his pants. "And I'll buy you as many gowns as I ruin. As long as you order gowns like this one."

Her lips curled up at the corners. "You like gowns with shocking necklines, my lord?"

"Mm. That, too." He reached out and touched the center of her silk bodice, then traced the tip of his finger over the long row of tiny jet buttons. She lay still as his finger traveled down to her ankles, but she shivered several times in between. "I like the buttons best. Small ones that go all the way to the floor."

"The style is not in fashion this Season."

"Hang fashion. I like buttons. I have no idea why, but on you they make me crazy." He shook his head and worked again on the much larger fastenings that secured his pants. His hands stilled when her fingers traveled the same path he'd just traced, long, lazy strokes from her bodice to her waist, then back up again. "Don't do that, Lily."

"Why not?" Her voice sounded almost like a purr.

"Because I won't—" He couldn't tear his eyes away from her slow, seductive movements to see if her expression revealed teasing or genuine interest. "Lily, stop. Please. This will ruin my plan."

"Plan?" Her hand stopped moving. "You have a *plan* for this evening? As in *schedule*?"

He nodded without thinking, his gaze still locked on the row of buttons. "A very definite plan."

"Just what does this—" Her breath came out in a small whoosh. Her hand started to move again, a little hesitantly at first, then she repeated the same bewitching strokes that made his mouth go dry.

He was naked. He didn't remember having taken off the rest of his clothes, but somehow he was naked. Then he realized why she had lost track of her opinion about his plan. Just to make certain, he glanced at her face, reminding himself that the buttons would still be there after he gauged her reaction to the sight of him.

He couldn't take his eyes from hers. Surely she'd caught glimpses of him before now. This couldn't be anything new to her. He had made love to her every night, stroked and caressed her in every way imaginable, encouraged her to explore him just as thoroughly, and taught her things about lovemaking even he didn't know. Yet he'd never displayed himself this way, never stood in the light and let her look at him. With everything she knew of him already, she somehow managed to retain her innocence, that wide, curious gaze that filled him with wonder and delight. He had to brace his knees to make certain he would remain upright. Her eyes touched him everywhere, moved in slow degrees over every inch of his body, then lingered for an incredible length of time on the most intimate part of him. He could *feel* her touching him with that gaze.

She repeated an order he once gave her. "Breathe, Miles."

He filled his lungs with air and placed one knee on the bed, then the other, then his hands were braced on either side of her shoulders. He lowered himself onto her silk-clad body in measured degrees, his skin so sensitive that he felt her warmth rise up to greet him before he touched her.

"Lily." He lowered his forehead to the pillow beside her, tried to remember what he had intended to do next. "I had a plan."

"I know." She arched up and he felt every one of the tiny jet buttons press against him. "This will be better."

He started to kiss her, but made himself stop. "I have to tell you something." His lips moved of their own accord to cover the pulse point on her throat. His hands began to move over her body. He couldn't help himself. Yes, he could. "It's important, Lily."

"Yes?" The question sounded more like an invitation. She pulled her head away, exposing more of her slender throat. "What is it?"

He could hear her breaths come in quick gasps, felt the rise and fall of her breasts beneath him, and knew the bodice barely covered them. His mouth moved lower. "I wanted this to be right, Lily."

"Then your plan is working." She arched her back again and he slipped his arm around her waist, pulling her closer, pressing erotic kisses across the exposed parts of her breasts. "The buttons," she whispered. "Undo them."

He heard his frustrated groan and made himself lift

his head away from temptation. He wanted to look into her eyes when he made his pledge. "No, not before I say ..." A movement from the edge of his vision distracted him. He watched her hand flutter across her chest, moving downward to work at the top button of her gown. He gritted his teeth and tried to concentrate. "I'm trying to say that I love you, damn it."

This time his groan became one of disgust. He'd said it all wrong. He'd stared at her chest and told her breasts that he loved her. She hated it when men stared at her chest. He'd even uttered a curse. He cursed himself.

"I love you, too, Miles." He lifted his head and looked up at her. She gave him an enchanting smile of warmth and innocence. "Now will you undo my buttons?"

He wanted to tell her there was more, that he wanted to say the words as they were meant to be said. He'd practiced them inside his head for hours. He just couldn't recall them at the moment.

Instead he used his body to tell her what was in his heart. He cherished her, lingered over her endlessly, filled with an emotion that went beyond the needs of his body to the needs of his soul.

Alone, he woke up the next morning.

His hand searched for her beneath the sheets, but he couldn't find even her lingering warmth. He was scowling before he even opened his eyes. She should know better than to sneak off this morning. He wanted to tell her that she was the center of his life, damn it. Damn it!

His gaze went to the window and he realized with a start that it was late morning. He never slept past dawn. The reason for this unusual occurrence made his scowl fade. Last night he'd gone to sleep at peace with himself for the first time since he'd met Lily. Not just at peace with himself, but at peace with his life. He'd held a beautiful Tiger Lily in his arms, knowing that her love for him would never wither or fade, that she would be the most radiant force in his life for as long as he drew breath. He wanted to hold her right now, this minute. He released a long sigh and rolled from the bed. He should have known she wouldn't be where he expected, no more than she ever did what he expected. It was part of the reason he loved her.

Jack brushed his hand over one shoulder to wave away a bothersome fly. The shouts of street vendors were almost lost in the din of carriages and carts that clattered along Bond Street. From his perch atop the duke's carriage, Jack surveyed the street with a half-interested eye as he waited for the duchess to conclude her business at Mr. Milton's engraving shop. The morning was unusually warm, and he shrugged the light cloak he wore onto the seat beside him. He glanced again toward the windows of Milton's shop. Posters and samples of the engraver's products filled the shop windows. He couldn't see the duchess or tell if she might be anywhere close to the conclusion of her business.

A sudden shout from the alleyway next to the shop drew Jack's attention. He watched as a printing clerk ran toward the carriage, his apron stained with black ink, a harried look on his face. Jack's hand moved toward the knife he kept tucked in his waistband.

"Ho! Are you the duchess's man?" the clerk called out.

Jack nodded, gripped by the sure knowledge that something was wrong.

"The duchess felt faint and she stepped out the back door for a breath of fresh air, but now she's taken sick for sure." He jerked his thumb over one shoulder. "She's back here, heaving up her breakfast."

Jack leaped down from the carriage and ran toward the alleyway.

"Around that corner," the clerk called out. He pointed down the brick alleyway then fell into step behind Jack.

Just as Jack slowed down to round the corner of the building, he felt something large and solid strike the back of his head. Then he didn't feel anything at all. He crumpled to the ground in a heap.

"These are very nice, Mr. Milton." Lily returned the sample invitations to Mr. Milton, then brushed a few stray specks of paper dust from her lavender gown. "How soon can the actual invitations be ready?"

"This afternoon, Your Grace." Mr. Milton gestured toward a green curtain that covered the doorway behind the counter. Lily could hear the muffled, rhythmic sounds of a printing press on the other side. The sharp, caustic smell of ink permeated the shop. "Time is so short that I took the chance you would approve the design," he went on. "My assistants are printing your invitations as we speak."

"I appreciate your efforts on such short notice, Mr. Milton."

"I am only too happy to oblige," Mr. Milton said. He gave her a humble bow, then stepped around the counter to stand before a wall fitted with shallow, tilted shelves. Envelopes in every size and shape filled one section of the shelves. He reached for a crisp white envelope lined with gold foil. "This envelope will match the invitation's gold border, Your Grace. Shall I add the appropriate number of envelopes to your order?"

Lily nodded. "You may send the envelopes and invitations to my residence this afternoon. You have the direction."

"Very good, Your Grace." Mr. Milton bowed again, then he escorted her to the door of his shop.

Lily stepped outside, still smiling over the results of the printer's efforts and her own. With that task accomplished, she could return home to her husband. It had taken every ounce of willpower she possessed to leave the warm cocoon of their bed that morning. Remmington held her even in his sleep. His hands caressed her whenever she moved, in what could only be an unconscious awareness of her body. The corners of her mouth turned up when she thought of the look on his face when he told her he loved her, when he literally *swore* that he loved her. She found it somehow endearing. As if to make up for his terse declaration, he'd murmured love words to her for hours, a few coherent, most not. Lily loved every one of them. She couldn't wait to hear what he would tell her this morning.

Lost in those thoughts, a moment passed before she realized her carriage no longer waited before the engraving shop. She looked up and down the street, but saw no sign of Jack or the sleek black chaise with the Remmington coat of arms emblazoned on the doors. A battered maroon traveling coach stood where her carriage should have been, and its driver started toward her. He wore a tan greatcoat that swirled around an expensive pair of top boots, and he tipped his wide-brimmed beaver hat.

"Good morning, Your Grace. My employer begs a moment of your time, if you wouldn't mind stepping over to his coach."

Lily took an immediate dislike to the man. Something in his demeanor set off warning bells in her head. She searched the street again for Jack.

"Your driver had to leave," he said, as if he read her thoughts. "If you will step over to the coach, Lord Gordon can explain everything."

"You work for Lord Gordon?" Lily felt a surge of relief when the driver nodded. She chewed on her lower lip, then followed the driver to the coach. The door opened, and Harry gave her a quick wave from inside. His usual cheerful smile was absent this morning, a solemn expression in his blue eyes.

"I hope we didn't startle you, Lily. I've just come from Lord Holybrook's, and I have urgent news." He rubbed his forehead, the look on his face harried, as if he were reluctant to divulge the information. "I went out there to get Lord Holybrook's opinion on a set of scrolls I'd just purchased, but a crisis struck before I arrived."

He opened his mouth as if to continue, but released a deep sigh instead. He shook his head, his eyes downcast. "I'm afraid there is no easy way to tell you this. It's your friend, Miss Stanhope. She developed a sudden fever last night and she's taken a turn for the worse. I'm sorry to be the one to tell you this, but Miss Stanhope's condition is dire. The physician does not hold much hope for a recovery. Lady Bainbridge says she's asked for you often, and she knows you will want to be with her before it's too late."

Lily's eyes grew round and wide with shock, not over the news of Sophie's fever, but over the fact that Harry would tell her such an outrageous lie. She'd received a note from Sophie two days before, saying her injuries were healing nicely. She and Lady Bainbridge planned to arrive in London that afternoon.

"I know this comes as a shock," Harry went on, "but I didn't know how else to break the news. You must return to Holybrook House with me immediately. I sent your driver to find Remmington to tell him that I will escort you to Basildon and the reason for our haste." Harry held out one hand to motion her forward. "Quickly, Lily. We must hurry."

Lily took one step toward the carriage, then stopped. She clapped one hand to her forehead. "The invitations! I must give Mr. Milton special instructions before I leave."

"This is no time to worry about invitations," Harry said. "Your friend is on her deathbed."

Lily backed away before he could grasp her wrist to pull her inside. "It will only take a moment. My father will be furious if I do not tell him the arrangements I made. His ball is less than a week away. The invitations must go out tomorrow."

Harry hesitated, then he nodded toward his driver. "Very well, but take Lando with you. He will make certain the engraver does not delay you any longer than necessary."

"I won't be but a moment," she promised. She turned and walked briskly to Mr. Milton's shop door, aware of Lando's shadow right behind her. Her heart beat faster and faster as she neared the doorway, and she knew he could sense her fear. She hoped he would mistake her frightened expression for worry over Sophie's health. Her life might depend on as much.

She pushed the door open and stepped inside. The bell over the door jangled and Mr. Milton appeared at the back of the shop. Lily walked to the counter where the samples of her invitations still sat in a neat pile. She turned them over before Lando came up behind her.

"I must leave Town unexpectedly," she told Mr. Milton in a clipped voice. "You must deliver the samples to my father at Crofford House, rather than my husband's town house." She reached for a quill pen that stood next to Mr. Milton's order register, then she dipped the quill in the inkwell and began to write on the back of her invitation. "You must also send this note along with the samples so he will know my preferences."

"But, Your Grace—"

"I do not have time to argue, my dear man. I am in a great hurry and cannot delay." She could feel Lando staring over her shoulder. Just to make certain, she glanced at him. Lando stood less then a pace away, intent on the words she wrote. She could see his lips moving as he read the message. She jerked her gaze back to the note and the words swam together in a dizzy haze. Only one image remained clear; the newly healed scar across Lando's left temple, one she felt certain was the result of a blow with a very old, very heavy candlestick.

Somehow she managed to initial the bottom of the note. The task forced her to school her concentration, to remember that she must act innocent and unsuspecting. She handed the note to Mr. Milton. Amazingly, her voice didn't quaver. "Please read it back to me, Mr. Milton. I want to be certain my writing is legible."

Mr. Milton scanned the note and shook his head, but he complied with the request. "Half pound paper. Almond in color. Remmington coat of arms on the envelope. Red wax seals. Yellow ribbon inserted in the seals. Lord Crofford will approve the final designs. Gold embossing on the coat of arms." Mr. Milton glanced up from the note and gave her a helpless look of bewilderment.

Lily spoke in a firm tone of voice, before he could make any further objections. "See that my father receives this note with the samples, Mr. Milton."

The engraver hesitated a moment, then he bowed to her wishes. "Yes, Your Grace."

Lily turned and walked slowly from the shop, aware of each moment that passed, amazed that she could appear almost calm in front of Mr. Milton. Lando kept one hand concealed inside his greatcoat, and she worried that he carried a pistol. It took her only a moment to decide that it would be foolish to ask Mr. Milton to help her escape this man. She knew Lando was capable of murder, that he would very likely shoot Mr. Milton before he could come to her rescue.

Her hand shook as she reached for the shop's doorlatch. Was Jack dead already? A sudden pain shot through her when she realized he must be. Jack would never leave her, no matter what harebrained excuse Harry gave him. Only one thought drove her past that pain. They would kill her, too. If she went willingly into Harry's coach, she felt certain she would never leave it alive.

There wasn't time to wonder why Harry would want her dead. Time was too precious a commodity. She had only one opportunity to escape, one hope that Lando wouldn't be bold enough to shoot her in broad daylight in the middle of Bond Street. The street teemed with people. All she had to do was open her mouth and scream. Someone would come to her rescue.

She'd barely opened her mouth when Lando's hand clamped down on her arm. Only a startled whimper of pain escaped her lips when something sharp poked her ribs.

"Don't even consider running from me," Lando warned under his breath. His hold on her looked deceptively solicitous, as if she'd lost her balance and he had taken her elbow to steady her. Hidden in the folds of his greatcoat, only Lily knew that he held a knife to her side. He tugged on her elbow and led her to the coach, then opened the coach's door and ordered her inside.

"She knows," Lando told Harry, as he nudged her forward.

Lily found herself staring into the barrel of Harry's pistol.

"Do join me," Harry said, with an inviting smile. He nodded toward the seat opposite his as she climbed into the coach. "Make yourself comfortable, Lily. I would really prefer not to shoot you."

Lily felt a shiver run down her spine. Even now, knowing that Harry was in league with a murderer, he looked boyishly friendly rather than dangerous and menacing. The carriage door closed behind her and she settled onto the seat, her gaze riveted on the pistol. "Why are you doing this, Harry?"

"You're such a clever girl," he mused. "I thought you would have that figured out by now." The pistol turned a little to one side as he shrugged. "But you thought you had everything figured out when your husband shot poor, demented Lord Allen, did you not?" His smile grew broader. "I laughed for days over that business. Things could not have worked out better for me. Lord Allen took the blame for Lando's bungled work, and Remmington relaxed his guard on you. I had almost despaired of taking you alive."

Still uncertain of Harry's motives, Lily phrased her question very carefully. "We don't know each other all that well, Harry. I cannot think of any insult I have dealt you. Why would you want me dead?"

"Ah, such a look of innocence," he drawled. "You fooled me a long time with your little act. I didn't realize your involvement in your father's business until the night of Lady Keaton's dinner, when you so neatly solved the riddle of my scroll. You were right, by the way. The words translated exactly as you said they would."

Lily felt a sinking sensation in the pit of her stomach. Remmington couldn't know how right he'd been that night, the worries she'd mistaken for possessiveness. She had indeed acted the fool. She wondered if he would ever know. Her gaze went to Harry, and she decided it would be wise to drop her act. She sensed that vehement denials would only weaken her position. "If you didn't know I was involved, then why did you have your man try to kill me?"

"Oh, you weren't supposed to die the night of the Ashlands' ball," Harry said, as if she should have known that fact. He gave her a look of mock regret. "How could you think such a thing of me, Lily? You are smarter than that."

Lily remained helplessly silent.

"Not so smart as you think?" he asked. His tone took on a clear note of gloating. "We planned to use you to control your father's activities, dear girl. As long as we held you prisoner, we knew he would do anything we asked, tell us any information we wanted to keep you safe. It's obvious that he dotes on you. I thought it a clever plan to turn Crofford into a double agent. That plan changed slightly when I realized you were a cryptographer as well." He smiled at her again, a winning smile of delight. "You are a very valuable lady. The French will pay me a small fortune when I deliver you to their hands. They are anxious to learn all the secrets you carry in that pretty head of yours."

Lily lifted her chin so it wouldn't tremble. "If I am so terribly valuable, why did you try to shoot me at Holybrook House?"

"Ah, that was another of Lando's bungles," he said regretfully. "He is a talented assassin, yet he seems to have a streak of incompetence where you are concerned. Not that you were the target that day. Remmington kept such a close eye on you that we decided it was time to re-move him from the picture. Unfortunately, Lando is more talented with a knife than he is with a pistol." Harry tapped his chin in a thoughtful gesture. "I must remem-ber to recommend him to Manton's for more practice."

Lily wondered what kind of man could plot to kill his own friend and not show so much as a shred of remorse when he admitted as much. Far from a guilty conscience, Harry's thoughts centered on ways to turn his hired as-sassin into a more talented killer. "You have me now," she said. "There is no longer any reason to kill Rem-mington."

"No," he agreed, "unless he becomes bothersome when you turn up missing." His hand brushed through the air. "Remmington should be safe enough. He will never suspect I am involved with your disappearance. No one will ever guess that I work for the French. Not even the bothersome Sir Malcolm Bainbridge. Lord Granger proved an effective distraction for Sir Malcolm all these months, yet no one but Lando knows of my involvement. Lando is one of France's top agents. You should be flat-tered that they sent the best for you. Lando will be the one to escort you to France, and I daresay the two of you will find much to talk about."

The thought of Lando escorting her across the Chan-nel made Lily shudder. She began to imagine the ven-geance Lando would exact for the scar he bore. "Why *do* you work for the French?" she asked. "What could make a man turn traitor against his country?"

Harry didn't take offense over the question as she'd feared. He merely shrugged. "Very simple. Money. The French have a great deal of it, and I was happy enough to relieve them of a sizable portion. I've already replen-ished the fortune my father squandered. Your abduction will be my last act as a traitor. I can live very comfortably for the remainder of my life on the prize they've prom-ised for your safe delivery."

She could feel an invisible noose tighten itself around her neck. "Where are you taking me?"

"To my town house," he answered. "I sent my mother and sisters along with most of the servants to my country estate for an extended visit. You will stay in a very cozy room in my basement until your family and Sir Malcolm complete their unsuccessful search for you. When they find your driver's body, they will naturally assume the worst and give up the search. Then it will be a simple matter to transport you to the coast, where you will board a ship for France. A week or two at most, I should think, then you will become a guest of the French government."

Lily wondered if she could stir some shred of pity in Harry. She studied his face, his demeanor, but she saw only cheerful determination in his expression. No regrets, no remorse, no feelings whatsoever that he was condemning her to a fate worse than death.

She began to pray that Mr. Milton delivered her note in all haste. Milton clearly thought her crazed to give him instructions that had nothing to do with her invitations. There was the chance that he would deliver the printed invitations and simply discard her message. She had to face the fact that this time Remmington might not come to her rescue.

Twenty

———— ✦ ————

"*I* woke up just as the two buggers tried to dump me in the river." Jack's hands were tightly fisted. He could barely contain his rage over how easily he'd fallen for the dupe. He'd failed his duty.

Both men braced themselves as the coach rounded a sharp corner. The speed Digsby demanded from the horses made the vehicle lurch to one side. Remmington righted himself and proceeded to load his pistols while Jack continued the tale.

"They'd taken the knife from my belt, but they didn't know I carry another in my boot." Jack found a grim smile. "I could tell they were sorry they didn't slit my throat in the first place, to make sure I couldn't come back from the dead."

"Did they say anything about my wife?" Remmington demanded.

Jack shook his head. "I heard only bits and pieces of

their conversation. None of it made much sense." He hesitated a moment, then said, "There's something you should know of the man who posed as a printer's apprentice, Your Grace. The man who lured me into the alley had a scar right here." Jack pointed to his temple. "The night we went to Crofford House, Digsby said that the duchess injured her attacker with a blow to the head. Fool that I am, I didn't make the connection until after I'd taken care of his hirelings."

Remmington felt his blood turn to ice. He checked the prime of his pistols, then checked them again. He needed to do something to keep busy, anything to combat his feeling of helplessness.

Was Lily lying in the same alley where Jack had nearly met his end? Was she alone? He knew she was terrified ... if she was still alive. He set the pistols aside, half afraid he would shoot himself by accident.

The coach rattled to a stop in front of Milton's shop. Digsby somehow managed to make it to the entrance of the establishment a moment before Remmington, to open the door without taking it from its hinges as Remmington intended. Remmington crossed the floor of the shop in three long strides.

Mr. Milton stood behind the counter. His eyes widened as Remmington bore down on him, but he hesitated a moment too long before he began to back away. He found himself hauled over the counter by Remmington's hold on his lapels.

"*Where is my wife?*"

Milton cringed over the roared question, even as he tried to find his footing. The tips of his shoes dangled a good inch off the floor. "She left nearly two hours ago! Oh, I just knew something was amiss. She acted so strange, and that note—"

Remmington set him down with a thud. "What note? Show me this note."

Milton scurried over to the counter. His hand trembled as he handed Remmington a sheet of paper. "This is just a copy, Your Grace. I sent the original to her father, just as she asked."

Remmington scanned the paper. "Do these instructions have anything to do with her invitations?"

Milton looked startled. "Why, no, Your Grace. They have nothing at all to do with her invitations. In fact, she told me just the opposite before she left the shop the first time, then moments later she returned and gave these orders that make no sense. She even acted different."

"What do you mean?"

"There was a man with her, and I just assumed he was her driver. Yet she kept looking over her shoulder at him, smiling the whole while and chattering on, with eyes as frightened as any I've ever seen."

"Did this man have a scar on his temple?"

Milton nodded. "I tried to ask her what was wrong, but she wouldn't let me get a word in edgewise. I knew right enough that she wanted me to act as if nothing were wrong, but I couldn't figure out why. She just said that she had to leave town unexpectedly, that it was very important that her note be delivered to the earl."

Remmington turned away from Milton. He could see Lily as if she stood before him, knew exactly what Milton meant about her eyes. What he didn't understand was how Milton could look into those eyes and not do anything to help her, how he could allow Lily to leave his shop with a man who terrified her. Milton would probably be dead if he hadn't.

"I didn't know what to make of it, Your Grace. I just tried to do what your wife wanted."

"I realize that, Mr. Milton." Remmington walked out of the shop without a backward glance.

"Crofford House?" Digsby asked, when they reached the street.

Remmington nodded.

• • •

He stalked into the earl's library less than a quarter hour later. Robert was there, along with his father. They both turned to stare at him.

"Lily," Remmington managed, through the constriction in his throat. "Did you get her note?"

"Something arrived from the printer about an hour ago." Crofford sat back in his chair, his grip on his desk so tight that his knuckles turned white. "What is it? What's happened to her?"

"She went to Milton's this morning to approve the invitations. Someone lured my driver into an alley and knocked him senseless. Before he took Lily, she managed to leave this note." Remmington tossed the printer's copy of the message on Crofford's desk. "What does it say?"

Robert rushed around the desk to look over his father's shoulder. He read the message aloud. "Half pound paper. Almond in color. Remmington coat of arms on the envelope. Red wax seals. Yellow ribbon inserted in the seals. Lord Crofford will approve the final designs. Gold embossing on the coat of arms."

"What does it *say*?" Remmington repeated.

The two men studied the note without a further word or question about Lily. Her note would tell them what they wanted to know. It had to.

Remmington began to pace.

Hurry! The word echoed over and over in his mind. He couldn't say it out loud, couldn't do anything to distract them from their work. The seconds ticked by. He wanted to shake them both. It wouldn't help. More seconds. The note had to be a code. It had to be! His silent demand turned into a prayer. *Please!*

Robert spoke first. "Seven sentences. Words in the sentences; three, three, seven, three, six, seven, seven. Three threes, three sevens, and a six in a seven-word sentence." He leaned closer to the note, studied it a good minute longer. "Damn it, Lily! Where did you hide the key?"

"Number the letters," Crofford snapped.

"No. It forms actual words. It can't be a cross alphabet, not unless she had a good hour to design the message." Robert glanced up at Remmington. "How long did she take to write this?"

"No more than minutes."

"Minutes." Robert stared at the message. "She can write a hundred codes in minutes!"

"Yes, but she knew she had only minutes," Crofford mused. "She wouldn't chance anything but a code she knew inside and out, one she couldn't possibly make a mistake on."

Remmington stopped pacing near the fireplace. The clock on the mantel continued to tick. Endless, endless ticks. He wanted to smash the clock to bits. He glared at Lily's father and brother. *Say something!*

"It might be a simple code," Robert said. "It might be a code so simple that we cannot see it."

"Oh, my God!" Crofford rose halfway from his seat. He sat down again just as abruptly. "Oh, my God." His pen underlined the first letter of each sentence. "H. A. R. R.Y. L. G. Harry, L. G. Harry, *Lord Gordon*."

They both looked at Remmington.

"Robert, come with me. Crofford, send for Bainbridge. Tell him I'm on my way to get more of my men, then I'm going to Harry's."

Lily angled her hairpin in a new direction inside the lock, unable to see anything she was doing. Her prison cell in Harry's town house was a small, narrow room dug deep into one wall of the cellar. It smelled of mold and mice. She'd caught only a glimpse of the damp brick walls and dirt floor before Lando pushed her inside, then the door banged shut, plunging her into darkness. The walls seemed to close in on her, walls she couldn't even see. She felt buried alive. It took every ounce of her willpower to keep from screaming, to keep herself from clawing at the door to beg for a lantern or candle. She wouldn't show them her weakness.

The cold that permeated the room seeped into her

bones, yet she felt a trace of perspiration on her brow, her skin made clammy by fear. The pin snapped in half, the third broken pin so far. She had no idea how long she'd worked at the lock. Time became elusive in total darkness. It felt like days. It might only be minutes. Still, her efforts must have required several hours. At some point the lock might prove too foolproof for her skills, but she wouldn't give up the effort until every last hairpin broke into useless nubs. Then she would know there was no hope of escape from this black pit. Then she would go mad.

She searched her hair for another pin, but started to panic when she couldn't free the broken piece from the lock. She wedged the good pin into the small opening and tried to maneuver the piece free. A sudden click made her stop. A little more maneuvering and she felt the lock turn into place. She'd done it!

Her hand felt for the latch, but she hesitated a long moment after she found it. Someone might be guarding the door, waiting until she tasted but a moment of freedom before forcing her back into the cell. She knew they would have to render her unconscious or worse before they returned her to this horror chamber.

She put her shoulder against the door and pushed it open, took a step forward to stand on the other side. Only darkness greeted her. It pressed in on her from every side, silent, black, endless night. Then a faint scurrying sound and a small, rhythmic clicking. Like small teeth. Like the sound of a rat. It came from inside her cell. A startled scream escaped her lips, even as she shoved the door back into place. Her shoulders collapsed against the door and a hard shudder racked her body. She listened hard for any sound. Not just for the rat, but for some noise from overhead that would say she had given herself away.

Nothing.

If anyone heard her scream, they must have assumed she found something unpleasant in her cell. She thrust her arms straight in front of her and spread her fingers wide, raking the darkness all around her, looking for something solid as she took a step forward. The steps were ahead and to her right ... or were they? Yes. Right. They were to her right.

Another step. Then another and another.

It couldn't be this far to the wall. She was going the wrong way! Her hand encountered something solid and she yelped, part shock, part pain from her jammed finger. A more hesitant stretch of her fingers and she felt stone. Brick. The brick wall opposite her cell door. She laid her palm flat against the grimy surface, a solid anchor in the dizzying black void that enveloped her. With her hand on the wall, she pointed her toe forward, eased onto her foot and shifted her weight, then repeated the same cautious movement with the other leg. Seven slow steps later, something struck her ankle, the bottom riser of the open staircase. She inched her way forward until her foot rested on the step, then she hiked up her skirts with one hand and used the other to balance herself on the steps above her.

A faint shadow of light showed from underneath the door at the top of the steps, no more than a gray shadow. What if that door was locked, too? The knob turned in her hand, but the door didn't budge. She straightened to lean against it, lost her bearings for a moment and almost fell over backwards. Only her grip on the doorknob kept her from tumbling back down the stairs. She waited until she could catch her breath again, then turned the knob and leaned her shoulder against the door. It opened.

She entered the basement of the town house. It seemed to be a storage area for the most part, but there were windows cut high into walls. They were covered with dust and dirt, but were windows nonetheless that bathed the room in the most beautiful light Lily had ever encountered. She wanted to laugh, but it was hysterical laughter and she kept it bottled tight inside her. She was a floor closer to her captors. Now they might hear her.

She rubbed her hands against her skirt and left dark streaks of soot and grime on the lavender gown. She didn't care that it was ruined. The staircase to the first floor rose before her. She fashioned her skirts into a large knot at her hip that left her legs and hands unencumbered. She reached for the fourth step and braced her hands to the far edge of the riser where a loose nail or board would be less likely to creak beneath her weight. She placed her feet in the same position on the first step, then began to work her way up the staircase, feeling like a large, awkward spider.

At the top of the stairs, a good inch gap separated the door from the polished oak floor. Lily knew this door opened onto the foyer. She settled all her weight onto the staircase so she could rest her cheek against the top step and peer beneath the door. To her left she could see a large arched doorway and she recalled a brief glimpse of a sitting room, ahead of her the front door. At the farthest range of her vision she could see the bottom riser of the staircase that led to the second floor. She turned her head and looked to the right.

More polished oak floor in that direction and a long wall with double doors in the center, perhaps a library, with another gap beneath its doors. The closed room had windows, for she could see sunlight reflected beneath the door. She also saw a momentary shadow and knew it was caused by someone inside the room who walked past the door. Harry, or Lando, or one of the two servants she saw when she first arrived, the ones who greeted Lando in French and deferred to him as if he was their leader.

She couldn't see any other movement, nor hear any sounds from anywhere in the house. If she could just make it to the front door without notice she would be free. Once she reached the street, they would have to shoot her to bring her back. She wouldn't return without a fight. Her hand reached for the doorknob. A sudden pounding noise made her snatch it away again. Someone was at the front door! More accomplices? What if they sent someone to check on her? Her heart beat harder.

A pair of scuffed brown shoes crossed the foyer and

stopped before the front door, then the door opened. "Maybe I help you, sir?"

The voice belonged to one of Lando's underlings. A movement caught her eye and she looked to her right. The library door was open now, and she saw the highly polished riding boots of the man who stood there. Harry or Lando. Her gaze returned to the front entry. In the second she'd looked away, another man had entered the foyer. She watched his booted feet cross the oak floor to stand not a pace from her hiding place. She released a silent sigh when he turned away from her.

"Tell Lord Gordon I am here," a voice announced from the doorway.

Lily covered her mouth and nose with both hands, terrified she wouldn't contain her sob. Only one thing kept her from bursting forth from her hiding place and throwing herself into her husband's arms—the knowledge that he would be dead before she reached him.

"Remmington?" Harry called out. The pair of boots near the library door moved forward. "Whatever are you doing here? Do come in."

The boots in front of her door blocked any view of her husband's entry into the foyer, but she heard his solid, familiar footsteps. The other three men stood within her sight, only one unaccounted for. Her gaze scanned the floor and she found the last pair of shoes near the entrance to the sitting room. Then she heard Harry's voice again.

"My God, Remmington! What are you doing with those pistols?"

Lily smiled, weak with relief. Remmington had the situation under control. She wondered if he had used that trick with his greatcoat to conceal his weapons. Now she could reveal herself. Just as soon as she felt able to stand. She still couldn't show any weakness in front of their enemies, nothing that might distract Remmington and make him vulnerable. She rested her cheek against the riser and drew a deep breath. It was all right now. She could take a moment to compose herself.

"I think you know exactly what I'm doing with these weapons. Take me to my wife. *Now!*"

"He won't be taking you anywhere." This from Lando. Lily could tell that he was the owner of the boots that stood in front of her door. She heard two sharp clicks. "We are equally matched, Remmington. In fact, the odds are tipped in my favor. If you will look over your left shoulder, you will see that my friend, Michel, has you in his sights as well."

"Do you think I am fool enough to come here alone?" Remmington sneered. "Take me to my wife, Harry."

It was Lando who answered. With a deafening pistol shot. Lily watched in horror as Harry crumpled to the floor. She could see his face now, but she couldn't see his injury. His mouth opened and closed, then opened one last time. In a matter of seconds his eyes glazed over and he stared straight ahead at nothing.

Lando broke the silence that followed. "I believe I mentioned the fact that he won't be taking you anywhere. I'm afraid Harry became a liability once he delivered what we wanted. An expensive liability. That shot should bring your men on the run, but I doubt they will be of much use with three pistols trained at your heart."

"You don't have enough weapons to shoot them all," Remmington warned. "You can shoot me and two others. That won't be enough. My wife will not leave here with you."

"Did I say she was here?" Lando asked. "Do you think *I* am fool enough to keep her within such easy reach? She is in a place you will never find her, unless I take you myself. If I don't meet the men who are holding her within the hour, they have orders to kill her."

"You wouldn't give such orders. Not after you went through this much trouble to take her alive." Remmington sounded sure of himself. Only Lily could recognize the trace of fear in his voice.

"Kill me and find out for yourself," Lando taunted. A silent moment passed, then Lando's voice turned triumphant. "A wise choice, Remmington. Now put them on the floor."

"Not until we come to an agreement. I'll act as your hostage if you take me to her. I won't order my men to shoot you unless you attempt some trick or shoot me yourself."

No, no, no! Lily didn't dare say a word, not when she knew her husband's weapons were lowered. Where were the others?

The sounds of footsteps answered her question, more and more until she saw too many boots to count. They stood a cautious distance from Lando and his men.

"Remmington! What happened?" It was the sound of Robert's voice.

"She isn't here," Remmington said. "Don't shoot him. Her life may depend upon it."

Lily knew this was her only chance. Remmington's men would be armed. They would have their pistols trained on the enemy. She said a quick prayer, then stood up and placed her hand on the doorknob, turning it until the latch rested inside the door. She backed down two steps, her hand still on the knob, then rushed the door as hard as she could. She heard a pistol discharge the moment the door struck Lando's back.

Three more shots were fired as she stumbled into the foyer. In that instant she saw her husband, his pistols raised instinctively to protect himself from Lando and his henchmen, yet his attention focused only on her face. He was vulnerable. She took a step forward, an overwhelming urge to protect him.

"Lily!"

Two more shots, and Remmington lunged for her, his weight forcing her to the floor, sheltering every inch of her body as she wanted to shelter his. He wrapped one arm around her head, lifted the pistol in his other hand, took aim, and fired. Lando fell to the floor just a few paces away, a fatal wound in the center of his chest.

"There!" she heard Jack yell. Lily felt a wave of relief

as she realized her driver had survived the morning's work.

"No," Bull answered. He leaned over the man named Michel. "They're all dead but this one, and he's got himself a nasty belly wound. He won't be going anywhere."

"You two," Robert ordered, pointing at Bull and another of Remmington's men. "Check the upper floors." He continued to bark out orders until everyone was occupied by his commands. Everyone but Lily and Remmington, who were occupied with each other.

Remmington turned to look at her, his gaze frantic as he searched her face. Then his pistols clattered to the floor. He propped himself up on one elbow and ran his hand over her. "Are you hurt? Lily! Tell me. Are you hurt anywhere?"

He checked her body for injuries with an impersonal touch, but he touched her everywhere. She placed her hand over his and made him stop. "I'm fine."

"Lily." He seemed to have trouble saying the word. His eyes held hers in a gaze that searched her soul. The lines in his face disappeared and his rigid body began to relax against hers. The tips of his fingers moved over the arch of her brow, her temple, the line of her cheekbone. He cupped her chin then spread his fingers wide as his palm moved lower, until his hand covered most of her throat. She felt his fingertip rub the sensitive spot where her pulse still raced in an erratic beat. *"Lily."*

The word held a wealth of meaning. All in one small word, in his expression when he said it.

"I love you, too," she whispered.

His arms wrapped around her, his hand cradling her head to hold her closer, his face buried in the crook of her neck. "I love you," he whispered. "I couldn't live if anything happened to you." He kissed her throat, her cheek, the curve of her ear, then he gave her more sweet, whispered words that filled her eyes with tears and her heart with joy.

"Ahem."

At last Remmington lifted his head to place his lips

against her own, a kiss meant to calm rather than incite. Lily made him deepen the kiss. She wanted him to possess her, claim her, make her forget everything that happened except what happened between them. She needed him to ease the lingering fear, the memory of the dark pit below them, the—

"Ahe-ahe-*ahem*!"

Lily opened her eyes. Robert stood over them, a dark, disapproving scowl on his face. She tried to extract her mouth from her husband's. Her feeble struggles had no affect.

Robert must have noticed her failure. He leaned down and poked Remmington's shoulder. Then he did it again until Remmington lifted his head. "Good Lord, man. Show some modesty. If nothing else, show a little respect for the dead. There are bodies all over this floor. It's ... it's sacrilegious."

"None of my men are hurt?" Remmington asked. His eyes didn't leave Lily.

"Not a one."

"You aren't hurt?"

"Nope."

Remmington nodded, then he gained his feet and drew Lily up to stand beside him. His gaze traveled around the foyer and he lifted her into his arms. "Put your head on my shoulder, Lily."

She started to look around and he turned so his chest blocked her view. He was scowling again, and Lily knew he didn't want her to look at the bodies. She nodded and laid her head on his shoulder.

He placed a kiss on her forehead. "Just look at me, Lily. I'll take you outside."

Two carriages pulled up just as they left the house. Several men Lily didn't recognize emerged from the vehicles, then her father and Sir Malcolm.

"Is everyone all right?" Crofford asked.

Remmington nodded. "Robert is inside with my men. I'll let him make most of the explanations. I want to take Lily home." He turned to Bainbridge. "Why don't we all meet at my town house after you finish here? There are things we need to discuss."

Bainbridge nodded.

"Did they hurt you?" her father asked, his face lined with worry.

"No, Papa, I'm fine." She smiled up at Remmington. "My husband saved me."

Remmington made a sound of disgust. "She saved herself," he told Crofford. "My life as well, I warrant." He looked down at Lily and shook his head. "Madam, you never cease to amaze me."

Lily felt a blush warm her cheeks. The look in his eyes reminded her of the words he'd whispered not so long ago. She wanted to hear them again. "I would very much like to leave this place. Could you please be amazed somewhere else?"

He studied her face for a moment, then lifted one brow. "I'm sure of it."

Twenty-one

---✦---

Robert swallowed the last of his brandy, then set the glass on Remmington's desk. "Damned inconsiderate, if you ask me. We've been here almost an hour."

"Have patience," his father said. "Your sister went through a terrible ordeal today. I daresay she's upstairs crying her eyes out, poor child. I can't find fault with Remmington for staying by his wife's side to offer her comfort."

Robert stalked over to the side table to pour another brandy, muttering under his breath. "I'll wager ten guineas he is not patting her hand and murmuring 'there, there.'"

"What's that?" Crofford asked.

"Nothing worth repeating. Would anyone else care for a drink?"

Crofford and Sir Malcolm declined the offer.

"We might as well get some portion of our business

taken care of while we wait," Bainbridge said. He smoothed the ends of his mustache with his thumb. "Remmington's brother, Trevor, is preparing his ship to sail with the tide tomorrow morning. I've already told him to expect a passenger, but I don't want you to take any unnecessary risks, Robert. We have only the word of a wounded spy that Lily and your father were their only targets. There could be others searching for you in France."

Robert shook his head. "Our armies are headed for a confrontation in northern Spain or the Pyrenees, in a battle that may decide the outcome of the war. My presence in Paris is critical. If the French were on to me, I would have heard from my contact by now."

"Unless the French have arrested him already," Crofford pointed out.

"Unlikely," Robert countered. "You don't know my contact. He is the last person the French would suspect of subversive activities."

"Very well then," Bainbridge said. "You sail with Montague in the morning." He turned to Crofford. "That leaves the problem of what to do with you, my friend. The French know of your activities, and they could very well order another agent to England to curtail those activities."

Crofford nodded. "I've considered the possibility. It seems best if I disappear for a time, yet I need to be somewhere where I can code and decipher the messages from our operatives, as well as the messages we intercept from the French." He leaned back in his chair and rubbed his chin. "The safe house in Brighton seems a likely spot. I understand it's all but impregnable. The only risk will be transporting the decoded messages from Brighton to London."

"I can ensure that the risk is very small," Bainbridge said. "It is better than losing your services entirely. You and Lily are the only ones who can decipher Robert's codes, and I think it safe to assume we will no longer have her talents at our disposal. Remmington is sure to forbid as much."

"What am I sure to forbid?" Remmington inquired from the doorway. His hand tightened on Lily's waist, and he led her to the settee where they sat facing Sir Malcolm and her father. Robert stood near the fireplace, one hand resting on the mantel.

"We didn't expect to see you, Lily," Crofford said. He frowned at Remmington. "She looks pale. You should insist that she return upstairs and rest to recover from her ordeal."

Remmington shrugged. "Your daughter insists otherwise."

"Lily looks fine to me," Robert said. "Not a bit pale. I say, Remmington. Your restorative powers must be something remarkable."

"I wish everyone would stop speaking of me as if I were a paperweight," Lily said. A deep blush covered her cheeks. "Robert, if you are curious about my health, you may simply ask me."

Robert inclined his head. "How do you feel, Lily?"

"Much better, thank you. Now may we speak of something important?"

Remmington directed his scowl at Robert. "Did you interrogate the wounded spy, or find anything else of interest in the house?"

Bainbridge answered his question. "Lando's man told us what we wanted to know, after I offered his life in exchange for the information. As it turns out, there was a fifth spy in Lord Granger's ring. Lando."

"But why couldn't we track him?" Remmington asked. "The other four spies or their messengers reported through Granger at regular intervals. Why not Lando?"

"Lando knew that Granger's indiscretions would attract attention from the authorities," Bainbridge explained, "and that it was only a matter of time before Granger gave himself away. Rather than jeopardize his mission, Lando severed his connections with Granger and created an independent operation with Harry's assistance."

"Harry acted as if he never had a farthing to his name," Remmington mused. "In that, he proved wiser than Granger."

"But why did Lando shoot him?" Robert asked.

"Lando had no intention of keeping his promises to Harry," Remmington said. "Once they had Lily, Harry's usefulness came to an end. If Lily hadn't escaped and knocked Lando off balance when she did, there is every chance that Lando would have left Harry's house alive." He felt Lily's grip tighten on his arm. He lifted her hand and held it gently between his own. "He intended to use me as a hostage. I had already agreed to act as one."

"Whatever possessed you to do anything so stupid?" Robert demanded. "I could not believe my eyes when I saw you lower your pistols."

"I couldn't be certain that he wasn't lying about Lily's location." He laced his fingers through Lily's, then reached over with his other hand to trace the delicate bones of her wrist. "At that moment, I would have agreed to almost anything if it meant her safety. Lando knew it. I would imagine he intended to use me as a bargaining tool, to negotiate his way onto a ship."

"You would have let him leave the country?" Robert asked.

"No. By that time I would have assumed the worst, that my wife was dead already. I would have killed Lando, or died in the effort. Without a hostage, Lando would not leave England alive."

No one spoke for a moment.

Lily's eyes sparkled with tears as she looked up at her brother. "I forgot to thank you for something, Robert. The time you spent teaching me how to pick a lock did not go unrewarded."

Remmington reached out to brush away a tear that spilled over her cheek. "Your father is right, sweetheart. You should be resting."

She placed her head on his shoulder, with one hand on his chest. "I can rest fine right here."

"We needn't take much more of your time," Bainbridge said. "What you need to know is that the French are aware of Lily's activities, her father's as well. Crofford intends to operate from the safe house in Brighton, and Robert will return to his post tomorrow morning. Naturally, I realize you will insist that Lily resign her position, but that will not ensure her safety. You must both be on your guard until the war ends."

Remmington considered those words for a moment, and the way his wife's hand grew tense beneath his. He tilted her chin up and looked into her eyes. "Do you want to resign?"

Lily bit her lip. "I don't know."

"Of course she will resign," Crofford said. "Lily, how can you even consider anything else?"

Remmington knew how. He saw it in her eyes. "I believe your daughter is considering *everything* else. There is more at stake than our lives." He stroked her cheek. "My men and I can keep you safe here. It won't be pleasant. You will be more or less a prisoner in your own home. But I will turn this place into a fortress before I risk losing you again."

She gave him a helpless look and shook her head. "I don't know."

He turned to Bainbridge. "I assume you can wait a day or two for her answer."

"You will do nothing of the sort," Crofford told Bainbridge. "You will tell them right now that Lily's career with the War Department is finished."

Bainbridge stroked his mustache again, his expression thoughtful. "I realize your concerns, Crofford, but I will not object if Lily wishes to remain with the Department. The French have no way of knowing if she resigns. She will be a target regardless of her decision."

Remmington watched Lily's face, her indecision and her fear. He didn't want to see her cry again. "Is there anything else we should know before you go, Sir Malcolm?"

It wasn't a subtle hint, and Bainbridge rose to his feet. "Nothing pressing." He turned to Crofford and Robert. "Gentlemen, I believe it's time we took our leave."

Lily couldn't help but cry when she said good-bye to her father and brother, uncertain when she would see them again. When they left, Remmington carried her to his bed, where he held her for a long time afterward. She hadn't cried at all when they first returned from Harry's. Her husband had kept her too distracted with fierce, possessive kisses. Then he'd made love to her, the emotions they shared so intense that she could think of nothing else. But now she could do nothing but cry.

"I can't seem to stop," she complained, wiping her eyes again with his handkerchief. He didn't seem to mind. He continued to rub her shoulders in a comforting motion. "I don't know what to do, Miles. So many dead, but it isn't over yet. Not the war, not the deceptions." She caught another sob in her throat.

"Hush, Lily. It's all right. You don't have to work for Bainbridge if you don't want to." He smoothed her hair back with his hand and pressed a kiss against her forehead. "You've already done more for the war effort than anyone could expect from one person."

"But I don't think I could sit idle while everyone else around me—" Another thought gave her pause. She leaned up on one elbow to search his face. "Will you continue *your* duties?"

"Of course," he said, smiling. "My current assignment will keep me busy for the remainder of the war. Trevor can take over my duties at sea, but I will not trust your safety to anyone else but me."

Lily didn't share his humor. "You will give up your work, but you don't expect me to do the same?"

"I just told you that I intend to fulfill my duties and

remain on my current assignment." The sparkle of humor and something a little more wicked lit his eyes. "A man cannot be remiss in his duties."

She turned in his arms until she came to rest on top of his chest, then propped her chin on her hands. "I'll resign if you want me to."

The humor faded from his expression. "I think your work is too important to give up entirely, Lily. I'll admit that I would be happier if you let your father take the translation work that comes from operatives other than your brother. I know the volume of messages that pass through Sir Malcolm's hands." His brows drew together in a frown. "Before all this started, how much time did you spend on translations?"

"Sometimes only an hour or so each day." She pursed her lips. "But oftentimes the majority of my day."

He began to rub her back as she spoke, his fingers lingering occasionally on the small, pearl buttons that secured the dress from her neck to her waist. "How much time would you spend if you worked only on Robert's messages?"

"A few hours, perhaps a day or two at the most each week." She felt her body begin to relax, and it seemed the most natural thing in the world to lift her lips and place a kiss on her husband's chin. There was always an element of fascination with the rough texture of his skin where he shaved. She reached up to stroke his cheek. She repeated the motion when she realized he liked the soothing strokes. She did, too.

"That sounds about right," he mused. "There will come a day when you will not want to devote much more than a day or two each week to your work."

His voice sounded deeper than normal and she recognized the desire that kindled to life in his eyes, a reflection of her own. "And what day would that be, my lord?"

"Well, I've heard that many new mothers like to devote much of their time to their babes. I just thought—"

She laid her fingers over his lips and shook her head,

unable to keep the disappointment from her voice. "Miles, I am not with child."

He pulled her hand away from his mouth, revealing a smile so handsome it made her ache inside.

"I know that, Lily." His hands cupped her face and he drew her closer until his lips were just a breath from hers. "However, I have a plan."

About the Author

Elizabeth Elliott took a turn off the corporate fast track to write romances on the shores of a lake not far from Woebegone. In her spare time, she works as a free-lance writer/consultant in the software industry. At home with her husband and sons, she is currently writing her next novel.

DON'T MISS THESE FABULOUS
BANTAM WOMEN'S FICTION TITLES

On Sale in January

LION'S BRIDE

by New York Times *bestselling author* Iris Johansen

"A master among master storytellers." —*Affaire de Coeur*

A magical weaver of spellbinding tales, enticing characters, and unforgettable romance returns with a breathtaking new novel of passion, peril, and sizzling sensuality.

_____ 56990-2 $5.99/$7.99 Canada

SEE HOW THEY RUN

by nationally bestselling author Bethany Campbell

"Bethany Campbell weaves strong magic so powerful that it encircles the reader." —*Romantic Times*

From nationally bestselling author Bethany Campbell, a gripping novel of romantic suspense in the tradition of Joy Fielding: Two innocent autistic children. A beautiful teacher. A hardened ex-cop. What they know could get them killed . . . _____ 56972-4 $5.50/$7.50

SCOUNDREL

by bright new talent Elizabeth Elliott

"Elizabeth Elliott is an exciting find for romance readers everywhere." —*New York Times* bestselling author Amanda Quick

Newcomer Elizabeth Elliott follows up her debut, *The Warlord* with this stunning romance in which a dazzling charade leads to dangerous desire in a world of war and intrigue where the greatest peril of all is in daring to love. _____ 56911-2 $5.50/$7.50